The Subject of a Portrait

The Subject of a Portrait

John Harvey

www.hhousebooks.com

ISBN: 978-1-910688-96-0
Cover design by Ken Dawson Creative Covers
Typeset by Polgarus Studio

First published in the UK by Polar Books 2014
This edition 2021

Holland House Books
Holland House
47 Greenham Road
Newbury, Berkshire RG14 7HY
United Kingdom

www.hhousebooks.com

For Julietta

Foreword

The idea that I might try to write a love-novel about the break-up of the Ruskin marriage came abruptly, near Greece's boundary with Bulgaria. We were exploring the mountain region of Karadere, which borders a surviving stretch of the primeval European forest. We had been following a steep stream down a high deep gorge when we came to a place where several waterfalls broke round a craggy projection into the water. I knew Millais' portrait of John Ruskin, standing amid waterfalls in a Highland glen. And it seemed to me that, all at once, we had arrived at that very place. I almost saw two men in long jackets, with a girl in a big skirt and a straw hat sitting by. One man would tell the other to stand a little differently on the crag, while he and the girl slipped shy glances. The picture flickered briefly like a film-clip in my head and as we carried on walking and talking it quietly turned into thoughts of a novel.

From teaching Ruskin and the PreRaphaelites, I knew the story. I re-read the biographies and in due course Julietta and I travelled up to Glenfinlas in the Trossachs, to look for the real crag. It was thought for many years that the original site of the portrait was lost when Loch Finlas, at the head of the stream, was dammed. But once a dam is built, as much water is likely to flow out of it below, as flows into it from the hills above. I had heard that the portrait-site had been rediscovered, but we needed still to find it, and the chapter where my characters push through bushes and brambles beside the Finlas stream, looking for a place to paint, recalls our own effort upwards, through undergrowth and foliage, till we found the spot. The water dashes round 'Ruskin's Rock' exactly as it did in 1853.

The glen – Glenfinlas – with its stream and string of cottages has not grown or changed greatly. The local grand hotel still stands, with its pointed-topped turrets of grey stone: it was new-built when the Ruskins and the Millais brothers stayed there. As my snapshot shows, the village graveyard still has its odd gravestones, horizontal and up on short legs, which 'John' in the novel remarks.

The subject of a portrait was one that Ruskin and Millais discussed. But also the subject of the portrait was John Ruskin himself. And one must wonder what Ruskin's full intention was, when he arranged for a young artist dear to both him and his wife to travel with them to the Scottish highlands mainly so the artist could paint his likeness. For company, and I guess for propriety, they took with them Millais' brother William – who saw he was not very much wanted, and presently left. The other three were all pleased, for different reasons maybe, when Ruskin insisted they move into a tiny cottage where Millais and Effie slept in minute cupboard rooms on either side of the sitting room, where Ruskin slept on the sofa. Clearly much could happen in this cauldron of claustrophobic companionship, given also that the Ruskins maintained their marriage on distinctly unusual terms. All three wrote letters about their stay, but as to the crucial private exchanges between them, one only can guess.

Even Queen Victoria guessed: she told others she could see well enough 'what happened in the Highlands'. Victorian society at large came to wonder also what happened – or did not happen -- in London afterwards. Nor do we know for sure, though the question, for a time, seemed momentous.

Each of the three was thrust into a dilemma. John Everett Millais had a precocious genius. He could draw as exactly as Dürer and had a wonderful love for intense but subtle colour. He had features in common with Ruskin: both had been child prodigies and both loved to get every detail exactly right. Ruskin needed to know the name of each wildflower he found in Scotland, as Millais painted carefully each corner of each petal. Working meticulously inch by inch from the top of his canvas down to the bottom, he must have wondered, how do I make this portrait a masterpiece while my passion for my subject turns steadily to fury? Ruskin's wife Effie had to ask, what is it in me that helped me not to see the ice-hole I had wandered into? More than the two men ever did, she had to ask, how may I change the foundations of my life?

The darkest question for history is how one should see and understand John Ruskin. He was a great writer on art and on society but he also had – as we might say – a complex pathology. It is not clear that he ever had full physical intimacy with anyone, though he did confess to practising 'the vice of Rousseau' (masturbation). Millais himself was uneasily suspicious of the obsessive personal affection Ruskin pressed on him (which Ruskin tried to continue even after Millais had married his own ex-wife). Sometimes there is a three-sided grouping: Ruskin was the brilliant only child of excessively doting elderly parents; he was happy going about in Venice with Effie and her admirer, the young Austrian, Lieutenant Paulizza; and he was perhaps, at the start, ideally happy with the chastely 'à trois' arrangements in the cottage at Brig o' Turk.

The most familiar charge against Ruskin is paedophilia, and certainly he had fallen in love with his wife Effie when she was twelve and fell in love with his later passion, Rose la Touche, when she was ten. His own father expressed his irritation with John's obsession with 'tiny virgins'. The psychoanalyst Juliet Mitchell suggested to me once, in conversation, that a part of Ruskin may have suffered arrest at that very early stage before the infant has determined whether it is male or female. What this might mean for Ruskin's supposed paedophilia is that in pursuing little girls (as he unquestionably did) he approached them as being himself a sort of little girl or little girl-boy. This fits the fact that he wrote whole long letters to friends like Joan Severn in baby-talk: anyone may read them, and their voice is that of a presexual child. If this sounds too weird or compromising, one need only think of the celebrated contemporary artist Grayson Perry, who overtly performs, in a big pinafore, his 'inner little girl' whom he calls Claire. A grown-up married man and artist can do that now, and integrate his hydra psyche, but John Ruskin couldn't do that in the 1850s.

However diverse the shadowed side of Ruskin's make-up, he did have a wonderful eloquence, an extraordinary genius for the appreciation of visual art, and a pioneering and courageous insight into social and political wrongs. Rightly the art school he helped found in Cambridge is now known as Cambridge Ruskin University while Oxford has its Ruskin School of Art. He was a great man. Even so, he also was a monster. The single worst act that I know of (it's not in the novel) was that when his wife remonstrated about their unconsummated marriage, he wrote to her father to tell him that his daughter was insane. In the circumstances, that letter seems not quite sane, but also it is malignant.

I do not claim, of course, that my John Ruskin, in this novel, is the real John Ruskin of history. A character in a novel, however historical, must be free to breathe and feel. Also, if you have an idea for a character in a novel, you surely should pursue your idea as far as it will go? What's the use of half-measures in a work of imagination? That's why, in this novel, I almost never use the name 'Ruskin'. 'John' gave me more freedom, for the world has many Johns: Everett Millais was John Everett Millais, I am a John.

But nor do I argue for a disconnect between my Ruskin and the real Ruskin. It is a question, how one should see the relation between a historical figure and their portrayal in fiction. I like to think that their relation can be like that of siblings – even twins, though not identical twins, since twins may be both the same and different. My John Ruskin can't be the John Ruskin but maybe he can be like Ruskin's brother, even his bad brother, an alter ego. In science fiction people invent parallel universes, and a historical novel about real people can only be, at best, a parallel universe, it cannot be the actual historical universe. Even so I hoped my fiction could shed some light on the true story of a great painter, and of our greatest art critic, and – it all comes back to this – on his wife's unhappiness, and her search for happiness, in one marriage – or another.

As to the illustrations in these pages, two thirds are real and one third fiction: that is, eight of them are images made by Millais in the years the novel covers, and four are collages I made myself, from nineteenth-century originals. These images are meant to conjure the shadow-world of Ruskin's psyche, while Millais' pictures show his tender humanity.

Otherwise... it did not worry me as I worked on the novel that the story had been told before. It was the great art-marriage-scandal topic of England's nineteenth century. What I did not know was that the story would be told again by someone else at exactly the same time. For it was only as my novel prepared to print (it came out in July 2014) that I heard of Emma Thompson's film Effie Gray, to be released that October. Probably it is as well that neither of us knew the other's take on the subject. We are not greatly at odds. Nor can either of us tell whether, when or how that story may be told again, though surely it will be, since it touches fundamental things that have gone right, and have gone wrong, inside the men and inside the women in these historic islands.

Part I
By Bridge of Turk

Everett understands love.

1

In the night before they left for the Highlands, she sat up stark awake. She had never had such a dream – in which a man made of mud was catching her close. He was tall and dripping, but stronger than her. In his clasp she herself was turning to mud, the fingers dripped off her melting hand. She heard the words in her head only after she woke, 'The King of the Night is waiting for you'. But who could that be? Her secret, her shadow? The darkness expanded to immeasurable size — till she heard John's long snore where he nestled beside her.

In the pitch-black she scarcely knew where she was. London, Scotland? Still she was calm. It was not quite a nightmare, for all the wet dirt. And tomorrow their journey would begin. They would climb in the Highlands, follow rivers back to their boggy beginnings — and with two young men for company.

In the morning, at King's Cross, she felt only excitement. She looked round at the jostling, sunlit crowd, the bevies of children, and ladies who fussed in colliding big skirts. Two rosy-faced men doffed tall hats to each other, while beyond them the funnel of the engine streamed smoke.

'It's like a picture by Frith.'

John nodded, but at the same time winced. She did not mind, she liked to name the artists he refused to admire. With energy she pinched his elbow.

'I'm glad we are going to my country, John.'

He started and blinked. 'We shall not be going anywhere if the brothers don't come. And then where will my portrait be?'

John's portrait – that too was their reason for travelling. Everett already had a brilliant name, he would paint John in a beautiful place they would find, while John was composing his lectures for Edinburgh.

'They will be here.'

She refused to worry, the air was too bright. She was aware nearby people glanced shyly at them. She turned her head, she could endure to have a famous husband – while John hardly noticed when he was noticed. He ought to fuss less. With his large nose he seemed to be sniffing his watch.

'Do you think I should ask Crawley to unload our trunk?'

'Be easy, John – the brothers are here.'

She smiled to see them, as they pressed to either side of a long lady in crepe. They wore identical light summer suits, and had identical German peaked caps on their heads. She knew Everett already, tall and thin as his pencils, with a shock of fair hair. His lean face was stern as he pushed through the crowd. William the teacher she did not know, but she saw he was fair-complexioned and handsome. He was tall as Everett but broad-built as a door.

'John, Mrs Ruskin, my brother William.'

'Mr Millais, a pleasure to meet you. This is Mrs Ruskin, whom I call Effie.'

The men shook hands, she dipped to the brothers. Everett turned to her. 'You are well?' His face was bright with recognition.

'Thank you, yes.'

But already he had returned to John, to praise a review which he had written. She thought, but Everett, I can see your bones. Had he lost more weight since last she saw him?

Beside them the engineer pressed a valve. A shrill whistle blew and a ball of white smoke rose into the sky. And still they had not decided, would they sit in an open carriage or closed? The brothers said open, John preferred closed.

'I'm for open,' she said.

'But your bonnet may be lost, my dear, and your hair blown all awry.'

'I shall tie my ribbon tighter, then – and you hold on to your hat.'

They took their seats in the train, she and John facing forwards with the brothers opposite: there was a zest in sitting with two handsome young men. It was innocent too.

John was explaining, 'We shall break our journey at Wallington Castle. Lady Trevelyan will make us welcome.'

Lady Trevelyan! She slightly frowned. John's lady admirers were half the aristocracy.

The train jolted into motion. Before long she was gazing down from a viaduct, at rings of tight houses with narrow mud yards. Women were walloping clothes into tubs, in the distance smoke teemed from factory chimneys. Then they ran into a tunnel, where smuts blew in their faces. Moving faster, they passed between wooded hills, where some hats took leave of their owners. A red parasol bowled away down a meadow. The carriage rocked as they reached the limits of speed, she clasped John's arm.

'Dear Effie,' he absently said, and licked his pencil's tip. He had his notebook out, she saw his lectures were forming.

It was hard to talk now, but from time to time one or other

brother would smile or nod to her. What now caught her eye, and her heart as well, were the glimpses she saw of the back of a family, milling in the next division of the carriage. A boy stood up shakily on the seat, another leaned over the carriage's side, and was quickly hauled back by his father's arm. A girl turned bright eyes to her mother's bonnet. Even the baby, in the nurse's arms, stretched fat frilled hands to the streaming air.

'Mrs Ruskin.' Everett held out a handkerchief to her. 'The wind is strong in your eyes.'

She swallowed, and thanked him, and took out a handkerchief of her own. She could pretend her tears were the wind's work. In courtesy she nodded again to Everett, then she took off her bonnet and lifted her head, so the wind dashed into her face. Let it blow, they were travelling free. She closed her eyes as if rapt, as if she washed her skin in air.

And when she opened her eyes, still, she met Everett's eyes, which studied her steadily.

*

At Wallington the Trevelyans already knew of Everett's fame. Especially they praised his 'Christ in the House of his Parents', in which the child Jesus has hurt his hand on his father's chisel, so a drop of blood splashes his bare feet also, while his mother, in blue and white, bends to tend him.

'Yes, it's a pretty fancy,' John said, 'But the strength of the painting is in its sharp sight of everything. His eye is a razor. It is like brilliant drawing, except the colours are so deep and rich. And Joseph – he *looks* like a carpenter, not a patriarch.'

'My own father posed for him,' Everett said quietly, 'The head, that is. I got a real carpenter in, for the arms.'

They were his only words: otherwise he let John tell his

story. She wondered, was this in modesty — or was it that he took their praise for granted? But why be modest, with such a talent?

Presently they sat at ease, in the long salon of the Castle. Lady Pauline and John drew apart, while Sir Walter spoke of his new teetotal campaign. He had an elegant, mournful face, while long moustaches rippled down his jaw.

'I shall work in the darkest slums of London. I mean to save many a ruined life.'

She quickly said, 'John would say, we should give them work, and better homes. It isn't enough just to give them less gin.'

Sir Walter smiled patiently. 'A noble dream. Your John has vision. Yet I fear he is not a practical man. Can work and houses be plucked from the air?'

She looked to the far end of the salon, where John and Lady Pauline stooped by a table. A large portfolio was open before them, in which she showed him, one by one, her drawings. John's finger hovered as he gently pointed out mistakes of perspective: she gave little nods. Then he gave her a sweetmeat, he found something to like. His face lit, he smiled, while she gazed up to him like a sweetheart.

She turned away. John, and his drawing ladies. She should not be annoyed, for he was like a saint and never seemed to flirt – but still he kept them in his track. He was a sort of a pied piper leading a dance, for the ladies of England with their neat portfolios.

'Hmph.' There was a grunt from Sir Walter, whose eyes had followed hers. He heaved up tall, on his wide horseman's legs.

'Mrs Ruskin, may I take you for a ride in my dog-cart? Northumberland also has its charms.'

The next morning, by the door of Wallington Castle, as they stood beside the coach they had hired, John turned again to Lady Pauline.

'If I send you pressed flowers that I find in the Highlands, will you look up their names and write to tell me?'

Lady Pauline dipped. 'To offer any help with your work is a privilege.'

John smiled with grace, and bent to breathe on her fingers.

From the coach she called out to him, 'Let us make haste, John.'

*

Their road took them across the bleak Cheviot hills. The surface was rough, and as the coach rocked she studied the brothers. William sat to the window like a lad, noticing horses and breeds of cattle, while Everett lounged back like a languid milord. Was he painting pictures in his head? She guessed he was filled with ambition like John — and otherwise cold at heart?

At Edinburgh they took the train to Stirling, then travelled on again by coach. Long hills lifted slowly, bare but for heather, and they saw no other travellers.

'The wilderness at last,' John said. 'The world is fresh, we are free of Society.'

They paused at Doune Castle, where they climbed ruined walls. Through broken battlements they gazed on the plain, where the river wound slowly, all bronze from the sinking sun.

William said, 'It takes your breath away.'

John nodded, 'It compares with the Roman *campagna*.'

She nudged his elbow. 'My country is beautiful, is it not, John? You aren't always fair to it.'

'Not only the country,' Everett said abruptly. 'Mrs Ruskin, will you stand by that old window?'

'Oh.' She was startled, for he had said nothing to her in the recent miles. But already he had snatched out a drawing pad. For a minute she was transfixed, his clear eye was cold and sharp as a knife. He made small movements with his pencil, then held the pad to John and William. 'Isn't that a picture?'

She was confused. His eye had been stark — had he made her a character piece, with her odd nose and troubled looks? And yet — a lady by a castle window — perhaps she made a touching figure, watching and waiting like a maiden in Tennyson.

He watched her still, with gleaming cat's eyes. She found herself blushing and coughing together.

'I must have caught cold from that draughty coach.'

John came to her aid. 'So my pretty minx will have *her* portrait also.'

Recovering, she thrust her arm in his. 'We shall be side by side at the Academy show.'

Yet this seemed not what he wanted. He turned stiffly to Everett.

'As for my portrait – have you thoughts as to which setting may be best.'

'Ah, that *is* a question. Still, don't worry, John. When we stop at Bridge of Turk, we shall find some good place in the glen.'

'In the glen! I had thought by a crag, or a peak.'

Everett frowned but William laughed. 'Oh, Everett doesn't like big skies. He likes a close small space, all solid with detail. He'll find some nook in the woods.'

She heard John whisper, 'Some nook in the woods!' He

had lost all colour. 'May we go to the coach?' he said shortly. 'I find that I have hurt my ankle.'

With a limp that was new he led the way down. William followed with a whistle, while she and Everett must bring up the rear. Everett seemed untroubled by John's dismay, but coughed as he handed her onto the grass. 'I think – you and I – we have caught the same cold.'

She dipped her bonnet at once, for what he said might be kind but was also familiar. She glanced sharply at him. He did look the gentleman more than the artist. Would he trifle with her?

She saw too that William had heard, for he paused, and turned, and gave his brother a keen, brief look.

*

At Bridge of Turk Everett insisted they would find a good place to paint, if they followed the stream that ran up the glen. He and John pressed on ahead, while she followed with William through the overgrown bank, thick with bushes and brambles and good Scottish thistles. Her thick woollen skirt protected her, though its hem was sodden and yellow with mud.

William held branches aside for her. 'Your health is mended, I think?'

'I thank you, yes,' she said. 'I have rubbed myself with olive oil, as Dr Simpson told me.'

William shook his head. 'Everett also has...delicate health.'

'He looks well enough today,' she mused, for Everett was almost lost to sight, pushing ahead through thickets. 'And *you* have good health, Mr Millais.'

'*Rude* health, I'm afraid!' he heartily laughed, 'I wonder I was not detailed to press back the brambles. Everett normally has me carry the bags. Men of talent, you know?'

'It's true I've never known John carry bags. His man Crawley does all of that. But – are you bitter? You have talents too, you draw and paint also, you have your music and mathematics...'

'I'm an usher — a school-teacher' he muttered bitterly, 'And otherwise — a Jack of all trades. Ach, these midges!' He flapped his hand angrily. 'You do well to wear your veil.'

'I know my country,' she said, 'But I swelter in these layers of linsey woolsey. Now why has John stopped?'

John gazed back to them gloomily. 'My friends, our path has come to its end.'

The ground had grown steep, the undergrowth dense, now the stream itself turned to a staircase of waterfalls. Above them loomed a rocky bank.

'That won't beat us,' Everett said. 'John, your stick, if I may.' Regardless of the stains to his suit, he scrambled up over boulders, through clumps of fern. He was limber and quick, and soon stood high over them. He held out John's stick. 'Hey, John, catch hold of the end of this.'

'Thank you, no.' John almost scoffed. 'If I can climb the Alps, I can climb a Scottish bank, I think.' He caught hold of a branch and pulled himself to the top, while William shinned up after him. All three of them then leaned down to her.

'My dear,' John said, and the hands of all of them helped her fly up the slope.

'And from here — where?' she said.

It seemed this must be the end of their walk. From the top of the bank they stepped out onto a moss-speckled headland of rock. In front was a waterfall, behind it the hill-side rose up like a cliff. Round the rock itself the falling water dashed and foamed.

'It's like poured beer,' William said, but John stepped out to the edge of the rock. 'No, but look at the rock-face opposite.' With his stick he pointed, to where the stone turned in folds and corners, like a heavy blanket half off a bed.

'The rock has kept the shape it had, when it still was a sluggish liquid – then here it fractured when it was cold.'

Following his hand they saw, in the weathered, lichened stone, the cooling lava it once had been.

She turned to William. 'John too is a teacher, and visits the schools. I learn greatly from him.'

William nodded, but her eye was caught by Everett. Gazing at John he took one step back, then stooped so his knee touched the ground. He held up his hands so his fingers made corners, like the opposite points of a picture-frame.

'Ah – ha,' said William, but already she knew.

'He has his picture.'

Everett had pulled out his drawing-pad, and a pencil.

'John, step back there, just as you were.'

John frowned, then said 'Ah!' and moved some paces back.

'No, John, there — near the edge — please.' He spoke crisply, John blinked.

For some moments Everett gazed back and forth, between John and his empty paper. He drew lines, paused, made more quick touches, and closed the pad with decision. Only then he looked round, shyly.

'I think it will do.'

She could see he was pleased. 'You have found your subject?'

He nodded cheerfully, while William said in her ear, 'He has every bit of it clear in his head. Everett is a daguerreotype machine. The painting of it now will be just filling it in.'

John however made a noise in his throat, they all turned to his sombre, not pleased face.

'This then is your "nook in the woods"? This damp, tight chasm, where the sun never comes.'

'Oh, but John!' Everett looked amazed. 'Where would you have me paint you?'

'I had said,' John spoke quietly slowly. 'I had said, I thought — the high places of the earth.'

'John, you are absolutely wrong.' He was suddenly fire, the milord and the lounger had disappeared. 'Look here at my sketch. Think how it will be! There you will stand, you will fill the frame. Mild as Jesus, above the plashing water. Behind you the *living* rocks – as you describe them in your books. Around you the plants, whose names you know. And the churning stream. Think, of all you have said about water, and how wonderful and hard it is to paint. I shall paint the water for you here as water *never* was painted before. Believe me, John, it will be a *stunner!*'

John looked unsure, but Nature must be on Everett's side, for at that moment the sun re-emerged, and clear bright sunlight fell on them all. It fell on John, so his figure, in his dark coat, glowed – on his quiet face and sandy hair. And on Everett, on his thin, inspired face: he looked like a young saint.

John looked at him too, he even seemed overcome. For a moment she saw Everett through John's eyes also. John would compare him not to saints, but to the young artists that he himself wrote about – the *beauty* of genius. Had the young Raphael looked like this?

John said, 'Oh, I do see, Everett. True, it is not what I expected – but yes, it will be a new thing in art. And painted in nature, in the open air! How often has that really been done? It can make a stir, I do believe.' He gave a sly smile.

'And truth to tell, Everett, as William has said, there is never a great deal of sky in your pictures. I was wrong to think of mountain-tops. In your pictures you look down more than up – but then you see *everything*.'

Everett started. Was John being critical? But far above them the clouds moved again, the sun became veiled. There was a gentle light now, and peace in the glen and in them.

'So then,' said William. 'Shall we fight our way up this river bank daily?'

'I don't think so,' said Everett. 'I am sure if we climb up the slope beside us, we shall come to the path that winds up to Loch Finlas. The glen has got so steep here, the path can't be far away.'

It proved so. They had to step on rocks and branches, and sodden sponges of moss, to get clear of the stream. Then they caught for tree-trunks, making their way like crabs up a slope of old dry leaves. At the top they found the path, which wound back down the glen, to the village and their hotel.

'Just look at us,' she said, 'We are like boys in the wood.' They all had wet feet and muddied trousers or skirt, and thistle-down and bramble barbs and crumbled leaves to speckle their clothes.

'It will brush off,' John lightly said. She thought, and I shall do the brushing.

They began their return, she chatting with William while John and Everett walked ahead. She saw a shine in their faces, when they turned to each other. They were together in this portrait, critic and painter, patron and protégé: they looked like relatives, uncle and nephew, like people who were close in a way that left her out.

After all, that pattern did not stay. John presently came beside her.

'My dear, I am so relieved that we have found the place.'

She was going to say she thought the choice good, but already he had moved on, calling to William, 'You are a fisherman, Mr Millais? It's not the season, I think, for salmon.'

'Oh, I shall find trout enough in the pools. A pike if I'm lucky.'

'Will you take my hand, Mrs Ruskin. The ground is rough from these roots?'

Everett joined her — and then was all courtesy. He helped her over low branches, and held others back. She asked, 'Is it true, what William says? That now you have seen your picture clearly, and all that remains is "painting in"?'

He laughed. 'In a way it's true. Also it's total nonsense. I would say I've seen the *ghost* of my picture – very clear, but thin. No body to it. The "painting in" is everything. Did you see those lichens on the rocks? They were nearly silver — with a speck of sea-green. And the way the stone glistened – it was white from the clouds we could not see. I'm sorry, these are small things. But the twigs of rowan made it – like looking through the finest net. And John — the man there — No, there is everything still to see. The "painting of it" is — he stopped, shook his head, sighed — *'everything.'*

He had grown fervent, even passionate, and she had listened, open-mouthed. He gazed to her directly a moment — then shrugged and shook it all off.

'If I remember, you play and sing, Mrs Ruskin.'

She started then. He was remembering the days when he had come to their home — when, at John's wish, she had posed for a figure in one of his paintings.

He asked, 'Have you seen *Linda di Chamonix?*'

'We went to it in Venice. Donizetti is sublime.' Under her voice, she sang a phrase.

'Don't stop,' he said. 'You have a lovely voice.' Before she could blush, he sang the next phrase, then stopped so she sang the one that followed. Briefly she let her voice fill, clear and liquid for all to hear. John and William stopped in their tracks.

'I adore *Linda di Chamonix*,' she said to them all. Everett gave a quiet clap of his hands.

William said, 'Oh Everett is at all the operas. He weeps, he sings. They give him the stories for his pictures. Of course he will only go, if he can sit in a box like a Duke.'

John gave an elderly smile. 'The popular opera? It's all right – for an evening.'

She voiced then two bars, from a trio by Gounod. The brothers caught it, and joined in. Quietly, for he did not like his singing voice, John presently joined them. So finally they made their way, side by side in a line, now talking now singing, to the grey stones of their hotel, which was like a stage-set itself, with its new-built towers and turrets.

2

In the hotel they found their names were known, as they had not been when they first arrived. Not to everyone of course, but as they lingered before dinner they were quietly approached. With apologies a suave man asked John if he were the famous 'Graduate of Oxford', the author of the celebrated volumes on *Modern Painters*. Another asked Everett if he truly were the painter of 'Christ in the House of his Parents', the picture which had caused such war in the press. Both men then begged to introduce their wives.

William, and she, were drawn into the company. John's introduction was almost offhand,

'Oh, and this is my Euphemia, whom others call Phemie and I call Effie.'

That said, one could think he went on to ignore her. She did not mind, she could fend for herself. She knew he liked a wife who could shine in society – so people would say, 'And how does a bookish man like that – genius though he may be – have *such* a wife?'

Or so she fancied they would say – let them say what they would. She had felt tired, now she came to life. Perhaps she was not a painter's model, but her eyes were bright, her head sat high, the husbands present were as courteous as their wives would let them be. She was aware of Everett, further down the table, speaking of his great friend Holman Hunt. John, she knew, would be talking of Turner, whom he had known, or of Fra Angelico or Fra Bartolomeo, or some other painting monk who once lived in Italy. For her part she would tell how they had climbed together on the Matterhorn, or how they lived months in Venice in a grand, damp palazzo, and kept warm by playing ball in the banqueting room.

'We called it our ball-room'. The table laughed.

She spoke with respect of John's book on Venice, and was lively about his foibles.

'He has a difficulty, in remembering people. It is worst of all if we go to a ball. He will forget who an Earl is, that he met the night before. Or he goes into a corner and takes out a book and reads it. Or he will take a tape-measure out, to measure how wide a column is. It isn't that he cannot dance.'

'But you like dancing, Mrs Ruskin?' the suave man quietly asked.

She ignored his twinkle and replied rather to Everett, whose eye was on her further down the table, 'I do, I can dance all night. I *have* danced all night in Venice.' She spoke with zest, so the table might guess the white satin she wore, see chandeliers sparkling over her head, and figures behind her that whirled in quadrilles. She did not add that John had gone home – having left her in the care of Lieutenant Paulizza, the Austrian officer of artillery, a gentleman of meticulous honour.

The brothers smiled to her through the company: they too liked parties. John, she knew, thought her worldly – and it was true, she liked laughter and balls and meeting limbs of royalty, and many things which were a trial to him. If her glance passed his, as the meal progressed, she never found him

18

gazing back – except once, and then his eye was old, cold, superior, beneath a raised and weary brow. As if he were someone not her husband, thinking there's that Ruskin woman again, making her sociable noise.

And now, when she looked, she found him in talk with a strange-looking man. He had a long, thin head, his skin was grey-white, his hair jet-black. There was something guarded in the way they talked, and in the way their eyes flicked round. They glanced often to a nearby table, where a family with fair-haired children sat. Did they joke? But when she looked again, the man had gone as though he never was there.

She blinked, there was something untoward. Never mind. In a very few days, the portrait-painting would start. Then she, John and Everett would be alone on the rock, for William was sure to go away and fish. And then, and then — it will be a summer of art, and new friendships too. A light like a sun would rise over her life.

*

John was bright as a boy. 'Come, you slow coaches, we must all make haste. Everett has his canvas ready, and I shall carry his palette and paints. Let us climb the glen, for this work to begin.'

At John's suggestion, they all brought drawing things. 'It won't be kind,' he had said, 'If we just stand beside Everett and stare.'

With their packets and parcels they processed up the glen. The cattle rolled slow big eyes as they passed. An old woman came to her cottage gate, and watched them grimly without a word. From inside the cottage a thin voice called,

'Get in, woman. They're off to bury their gold, nae doot, and dinna want their doings seen.'

They climbed to where the alders gave way to birch-trees, then they knew they were above the site of the portrait. They turned from the path and pushed downwards through bracken. Carefully they descended the last sheer slope of fat wet moss, to emerge on the rock that jutted into the stream.

'Here I shall stand.' John took up his position at the edge of the rock.

She said, 'John dear, there's hardly room for us all.'

In truth, when Everett unfolded his easel, they found they were hemmed in precariously. Everett tightened the clamps that held the canvas.

'Would you step to the edge, John? In front of the waterfall.'

'Take care,' she said, 'the lichen is slippery.'

Warily John stood on a lip of the rock, over a gap where the water foamed. The others pressed back in a wobbling huddle, to leave clear space round artist and subject.

'Could you turn a trace towards me? No, back a little. Thank you.'

'What about John's cane,' said William. 'He can't just hold it straight like that.'

'John, might you – no, that's no good. Might you rest your cane behind you?'

The cane was a problem to them. Everett sniffed.

'I shall paint the cane in later.'

He took a pencil. Then, for a long while, he only looked. At John, at the waterfall, at the branches and rocks. William murmured to her, 'We take our time.'

Finally, Everett's pencil made a mark on the canvas, then, between pauses, he drew more lines. There was no sound except the plash of the waterfall, and a gurgle where the water sucked under the rocks.

'Thank you, John. I have you now.'

Everett sat back, they leaned to look. The outline of John was razor clear, from his whiskers to the instep of his shoe. Behind him, in outline, ran each curl of the waterfall, and the line of each twig that hung over the rock. Everett gravely made ready his palette. He set out small dabs of blue, yellow, white and red, then sat himself round to the canvas again.

John said, 'Shall I stand by the water still?'

'There's no need.' Everett picked out a fine brush. 'I shall start with the foliage at the top of the frame.'

He had mixed a puddle of grey-green viridian, and placed a small dab at the top of the canvas.

She was surprised. 'But won't you paint John first, as the man in the foreground?'

'Oh, Everett doesn't paint like that,' William said. 'He'll start at the top and work his way down. With luck he'll complete an inch a day – or half an inch.'

'Well, but —' John said, from behind the canvas. 'And shall you paint me one inch to the day?'

Then Everett said, 'O, but John — I'm not sure that I can paint *you* just now. I may need all our time in Scotland, to get the rocks and water right. Let us see how it goes. If need be, I shall paint you in, in London.'

She saw John was speechless — smitten, aghast.

She said, 'But you cannot mean — that John will stay just an outline. Just a shape, until all the waterfall's done?'

Everett gave a wise, mild smile. 'Of *course* John is the important part of the painting. That's why it's best I paint him last.'

She heard John breathing heavily.

Everett said, 'Believe me, it is better so, John.'

John shrugged with big arms, looked to Heaven, looked down. He sighed, he would endure the wait.

It had to be. Everett seemed hardly aware of them, as he began to paint a slender twig of birch, which just crept in sight at the top of his canvas.

'Well,' William said, 'John said to bring our drawing things. Let's all of us daub! It'll give Everett peace, and us something to do.'

She shrugged. 'There's not room on this rock for us all to sit down.'

'We don't all need to be here.' William waved up at the mountain-side. 'I shall work in water-colours, up on that bank.'

'I shall stay here,' John said, 'I dearly like those gneiss rocks opposite. I shall draw them as best I may.'

Presently they were distributed. She sat back on a root, tracing a stone-crop.

'Effie dearest, might you come and sharpen my pencil.'

'Most willingly, John. William, I hope those leaves are dry. You look the picture of comfort.'

'Oh, I don't believe in sitting cooped-up. Your body must be easy, if you want to draw well.'

'Concentrate, William,' Everett called, 'Or the picture will look as if it's done with your feet.'

William made a pout. There was quietness then, as they bent to their papers. She looked about her. Through the canopy of birch, fir and rowan, rods of sunlight picked out the crimson neck-cloth that William wore loosely, the black coat of John, Everett's crest of hair. The scene was all artists, and dappled sun and shade – except for Crawley, higher up the bank, who tamped his pipe with a stick.

She sat again, and tilted her straw hat at an angle, so she could watch Everett from its shadow. She thought, dear Everett, you're thin as a pin. And his temples were high:

would he go bald early? Then his odd crop of curls stood up like a crest. With his neat nose, he is like a bird, as he pecks at the canvas with that tiny brush. And with his eyes bent down so close to it — he will have to wear spectacles soon.

He was completely absorbed, he had no eyes for her. Still her gaze rested on the sight of him as if her hand lay on his hand.

She returned to the white spiky petals of the stonecrop, but kept rubbing out details. She wondered, why do I draw at all? I cannot draw as John does, let alone Everett. She frowned at the stonecrop, was busy with her rubber again. She was growing more agitated. For if Everett painted only the background, she and John would hardly need to be there. So Everett would be lost to her.

Till she looked up, and saw Everett gazed hard at her. Was he taking a rest? His brush and palette were down, he had sat round. She was aware of the hump of John beyond him, bent and busy at his pad. But Everett stared, and with a frown. Not as if he drew her, but as if she were enigma to him, a puzzle that he could not guess. Or could he see behind her guard? His eye was so keen, he could see through her clothes and through her body. If he robbed her of her secrets — would she get up and go?

But his gaze, after all, was for a second only. Quickly he smiled, and stretched his arms, while she returned a casual nod.

He had picked up his brush, she returned to the stonecrop. Only the petals shivered and blurred, her pencil trembled. She was shaking still from the shock of his look. This was not good. What was he to her?

'My dear,' John called, 'Would you see my drawing?'

She stood, and went, and bent to look. But it was strange,

John's drawing, as they always were. Somehow he had made the rough rock smooth, so it hung like uncooked chicken-skin. She saw a lipless mouth, the pits in the stone were like bead-eyes.

'That's clever shading, dear,' she said.

'Well,' he said, pleased. 'But now let us see how a master does.'

With a nod to Everett he went and stood beside him. 'Now that is what I could not do. It is finer than Dürer! My dear, come and look.'

She bent to see. In the top corner of the nearly blank canvas of Everett was a patch of silver-white glowing lichen, and a flower-stem with tiny petals and leaves, standing out sharp against damp leaden rock. It was brighter, more brilliant, than the flower itself, when she found it on the opposite slope. It left her work nowhere, and John's work in a goblin dream.

'It's a wonder,' she said, but she hardly had voice. His sight was all for his art of course, and not for her at all.

'Oh, it's just work,' he said with a gentle brief glance.

*

She was uneasy all evening, they hardly spoke over dinner. Only in their room, as she sat rubbing olive oil into her neck, she broke out abruptly, 'But will Everett be up there all day by himself? Painting the "background" grass by grass, with no one ever to exchange a word? That could be miserable. We will go to visit him, I hope.'

'When he invites us,' John quietly said. 'An artist must be left to his work, and not disturbed by a rattle of chatter.'

Did he say that to annoy her? But then he went on, 'He will miss us, I think. Let us wait till he says. And I shall miss my protégé. You will miss him too, I think?' His eyes narrowed a trace.

' Your protégé, John? His talent is his own, I think. His genius even, as you have said.'

'Yes, but I too had a hand in his fame. He nearly was lost before I wrote to *The Times*, when his painting of Our Lord had made that scandal. It is fair, I think, that he paints a picture of me.'

'Whether here — or months away, in London.'

John shrugged, he was unwilling to be provoked now. He smoothed his nightshirt down, and placed his nightcap on his head.

'My dear, shall we say our prayers?'

All white as a ghost he knelt by the bed, and she all in white knelt close beside him. He thanked God for his care of them, and ended as he always did, 'And most we pray, dear loving Father, that you safeguard your children, John and Euphemia, and preserve them in purity all the days of their life, for thine is the kingdom, the power and the glory, Amen.'

'Amen,' she said, as she always did.

They leaned back side by side on high-builded pillows.

'My dear, I am more than overjoyed, that my portrait is begun.'

'I am happy for you, John, and for all of us.'

Then he turned smiling to her, and burrowed his big nose into her cheek, and blew in her ear. He gave tiny kisses, butterfly brushings, but she found she was cold to them. Still she said tenderly, 'Sleep well, dear John.'

He worked in the bed, and settled as always, curled up small with his head on her breast. She stroked his hair absently, for this was their life, and presently his slightly blocked snoring began. She lay wide awake, thinking, Everett.

She pictured him painting by himself on the rock — gazing at a place where the waterfall splashed, and working so slowly on that pelting rush. But the loneliness of it — and he never would know how she felt for him.

John gasped, and abruptly sat up in bed. She saw he was shuddering.

'There, dear,' she said, and stroked his elbow. 'The dream was bad?'

'I have been — in the Snakehouse.' He made a retching cough.

'John — what is it that happens in the Snakehouse?' He had used this strange name before.

He clutched her arm. 'Oh, my dear wife, you must never ask that. It must not be told.'

His trouble calmed as she held him, while she felt like the mother she never could be. It was so strange. He was the age's clarion voice on art, and read in London and Windsor and in New York. And he was her John, whom the world did not know, coiled up helpless in her arms. No one she knew had nightmares like his.

'What, John?' She had missed his words.

'Wa — ma —' The mumble was soft as a babe's. He was returning to rest, his head on her breast, while she lay now calm. As if she lay in a barge, like Tennyson's Lady of Shalott, drifting beneath a sky of stars. Her griefs were quiet, like a distant dog that had gone to sleep. She wondered who the man with the thin head was, with whom John talked sometimes in the hotel.

'It must not be told'

And as to Everett — if she hardly saw him, because he was busy painting, well, but it was for the best. He had caused her a strange disturbance, as if the world could split open, and all its secrets fall out — its secrets, her secrets, their house upside down. It was best she spent her days with John. It made her sad, but she was safe.

All her tiredness came together then, like the calm deep sea of sleep into which she slipped unknowing.

3

And in the following days she saw small sign of Everett. He left in the morning before they had breakfast, and came in, in the evening, when the dining room was full. John worked in the morning on his lectures for Edinburgh, while she read, or tidied, or sewed, or mused, and later they walked, by the loch, on the hills.

Only once, when John said he must find a book in the hotel library, she locked their door on the inside and carefully slowly she took everything off. She laid her gown, her petticoat, her drawers on the bed, then took a breath and stepped before the mirror. So she saw herself, all white. But what could be wrong? She did not understand. What was it God had done to her? Or not done? What was it that John could not love?

But she must not stay, John would come back. Quickly she dressed and faced herself again. She was handsome enough. She squinted to catch her odd, piquante profile, then went and unlocked the door.

When John came, he did not sit to his work. 'My dear, why don't we take a walk up the glen? We have not been that way for days — and I have a mind to see how my "portrait" does.'

After all, it could be a good day. From the vestibule they stepped into dazzling sunlight. 'It's heavenly,' she simply said.

As they walked he held his forearm to her. 'But isn't that extraordinary!'

They were passing the small graveyard of the village. The gravestones rested flat, up on other short stones, so they seemed to have legs.

'It is as if the dead here may linger in the air, not the clay. I have not seen that anywhere. I love the fancy.'

She nodded. 'I have never thought much about graveyards'.

As they walked he continued to notice everything, so she felt small beside his quick eye. 'See, dear, how the alder is covered with lichen — and of such a sweet and silvery tone.'

'And John — what a horde of buttercups!'

'Buttercups?' He picked one. 'It's butter, sun, and gold, and wax. But is it crowfoot, or spearwort — or common meadow buttercup?'

'Lady Trevelyan will tell us for sure.'

'You're saucy, my Effie. Lady Trevelyan is our dear good friend.'

Always he must know the right name for everything. John, she thought, you are a schoolroom on legs.

The path climbed up between birches and fir-trees, and she listened for the sounds small animals made.

There were scampering, chatterings, she saw tiny claws to either side of a birch-branch. Then she saw a red squirrel run along a high branch, while its tail made a smooth wave in the air.

'If we're quiet, they will all come out.'

There was a faint strange cry.

'That must be a pine marten.'

They both were still. Would a mole lift its snout from the

leaf-mould? A woodpecker went tap-tap in the distance.

'We should get on — please.' John did not care for animals as he did for trees.

Climbing steadily, the path brought them to the edge of a steep-falling bank. Below them they saw the first of the pools, which led back, by way of waterfalls, to Everett's rock. There were bare bodies there, splashing.

'Why it's Everett and William!' John leaned to look. 'So that's what he does, when he says that he paints.'

The white figure of William flailed swooshes of water, up over Everett who stood on the bank, naked and hugging himself as if cold. She looked quickly away, and saw him now inside her eyelid, white and thin as a skeleton.

'My dear,' John said, 'There is nothing amiss. People used always to bathe in the buff.' He frankly gazed. 'How they play — the young cubs!'

She allowed herself to glance quickly once more — in time to see Everett crouch down low. But his eyes again! For he looked up as he began his run, and she saw that he saw her. He tripped in his run, and launched forward awkwardly splett! in the water.

An odd commotion. William staggered, someone shouted. Everett broke surface with his back towards them, hump-backed, crouching in the shallows. When he turned pain stabbed like a railing stuck through her. His face — eyes nose and mouth — were scraped off leaving an oval of blood. She could not breathe.

'Aaaah!' John wailed, while she was fainting, panting, and running full-pelt down the slope. It is my fault, I made him trip. She would fall herself, in the slithering mulch of leaves and moss.

She and her big skirt were quickly there, where Everett sat

shivering on a rock, with someone's shirt wrapped round him. His face was rivers of blood and water.

'Your nose is smashed.' William sloshed water in his face. 'Yugh! Horrible! Get your trousers on. What happened? You knew that rock was there.'

Taking care to look nowhere but in his face, she dabbed with her handkerchief, which immediately was a dripping ball of red. On the bridge of his once-fine nose there was an open gash from which blood burst. Even as they watched they saw his nose swell and bulge.

'John, your handkerchief.' John had worked his way down, from tree to tree.

'Hold it tight there.' She had bunched the cloth hard. 'We must stop the bleeding.'

Everett pressed the red pack to the wound, while John peered in. 'Your eyes are untouched. That is the great mercy.'

William turned to them. 'Everett has accidents. He's careless, in day-to-day things.'

They let William get Everett dressed, while she rinsed the bloody shirt, which turned out to be William's. Then all of them asked Everett to lean on them as they helped him climb the slope.

He held her hand tight as they came to the top, and in time she was his only support. For John led the way, and was talking to William, who was stripped to the waist, and carried his well-wrung shirt like a flag, letting it dry in the sun.

'Let me sit,' Everett said, 'I'm about to faint.'

It was odd his fainting came after the fall. She sat beside him, till he was ready.

'Take my arm,' she said, but she held his, as they walked back to the village.

*

The hotel doctor seemed very Scottish. He fastened a plaster, and told Everett his nose was severely bruised.

'It's broken, no?' William asked.

'Eeeh!' the Scottish voice keened. 'It's too early to say if it's brrroken *as such*.' He fingered his chin. 'It *may* be the line is spoiled.'

By now all of Everett's face was swollen, and his eyes tight slits between puffed lids. But he had his strength, and walked beside William.

'I shall order a hamper from the kitchen,' John said. 'Good food and ease will make us whole. Let us dine by the stream, in the dappled shade. There Everett may rest while we supply him.'

While John's man Crawley lugged the hamper, they crossed to the meadow of lush ripe grass, where the stream from the glen ran into Loch Achray. Everett walked with William, while John came beside her.

'Such a tragedy,' John murmured.

'Why a tragedy, John? The swelling will pass.'

'But his beauty will not be as it was. For he was as an angel, perfect in looks as in his art. I grieve as I would if my own son was hurt.'

'Well, he is a man. He will be all right, I think.'

John raised a brow.

Beside the stream they spread the cloth, and, kneeling down, she served them from the basket with cold chicken and hard-boiled eggs, and bread, honey and apples. By John's special order there was a bottle of sherry labelled Ruskin and Domecq: they drank it from tankards, which otherwise they filled with cold water from the stream.

'You are eating that chicken well enough,' William said, while John gave Everett more sherry for strength.

'My skin wants to tear,' the artist moaned. 'The swelling *hurts.*'

She saw mischief prepare in William's face. 'You know brother, this may be the making of the artist in you. Your pictures were too pretty before — and that may be because *you* were too pretty.'

'William!' she cried, but John was thoughtful. 'There may be truth in William's thought. The great Michelangelo — may it be that some of his *terribilità,* as they call it, came from his knowledge of his ruined face. For his nose was truly smashed in flat. Let us thank God that is not your case.'

She winced, while, unseen, her hand reached towards Everett. John, in the meantime, had a new idea, and presently he and William stood in the stream with their trousers rolled high, and began to heave boulders from the bank.

'What are you about?' she called.

'We are building the new Bridge of Turk.' He splashed one stone down on top of others, so they showed above the stream. 'But I'm glad you are amused, my dear.'

'It's your legs — they're so white.'

John's legs were lean, with knobbled knees, but showed hard muscle at the calf. He smiled and lifted another stone.

Everett turned to her the red-white bloated bag of his face. He had tiny slit eyes.

'You are kind, as Beauty is to the Beast.'

Very softly she said, 'Well, but I too may be a Beast'.

'No, you are beauty,' she thought he said. But had he said it, or anything? His voice was so soft. He turned from her to face the river, his face bulged in a puffy frown.

'Dear boy, you are in the best of hands.' John came splashing up out of the water. He rolled his trousers down and put on his shoes. 'But I must away. There is something I have a mind to do, and there is no time like the present.'

He sparkled as if he set a puzzle to guess. Then quickly he tramped away through the meadow, leaving two tracks in the grass.

*

William joined them and threw himself down on the tussocks.

'John is pleased with my work.' He stretched his arms wide. 'He said I showed the makings of a master-mason, and could have done wonders in the age of cathedrals.'

She made a wry face. 'John will have us all to work at his bidding. As you paint his picture, Everett, on his commission — and as I do what he bids me do. When he gives his lectures in Edinburgh he will have me stand by the doors I know, and after I shall serve tea to his friends.'

They talked at ease, so she thought I love to be with the brothers. Stretching out she rubbed her back on the grass, gazing at redness through shut lids. She heard a skylark far off, and breathed a smell like hay.

Everett also lay back and lounged. 'Well, I needed a loose. When you paint all day, your eyes get to feel like pickled eggs.'

He had pulled his German cap over his face, she had a mind to tickle him with a long grass.

So John found them: he came back in high spirits. 'Companions mine, I have found us a cottage. Come, let us look.'

She blinked and frowned. 'A cottage? The hotel is well enough, John.'

'But my dear, it is as you had said. The hotel costs a great deal, for a long stay such as ours must be. I had inquired for a cottage. William may stay in the hotel, it is true, since he must leave before we three. I spoke to William as we worked in the stream — eh, William?'

William too was blinking, but John went on. 'For Everett's work needs many weeks — even the background, since he is thorough.'

Already he walked away through the meadow, so they must follow. She came beside him.

'John, it is odd — to change everything all in a hurry like this.'

In a low voice he said, 'My dear, you have seen how Everett is hurt. He needs our care. William is rough with him — and Everett is a fragile youth.'

'Fragile? I am not sure of that.'

John smiled, while she still was thinking, we three shall live together in a cottage. It was wonderful, and full of peril and strangeness.

'It's only two doors up.' They had come to the main track through the hamlet, and stopped beside a white thatched cottage.

'This is the schoolmaster's house.' John waved to it. 'But it's summer now, and Mrs Stewart is glad to let it.'

He tapped on the door, and Mrs Stewart, a brisk body, let them in then stepped outside.

John showed them round. 'The school-room is behind the cottage. We may have this sitting room, and the two small rooms that open from it.'

The sitting room was neat. Through the narrow doors to either side they could see the ends of bedsteads.

'I thought I could sleep on the sofa in here, and you, my dearest, could have this small room for your "boudoir".'

'But John, it's hardly more than a cupboard.'

'That's a charming little bed, dear, and better than I shall have.'

'"Charming"? I can touch both walls as I lie in it. And why

should my husband sleep out on the sofa? That "cupboard" on the other side has a bed in it too.'

John said airily, 'Oh – I thought Everett could sleep in there.'

'Everett? I see, this is what you meant. And we leave William out, to stay in the hotel by himself.'

John made a patient, even saintly smile. 'William says he enjoys the hotel's comforts. And soon he must leave. Ask him, my dear.'

She turned to William, whose face was puckered and dry. 'I prefer the hotel, Mrs R, to be frank.'

She looked then to Everett, who met her eye quickly and looked away.

John's fingers hovered near his teeth, like a child watching big people make a decision.

She looked round the small room, with its embroidered cloths and vase of flowers. It was simple, clean and bright. She saw the choice was hers, and full of doubt and danger.

'And the rent, John?'

'Oh, that? We can have it for five pounds a week.'

'Five pounds a week for three cupboards in a row? Take me, please, to Mrs Stewart.' She braced herself for the duel of pennies.

In the event Mrs Stewart did not fight hard. Perhaps she hardly believed herself that she could find five pounds a week.

'Below one pound and ten shillings I canna, nae, I willna go.' She jerked the pelmet sharply straight.

'Oh, I'm so sorry. I should have loved to live here. But for a time like two months — a pound a week is *all* we can find.'

She waited by the door, for Mrs Stewart to let her out.

'Two months, did ye say? Will ye wait, if you please. I needs must speak to Mr Stewart.'

So they agreed. She stepped lightly as they started back down to the meadow. John came beside her, pleased as she was.

'You have made a handsome bargain, my dear. You are so good with money, and I am so bad.' He was far from contrite.

'You do not need to be so, John. You always leave such things to me — or to your father. Five pounds a week! Where was your head?'

But John was carefree, now the plan was made. 'And Everett's genius will be in my hands, the whiles he will be painting me. For I shall have my work to do.'

'You mean, for your lectures in Edinburgh?'

'No, dear goose, I mean my work of saving Everett. For I see what he is capable of.'

'Are you sure, John, he will let you "save" him?'

'I know not, but I am bound to try. Oh, Effie, it is as if we had the young Raphael himself, living with us like a son.'

Sharply she said, 'Do you wish you could adopt him, John?'

He only laughed. They had come where they had sat before, where Crawley was packing their plates in the hamper. The brothers were speaking together, closely, near the water's edge. She could see Everett's swollen face was displeased. Then they both glanced to her — a pointed look, quick and away. So she knew they were speaking of her, and William gave Everett warning.

John in the meantime had picked up a pebble, and sent it skimming across the stream.

'Ducks and drakes!' cried William. He broke away from Everett. 'Do you know, John, what skips the best of all?'

'Why a smooth round stone, all thin and flat,' John answered from the shallows. He had his shoes off again.

'Why no, Mr R. Crawley, hold!' William strode to the hamper and took out a plate.

Everett started. 'You don't mean dinner plates, you great buffoon.'

'You priceless idiot,' William replied. 'I mean broken china.' He raised the plate high and brought it down on a stone.

'William!' she cried.

'No fear, Mrs R. I shall pay for the plate.' His face was grim, he would not stop. He broke another, and another. Then he picked a gleaming, jagged shape, and with a sharp flick sent it spinning. It skimmed, tripped, bounced ten, now eleven times.

'Bravo, William!' John joined him. 'A revelation.' He picked up a shard, and sent it skimming and hopping like William's.

'Oh stop!' she cried. It was the housewife in her. But John was taken with the game, and Everett, in spite of his hurt, joined in.

Watching from the bank, she glanced at each of them. William was grim and hurled his shards with a twist. Everett would not meet her eye, and his swollen face, from the side, looked like a mask. And John seemed as happy as a child at play, breaking plates and chucking pieces. Often he gave Everett a sidelong look, which was shy, sly — she could not fathom it. He had got what he wanted, she could see. But *what* did John want, getting the three of them into one bucket? There were plans in his head which she could not guess. But for herself — it was wonderful. She had not lost Everett after all. Instead they would be living in the same room, almost. Was this unwise? Time would show.

But the china skipped: she would not be left out. She

smashed her own plate, and while Crawley, who squatted on the bank, shook his head, she sent sharp-edged diamonds and slender white triangles hopping, leaping, skipping on the sparkling shallow water.

4

They moved to the cottage, where she and Everett slept in the tiny cupboard rooms and John on the sofa in the sitting room between. All day Everett would be out painting, while John worked by the sitting-room window, and she made the cottage nice with a vase of long grasses, and flowers from the garden.

Or, when it rained all day, as often it did, they were all in the cottage —for William joined them. Everett offered to help with her drawing. They set their chairs side by side, and drew William where he lolled across John's sofa, with whisky in a glass beside him.

'Get comfortable, William, and then be still,' Everett spoke sharply.

'There's no "comfortable" when you're shut indoors all day. But I give you good health and damn the French!'

John quietly laughed where he sat by the window, writing letters.

Everett drew his chair closer to hers. 'Just get his posture. Round shapes, balloons, for his head and his body, and lines for his legs like a match-stick man.' His voice was gentle, with a soft catch in its timbre, and so close in her ear it might be in her head.

'Now let's put some meat on William. Let's give him calves, thin and faint — *now* we draw the trousers in.'

She had half-closed her eyes, for her pencil seemed to move on its own, as if she were drawing from Everett's sight.

'That's better — oh, that's *good*. You should come and see, John.'

John had turned to watch them. He sat back as if throned with his hands on his knees. Yellow hairs in his brows spiked down over his eyes in a way that gave him an elderly look.

'It's because you're showing me,' she quietly said.

'It *isn't* just that. You have talent, I do believe.'

John blew his nose, and made no move to see the drawing. 'This rain, now, Everett — it would do for your "Deluge".'

'Your "Deluge"?' she said.

Everett sat back. 'That will be my *big* painting — a true epic in oils.'

John stood, their lesson was interrupted. 'Everett has told me. He will show the world in the Flood, in a great panel with different sections. It will be a scene of catastrophe, with all the world drowned and mankind chastised for its vanity and sinfulness.'

'Oh how terrible!' she said.

'Terrible!' John stood. 'It is the greatest of subjects. And it will have such cloud-painting as never was done. It will leave John Martin's "Deluge" nowhere.'

'Cloud-painting, John? And with all the world drowned.'

'You are not pleased?' Everett had stood beside John.

She gazed at them. If she did not take care, Everett could be her enemy for ever. Still she said, 'It sounds heartless to me. And vain in the artist, to enjoy such a thing.'

Everett's jaw dropped, while John exclaimed, 'Heartless? But the terribleness *is* the greatness! Our geology teaches, there *was* once a Deluge. Such a thing shows how vast our universe is, where worlds may be snuffed out in a twinkling, and Nature care not a jot. No, nor God neither. To face such a thought you need flint and metal in you.'

John glared as from a pulpit, while she was browbeaten, at a loss. To Everett she said, 'I am sorry...'

'What!' William stood as well. 'You must never say sorry to Everett. You did him good. Now he's famous, no one tells him the truth. And if you have saved us from his gloomy, sodden "Deluge" — it's as good as if you saved us from a real flood.'

'For shame!' John cried. He looked between them, but Everett's face was uncertain now. She saw the "Deluge" hovered further off, she had spoiled John's plan for Everett's art. Neither man was her friend now.

'Mmmmph.' John grunted. She saw his hurt, he would make her pay for what she had done. But for now, with dignity, he picked up the Scotch plaid, which they had bought in the nearby town of Callander, and wrapped it round his shoulders.

'I shall away to the hotel, to see if the proofs of my book are come. The proofs of a book by a heartless critic, who smiles while the world is drowned.' He looked dignified in his tartan toga, like a sort of Scottish Roman.

'John —' she began, but he ignored her.

As he stepped into the passage which led to the door, they heard a faint tapping on the door itself. Perhaps their visitor had tapped before.

They caught John's voice as he opened the door. But at once his tone changed, it grew soft and silvery, and quiet so they could not catch a word. A faint voice answered, then John spoke again with a music, a lilt.

She moved so she saw them through the door-frame. John, in his plaid, stooped over a tiny figure in a clear blue hood and cloak, who shyly held a big basket to him.

'I thank you, little maid,' he said. 'Oh, but what a heavy basket it is! And you have carried it all this way!'

'John?' she inquired.

'My dears.' He turned. 'This little maid is the housekeeper's daughter. She has brought us the fruit from the hotel, which we ordered. And in this rain too!'

'It's a soft rain,' the small girl said.

'By no means.' He took the umbrella that leaned by the door. 'I have a gamp. For I was going to the hotel myself. I shall escort you all the way.'

It seemed he had forgotten the rest of them. He put the basket down, and opened the umbrella, and held it out over her head.

So, as she watched, they walked away, John talking still in the same strange, milky, singsong voice, as his tall figure bent to the tiny girl. It was as if they were grandfather, granddaughter, walking like a couple.

She came back in the room, with the fruit, to see the brothers still at odds.

'I spoke out of turn.' She was abashed, distressed. Everett was staring with hard eyes.

'No.' His face changed. 'You did not. Nor did William. I don't know if I am a painter of Deluges. Anyway I shalln't paint it today.'

She sighed and shook her head.

'Don't be so sad. Instead, I shall paint a picture of you — with foxgloves in your hair, if I may.' He took the small bunch from the vase where she put them. 'Please.' Courteously he gave them to her.

'Thank you.' She was confused, her eyes pricked, she wanted to cry. He was not her enemy after all.

'It is your painting,' she said softly. '*You* arrange them, if you will.'

She sat on a chair, very still – as if dead, almost, while he hung the flowers to the side of her head. His fingers moved gently, so her hair barely stirred.

'Will that do, William?'

William had been watching keenly. 'Excellent. They look so fine, I shall paint Mrs R as well.'

'What, both of you?' she cried. 'I shall shrivel to nothing. Please no, I'm out of sorts.'

'Nonsense, you'll be the Muse of Art. It'll be like the Academy Schools. But what will *you* do? Will you sit like Linda, at the end of the opera?'

'Not now. I'm fretful. I shall do my work.'

She picked up a red skirt, which she had been stitching, and made herself comfortable in the chair.

'Please move only your hands, nothing else.'

The brothers leaned pieces of board on chair backs, and drew up stools on which to sit. They opened their painting boxes, and took out their palettes.

'Look at that,' said William. 'I use wood for my palette, as honest painters always have. But for his best palette, to use indoors, our Everett must have – *porcelain.*'

She looked at the oval of shining white, which was unchipped and spotless – Everett must guard it carefully. She murmured, 'It's a lovely piece of china.'

William jeered, 'It's not a tea-set.'

Everett ignored him and they both fell silent. There was quiet in the cottage. She heard their breathing, and the patter of the rain where it blew on the window. A log broke in the grate, the timber of the cottage quietly creaked with the wind. When she stole glances at the brothers, their eyelids were feathered, gazing down to their paintings. Or if their eyes met hers, they were cold and careful: she was the subject. She let her thoughts empty, so peace enveloped her.

William put his board down. 'I've caught you, I think.'

Everett leaned over. 'You've got the hand. But look, the upper arm is too long. Scrape it out from the shoulder. You must do it again.'

'Who are you telling what to do? I'm not scraping anything out. Besides, it won't get better if I go on.'

'Can I see? May I stand?' Everett nodded, and she went where she could see William's painting. The brush-strokes were bright and brisk, perhaps he caught her thoughtful eyes – or had he made her slightly squint?

'The foxgloves are a wonderful pink.' She fingered her scarf. 'Maybe my jabot is not so green.'

'It's a sketch,' said William. 'I like a quick sketch. You can kill a thing, getting the details right.'

'You don't have to kill it,' Everett said.

'I haven't your patience. You'll be sitting here for another hour, Mrs R.'

William wiped his brush on a rag, and was away through a door. They heard him rummage in the cupboards of the schoolroom beyond.

She sat again. She adjusted her pose to Everett's words, then said, 'I'm ready.'

'Thank you.'

The air had changed, now William had gone, and she and Everett were alone in art.

'Are you painting my fingers?'

'How do you know?'

She did not answer. He must be drawing her very gently, the passage of his gaze felt like a caress. Her fingers stopped sewing, the work lay in her lap, as she passed into a shadowy place. The eyes of this man touch me here, and now here. With a slight ache she said,

'William tells me he has hopes of marrying shortly.'

'Oh, William? Yes, he has his Enid. They plan a big brood — little boys in sailor suits, little girls in ribbons.' He studied his picture. 'And you? May you and John begin a family, now you are home from Venice?'

She was suddenly caught. 'Oh! We have no plans.'

'But one day?' His smile was kindly, so her eyes must smart.

'John does not like children. He calls them bits of putty. He says their eyes are like rat's hair.' She sat now thin as a stick.

'Like rat's hair?' He frowned. 'But *you* like children?'

'We shall have no children.'

He stopped work entirely. It seemed his gaze enveloped her, so she sat inside his eye. Her skin burned, they were on the momentous edge. She should not speak but his eye was lifting her silence from her.

'We live like angels.' It was almost a whisper.

He blinked: it was better he did not understand.

'It is John's wish. He wants my figure not to spoil, and for me always to climb the Alps with him.'

She saw his understanding grow. 'You mean —' He stopped there.

She dropped her eyes. His lips moved though no word came.

There was a stamping outside the door.

'John —' she began.

46

He opened the door and came in dripping, with a big parcel under his arm.

'The weather of your country, wife! It's a hundred yards and I had the gamp, and still I'm wet right through this plaid. But look — they are come!'

'The proofs of your book?'

He smiled, his anger was long forgotten. He let the umbrella drip into the fireplace, and hung the wet plaid across a chair-back.

'Yes. Oh, but what's this? You are painting already. Why, bless my soul, it's a picture of you, dear.'

Through his words and stampings she had collected herself. 'Do you not think, John, it is a graceful study? I think he has caught — my curious features.'

John raised a pale blue eye to her, and lowered it again to the canvas.

'The likeness is – good.' He bent so his nose nearly banged the canvas. 'The foxgloves are beyond compare. I have one query. That pucker at the neck – is that exact?'

'Ah!' Everett picked up his palette knife, but John stayed his arm.

'Don't touch it. Allow me to look more.' Behind John his plaid dripped a puddle on the floor, and the smell of wet wool enveloped the room.

Abruptly he turned. 'It is a perfect gem. I shall buy it, if I may. For fifty pounds, maybe? I think that's fair. What do you say?'

'Most pleased...'

He scooped it up, and leaned it on the window-sill next to his table.

'I shall hang it, my dear, where we may always see it.'

Still she felt that, with his words, he had picked up the

picture, and her, and Everett, and placed them in separate pockets of his large frock-coat.

He moved the chair with the plaid, so he could stand in front of the fire. 'It itches,' he said, meaning the tartan. He lifted his coat-skirts to warm himself better.

The inner door opened, and William came back. 'Look, I found rackets. We can play in the school-room.'

'A capital idea — but another day, William. First I have to see my pages. My dear, might I have a knife?' His eye called her to duty.

He slit the string, undid the wrappings, and brought before them sheets of paper. He held one up, it looked big as a poster, with a column of print from top to bottom. He looked close. 'Uh!' he had caught a mistake. He took another, then another, absorbed, content for the others to watch. Before their eyes he spread the sheets, across the table, on chairs, on the floor, where he crouched to inspect them. From time to time he looked up quickly, smiling, while all round him the floor became covered with paper, as if the rain outside had come in as snow.

Over the papers she glanced shyly to Everett, who looked back with a face more white than the paper.

Finally John gathered the proofs together. 'My friends, I have detained you — and filled this space. I am sorry. But also — I am in a humour to celebrate. We shall make a party on the morrow. We may order what we wish in the hotel.'

He sat back in a chair — and continued to read. William left, she set the table. But as they ate John read, and after the meal, looking up from time to time to murmur, 'My dears.' She and Everett read Ainsworth and Mrs Trollope desultorily.

At last John yawned, and stretched so his great arms filled the room. She and Everett retired to their opposite cabins, while John laid his length along the sofa.

Through the door of her cell she heard his snoring begin. Briefly he whimpered 'Wa — ma —', then the slow clogged roar from his windpipe resumed. His dreams would not be bad tonight.

But she could not sleep, she would not sleep again. Her hearing, like a ghost arm, stretched out through the cottage, till she knew she was listening at Everett's door. She found dead silence, so she knew he was awake.

5

'No rain today,' William said at the door. 'Shall we take a turn?'

'Let us,' said John, 'I have yet to make the list of what I want for tonight. It's too damp for painting today, I think, Everett.'

Though the rain had stopped, they walked through moist air and the smell of wet soil. The clouds, it seemed, had come down to earth, and lay in drifting rags across the fir-trees. Humps of hill-top bulged above them, like mountains in Germany.

They passed piled stones beside the path, and William and John began building again.

'A monument,' John said, 'to our presence, and labours.'

Everett hung with them, but she walked ahead. She needed a distance, she was shaking still, from her words to Everett the day before. Had she truly told him she was virgin still? If he understood her, what must he think? He must wonder how she was content with this.

There was a commotion behind her, a shout or a cry. She turned and saw the three men bent in a huddle.

'Oh, it's just Everett,' William said as she came. 'He's crushed his thumb.'

Evidently Everett had joined in the building works, he stood red-faced, with smarting eyes, clutching his hand inside his coat.

'Let me see.' She pulled the hand into the light. 'Oh, but

what have you done? Can you move the thumb?'

William looked in. 'You'll lose that nail for sure.'

'I am perfectly well,' Everett said with annoyance. 'Two hurts in as many weeks. I have become ridiculous utterly — the clown of Glen Finlas.'

'Well, not for me,' she said, but smiled as well. 'We'll poultice it, and wrap it round. It will be better soon, I think.'

They returned to the cottage, where she made little fuss as she bandaged his hand, since Everett was on his dignity.

'I ask too much of you,' he said as she finished. 'But I thank you from the bottom of my heart.'

She bent low, for she had blushed at once.

John held up his list. 'I must be off to the housekeeper, in the hotel. But first, my dear, may you fetch your scissors?' He stroked his hair. 'I have grown lank, and I should like to be smart. In truth a trim would do no harm, to William and Everett either. Let us not look Bohemian as we meet tonight.'

The brothers blinked and William said, 'Our hair may be cut in the hotel, I am sure.'

John raised his palm. 'By no means, when we have the best skill here. My dear — let us show your talent. I don't know where I should be without you.'

He pulled their trunk forward from the side of the room, and sat there very tall and still.

She fetched her scissors, and snipped in the air to flex her fingers.

'Lift your head, please.' She set a towel round John's neck, and began to clip his sandy strands.

'My turn next,' William said, 'Everett, leave that scab alone.'

'It's tender.' His finger hovered at the bridge of his nose.

'Puh! The swelling is nearly gone. It's your hand that's the latest drama now. You are a walking Casual Ward.'

John prepared to stand. 'Thank you, my dear.' He smoothed the longer hairs past his left ear. 'Ah, those little nimble fingers – what busy mice they are!'

She lightly dipped as he put on his coat. By the door he bowed.

'My friends, adieu.' He paused in the doorway, for the sky darkened again. As he left, rain pattered on the window panes.

She raised her scissors coaxingly. 'William?'

He in turn sat, and held the towel to his neck. He was docile while she began to snip, but then he made noises.

'Plink. Donk.'

'Are you well?' she asked.

'Cloinggg.'

'It's all right,' Everett said, 'He's being an orchestra, warming up.'

When she pushed his head down to clip his poll, he made dewlaps as he sank his jaw deep into his chest.

'Fig-aro. Fig-aro. Figaro-Figaro-Figaro.'

A hum-and-buzz *Barber of Seville* began. She sang herself and snipped in rhythm. Everett hummed also, while, as if in respect for them, the rain outside paused.

Clip! She snipped strongly, on a closing chord. 'Oh dear. William, I'm so sorry.'

William loosened the towel and stood. They all surveyed the bright curl, that had lived on his forehead, lying on the open pages of *The Witness*, which she had spread on the chair beside her.

'Thank you – I needed a change of style.'

She was rueful. 'Your hair looks nice, though.'

'He still has too much,' Everett called. 'You didn't take off half enough.'

William thumbed his nose to Everett as a boxer might.

'Everett.' She turned to him invitingly. 'Will you be cut?'

'Closely, please.' He clutched the towel with his good

hand, while the bad hand, bandaged, lay on his knee.

'Your poor nose.' She looked close. 'But what a thicket your hair is!'

Carefully she worked with the comb to part it. His head became totally still when she moved his hair with her fingers also. Her finger-tips tingled, for his hair was fine as feather-down. She brought the scissors close.

Everett asked, 'Will you parents come to John's lectures in Edinburgh?'

'My mother for certain, and my little sister Sophie. John has asked for her, she is very dear to him. Whether the rest will come over from Perth – '

'You've told me of Perth.'

'I wish I could show you the old town,' she murmured. He had still not moved. Her fingers roved absently over his head.

'Hem,' William coughed. She began to snip.

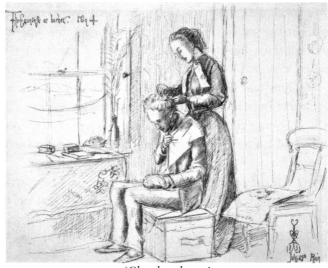

'Closely, please.'

'John doesn't like Perth,' she said, 'But that's because his parents won't go there.'

'Why's that?'

'His family lived where we live now. Yes, the same plot, though the house was rebuilt. But something happened to John's mother in the old house – the most hideous thing that could happen to anyone.' Snip went her scissors, along Everett's forehead.

'Say,' said William, 'I like a gothic horror.'

'William, I cannot. This was a true horror, not something in a story.'

William could no longer sit. 'I'll look at the weather.' He opened the door.

'William!' she cried. The gust blew cut hairs all over the room.

'I'm sorry. But Crawley can sweep them up. There's another storm coming for sure.' He closed the door and sat again.

The light in the cottage grew yet more dim. She fell quiet, attending to her hair-cutting, and Everett it seemed could no longer speak either. Between snips she softly parted his hairs, her finger-tips moving like breath on his scalp. She knew he could tell what her fingers said. I care very much for your wounds, they said. I have trusted you as my most dear friend.

The light was sinking, her cutting had slowed. He was holding his breath, as his hairs themselves leaned in to her touch. Through the hairs, through her fingers, his message came – and I, I hurt with care for you. Any secret you tell is safe with me.

From far off came a roll of thunder, the air in the cottage was close and warm. William drummed his fingers on the table.

'Not a lot of art today, then, brother.'

*

John returned, and later the baskets from the hotel arrived, with cold cuts, a game pie, cheeses, tarts, fruit, and bottles of wine as well as sherry. William went to the hotel to bathe and dress. By late afternoon, when he came back, they all were smart, as if they were visiting a grander house. With clinking glasses they toasted John's book to be.

'What's it about?' William asked.

'Venice,' said John.

'Oh. Abroad. Who's for battledore and shuttlecock?' He held up the rackets he had found before.

'And why not?' John caught the spirit at once. 'Stir your stumps, Everett, you are in a study. I shall be the London Gamecock, and you can be the Jersey Stunner.'

In the school-room they pushed back the few desks, and strung the net between the window-fastenings. John took off his coat, and they played in changing singles and pairs. She must put by her cares — and her zest quickly woke: her long skirt would not stop her from darting and sprinting. She stretched high to snick the shuttlecock down, and swooped to catch it before it hit the floor. William lobbed it up, and bounced it off the ceiling. In spite of his hurts Everett too sprang to life. He stretched long thin limbs, to bat the shuttlecock straight to meet her. And John whipped and slammed it fiercer than anyone. Age was going to put down youth, and literature show it could answer art.

Back in the sitting room they sat to eat and drink, and got caught in a passion of toasting each other. Everett held a tankard high.

'A bumper of sherry to you, Sir John, and to your good reviews.'

'And to your sales.' William toasted again.

'And to your painting, Lord Everett.' John raised his cup high.

'Which is of you, sir.' Everett toasted again, then turned to her. 'But Countess, will you honour us with a sentiment.' His eyes were excited, even wild.

She stood. 'To all our talents, in the world and at home.'

From gallantry perhaps they all repeated her toast, and dashed their tankards together.

Everett took out his sketching book, and between sips and toasts began to draw busily. His hair flew, his pen danced. This was not his normal style. He looked often at her.

John watched. 'You are inspired. These are studies for your Deluge, maybe?'

'They are studies of your lady, sir. As I would dress her, were she off to see the Queen, because indeed you became Sir John.'

'Indeed!' John blinked. 'May I see them, please?' For a moment he looked irate.

Everett gave him the sketch-book. 'I wonder, should I leave off painting and turn jeweller, do you think?'

'May I see?' she asked, 'If they are of me.'

They all came round the sketch-book which John held.

'Hmmm,' he rumbled. 'These are works of what the poet Coleridge called Fancy.'

'I'd call them rum,' William peered. 'With sherry mixed — from the vaults of Ruskin and Domecq.'

As she looked the cottage darkened round the bright sheets. For the drawings were of her. She saw her nose, with its impudent tip – but ears of wheat grew in her hair. She wore a chain of flower-bells. The necklace he had drawn was made of live birds.

Everett looked to her. 'And your bracelet is a lizard, scuttling up your arm.' As she looked the lizard moved, it was alive.

'They're *magic* drawings — and so elegant.'

John gave a quick laugh, like a rattle. 'They have caprice.'

Everett stood. 'Brother, I challenge you. Back to the battledore.'

The brothers went to the school-room, while John picked up a proof and scanned it. She still held the sketch-book. She saw the gift he had made to her, he had dressed her in the animals that strayed within the woods. He had made cornflowers grow in her breast.

There was whooping next door as they began to play She sat back with closed eyes, for the wine worked in her. The cottage swayed, its woodwork stirred. Did she hear small feet, behind the wainscot? She blinked awake, for John had put his proof-sheet by, and was speaking to her.

'Do you know, my dear, I'm half in love.'

She came alert. 'In love!'

'I mean in a pure and innocent way.'

From next door they heard William shout, 'Yours!'

'May I know, John, whom you love?' Was he jealous, suspicious? Would he make her jealous?

John lazily swilled his sherry. 'Oh, I only mean the little maid, who lives in the hotel. Do you know whom she reminds me of?'

'Do you mean my little sister Sophie?'

'Now *there's* a thought! But no, I didn't mean sweet Sophie. I meant, my pretty goose, that the little maid reminds me of *you*. When first we met, and I so fell in love. When I wrote that story for you, called The King of the Golden River. Surely you were the same age then?'

'I think not. I was twelve. She isn't yet ten.'

'Are you sure? I'm so old, I can't tell these things. But that is the age where beauty dwells, we spoil as we grow big.'

Both brothers next door hollered 'Mine!'

John sipped sherry, she sipped too. Love, in love. She must not think it, she was wed. But the air had grown very close in the room: the rain-clouds must be piling again, high up through the darkness over the cottage. Would Everett's Deluge come after all, and cataracts pelt them from their home? She needed a drench, she was burning hot.

But had she dozed? If so, it was for seconds only, for John sat just as he did before, nodding and smiling over his glass. He caught her eye.

'My dear, I have such hopes for this book. And for Everett's painting, and what the world says of it. We are truly blest.'

'Let us give thanks, John.'

But if she had slept, what was it that woke her? It was not the brothers, she knew their shouts well. It was rustling feet, a swish of tails. The animals had come from deep in the wood, and got inside her. Everett's drawings had let them in. Their soft quick claws tripped through her womb, but she had no fear. Scamper. Run. Go where you will. They could take the pink inside of her, and turn it to the outside. The cottage walls dissolved, she saw tree-trunks crowded with whiskered faces. A slow drumming began: boum, boum. A slant-eyed demon was coming to her.

She said aloud, 'But the animals *are* the demon, I see.'

'Effie? My dear?'

'Oh John, I'm with you! Such a strange place has visited me.' But who could the demon be, she must ask.

John smiled to her, patient and bright. Everett, in the schoolroom, shouted, 'Mine!'

6

What was strange, through the following days, was how the word 'virgin' hung in her head. She looked again at each woman she saw. A party came out, as she passed the hotel. A child bawled in the arms of a nurse, while the mother, quite slender, stepped lightly ahead. Yet it was the mother who had been rent by love. And rent again — she may have shrieked for hours — while the infant was fetched out of her. Oh, she and John had been frightened of that. The pain, the howling, the blood and the after-mess. Or she watched other wives, when they stood and talked where the wagon of the carrier stopped each week. The wives of men. She too was a wife, but the other wives stood across a chasm from her. If you listened hard at night, maybe, you would hear the soft crooning moan of all the women in the beds of the world. Their husbands loved them. And she — where had she been, the last five years?

The strange fever, that overwhelmed her in the cottage, roamed through her all the following days. Especially she felt like a roast in the tiny church, beside the loch, where they worshipped on Sundays. The tight pews were packed with guests from the hotel – bald stately men, ladies with ostrich plumes.

'O Lord, save thy people,' the precentor chanted. He had eyebrows like a hedge: his terrier, beside him, howled when he sang.

'And bless thine inheritance,' she moaned with the congregation. She sighed as she saw nearby a lady's mantle of Maltese lace. Lace would be so cool, if you wore on your nakedness only lace.

They stood for the hymn. 'Christ hath a garden walled around,' John boomed beside her. When he sang, his nose looked as though it had only one nostril, gaping like cavern. Why cannot I like John more?

'Like trees of spice his servants stand,' the brothers sang, standing opposite. Everett was a tree of spice – his throat was soft and white as cream. But why must he play with that wound on his nose? The scab would come off in church. His eyes — she could fall into his eyes. If he stole her away – to Arabia and the lands Lord Byron knew, to ravish her amidst the scalding sands... John, you must guard me, *you* are my husband.

They sat, the precentor hoarsely called, 'We are greatly honoured to have with us today Dr Muir of Stirrling.' But he was fat, Dr Muir, and red in the face, and sweating like a hog in the fire that burned her also.

'I take my text, brethren and sisters, from the Epistle to Titus, Chapter III, Verse 4, "But avoid foolish questions, and genealogies, and contentions, and strivings about the law".'

He looked enraged, burning red and frothing with spit. He talked of angels, so she remembered John saying that angels know not carnal love. She thought of *Paradise Lost* – then thought, John is wrong. Milton's angels love – she remembered Raphael, 'the affable archangel', chatting with Adam and Eve in the Garden. The archangel blushed as he told them how angels loved. 'If spirits embrace, total they mix...easier than air with air.' She looked at John: you must give me love, my lord. How can I be true if you give me no love?

Dr Muir had become a distant drone. She writhed her back, stretching her neck across the pew-top. Half-closing her eyes she saw the angels. They must be all of a hundred feet tall, yet they fitted inside the church, hovering slow on gigantic wings. Their robes were made of pliable light, which brightened to blinding as they entered each other. Then their hair stood tall in flickering spires, while through their merged forms there were sparklings, flashes, like the fireworks in Vauxhall Gardens. With dazzled eyes she saw them part, though still with their wings they cloaked each other, caressing to a swooning music which closed her eyes in happy tears.

The congregation and Dr Muir returned, but she had seen the lust of angels. She knew what no doctor of theology knew: there is no sweetness like angel love. John had been wrong – could she teach him his error? Her eyes strayed to Everett. At any moment she would up, and dash from the church.

The congregation stood, Dr Muir had finished. They shuffled in a queue to the open air.

John saw her glow. 'Yes, dearest, I agree, Dr Muir was ingenious. Still I question his reading of Titus III.'

She nodded as he explained, and took large breaths.

'Also, John – it's so nice, walking beside Loch Achray.'

Through sunlight and dapple the congregation strolled, while the carriages, returning to the hotel, moved through them and away at a leisurely pace, with their windows down to let in the air.

'A capital day,' 'A splendid service,' the brothers said as they came beside them.

'Good Heavens,' said John, 'There's Crawley, talking with the hotel maids.'

As she watched, the two girls kicked off their slippers, to walk barefoot through the roadside grass. What a lovely idea, she ached to be a common girl.

At the cottage they brought table and chairs outside, and ate at their ease the cold meats she set.

William sighed. 'I'm sorry to be going.' He was to leave the following Wednesday.

'Take heart,' said Everett, 'The Countess will be with you as far as Perth.'

'And I look forward to my journey with William.' She would travel with William as far as Perth, to pass some days with her family. 'Mrs Stuart will be good company too.' Their landlady, the school teacher's wife, would come with her to see her chaperoned.

'We are grateful to Mrs Stewart,' John said.

'We *are*, John,' she said, making fun of his solemnity. 'But William, I am sad that you are going. We shall miss you – and the fish you caught.'

William muttered, half to himself, 'I'm not even sure I ought to go.' He looked at Everett, who, abruptly, got to his feet.

'Well, I'm off up the glen. It's a fine day for painting, Sunday or not, and I'm half way through a delicate lichen.'

William stretched and yawned. 'I'll get back to the hotel. To be honest, I'm inclined to a nap.'

She and John were left, at ease and replete on a beautiful day. But John she saw was far from sleepy. A vibration began inside her.

'I'm hot out here. The cool in the cottage must be delicious.'

She stood but lingered. She waited till he raised his head, then nodded and went indoors. 'For it has to be John,' she murmured over. She was married to him, there was no other way.

He stood. 'And I should return to my Edinburgh lecture.'

'It is the Lord's day, John, and not a day for labour.'

'Yet Everett works – and I shall jot.'

Let him jot. She must compose herself. She went inside her tiny room. So, at last, the time has come. Her heart was sounding, her breathing shallow.

On the bed she arranged herself, and lay some moments simply still. In her head she called, 'Come John,' as if her thought could bring him there. For he had sat to his papers beside the window. She heard the quiet smacking sound as, several times, he moistened his lips.

Softly she said aloud, 'John.' The door was ajar, the sound should reach him. Perhaps too he did hear something, for the scratching of his pen-nib paused.

The pen-nib resumed its rub on paper.

'John,' she said again.

A chair-leg scraped. 'Euphemia?' He would be standing, with his head cocked up to catch her answer.

'I am here.' Her voice had sunk low.

She lay still, waiting, and presently the light changed in her cell. John filled the doorway.

With a tremor he asked, 'Are you well, dear?' Though the sheet covered her, he would understand she wore nothing beneath it.

'Come to me.' She moved in the bed, showing where her hips and shoulders were.

'Make me your wife. It is time, dear.'

He stood stock still. Her heart beat so loud he must hear

it too. Slowly she drew back the sheet. With a final flick of her foot she uncovered herself.

'Take your wife, sir.'

Hoarsely he said, 'It is the Lord's day.'

'In the eyes of the Lord we are man and wife.'

He made that gurgle-suck noise with his nose. 'Be covered, I beg.'

She saw his distress. What devil made her part her legs, and slowly swing her knees apart?

'Ah!' He drew back, as though a serpent crouched there.

'Why, John?' she cried. 'What is the matter?'

He said in an odd, soft, mealy voice, 'It is how you are made.'

'So you have said, John. Tell me clearly' – she rose till she stood up on the bed – 'What is the fault you find in me?'

He rocked, his hands played, he looked blind with dismay. Above him she stood tall and bare as Eve.

'It is – the hand of Nature sometimes errs — I can not – ' He seemed to choke.

She stepped down from the bed. But what had he seen? He winced away, he feared her bare skin touching his clothes.

She felt cold now, exposed. He sat down on the bed as if his strength had failed. With tears in his eyes he reached and gently took her hand. Unhappily she let him take it.

'Dear wife, let us not go down this road. We are given to bear – a great affliction. That is your tragedy, and mine also. Yet still we are a loving husband and wife.'

She shook his hand off and bawled out loud, 'What is it that is wrong with me, that no man may love me?'

He looked up with frightened eyes, his limbs and body folded small: his years, his age, his strength, had gone. She wondered, what would he do next?

It was shown to him, what he would do. He rose, and turned, and knelt on the floor.

'Pray with me.'

She did not kneel, or take his hand. Still he raised his head,

'Dear Loving Father – Maker of Man and Woman – we beg that Thou shed thy healing light, even upon thy daughter Euphemia. Bind with thy grace her wounded faculties –'

'John!' she interrupted him.

He reached out quickly and grasped her wrist. 'Kneel thou down and pray with me!' He pulled at her with a surprising strength.

She snatched her hand free. 'Do you dare, and in front of me, to pray for my brain?'

It seemed his temper flared at last. He stood, he shouted, 'The curse it is to have a wife, who is *both* mis-formed, and mad!' He raised his head to the ceiling, 'Great Lord of Hosts, how have I offended, that you visit your wrath upon my house?'

He stayed standing, gazing upwards, in his strong demand. She pulled the bed-sheet round herself and moved further off.

A change came: his jaw dropped, his hands hung down. He looked as though he truly listened, to the space above where no voice spoke.

'Aaah.' As his head swung down he sighed at length, to pour out all the air in his lungs. He reached for the back of her chair, and sat, his head so low she saw only his hair. He was nowhere still, tiny shivers or trembles ran through him as though he had insects under his skin.

'Are you well, John?'

He lifted his head, to show a white face, ravaged. Hoarsely he murmured — to himself, not her,

'It is my vice. I have offended — grievously.'

She knew of no vice or sin he had. 'I know, John, you are in constant prayer.'

Still blind to her, he climbed to his feet. 'I have sinned and I sin every day.'

There followed a curious moment. He turned to her frowning, then his features melted, so she saw his chagrin, shame. She wondered would he start to cry, but instead he slowly raised his hand. Her face had been touched by a blind girl once, damp fingers feathered on her cheeks. John's hand was clammy, boneless, like the paddle of a squid: his mouth was puckered tiny, like a small boy trying to whistle. He was not a man, what *was* he? She felt a spasm of revulsion, as if she could vomit at his touch.

'Get from me, John!'

He blinked, affronted. 'What?' he demanded. 'Do *you* spurn *me*? Great God, how I am troubled with torment and affliction!'

Her vision came hard and clear. 'Speak plainly, John. Am I that torment and affliction?'

His lips munched in perfect anger. 'You are all and worse that my mother told me. Begone from my house!'

Oh, indeed – well, she would oblige his mother. She put her hands on her hips and jutted her chin. She would give him the harridan.

'No, John – remove yourself. This is my boudoir, this *drawer* you have put me in. You have no rights here. Quit my room.'

He stared then, surprised. His hands fluttered, his lower lip trembled. Still he paused by the door, calling out in a high voice, 'Father, I do not dispute your justice. Yet whether, sir, I deserve this *scorpion* you have loosed upon me –'

His voice broke on a high note, he was gone.

'Dead.' She threw herself back full-length on her bed. Dead. Dead. As a husband he is dead to me. She lay panting, repeating his epitaph. Till the new thought rose, which had waited all day. Everett dearest — *if* you want me, I am yours. I may be married to John till the day I die. But if my 'oddity' does not appal you – then I am yours, in the woods, in the meadow, or in this cottage if John is out. Or in the vestry of the church if we find it is free. Nor do I care if you love me or you don't. You may use me and leave me, so you use me with desire.

She listened, but there came no sound. No thunder-clap, no bolt from God. John, she guessed, had gone off on a walk.

At leisure she dressed, and put up her hair. She was handsome enough, if she tilted her head and studied herself through half-closed eyes. She opened the door and stood in its frame: the treacherous woman, the woman of lust. The late daylight did not blink, the topmost leaves of the trees were still. A crow cacked to other crows, flying towards the rising dusk.

Nor could she know when her trespass would be, since she was leaving for Perth. Well, she would return, to the cottage where there waited her husband and — maybe — her lover? And if this 'lover' did not want her and had been simply flirting — well, she would use her wiles. For the king of the night is waiting for me – though is he love, or disgrace?

7

His brush nipped canvas as he sat on the rock. All round him the waterfall dashed and creamed, so he could have been sitting in the prow of a boat. He thought, I miss her voice too, with its Scottish lilt — do you call it a brogue? The unrest in him was worse now she had gone.

Oh, but the painting. He was pleased with this branch, glistening still with wet oil. You could think it stood in front of the canvas, its leaves climbed out in a staircase of fans. The last leaf touched the outline of John — of the white silhouette where his head was to be.

But how had things gone so far? Some trapdoor in his heart had opened, the first time he saw her — with her odd 'piquante' features, and her sad perplexed look like a woebegone elf. Then up she jumped to dance or sing, she laughed and made jests, and was quick to say her mind. He saw at once there was an enigma in her. He must take care — the wife of his patron, of his protector. Scandal must not lie ahead. But to find she was maiden — how did they live so?

And John — John had command of the world's taste in art. John meant to tell him how he should see. I will *not* be his pupil he said each day, then listened to some new thought of John's. But what John did — or not — with his wife! It must make you mad to think it — her white maiden body lying unused in bed, her breasts slack and cold in frost-white sheets, the wrong, the shame, the pity of it. If he thought too long, he would punch John's head. He would take him by the collar, and shake him so he rattled and his follies fell out for all to see.

Would he help her himself? Help her — or harm her. If he led her to scandal and grief and disgrace... But how had she stood for it? She was under John's spell, in his prison.

But where was his mind? Yes, that branch stood out from the canvas, but it made the dark rocks behind it look flat. He must push the space back, but how would he do that? This was the problem with his famous technique. If every detail is microscope-clear, then they all seem the same distance from the eye. Depth, I must force the space back and gain depth.

He sat back with a sigh. Gain depth. He was tired, he had not paused for an hour, neither in painting, nor in turning in fruitless circles of thought.

'A difficulty, Everett?'

Ah, so here was John — a dark figure spidering down the slope, stabbing here and there with his cane.

'Good day, John!' After all, he could not box John's ears. And he must show no sign, of what he had learned in secret. John looked pleased, so he called out, 'Scribble, scribble, John?'

John smiled as he jumped the last gap to the rock. 'It's true my pen runs on these days. Why, my lectures almost write themselves. But do you know what those Edinburghers have done?'

He sat down on a stone, so he talked between his pointed knees. 'They had a beautiful city, below that old grange they call the castle. And in the heart of it they have placed — a railway station. I compare their city to Verona, which has no steam-engines at its core, but every house-front thick with art.'

'And will your audience be pleased to hear that?'

'No — but they will not be bored, nor count the minutes till I stop. Oh, but your painting — you have been busy, I see. Everett, that mountain ash is superb! Those flattened fans, they reach like hands. And the difference you make, between the topside and the underside of the leaves.'

'That's why they shimmer.'

'It's not just the hue. All leaves are reflective, and catch different lights. But forgive me, again I am playing the pedagogue. Oh, I have become a pedant of sight!' John made a rueful mouth, and sat down on the rock so he hugged his knees close. 'Dear friend, I love these bachelor days. You paint, I write, we meet and talk. I suppose it's because I had no brothers — now we two live like brothers in art. I don't know if I have been so happy.'

Sitting forward, John dug his chin into his knees, and gazed into the waterfall. Seen side on, his head was like that of sheep, with his lumping nose and shrinking chin. Ah, John, it's well I don't paint you in profile.

John mused, 'Water is the most protean thing. You will catch its soul within this painting, as water has never been caught before. I do command it.'

'Do not command me.' He spoke quickly, quietly. He was glad he spoke, even a patron must be kept in his place.

John blinked and said softly, 'I beg your pardon.' Then his face changed, he looked aghast.

'John?'

He turned to follow John's stare, and saw between the

roots and stones the small blunt head — flat, wedge-shaped, with black bead-eyes. It swayed a little, he caught the flicker of the darting tongue.

'That's an adder, isn't it?'

'It is — a viper.' John was hoarse.

Both had risen, while the snake slid in a flow like water out of the root-clump and onto their rock.

'Ah!' John had retreated, he trembled and tottered on the brink of the fall.

'John — your cane!'

It came to his hand. He brandished it, stamped.

'Strike home! Strike true!' John called behind him.

But the snake had slipped off, with a sideways flick of its yellowish tail.

'It was just a poor worm. I won't hurt your cane.'

John took the cane back, and leaned upon it. Domes of moisture stood on his brow, he was in a cold sweat.

'Everett, you saved me. Oh, you are strength and I am weakness.'

'I am shaken too. Well, but I have done for today. I must stop and think how I go on.'

He unscrewed the easel's clasps, and wiped his palette clear with rags. John, beside him, was still in a dither, his hands making small flaps.

'Home, John,' he said.

He had his easel folded and slung on his back. They were ready to climb to the path.

'Stamp your feet as we climb up. If any serpent's nearby, it will scuttle away.'

'Yes, Everett.' John spoke with quiet obedience. If they were brothers, he had chosen to be the younger brother.

Stamping their feet, making a racket through bracken and

stones, they cautiously climbed the mossy, leaf-strewn, fern-grown slope.

*

He must not speak of her to John, he would give the wrong sign. But in the evening as they drank sweet sherry, after eating the meal that Crawley had made, he found he said — before he could stop — 'It's glum without the Countess here.'

'Goodness!' said John. 'We can pass a day or two without *women*.'

'I don't call your lady "women".'

'No, she is my own clever monkey. She is my sweet little clever-paws ladykins.' John watched him keenly, did he speak to provoke?

Everett's sight went red, he stood at once. 'Forgive me, John. I have to say — I take exception — to the tone you take of and to the lady.'

'Of and *to* "the lady"?' John himself sat up tall. '*You* take "exception" to the "tone" I use when I speak of my wife.'

'I speak from my reverent respect for her. I honour her — as I honour you.'

But he lowered his head, he was wrong to break out. This could lead — in wrong directions. John watched his uncertainty, then said with a weary, supercilious voice.

'Oh, do sit down, Everett. Frankly I demand it. Be seated, sir! Thank you. I see you must be told that I love my wife, as my true companion on our pilgrimage. She knows the ways I show that love, and the joys we share as few may do. She and I have walked from end to end of the Alps.' John studied him. 'But I forgive your impudence, for the fault is mine. I have allowed you to live too closely with us.'

John eyed him severely for several moments. 'But there is

something else I have on my mind. As you know, I write a good deal of churches. And yet I have never designed a church. Some of your drawings have made me wonder —'

'I'm no architect.' He spoke shortly, interrupting rudely.

'No, nor I, though I write of buildings. But those drawings you did, of those animals for my dear to wear — oh, *please* be at ease, you have ants in your pants — they did make me think. I see that among your other talents, you could design *wonderful* carvings.'

'Carvings?' He must make his own face stone.

'Let's make the test.' John's fingers fluttered like insect wings, bringing Everett his drawing book and pencils.

'Look here, John — I'm not for churches.' Churches — good God! — he was thinking still.

'Trust my foresight. Let *me* draw the arches. You can fill the figures between.' John's sandy-haired head bent down before him.

'There, now — decorate those shapes!'

Everett looked — and on an impulse started to draw. For the idea had come, which would answer John, and confound him too. Then he paused, with an oath, 'Dammit, no!'

John looked up startled from the book he had taken.

'I shall do it a good size, if I do it at all. What I need is wood, to make a stretcher.'

John got up happily. 'There's my brave Everett! And there are boards in the school-room, I am sure we may take them. I shall help you, for I can be a good handyman.'

They took the boards and planks they found, and nailed them together in a big rough triangle. To this frame Everett tacked strips of canvas, over which he pasted paper.

'What paper's that? That's not Whatman's.'

'It's grocery paper. I found it in the scullery.'

'Grocery paper! And I thought I knew all about art.'

'No, it's good, for quick work like this. I shalln't use oils, I'll paint it in turpentine. You'll see, it'll turn out well. But that's for tomorrow. We must let it dry.'

'You're the painter. But isn't it wonderful? After all, we *are* making a church together. And what figures, may I ask, will you paint within the arches?'

'Oh, since it's a church — I shall paint angels. Or one angel, that I heard of lately, but several times. You will see, John.'

'Bless you, Everett.' John spoke like a priest, giving benediction. 'Now let us retire — for you work tomorrow.'

Yes, he thought silently. And you will see who that angel will be. It ought to please you, but I fear it may not.

*

He woke in the dark — or had he been woken? It was odd, the faint cry. Could the house be haunted by the ghost of a child?

He opened his door. In the summer night there was not complete dark, and he saw there was no one in the sitting room. The sound must have come from the place where John lay, for in Effie's absence he slept in her cabin.

He heard no more cries, and was closing his door when — 'Oh!' — he heard a rending shout. This was John for sure, and the next moment the door banged sharply open, and John stumbled out, white in his night-shirt and night-cap, to the table where he fumbled with the lucifer matches.

'Oh — oh — oh!' He was shivering.

'Let me light the candle, John. Sit and take breath. You had a bad dream.'

In a weak voice John murmured, 'Ebewett', and sat back

on the sofa. Everett poured a tumbler of sherry, which John cupped in his hands.

'They have returned, my familiars. I thought they were gone from me, up in these hills. But they writhe, they hiss —'

'Do you mean serpents — such as we saw in the rocks today?'

'Not such, though that one caused my dream. No, but these are the giants of the race, and my companions from the pit of Hell. Yet their house is but a round, plain house, of stone and set in a barren plain. And the little maid, when she came among them...that sweet dear maid, amid their coils...' He shivered, all his body shook.

He waited for John to say more, but John had sunk within himself.

'Be easy, John. I slept badly too.'

John looked up, but scarcely knew him. Presently he stood.

'We are a battle-field. But I thank you, Everett, for your comfort.'

He was himself again. They retired into their opposite rooms.

*

In the morning, nothing was said of the night, and John was again full of words for Edinburgh.

'They have called their town "the Athens of the North", and filled it with columns and pediments. But I shall tell them what I think of the Greeks. For what is the Parthenon, but Stonehenge plus Ornament?'

Everett looked up from his cold meats. 'You prefer the pointed arch?'

'Of *course* the Gothic arch. It is the form God loves. It

bears loads best. If you come back in a thousand years, all windows and doors will be gothic in style.'

'That's more than I know.'

'Most leaves of most trees are of the gothic shape.'

'That's true.' John always could surprise him with odd new thoughts which were not nonsense, quite.

They turned to the window. The sky outside was deep blue-black.

'Not a good day for the glen,' he said.

'But a capital day for painting indoors. I die to see your "angels", Everett.'

'Ah, my angels.' They were less clear now.

'I shall not distract you. I shall read for my lecture within my chamber.'

While John read in the little room, Everett dipped his brush in the turpentine, and approached the great triangle which leaned on the fireplace. He had traced the arches the night before. The space between them would be dark green, to suggest glass. But over against it would be — the angels. She had said something odd, before she left, about the love that angels know. And these angels which he drew for carving — they swooned, leaning close so they almost kissed, with eyelids closing drunk with love. They were thistledown creatures — however could they be cut in limestone? He was in a trance himself, his eyes half-closed, his own mouth pursed as he drew their lips.

'Everett — they are transcendent!'

He turned, startled, he heard no approach. But John was shaking his head with pleasure.

'You like them? I feared I had given them *earthly* passion.'

'Earthly, celestial — is there so great difference? Love is love — and the beauty, oh but the purity of it! I was right to set you on this track. Let us sit, to admire them better.'

John pulled the sofa round, and pressed Everett to sit so they sat side by side. They gazed at the large triangular painting. In the dim room the angels glowed.

I feared I had given them earthly passion.'

'There is but one observation I would make.'

'Yes, John?'

'I take it as a compliment to my lady and to me. Of course I saw at once that not one but most of the angels you drew have the sweetly scooping profile which graces — my wife.'

'Oh —' He had not meant John to notice so fast.

'Yes?' With a kind of mischief, John watched him and waited.

'I respect —' he began, then stopped. He was blushing. For he saw clearly now what his paint-brush had said. He had declared his fascination with her, made it obvious for all to see.

He must face John. 'It is true I have paid tribute to her grace. I hoped it might not displease you.' Though this was not truth — but John did not seem, after all, dismayed.

'I thank you.' He raised his hand. 'About your regard for — "the lady" —'

'John —'

'Allow me to speak. For I have noted you have a — friendship. I am glad too she should have young companions, when I am busy for hours upon my "scribbling". I understand too that the pair of you are — young in heart and mind, and body — in a way that I was never, quite. And if you strayed into the heart of the woods — if you chanced on a nook among the sycamore trees —' He paused with an odd, sly, meaning look.

'John! I pray! What do you say?' They were on the edge of unspeakable things. John's eyes glittered, he had a smile of teeth — there was danger, trickery, forbidden paths.

Slow and clear he said, 'I am all honour, John.'

'But of course you are, my dear.' John sat back, he seemed at ease. 'It is our kinship that matters most. For there is a providence in our coming together.' His voice grew musical. 'I have dreamed that we two could change our age.'

Outside the clouds thickened, so the light sank to a yellow glimmer. 'Let us think of the churches and schools we could make — that you could embellish, with paintings and with carvings too. We could fashion in England the City of Heaven, and Cheapside be Jerusalem.'

He sat larger so their shoulders touched, while his voice sank deep in tenderness. 'I even feel — that where we touch, our souls may join.' His arm crept shyly round Everett's shoulder. 'Dearest, we must cleave to one another.'

Everett stood abruptly, even as John's grasp sought to tighten. 'I shall light the candles. It's dusk in here.'

John stood also. 'Is something amiss?' He seemed astonished. 'Had you thought I meant — another thing? There is a manly love we must not soil — the love of comrades in arms, of knights on a quest.'

'Yes, well I have known of some valiant loves. They thrive well enough in the drawing schools. I am no prude in my morals, but it is not my taste.'

'Had you thought I wanted — my gorge rises — filthy buggery? Man mounting man like monkey on monkey?' He laughed freely. 'Like Jolly Jack Tar and the powder-monkey? There is a different, nobler love, within the world of aspiring men. Ignoble man, your soul is base. You are unworthy of my love.'

'I fear I am.'

'You have soiled your soul with unclean living. I had heard you had been among the fleshpots. You, and that Hunt, and the beast, Rossetti.'

'Thank you, John — that is not your concern.' Leaving John where he stood, he stepped into his own small room, and pulled his trunk from under his bed.

'What are you doing?' John filled the door. 'You are not packing to leave?'

'I shall stay in the hotel for a time.'

'By no means. You will do as I direct. You are engaged on my commission.'

'A commission may be cancelled.'

There was silence then, in which he lifted his coat that hung on the bed-post, and shook out its creases.

'Do not go.'

He folded trousers.

'Do you dare defy me? I have a voice in the world of art, which you would be wise to heed.'

There was a longer silence, in which he collected his comb and shaving pieces, and placed them in their case. Then the hairs at the back of his neck stood clear, as the strangest voice said, small and weak as a child,

'Ebewett — don'lea'me — all on my owny.'

He turned. John's face was crumpled and pouting.

'Don'go, Ebewett. Be like bwother to Johnny.'

'Forgive me, John.' He came out with his trunk, and waited for John to step aside.

'Sir!' John cried, stepping sharply back. He shook his head quickly, and regained self-possession. 'Pardon *me*! What I said was far from urbane. You know what Coleridge says of genius — the vision of the child with the powers of a man. I fear such a child lives still in me.'

'I know not —'

But John had grown brisk. 'I'll help with your trunk.' He showed no embarrassment. He even seemed to watch, amused, the unease into which he had thrown Everett.

'I can carry my bags.'

'True enough. But I may carry your paint-case.' He hurried Everett on his way.

They walked in silence towards the hotel, beneath purple clouds as low as the house-tops.

At the hotel, John said, 'Have a good night. I trust that tomorrow will be good for painting. I shall visit you at midday, with luncheon and with Crawley.'

'Thank you. I shall make my own way to our rock.'

*

But John did not come. Everett painted all day with no pause to eat, and returned to the hotel as the sky darkened again.

Did he look so strange? Ladies made way for him on the stairs with a startled, even intrigued expression.

'An *odd* young man!' one tenderly said.

In the half-stairs mirror he saw himself — a scampering figure thin as a fly, with his hair awry and a face of distress.

In the hotel room he briskly unpacked. Unwrapping his canvas, he leaned it face-up on the seat of a chair. Though his head spun, he would make himself work. There was John's head, in white silhouette, surrounded by a dimness of branches and rocks. As to flatness — now he saw the answer. The lichens were the key, in their silver-whiteness. He would keep them bright on the nearby rocks, and erase them from the hollows. Where the space was dark it would recede, he was stupid not to see it before.

Oh, but her — Mrs John — and then, John. He went to the window, and rubbed the pane hard, as if he could clear the dusk itself. Against ponderous clouds a page of newspaper flapped white in the sky. He peered where he knew the cottage must be, and through branches made out a window. John had lit candles, he would have sat with a book. And Effie? She was far removed.

The thought came with a sudden pang. I have shut myself out, I cannot go back. In rashness, impatience, he had cut himself off. In the cottage they had been together, in the morning, in the evening... But had she, then, *such* a hold on him?

As he stood by the window the downpour arrived. It was like a drum band, sharp on the panes and deep on the tiles. The cottage, and all lights, disappeared, while the wild thought came: Dearest, I would surround and swallow you as if I were all made of rain.

When he looked round, in the dim-lit room, he found his painting of John gazing back. Mild as milk two pale blue eyes began to glow in the blank white head.

8

She arrived home late and tired, and it was only over breakfast, the following morning, that she asked as lightly as she could,

'Where is Everett, John?'

'Everett — oh, he moved back to the hotel. He found he much preferred to stay there.'

Her small gasp was like a yelp — as if she dropped an axe, and looking down saw her foot cut off. How ridiculous — was Everett her foot?

Over the bread-crumbs she would glance at John, and notice again the things she never could like in his face. That scar from the dog-bite next to his mouth, where he had stitches as a child.

'Dear — your father's finances have begun to mend?'

'Yes,' she said impatiently, 'John —'

'My dear?'

'Did you in some manner — make Everett go?'

'What a thought! I should love for him to stay with us always.'

But still, as he eyed his plate, she saw his neck and cheeks grow red. He fetched a book and read as he chewed, while the wind rose outside. A fitful light fell on tea-cups and marmalade.

There was a tap on the door, she hurried to open it.

'Everett — I am so pleased to see you. Pray step inside.'

'I'm burdened like Bunyan, I won't take it all off.' He was ready for the glen, with canvas and easel strapped to his back, and palette and painting-box under his arm. 'I stopped only to say, Welcome home! You are well? You had a good journey?' He called through the house, 'Morning, John.'

'Everett.' John did not stir from his book.

'Do stay.' She stepped back, so he could enter.

But he hung on the step. He looked urgently to her. 'I must hurry — the weather's set to get worse.'

She watched him walk away, a square bundle with legs: I never should have gone from this house.

'Come inside, will you?' John called. 'There's a draught from that door.'

'I shall walk up the glen.' She reached for her pelisse and her wideawake hat.

John stood at once. 'Excuse me, you may not go. It is an evil wind. Pray make the house neat, it needs your touch.'

She blinked, but paused, and bit her lip. She had better not run hurrying after Everett. John had returned to his book, and presently she hung her hat on its peg.

The wind increased, the daylight dimmed. She lit a candle for John, then sat on the window-seat, gazing where the aspens thrashed — blow wind, bear my love to me. Looking round, she saw John's eye was on her, through the spikes of his brows, glittering as the candle flickered.

She turned back to the window — but here *was* Everett. No more painting today. He stumbled down the path through an onrush of dust, huddling his wrapped-up canvas before him. She rose, knowing he would stop.

He did not. He glanced at their door with a sharp, starved

look — then jutted his mouth and went on, the easel wagging on his back. He was lost to sight in a whirlpool of leaves.

Her heart tore as no grief had torn it. She knew then John had warned him away. She looked round and found John, watching her hot-eyed.

'Why are you staring?' she snapped. 'I thought your lecture was all your thought.'

He looked down then up as her cape swirled past.

'I forbid you to go out in the teeth of this gale.'

'John — I went.'

She strode up the path, and came out on a height above the glen. The trees below wheeled like blinded bears. She walked back and forth quickly, hands held to her mouth. Everett, you are my own true love.

The rain came sharply, like tiny stones. Yes, drown! she thought, looking over the glen. In her mind Everett's dream of the deluge came true, she saw floodwaters swell, steeples taper and vanish. Any cruel thought was free to her now, unhappy as she was.

*

And yet that evening, and the following evenings, Everett would visit them in the cottage.

'*Still* it hasn't stopped.' Everett turned from the blackened window. 'Will it rain for ever? Four days on end! You sink in the ground, the river's in spate. Where does the water come from, Effie?'

'Och,' she crooned, in her strongest Scottish, 'For water we are weel provided.'

They paused, as a new gust pressed the walls. The door juddered, the window-panes tinkled. John poked and banked the smouldering peat.

'These are dreadful times. In Newcastle the cholera is raging worse. They didn't take good measures. There'll be an epidemic.'

Everett muttered, 'The Government lets the provinces rot.'

John made a mouth. 'I don't blame the Government. I shall fear if London grows too strong. I want each region to have sound Commissioners, to see to each need, and make justice for all.'

'I expect you're right.'

Everett's eyes turned now to her, with a look — could it be, of hunger? Just this look made her breath come short.

John stretched his arms. 'I have a remedy for our idleness. My mother has sent me a sermon — I shall read it to you. No? Effie, *you* will hear Dr Snell?'

She stood and stretched. 'I don't think I shall attend well, John. I'm all of a fidget, with being cooped up. And the schoolroom drips — because the thatch is wet through — we can't play battledore. I feel I'll burst.' As she crossed the room, she knew John stood up. Would he forbid her again to step outside?

But outside their door she saw absolute downpour, and the path turned to a torrent.

John sat again. 'We are safest indoors. That pelting black rain is filled with infection. Sit by me, my dear, while I read.'

She watched him pat the place on the sofa beside him.

'Do as I bid, if you please.'

She only stood.

Tartly he said, 'Euphemia!'

Everett sat tall, 'John —'

She saw everything could go bad quickly. 'Read to us, dear. You read so well.'

She went and sat by John, but he put the book down. 'We

are not worthy of Dr Snell now.'

'Then I shall read.' She took a book embossed in gold, and read to the moan of the wind in the chimney, to the rattle of rain-shot, in gusts, on the glass.

'Deep on the convent-roof the snows

Are sparkling to the moon —'

'"St Agnes' Eve"', Everett murmured. 'You read Tennyson beautifully.'

He nodded as she read the first two stanzas, and when she paused he took the book and read the last lines out himself.

'For me the Heavenly Bridegroom waits

To make me pure of sin.

The sabbaths of Eternity,

One Sabbath deep and wide —

A light upon the shining sea —

The bridegroom with his bride!'

The bridegroom was Christ, but still, as he read, he gazed to her with brilliant eyes.

John had made small starts all through the reading. 'Tennyson is noble,' he said at the end, 'but I am not sure his piety is always pure.' She mistrusted the spark that came in his eye. 'But still' — he surveyed them both — 'his mood of sad peace is such as we all may shortly feel — when Effie and I take our leave of this place.'

'Take our leave?' She was startled to the core, and Everett stared. 'You said we should stay all summer long — till Everett finishes your portrait.'

'But Everett is, as he warned us, slow — and we see I am not needed for my portrait.' He laughed. 'I am a white shape in the scenery — Everett will "fill me in" in London. Besides, I must study the buildings of Edinburgh, if I am to speak to the Edinburghers of architecture.'

She wondered, what went awry while I was away? All their summer plan was changing.

'So you mean to leave Everett all alone? By himself all day up in the glen, and all alone in the hotel at night?'

Everett swallowed, while John looked between them with a glint, as if he fed on their surprise.

Everett stood, and pulled the cape of his coat round his shoulders. 'It's time I went back.'

'Oh — wait till the rain stops, please.'

'This shower has stopped. And the wind is rising to bring on the next downpour.'

In evidence, twigs whipped the window panes hard. Wind boomed in the chimney. The door, when he opened it, banged from his hand and his painting of herself, with the foxgloves, fell down. In an instant the room filled with rain, twigs and leaves.

'I must brave it, before we have pitch dark. I shall visit tomorrow. Take good rest.'

'Tread carefully, please. You could slip in this mud.'

He laughed, smiled, waved, went.

They shut the door fast. John poked in the grate and a ball of smoke blew back in the room.

'This rain is washing our world away.'

She set her portrait back on the mantle-piece. 'How could you speak to Everett so? You brought him to this *sodden* place, and now you are going to leave him here. Painting *your* portrait, if you please.'

John only, sadly, shook his head. 'Everett, Everett. I fear that young man is lost to me, whether I am here, or far away.' He heaved a great sigh. 'I had built such hopes on him, for the future of our nation's art.'

'Oh. You mean you cannot bend him to your will.'

'Not yet.' He looked up, even with a twinkle. 'True, I have not given up all hope. Maybe in London, when I visit his studio daily... Who knows? We may come to be — in tune.' He gazed mistily towards the future. Did he also gloat, that he would see Everett often then, when she could see him never? She heard the noise, as she ground her teeth.

'The point is, John, what happens now? Do we leave him in the pouring rain, where his painting too may get washed away?'

'Oh, the weather will mend. And we are not going tomorrow — you did not think that surely, my goose? In any case Everett must finish the portrait, for now his art is mine to command. I am paying good money for it.' He took her hand and shyly rubbed it. 'Be easy. After Edinburgh we go back to our little house. Our crib. Our nest. Herne Hill is so cosy, and dryer than here.'

He stooped closer. 'I'm sorry. *What* did you say?'

She had barely whispered, she spoke clear now. 'I said I'd rather go straight to Hell.'

Her own words startled her, loud in the room, and they jarred on John, she saw. His blue eyes stared. 'That is a terrible thing to say. You do not mean it — you speak to hurt me.' He stopped to ponder, and presently said, 'But I understand. It is because my parents live close by. You see my mother as a tyrant. Do not be unhappy, you need not see her. I shall visit her daily to make your apologies.' He smiled, as though she should be pleased.

'It is not your parents, it is you, John.' She had not thought her voice could be harsh as this. It was a new voice, and a blade.

He was gazing at her, his mouth ajar.

She turned aside with an angry shrug. 'We had better rest. Good night, John.'

'You are right,' he said breathlessly. He moved towards the room that had been Everett's: on the threshold he turned, to look to her uncertainly. She had never seen him so at a loss. Then he went in and closed the door. They had not even said their prayers.

*

When she woke in the night it was quiet outside. The wind had dropped, no rain beat down, instead she listened to falling water. Drop. Drip. All round the cottage, from the soaking thatch, water fell softly on flagstones and earth. From the trees beside the path it splashed. Faintly she heard the tumbling Finlas, and somewhere a dog, a lowing cow, as the animals woke to the end of the flood.

She lay in pitch-black with open eyes, while in space and peace the thought collected: if John died I could marry Everett. She woke to the enormity: she had thought of John dead with no atom of grief. Thought? No, it had been a wish. What was happening to her — was she joining the bad? She thought of those women in Scottish legends — women of vengeance, impassioned, ruthless, they would use the dirk they kept in their plaid.

There were other noises. She sat up in bed, hearing steps. Had John dreamt again? But she heard no alarm, only softly padding footfalls. He was walking barefoot in the sitting room. Perhaps he trod carefully, not to wake her. The steps paused at her door. She was in a sweat, he must not come in.

He did not come. He cleared his throat several times, and made that noise with his nose which she always disliked. John, she thought — we are both in trouble.

The quiet sounds stopped, he must be back in his cabin. She heard wood creak as he lay on his bed.

She listened once more for the dripping water, but caught no sound at all. True stillness at last. Then she heard a cock crow, cock-a-doo in the distance. The shape of her window had begun to gleam when, finally, she slept.

*

The morning was clear. Barefoot herself, like the hotel girls, she walked in the garden behind the cottage, through long grass wet with rain and dew.

'Euphemia.'

'Doesn't the world smell wonderful, John? You can smell the earth — but the roses are wrecked.'

She paused when she saw his face. He looked stricken, even aged — in a strange way handsome. He wore his black frock coat.

'My dear.' His voice was grave and gentle. 'May we sit on the bench beneath the trees?'

'It's much too wet.'

'Even so I should like to sit.' There was a catch in his step.

'Are you well, John?'

'I am perfectly well. I shall spread my coat for you, as a courtier would. Be seated, Countess — as Everett calls you.'

He sat beside her, in his shirtsleeves in sunlight. Their bad night had taken its toll on him.

'What troubles you, John? Is it what I said, about our home? I am sorry if I upset you.'

He nodded slightly. 'Yes and no. Our words last night brought my thoughts to a head. I know the problem is not my parents. The true question is — as we both have thought — that it may be we are not well matched.'

She went completely still.

'Nay, more than that. Last night, in my thoughts, I saw

91

myself as in a glass. Maybe I am that sort of man, who sadly perhaps should never be married.'

'John —' She stopped herself, she must simply wait. He saw the truth. He would agree to part. It would all be easy, after all.

His blue eyes were grave. 'For I have not given you what a wife — *desires*. Instead I gave you my reproaches.'

Gazing downwards she said, 'It must be a very serious thing, that you have not wanted to make me your wife. I believe I have lived — in an unjust grief.'

He nodded. They sat side by side, their hands close on the bench.

'And I have been thinking what we should do. I have travailed through the watches of the night. Most earnestly, even abjectly. I believe the answer was shown to me.'

'Yes, John?' She turned towards him with all hope.

'God has made a place for the likes of me. I see I may be that kind of man, who perhaps should dwell in a monastery. Grieving for his fallen nature, praying to make his soul come good. I have thought I might be' — he gave a short, sharp clap of laugh — 'a *Protestant* monk! And do you know there is in Switzerland a Hermitage — near Sion, we have seen it — in the Alps that I love —'

She must interrupt. 'What is it you are saying, John?'

'I am saying — may it be my dearest wish! — that I should withdraw into a Holy House.'

'I see. I know your piety, John.' But her heart had chilled. 'And may I ask where I should be?'

He blinked. 'You? Oh.' His brow narrowed. 'Well — you shall stay my wife. You will live in our house in Herne Hill. You will enjoy it more if I am away. And I shall give you a competence for all of your life.'

'Thank you, John.' She said the words over in her head, and then aloud as well. 'You would have me live there, a sort of widow. And a hermit, like you. And the world would say, oh, she's that woman, whose husband fled from her into a monastery.'

He bridled. 'And do we care what "Society" says? We speak of conscience, and sacrifice. You may live in virtue so. And my allowance will provide for you.'

But his eyes had narrowed. Whenever he spoke of 'Society', it was to mock her pleasure in being with people. There was a question she must ask, she had rehearsed it in her days away.

'If, John, we are not well matched — and if we should live in separate places — may it be that our marriage should be ended?'

His head reared back. 'Do you mean — dissolution?'

'If that is the word. I know not —'

His eyebrows bushed. 'Indeed you know not. Dissolutions are granted almost never, and beyond that they are a blasphemy. We have sworn our pledge before the Lord. It is a sacrament. We are married until the day we die.'

He gazed directly, as if he were the church in person. A glint came in his eye. 'Are you shy of leading a pure life?' She saw malice.

'Are you asking, do I choose to be a nun because you yearn to be a monk? In short, John, no.'

He started: her words, or tone, surprised him. 'I am speaking of our future life, and your dislike of living with me. What would you have me do?'

She flounced round. 'Oh, go there, John. Get to your monastery!'

'Say you so? I do not think you mean it well.'

He turned from her. Then it seemed all his body lifted, to fall away in a sighing shrug. Was he talking to himself?

'Well, well. Who knows? It may be I too am not for the cloister.' A small look, puckish, played in his face. 'I am a priest of beauty, more than virtue.' He even smiled, with a kind of mischief. Then she was not sure where they were.

'Shall we breakfast, John?'

Strangely, he seemed already refreshed.

'Hm. Do you know, I think I shall breakfast in the hotel. I shall be busied there through the day.'

'In the hotel?'

'In the library there.'

'Has it so many books?'

He had stood, and settled his coat on his shoulders. 'Oh, there are gems within the hotel. I had better be off.' He gave a quick bow. 'Let us meet for dinner.'

Before she knew it he had slipped away through the garden gate, and vanished among the sycamore trees. But why so quickly — where do you go, John?

She waited a pause, then got up and followed in his tracks. She remembered the tiny girl John 'loved'. It must not be that he hunted her.

John walked fast, she knew. She thought she had lost him. Then she saw him before the hotel steps, where he greeted a man. She saw, it was that man with the long thin head, with whom he had talked before. His skin, in the daylight, looked yellow or green. He was dressed in black, and held a large black cloth. It was not a cloak, it looked like a black sheet, she could not think what its purpose was.

He looks like Death, she said to herself. Again they talked closely, as if they plotted bad acts. What was John about?

'Good day.' It was the man's voice, he seemed to have a

frog in his throat. But he was animated enough, as he turned from John, and, waving a long arm, greeted a party at the top of the steps, who, it appeared, had come to meet him. Their skirts and coats surrounded him, but his thin head showed above them all: it seemed a head made of bone and jet-black hair.

John, meanwhile, slipped into the hotel and was lost, while she stepped back beneath the branches, and turned to make her way home.

9

She went back into the cottage with John's words echoing in her head. Not well matched, dissolutions... She did not know if hope was given, or taken away. She ate ham and drank tea by herself.

There came a rap on the door. She knew at once who it was.

'Oh, I am so glad to see you. Won't you step inside?'

Everett stayed on the step. He was without his painting things.

'John is in?'

'John is away to the hotel library. I doubt I shall see him before it gets dusk.'

He hung still on the threshold. 'I should not come in. I came to say, shall we all take a walk? It's true this is the first good day for painting. But I thought, I'll take a loose.'

'Oh, let us walk! I have longed to for days. I shall fetch a shawl.'

He waited courteously. 'Should we not tell John?'

'We cannot easily.' She paused — then faced him brightly. 'And I shall decide with whom I walk. Will you wait a moment?'

She went back into the scullery, and put bread, cheese and apples into a basket. She put on her thick jacket, and her wideawake hat, and pulled on her boots for the slippery path.

'Give me the basket.'

They began their walk. The sun was high now, and from the meadows beside them — from the fields and trees as far as she saw — wreaths of gleaming mist rose thickly. Or rather,

'The whole world is *steaming*.'

'It's a *very* wet world.'

She was dazzled by the sunlit mist, which smoked from the ground as though a stove were lit under it.

'It's wonderful.'

'John is well?' he asked. It was the merest courtesy, she need say nothing. But she described John's scheme, of escape to a hermitage. Everett was not impressed.

'A Protestant monastery — away in the Alps?'

She mused, 'But still I wonder — what John said may be right for him. He is a very *different* man.'

'I fear he would feel as most men would, if he saw the two of us walking so.'

'Do you know, he might not? He is very little jealous. It was a wonder in Venice, how he let me walk out with officers, with gentlemen. He trusted me. As to what other people thought — why, he simply made jokes about it.'

'Did he?' Everett drew a long breath. 'I would not do that, if I were he.'

'Dear Everett,' she said, 'I missed your company when I was away. I missed it dearly.'

'And I yours — very much.' He had stopped, and looked at her intently.

They heard a quiet cry overhead.

'What was that?' Everett squinted up into the brightness. At the top of the sky, two tiny birds circled, and gave again their throbbing cry.

'Are they hawks?'

'They're eagles,' she said.

'Eagles don't make that little odd noise!'

'That's eagles.'

They both craned upwards, following the birds in their looping flight.

'I'm a city lad.'

'I thought you were from Jersey.'

'We came to London when I was small, and we've lived there ever since.'

They had come to the trees. Here the path was more muddy and every dip had a puddle, so their going was slow. At times she took his arm, to steady her tread. They were walking like friends who were very close — as if she had never been away, as if he stayed still in the cottage.

'You are the perfect gentleman.'

'Good Heavens! I don't like the sound of that. I was expelled from the first school I went to.'

'What did you do?'

'They say I bit the teacher's hand — like a dog, so it bled.'

She smiled. 'How old were you?'

'I don't know. I was an infant, surely. After that, I had tutors at home — I dare say that helped to "spoil" me. I told you before, I behaved like a prig.'

'Do prigs bite hands? What other adventures did you have?'

'Oh, not much. I threw a palette at someone's head. A friend of the family, and he bought my pictures. But he fussed so much. And at Sass's they held me out of the window — by the heels. I was brought in in a faint.'

'Why did they do that? Did you throw things at them?'

'No, I simply out-drew them all.' He paused, and laughed

again. 'So you see — I'm proud as well as bad. Or conceited.'

'You're not conceited. Or you only pretend to be. And when I think what you have done.' She mused. 'I think, of all your pictures, I like "The Huguenot" best.'

'Why?' he asked.

'John would say, because the flowers and the wall are painted so beautifully. But I would say, the lovers gaze with *entire* love. And you see her fear that he may be killed, and how he works to calm her fear. It moves me just as opera does.'

'Opera?' he said, 'But I was thinking of *Les Huguenots*. Of course.'

'Meyerbeer,' she murmured. Quietly she sang some bars. At once he joined in, their voices strengthened together.

'Capital!' he said, then he began to sing from Donizetti's *Martiri*. She joined him in that. In turn they sang snatches, or began new arias and let the other continue, like batting the shuttlecock back and forth. The woodlands were empty, their voices filled. Rossini, Bellini, the new men... Strongly but tenderly, with looks to each other, they sang together, as they gently climbed, 'Va, pensiero' — 'Fly, thought' — the chorus from *Nabucco*.

'Our notes are filling the greenwood,' he said. He had a beautiful baritone — she had never heard him in full throat before.

'A crescendo will get us to the top of this glen.'

A descending countryman, in faded plaids, made them quiet, he looked so dismayed. She greeted him in her strongest Scotch, and then he seemed amazed by that.

'Good day to ye,' he said, through a slit-mouth dry as his narrowed eyes.

'It is a good day,' she heartily said.

They paused to eat her apples and cheese, sitting on a wet tree-trunk. The scent of pine was strong. They were in the deep shadow of the taller pines, but around them slender rods of sunlight would appear and fade as the branches stirred.

'And I love the care you gave to the clothes in "The Huguenot". Her lovely lace collar, the puffed sleeves of his coat. You care for clothes in all of your paintings.'

He was rueful. 'Some would say I give them too much care. Well, I like to get them right. But you too — I have seen — you have a wonderful sense of colour in clothes.'

'Truly?' She was pleased to the core. He — she — they loved colour so much. 'I love nice stuffs. In Venice I found silks, you would not believe — and point lace, in all London there is no such work. John would say, there is vanity in clothes.'

'There is,' he laughed. 'And where artists be, without the vanity of clothes? Titian loved velvet. Watteau loved satin. And if you *love* colour...'

'Yes,' she said, for she saw it — the impossible dream. If the two of them could be together, she would help him with the clothes. She would hunt out old velvets for his history scenes, and corduroys for his modern pictures. She would stitch and embroider, and help to make the picture's beauty.

She gathered their remnants into her basket: they resumed their climb. When the path was difficult they took detours through the sodden leaf-mould. Often he held back branches for her, and their eyes met in her tender thanks. She grew deeply serious. Making their way side by side uphill, they were two halves of a single soul.

The trees thinned, the light grew. They had reached the small loch at the head of the glen. All round them were hills, with firs and much heather. High in the sky the eagles they

100

had seen before circled slowly, and gave their faint cry.

He murmured, 'Loch Finlas.'

She said, 'It's so beautiful.' The water's surface was gold light.

They sauntered on the bank. Yes, the loch had its beauty but that beauty was sad. Glancing at his sensitive face, she felt she must faint from hopeless love. It was not the loch, it was he who was beautiful. She could die there, on that spot, from love.

In time he said, 'We should perhaps turn round.'

They started back. Her heart was too full to speak, and he was pensive, sombre.

'There!' He startled her. She turned too, so both of them saw the eagle's dive — on a slanting curve from the top of the sky. She saw the hooked beak, the lifted wing-tips, with long dark feathers spread like fingers. It shot within a copse of trees.

They listened, but heard no cry, no sound.

He said, 'It will come out with a vole in its beak. Or a pine-marten maybe.'

The eagle did not reappear. They moved nearer to the copse and tramped through the bushes, but the bird had disappeared.

'Strange,' he murmured.

They started on the path which led back down the glen. It was steep at first, sinking down between banks, while the light grew dim from the tree-tops over them. They had ceased to speak, he even looked angry. But she knew what she wanted — for him to seize her under the trees, and brand her cheeks with burning kisses. She had read too many novels: it would not happen. They both were honourable. The sadness of it thickened like lead in her head.

Their way bent to the right, they saw black water glistening. 'I don't remember this,' she said.

The dip in the path was filled, from side to side, by standing water, with edges of glistening trodden mud.

'We cut through the woods, that's why,' he said. 'Look, if I hold this branch, maybe we can get by on this side.' He inched precariously along the slippery brink.

'Take my hand.' Gripping the branch, he reached his other hand to her. 'Trust me.'

With his support she began, leaning above black water. When he drew her close to him her feet slid in the mud: she was falling. She remembered her dream. She gave a pull, so he came too.

She landed on her back with a wide loud splash, and he fell on top of her. There was a breathless moment of confusion, apology. Then he had kissed her or she had kissed him. He dripped muddy water, as she did too. His hot mouth was devouring her face — or she ate his. When he paused she clasped his head in both hands and brought him back close: so she kissed her muddy lover again as she lay on her back in shallow water.

'We're mudlarks,' he said. 'It's thick as treacle.'

'Soiled.' The relish of it. 'We're black.'

Shining wet, with gouts of mud clinging to them, they knelt up tall in the chilly pool, where she raised her numb head blindly to him to bury her face in his for ever.

'I love you truly, Euphemia. I did not know till now how much.'

'I — I knew how much I loved.'

As he helped her to her feet, they broke out in laughter.

'We are *covered* in filth.' Each other caught the laugh, they shrieked together.

Dripping thick blackness, they squelched to the further side of the pool. Beneath her clothes icy trickles ran down her skin, from pockets and pleats where the water caught.

'We must get you home quickly,' he said, 'You could catch your death up here.' He hugged her close to warm her through.

'I'm not cold,' she said, 'But we had better go back. What John will say — when he sees us thick with dirt —'

'Oh, I shall say we had an accident. We did. And he knows I have accidents.'

'*I* am one of your accidents.' She curled closely inside his arms, they stopped to clasp and kiss again.

They walked on quickly, not to chill. It seemed their clothes would be sodden for ever, but the pool was shallow, and in places the cloth began to dry. There the mud turned to a grey dust, some of which she could brush off.

'We must think what we will do.' He spoke with solemnity, he meant in the future.

'But not now.' She touched her finger to his lips. 'Don't say things that will scare me to death. Let's just be — where we are. It's so precious.'

'It is.' He was glad to leave the future. They kissed again, and walked on entwined. From kissing him she had the taste of earth in her mouth. It was his taste too.

They met John by the churchyard, in the dim late afternoon.

'You're safe? I'm glad, I was coming to look.' There was a tremor in his voice. 'Oh! But what's happened to you?'

Everett began hoarsely, 'I'm afraid - '

But she said over him, 'John, we had *such* a fall! Everett was helping me past a place — but I lost my hold, I fell in the filthiest huge mud-puddle — and I pulled Everett so he fell too. Look at us! We're creatures of mud.'

'You're creatures of earth and water,' he said. '*What* a mess! You and your accidents, Everett! But you must both be freezing — let's hurry inside.'

In the cottage they lit a fire. 'I must take off these wet things.' She disappeared inside her cupboard room.

'I must change too,' she heard Everett say. Then there was quiet, he had left for the hotel.

'That's better,' she said, emerging dressed. John watched her with a curious smile — was it knowing, questioning? He did not seem upset. He made tea for them. Then Everett came back, washed and smart and filled with light.

'What an adventure!' Somehow, as companions in disaster, they had sat side by side on the sofa — but smiling and glowing as if they had swallowed the sun. There was no help for it, they could not look grave for you cannot hide happiness. John can see it, what must he think?

Nor did John seem upset. He watched them with nervous gleaming eyes, in agitation he dropped his cup on the rug. He looked sharply up as he bent to retrieve it. His eyes jigged, he could not be still, his look was — exhilarated.

'This place is enchanted,' he said, and sighed. 'Here we all may trip and slip. What days these are!'

She glanced to Everett, and then caught John watching with a new look again. With a glittering relish, though his mouth was pulled down like the grin of a shark.

'We must rest.' She stood, though she was leagues from feeling tired.

'I must get up early.' Everett had stood. 'I must get on with my canvas tomorrow.'

'And I shall slumber too,' said John. 'I cannot write lectures every day.'

They bid Everett farewell.

John said, 'You went walking in the woods?'

'I proposed it, John. The sun was so fine, after all these storms. You disapprove?'

His eyes glistened sharply, like new-cut gems.

'Oh by no means.'

With relief she went to her room. There she lifted her head and shook back her hair. Sleep? There would be no sleep tonight. Her blood effervesced. She and Everett were lovers. Everything that had been impossible was dashing pell-mell towards them now.

When she lay down she felt a pain. Below her gut a sharp hurt like cramp came and went. The bed was hot, she was burning or melting. What disturbance was this? — as if her own body could yawn like a pit. She had forgotten her — peculiarity, Everett's tenderness had made her forget. If Everett saw her as she was — then would all their love be lost?

10

John paused in his lecture. And would his sweetheart come today? For a moment he saw her, in her sky-blue dress.

But on with his argument: he must settle with those architects, who still built houses like Greek temples. He dipped his pen in the inkwell. A Grecian style on a modern building — why, it is nothing but a spiritless shell. As a leopardskin hearth-rug is to the leopard, or as stuffed scales in a bottle are to the serpent....

He said over his own words with pleasure, then wondered — would she not come today? Had they ordered nothing? *She* was out, there could not be a better time for a visit.

His fingers drummed — he must broaden his attack on the shout architects made about volumes and spaces. The true life of a building shows on its surface, even the Greeks painted their temples rich colours. He would change the value set on 'decoration'.

He had found his thread. Sentence led to sentence like doors opening towards larger doors — they led to a painted wall in Italy, storied like a picture-Bible. Till he put down his pen. He could rest, now thought had taken a stride. As to his lady love — he would seek her out. He got to his feet, his heart beat loud: for once, he would act.

He smoothed his coat and hair, and adjusted his cravat, in *her* mirror. And where was his wife, if you please? Had she 'taken the air', in order to prattle, up the glen, with Everett? He thought of their petty amour with derision. The silly, romantic chit, she cannot love Everett with the high love that I do. He and I together — we shall build the Heaven of Art in England.

But if their bodies twined, if their lips met — the baseness and soil — his member stirred. The treachery and vileness — the excitement — of it. No, but they would not go that road. His wife understood honour, he must give her that. And their maudlin flirtation — why it gave him the right, to find his own pleasure where he would.

Yes, but if as they talked she caressed his Everett — if her finger touched his cheek — his skin was cream, his hair spun bronze. His eyes were topaz. If she stroked him with her kitchen hands — Jealousy, how you work in us! Genius youth, I have lost you now.

But Everett — why be jealous of Everett? Maybe once he was maiden-fair, but already he was more than half a man. He had the un-sweet voice of a man. Soon he would be — the male beast. Oh, animality — the pink stick of a dog in the street, two flies on a pane, the stallion rammed into the dripping mare. But away with brutishness. The perfect beloved must be young and new, delicate-fresh from the Maker's hand. The tiny body not yet awake, perfect in shape — a fine gold down just appears on her lip. Lower, there is Heaven's gate: he must never approach it.

He saw himself in the mirror. I have a fine look still, with my off-red hair. Today I shall play the game of games.

He took his cane, and broad-brimmed hat, and pulled the door wide — but on the doorstep stopped, blinded by beauty.

There was the thinnest of mists, lit incandescent by the sun, and a visionary light lay on the pastures. Total stillness, and no bird sang.

Walking down the village, every bush shone with cobwebs, jewelled with dew. Beauty sparkled which way he turned.

But why is it that the youngest bodies — in beasts as in men — are so utterly beautiful? Is it because they are helpless? They have no other shield but beauty. So parent creatures cherish their young — and the malformed infant is expelled to die.

He saw the hotel, its grey stone walls — like an opera castle with its cone-capped turrets. Where, in that fastness, is my sweetheart hid?

In the forecourt he passed a dawdle of gentlemen — rank, at their ease, in a reek of tobacco. They stabbed the gravel with canes, or roared at a dog which they chose to call 'sir'. One had his cravat loose, so you saw the jet growth on his matted chest. The same hair curled from his nostrils and cuffs, and stood on each joint of his meaty fingers. Male-animal grossness! And these were the 'quality' his wife admired.

Entering the lobby he turned each which way — how, in this labyrinth, would he find his dear? His path was blocked by the human menagerie: sweating clerics, beanpole flunkeys, pretty coy women like monkeys in bunting, mountains of shawls with old sows hid under them. Animals all, stood up on their hind legs — inside their adornments they steamed and stank. The Church Fathers knew the vileness of the grown human body. Only in art could it find beauty.

But he saw his friend, with the thinnest ever of human heads. He sat next to a brood of golden-haired daughters, cherubs in taffeta, while he leaned affably to the parents. They two were kin, as he passed they narrowed one eye to each other.

He knew where he must seek his beloved — in the back-corridors. Though how could he, a gentleman, step behind the green baize door? To anyone who saw him he would look both fool and clown. But it had to be. Couraggio, he *was* a man! And a man in love, to boot. He would step quickly.

With an urgent face he entered the narrow, low-ceilinged passage, between airing cupboards and hangers for aprons. But what an adventure! His heart clanged in his chest

'Sir?' He met the astonished face of the cook, red, hard and glistening. Large copper vessels vapoured behind her, bevvies of kitchen-maids chopped as they chattered.

'I am seeking, by your leave, the house-keeper's room.' He had spoken to her only in the lobby before.

He was given directions — though he had little wish now to face that tyrant.

Oh where may my true love be? In the darkest of dungeons I shall find her.

He braved the stares of maids carrying laundry, and nodded shortly — man to man — with the boots. He was discomposed only when he turned a corner, and —

'Crawley!'

'Mr John!'

'Why are you here, Crawley?' He meant to be severe, but his own voice rode high.

'Oh — I came for firewood.'

He thought, firewood here — among the airing cupboards! Also Crawley had no basket. And in high summer? But he said only,

'Well, I shall look forward to a good blaze tonight. Crawley.'

'Mr John.'

He felt Crawley's eyes on him, as he quickly walked away. Well, let Crawley think what he would — he values his place.

He passed sculleries and store-rooms, and came out in a yard.

Dear heart — suddenly she was before him, playing with a hoop beside an old dog-kennel. She is exactly a Fra Angelico angel: with that straw-gold hair, those pale eyes, that white sweet face so slightly plump.

She looked up as he came. 'Hello, Captain Pancake.' Ah, his joke-name.

'Sweet Polly, I grieved you did not come today. I have missed you this many a day. I feared you were ill.'

'No, I'm *very* well.' Her voice as always was neat, and English not Scotch.

'Oh, I'm so glad, I could hop and skip.'

He would cut a small caper to make her laugh, for his feet were quick. But there was a shatter of horse-shoes on flag-stones, as a wagon heavily swayed in through the gates. A voice in the hotel called, 'The carrier from Callander!' Men in waistcoats and aprons came out, and began to unload large baskets and crates. One looked at him oddly, and spoke to another. But how should he care what skivvies thought?

'Why did you not come? Each day, to bring you, I sent for fruit.'

She blew out her cheeks in a funny way.

'Did anyone tell you not to come?'

He found he was trembling with indignation. If someone should try to keep her from him…

'Well, well.' He restrained his hand from her yellow-gold hair. 'Is your mother within?'

She nodded.

"Will you ask her, may I take you for a short walk? Just to show you the flowers in our cottage garden? And others I know of in the glen. Say, my good wife will give you tea, and she will bring you back herself.'

She tripped into the hotel. Then he was nervous — would he rouse a she-wolf? It was a brave thing he did, confronting the mother. But a shrewd move also — as the Scots say, canny. He knew how to be suave. When he wished he could speak in a voice like treacle, so all the mothers in the world would send their babes to learn from him.

Briefly an erect woman came to the door: she had a worn, stern face. But they had spoken before, and from a distance he smiled and raised his hat. She slightly smiled, and returned inside.

His Polly came hopping back. 'Mamma says you may show me, and give me tea too, so I do not come home too late.'

'You shall not. Let us be on our way.'

Near the gate the men had set up planks, and shouted as they rolled barrels down from the wagon. One of them called out, in strong Scottish, to her.

She lifted her tiny perfect nose. *She* was walking with a gentleman.

As they walked through the village, he reached into his coat. 'Look, I have a flower pressed flat as a wafer. It was posted to me by Lady Trevelyan.'

'Did she press it by sitting on it?' She gazed to him with roguish eyes, so his soul melted in adoration even as he winced at the childish joke.

'Look, there is our cottage. That is where my good lady will make tea later. But let us see first the flowers of the glen.'

Pausing now to look at the bluest cornflowers, and now

at a deep-red peony, he led her clear of the village. The thin mist had lifted, and, walking with her, he pointed to the beauties in all they saw. The breeze made ripples race through the grass, which itself was as fine as her delicate hair. On the wooded hills, the shadows of clouds made odd dark shapes that moved like reptiles.

She looked where he pointed, and smiled to please him.

'Do you see?' he asked.

'I see you are kind.'

Such beautiful words! And Nature herself now blessed their meeting.

'Look, sweet maid — there is a wonder!'

Led by his arm, she gazed as he did. Above the highest hill a great cape of cloud rose as they watched and slowly curled over like a wave of the sea, till it made the shape of a giant conch. It seemed as big as half the sky, lit by the sun to blinding whiteness.

'I have never seen that,' he said half to himself.

As she gazed he gazed at her. At the back of her neck — that slender stalk with its two fine cords, she was the most delicately beautiful thing that ever he saw in the world. In loving her he loved the art of God. He imagined her tiny shoulder-blades, sliding within her dress.

The clouds above changed shape again. 'Here,' he said, 'We have come to the forest. Just a little way within, there is a woodland glade I know —'

*

He stood in the woods, his hands over his eyes.

'Nineteen — twenty. I'm coming to catch you!'

He stalked the clearing. Where had she hidden — among the tight berries of mountain ash, behind the white gleam of the birches? If he glimpsed her, he would give chase.

'Booo!' From behind a holly bush she jumped on his back — suddenly so he staggered. She held tight round his neck.

'Sweet Polly, let me rest a moment.'

He was winded, and sat on a bank. She watched him catch breath, then with a bounce she sat in his lap.

'Poor Captain Pancake. I have made you tired.'

'And you hair is awry — here, let me make it smooth.'

With trembling stealth he smoothed the hairs, which were silk spun finer than a breath.

'Hey, Captain Pancake!' Abruptly she leaned back, flat across his knees, so she gazed past his head and laughed at the sky. Then all her white throat was exposed to him.

'Pray, what do you see?'

'I see funny clouds, like you do. There's one up there just like a pancake!' She squirmed with giggles at her joke.

He cocked his head to try to see it. 'Sweet miss, I know as much of clouds as any man that lives. In truth, I am Captain of the Clouds.'

'Captain of the Clouds!' She mimicked him, then sat up straight in his lap. 'That's a funny thing to be captain of!'

'But so it is. But look, dear heart!' He helped her stand. 'That is what I have been seeking.'

He crossed the clearing, and knelt to delve among the grasses.

'This we call deadnettle. If you gather a pinch of these hooded white flowers, and suck at their base, you will taste the sweetest nectar in nature.'

He gave her to suck from the tiny white tubes. 'But this is not what I sought. *Here* they are! I glimpsed their crimson as I sat. Do you know what these are?'

He held up the stem, with its polished red beads, that were

peppered with tiny black dots.

She looked. 'They're just like baby strawberries.'

'And so they are — wild strawberries! But do you know the magic of their taste?'

She slightly frowned.

'Look, I will give you one to try. But you must pay me something for it.'

Her face fell. 'I have no pennies in my purse.'

'Then we must find something more precious than pennies. I will give you a strawberry if you give me a kiss.' He turned his cheek, and closed his eyes to prepare for delight.

'I like them,' she said, 'Will you give me another.'

Humbly, as in an extreme of prayer, he bent his forehead before her face. She gave a fuller kiss, and at the soft touch of the tiny moist lips he was unmanned.

'Are you crying, Captain Pancake.'

'But you can make me well, sweet Polly. Here, let me give you all my fruit.'

He stood again. 'Come, let us go to the heart of the woods.'

As he took her hand to resume their walk, his brow burned red like a brand of fire. I am blest beyond all men's deserving.

He bowed as he led her beneath low branches.

11

He should be painting, he could not paint. He only sat, gazing into the white blaze of foam. Dashing frothing splashing water hurled itself towards the rock, but he had passed into a trance. He saw her still, in other water, as she raised her face with years of no-love in her eyes. It was that look that melted him, and bound their bond for ever. At all costs you must leave John, he gives you nothing a husband should.

And what could they do? She was John's wife, that could not be changed. If they ran away to a distant city — still the scandal at home would be epidemic, and her name would be destroyed.

What was left? Love in the woods, if they gave John the slip? So he 'helped' her, and was free to continue his fat life in society. It was sordid, bad — or a wonderful interlude. An oasis of love. Passion is passion.

But he was making odd movements — what's the matter with me? Puffing and blowing, working his mouth. He screwed his eyes shut, like a poor soul striving to hold back tears — which was his case, he had a mind to bawl.

He returned to his canvas, and the threshing water. Staring hard till the water streamed through his sight, he found the shape of its fury. There were folds and domes that came back with each splash, and other places where falling water thinned, so you saw brown rock as if through old glass. He dabbed tiny white points, his canvas flowed —

Till he stopped, he could not paint today. He packed his easel and painting gear, and began to clamber up the bank. The noise of the falls still boomed in his head, but even so, near the top, he caught quiet voices. Through a screen of brambles he made out John. He wore his smart black coat, coming slowly up the path with the small girl who brought fruit from the hotel.

'Stay!' John stooped to pick a flower. Bending down so his nose nearly bumped on hers, he pointed among the petals. John is such a teacher!

John continued up the path with his tiny pupil, and he himself, with his painting things, walked down to the village. So — she will be alone. Crawley will be with the hotel maids. There was no question, he must go to her.

But John — he walked fast — does he know desire? He is a womanish man. Does he love men or boys? Or — he remembered John's zest, when he and Effie came home soaked but happy. Is John one of those men who cannot perform but is willing to watch?

But he must not whisper a word of this, now that he saw the cottage door.

He tapped and when she opened it, and gave her small gasp, there was no moment before they embraced. He was startled by the force of her mouth.

'Most dearest Countess.'

For some time there only were enfoldings and claspings, and slow shakes of their heads with eyes half closed, and intakes of breath and whispered dearests. No problem could stop them, there was only love and they were lifted up weightless by love.

When they had sat, their chairs drawn close, she softly butted her head in his chest. Then she screwed her hair hard into his chest as if she would bore her way to his heart. It must be late afternoon outside, a light like honey filled the room.

She mused. 'In my dreams I think, may we not sail away? To Florence or Rome, where painters live with their mistresses — and just paint and love all the live long day.'

He smiled with enigma, but in any case she went on, 'But I know you must make your art here, where your fame is just beginning.'

'Well,' he demurred. 'I don't need to stay here. My friend Hunt has just left for the Holy Land — and his art will be the gainer. Will you come with me to the Holy Land?'

He met her steady listening eyes: there was something here — in his love, in her — which he must not defile.

She touched her finger to his lip. 'And there is — the scandal, and what it would do, to you — and me too.'

He ground out, 'The world is a grinning hypocrite!' He stroked her cheek. 'What I do know is, we must not act in haste. We must speak to others — about your marriage, about what can be.'

'Yes,' she said. Her eyes wetly burned and her face drew closer.

'We must do what is right and not be impatient,' he quietly breathed inside her ear.

'Yes,' she said, half-closing her eyes as she tilted her face to meet his kiss. 'No impatience at all but only care.' His arms closing round her drew her to him while her arm round his neck pulled him upon her. Their embrace leaned over, till they hovered half off the sofa. Gently he lowered her to the carpet — then she gazed just as when she lay in the water, her eyes veiled with tenderness. Her finger-tips touched his face as if she felt him because she was blind, while his skin became sensitive as it never had been. He kissed her brow with careful love, as he stroked her shoulders and her bust and caressed her stomach and waist.

'My dearest love, please.' Her breathing was louder, her chest heaved. She was flushed and no longer met his eyes, but only looked upwards to the ceiling. Her back had arched, she had begun to pant.

'Dearest —' Her face was marked with chagrin and pain.

'I cannot — I cannot.' She gave a groaning sigh.

While he was all tenderness trying to help, she rose to sit on the sofa's edge. She cried in big irregular sobs.

'You are right', he began, 'I should not have — forgive me —'

She pushed back her hair and looked to him with stark red eyes. 'There is nothing to forgive. I do not think we should not, I think we should. But —' She gave a single explosive sob. 'I cannot go there. You might not even like me.'

He blinked, he did not understand. Her eyes shone.

'Dearest Everett, I thank you from the bottom of my heart for your love. It has been the most wonderful gift in my life.'

He was on the brittle edge of grief. 'Are you dismissing me?'

'Never, I must not and I dare not. But I am where I am. I am married to John, I gave my promise. I see I shall go back to London with him. It breaks my heart, but — it is God's will.'

He sat up. 'I don't know that. I don't believe it.'

'Dearest Everett.' She laid her hand on his wrist. 'I wonder whether, because of your talent, you have been a little spoilt. There are some things one may not have, though one is sick with longing to have them.'

'Now I shall cry. I shall jump out of the hotel window. I

shall run up the mountain and jump off the top.'

She smiled beautifully and sweetly pleaded, 'Don't jump out of the window, dearest.'

He saw he had come to an edge. He spoke. 'Do not go back to London with John. I don't say run away with me. You must take great care. But I shall wait. And I shall do all that I should. You have my heart.'

Then both her hands took both of his, she mouthed a kiss and shone her eyes, which had filled again with standing tears.

He was grave, still waking to what he had said. Had he — proposed? What had he said, was it something or nothing? But he held her closely, and slowly they came to be at ease again. Her body settled into his, he smelt her hair and stroked it lightly, and she again caressed.

'What's that?'

There was commotion outside. She stood, 'John has come!' Her face became alert and pointed.

They both stood, absently smoothing their clothes.

But would John knock on his own door — and so sharply?

Everett opened the door to see — faces. A grim fair-haired woman, another with a sallow, crumpled face, and a lantern-jawed man who looked perplexed. They were not dressed like quality.

'How may I assist you?'

The man said, 'Your pardon, sir — is the wee lass here?'

'The lass? Do you mean little Polly, that brings our fruit?'

One of them said 'Aye', all three came closer.

'Why no,' he said. 'My friend has taken her for a walk in the glen. He was showing her flowers — he is a dedicated botanist.'

The strangers looked at each other. The fair-haired

woman faced him solemnly. 'Where are they now?'

There was a pause — then Everett reached for his cap. 'Let us find them. They won't be far off.'

'Thank you, sir.' The man turned to lead the way.

To Effie Everett said, 'I shall bring Sir John home soon.'

She nodded. 'You had better go. He can forget himself when he is lecturing.'

As they started up the glen Everett spoke of John. 'He is an inspired teacher. He has a way with small children which few learned men have.'

The woman stopped him with a man's noise like 'Humph!'

Everett turned and waved to the cottage. She waved and stayed, watching.

*

As they climbed among the trees, the gold light of late afternoon faded through rose to a blue-grey dimness.

To break the quietness he said to the mother, 'You are from these parts?'

'No, I'm from Derbyshire.' She stopped there.

Though at first he had no alarm, as they tried different tracks and then moved to higher ones he wondered, had there been an accident? In the stream, on the rocks? Was John hurt, and the small girl frightened? Or had she been injured in a fall — and John could not leave a child alone. There were no 'banditti' in these hills, but what if they met a troubled person? Were there animals that could hurt them?

Ridiculous fancies — for sure they would find the couple well. Yet the light was gone within the woods, and the sky an unfathomable velvet blue. The mother grew more agitated, and her friend encouraged her.

'Ye canna trust a man with pale eyes and sandy hair. Do

ye no remember Judas? Och, I misgive.'

Everett said, 'Maybe they are already home. They could have passed us going the other way.'

The man frowned. 'I would have caught them. I know the glen, with its winds and tracks. Huist!'

They approached a clearing, and he signalled for the others to come beside him.

'There's John,' Everett said, 'What is he doing up there?'

They looked out across a hollow of ferns. On the far side, the ground rose in a rough mound or hillock, where only grass grew. Very low, in the dark-blue sky, a gigantic burnt-copper moon was rising. It just cleared the tree-tops, and against its disk he saw them dancing — up on the mound, the tall man stooping to his tiny lady. When John passed the moon, his limbs looked bony as a mantis. He did not hold her closely, but he stooped to hold her rightly, elegantly turning to the new dance, the waltz, which it seemed he had taught her, for her own small steps had grace and politeness. His lips moved, maybe he hummed the music. As they watched the dance ended. John gave a deep bow, while Polly returned an elegant curtsey.

'The child looks well enough,' the man murmured, while Polly's mother strode through the ferns.

'Polly, come down here.'

But already she came, with ladylike steps, conducted by John — who let go her hand, and stood looking at them, for a moment confounded, like a caught child himself. His voice came thin, from airless lungs.

'Mrs Boyce — I fear I have detained your daughter. I had meant to give her tea by now. I have striven to give her good instruction.'

The mother ignored him, in talk with Polly. The man hulked over John.

'Do ye no ken the hour, man? What in God's name were you thinking of? The wee child's mother was beside herself.'

John stood with a lowered head, sheep-faced, contrite. He repeated in a crumbled voice, 'I am at fault. It did grow late. But I meant good, and the child is well.'

The mother said clearly, for all to hear, 'Polly, from now on you do not leave the hotel. Do you hear me? And you sir — if you seek to lead Polly again from the hotel, I shall away to Callander for the constable.'

Everett started, to hear such words to John — a gentleman, and from a housekeeper. But John it seemed had abandoned his body, as though it were nothing but empty clothes, which someone had hung from a hook by the collar. His fallen head was meek as gruel.

'I am sorry. Truly I meant well.'

'Ough!' She pulled Polly away by the hand, while her friend hurried after. The man lingered.

' I don't know, sir, if you are man or goblin. As I gather, you are soon to leave Bridge of Turk. That is the best thing you may do.'

John's head stayed down, they saw his nose through his hair.

'Och, he's no a man at all.' The man shrugged furiously, and paced after the women.

John raised his head shyly. 'Have they gone?'

'What possessed you, John? You know the time. What on earth did you think would happen?' He thought, I sound like my own father — but John seemed half a child.

John pulled on his sleeve. 'Don't be cross, Ebewett. The tempest is past. We shall leave here, and they will forget.'

He in turn took John's elbow. 'Let us get to the cottage.'

As they walked John grew ever more sleepy, lolling his head and half-closing his eyes.

Everett had to stop. 'John, are you well? What has happened?'

'My dear — I am *destroyed* with happiness.'

'Have you taken opium?'

John turned as if he would embrace him. 'It is love, not opium. Just a moment, look — I kept her wibbon.'

He made wide eyes, holding the ribbon aslant on his forelock. Did he mean to mimic the child?

'Please, John —' He moved quickly on, but John stumbled in the leaves and leaned heavily on him. A small voice said,

'Ebewett —'

He did not answer.

'Le' me be your bad girl.'

Away in the trees, a fox gave its thin bark.

'Oh!' John shrank as if frightened into his arms. Everett stepped back, so John nearly fell. He thought, John's insane.

'Get a grip on yourself, man. This is worse than unseemly. You have made a ludicrous show of yourself.' He surprised himself with his own harsh bark.

John drew breath sharply. He had stopped in his tracks, astonished.

Everett pointed. 'That must be the path.'

Between shimmering birches they glimpsed the moonlit track.

'Make haste,' Everett called sharply. 'We should leave this spot. And you must let such little girls be. What the dickens is wrong with you?' The indignation of weeks filled his voice.

John, in deep dapple, stood still as a stake. He stayed so. When he stepped into the moonlight, his softness had gone. He was gaunt, scorched white by the icy light.

'You're right, we must quit this place. We can't stay where these oafs will clack. We'll pack our trunks and get far off.'

'Steady, John. I need some time here, still. I haven't finished the background.'

But John had grown supercilious. 'Oh, you can stay, Everett. As to the "background", you don't need me for that. It's all botany and boulders, after all — and your priceless dashing water. You shall add me in — as you said — in London.'

'Even so I had thought that we travelled together.'

John stooped towards him with a deep-grooved smile. 'My dear, don't you think we have been "together" long enough? The three of us — or should I rather say, the two of us?' His eyes shone white like china eyes.

Everett started. 'Do you refer — to your lady and to me?'

'Oh, I blame myself. You remember Vasari? He who takes a young painter into his house — he should look to his wife.'

'The lady is all honour. And as to myself —' He paused, for the voice of William said loud in his head, say nothing rash, you will do yourself hurt. But he must speak. 'As to myself, I will not be blamed for behaving with kindness to a clever young *beautiful* woman whom you have treated with cruel neglect. With shameful indifference. I have not known any man slight his wife as you do.'

John, in the pale light, seemed to grow thinner.

'Do you say so, Everett? Thank you for that lesson. And is friendly "kindness" all you have given?'

'I know she will never betray you. That is your good fortune. Because one might think, from your carelessness of her, that you wanted for her to get into a scrape.'

John gave his odd, loud, nasal snort. 'I don't give two ha'pence for your opinion. Be assured that in future my wife shall have my best attention.' He stood grim like some old totem of savages. 'Mine, not yours. You will speak no more with her when I am not by. And when we are gone, I forbid you to write to her. I shall forbid her likewise to write to you.'

He was shaken. How had he not thought, that John might in time play the righteous husband? His own rash words had brought this on. Coolly he said, 'I shall not inflict my company where it is not wanted. And for letters — is she not her own mistress, as to whom she may address an envelope?'

'No, sir, she is not. She is my wife, and will act as I direct.' His voice had a clang. 'Attend me now. When we leave this place you shall not see my wife again, in any circumstance whatever.'

He had fallen into deep dejection. 'I do not think I shall see either of you again.'

'Oh no, Everett. Me you shall see on many a day. I shall wait on you, in your studio in London, for my portrait to be completed.'

It amazed him still to see John, who had been so pitiable, pretending to command him.

'I should tell you, John, I have no mind to continue that work.'

'And why not, pray? You have taken my coin. You have given your word, and I shall hold you to it. There is a side to things you should remember, Everett. For all your talents, your purse is light. And I have a voice — I can make your fortune, and mar it too.'

'You think I shall buckle because you have influence — and because you are rich?'

'I am more than "rich", Everett. My father's fortune is mine to spend, and I am free to do as I please in life. My wife was penniless when I contracted to marry her, even so I settled ten thousand upon her. Were she to forsake me, she must pay it all back, and that she never can do.'

It was like being struck with a weight of cast iron, this reminder that all life turned on money. And it came from

John, whom he had thought unworldly.

John stepped closer. 'I do not say you are mercenary, Everett — only that you are not a fool.'

'Still the choice is mine. The portrait will wait on my pleasure, not yours.'

'And so it should.' John gave an odd chuckle. 'And that gangling *goatherd* friend of yours — that just led you to me through the glen — he may think I can't play the man. But I shall show, I can play the man. And do it as well as the best of you.'

'Good, John. That would be best.'

'Sarcasm, Everett? Would you dare to judge me?' His moon-white face leered — then recoiled. 'Will you hit me?' His voice went high, he shrank as he backed away.

'I was not going to —' But he was perplexed — had he raised his fist?

John straightened. 'Let me pass, please.' His voice was tremulous.

Everett stepped back. 'There is room enough.'

John passed him, then turned,

'The great artist of our time? We shall see how you do. You may yet fall to making your bread by painting heiresses to please their mammas. Or by drawing cartoons for novels — or even for *Punch,* like your friend John Leech.'

John started downhill with his Alpine stride.

Thank you, John, he murmured. You can go to the deuce, and take my canvas with you. And as to your orders — I shall not be stopped. I shall take your wife, sir, and make her my own.

He waited till John had got clear ahead, then, at his own pace, walked down the hill.

12

'But to leave in a week,' she said, 'How can we be ready?'

'With the greatest ease. My lectures I may finish in our rooms in Edinburgh — while watching the city I am speaking of.'

'And your portrait?'

'Oh,' he said lightly, 'I'm not needed for that. Everett will paint me in London, not here.'

Still it was as if the sky fell in. The weeks of late summer had stretched before her, in which at times she would contrive to see Everett. Now those weeks disappeared, and Everett with them. She was suddenly desperate.

'Must you go to the hotel?' she asked in the morning.

'By no means, my dear, my work there is done. Now I must sit to my lectures all day — here, at this table, with you by my side.' He patted the chair that stood near his. 'You may read Sir Walter — and look up dates when I ask you to.'

He did not stay to see her dismay, but took up his pen and began to write.

She wandered in the room. Would he hold her by his side, all day and all night? She was all at once in prison. What had passed, when Everett met John on the mountain? All she knew was that John's small pupil had come home well and happy.

John wrote, chewed his pen, and wrote again. She sat and read: she dusted and tidied: she went to the scullery. She stood and watched John, or she gazed from the window.

At last she said, 'I must take some air, it is close in here.'

'I beg you will not. I need for you to find a name, in among my Venice papers.'

Yet he delayed to give the name, and when she hemmed and coughed he said, 'Pray return to Sir Walter, my dear. He is a most improving author.'

The words sounded like an order, and his face grew elderly as he handed *The Antiquary* back to her. The words danced, she turned the pages backwards. When she looked up to find John watching, he gave his little v-shaped smile.

Finally she stood, and put on her pelisse and her wide-awake hat. Then John yawned and stretched his arms, and stood up from his papers.

'My dear helpmate, I have wearied you. You are right to rise. May I bear you company? I too need a pause.' Was mockery hiding in his voice? The courtesies oozed like thin syrup. With ceremony he held the door for her, and they walked up the glen.

She paused on the path to breathe in deeply the scent of pines, and lightly asked, 'Shall we go down to see how Everett does?'

'Let us not disturb him. He must increase his pace a little.' He laughed. 'He is hardly the fastest painter I know.'

'He is the most careful, I believe.'

'And so am I a careful person, of all that is so dear to me.' The wave of his stick included her in its curve, which ended by pointing down the slope to the falls. 'Also, he recently took rest for some days. It is fit he is left to make up for lost time.'

So she knew, he would not let her meet Everett again.

With courtesy he took her arm, but his hold on her was hard. His blue glance was keen so she dared not gaze to where Everett painted, though her nerves ached to do so like threads of cotton being stretched till they snapped.

*

She could not follow his changes of mood. On their last Sunday, in church, he was bland and serene. At the church door he greeted Everett, as one greets a long-lost friend.

'Everett, my dear! Pray walk with us on this beautiful day.'

'My pleasure,' Everett said, and gleamed to her.

At once she said, 'And dine with us too. Will that not also be a pleasure, John?'

She feared his answer, but he lightly said, 'A capital notion! Will you, sir?'

'I thank you both.'

'That is well.' John turned to the loch beside them. 'But hold — it is early yet. Let us take a turn on the waters of Loch Achray.'

She frowned. 'Boating, John? You have not liked to go boating before.'

It was, though, a beautiful thought. The air was still and the loch seemed made of dazzling sunlight: it stretched endlessly from them into a thin shining water-haze.

'My dears, the wind is in my sails. I have had my griefs, but my lectures go well. We are almost gone and I am impatient for Edinburgh. This will be my present to us all.'

She started, for Everett's hand had clasped hers, and gripped hers so it hurt.

As they walked to the hotel's landing stage, she saw, among the people strolling, that man John knew with the very thin head. Again he wore black and carried an instrument like a weapon: it was three spears in a bundle. But no one spoke to him. Did they see him at all, or was he a spectre?

She took Everett's hand quickly, and squeezed his fingers with all her force.

At the landing stage below the hotel, John spoke across her. 'In the last of my lectures in Edinburgh, Everett, I purpose to speak about Pre-Raphaelitism — about you yourself, and your Brothers in Art.'

'Good,' Everett said shortly, quietly.

John paused for him to say more, but he did not. 'And I stand in need of your advice. I am right, I believe, that the first three Brothers were you, your friend Hunt, and Dante Rossetti?'

'Yes.'

'Though your style and Dante's differ greatly. Yet you are true comrades in this Revolution of Art?'

'Yes.'

'That is how it should be. In art there cannot be one right style.'

Everett did not speak.

'No, indeed,' said John.

At the landing stage a handful of boatmen lounged. They wore plump Scotch caps with balls of wool in the middle. John engaged two, and stepped precariously into the swaying boat.

'My dear, sit by me. So we face Everett where he sits in the stern. Oh, be careful, dear friend! You're rocking our boat!' He laughed as the boat both swung and tipped, and Everett stumbled to his seat. 'We're shipshape now. Oarsmen, would you?'

With graceful ease the oarsmen heaved, and the boat slid smoothly into the loch.

'Stay here,' John called. 'The water's like glass.'

In the still heat the boat seemed to hang in mid-air, with blue sky and white cloud above and below them. John stretched his arms wide.

'To me this is a visionary moment. Our stay is coming to a glorious close.'

He scanned the far bank, lifting his head as if he saw through his nose.

'There's the chapel, Effie. Those reeds over there mark the mouth of the Finlas.'

She could look only to Everett, who gazed back to her with such eyes — as if famished hunger sat in the stern. Was he thinner, more pale? His eyes said, Why do we not meet? Why do you not come?

She must look away, for John watched. He smiled, they smiled, though Everett was beset by midges.

John mused, 'My dears, our time here has been — an interlude in the life we knew. I think we each have made discoveries — that our wants reach further than we knew. But after all, things stay as they were. There is no harm done. And each of us carries away — a trophy.'

He smiled — a strange smile, elderly and knowing, and young and teasing.

'What do you mean, John?

'A trophy, a treasure. It may be a knowledge. It may be a picture, as Everett takes his canvas back.'

His eye was bright as he looked at them both, as if each must know what he meant.

She fidgeted in her seat. Everett flapped at the flies.

'Everett — it occurs to me, might you bring your canvas when you come to the cottage? It would be so kind. So we may see it with good leisure.'

'I will.'

John leaned over the side of the boat. 'But the water's so still — and such deep blue. Look at the clouds. You could think they were monsters, deep down under us.'

Before leaning to see she cried out with her eyes, My dear true Everett, I shall come to you. My heart is sure. John will not prevent me.

But how could she see Everett? John was a gaoler, and so few days left.

John trailed a finger in the water. 'Ah, Everett,' he crooned, 'You couldn't catch those beasts with your rod and line. But we escape them.'

'I can't catch these midges, that's for sure.' Everett waved his hand sharply. 'May we move, please? We are becalmed.'

'My fault. Oarsmen, please.'

As the water stirred, and the boat slipped forward, she gazed deep down into endless blue, where the largest cloud stretched and turned, an arctic bear in a cage, reaching out a blind white paw.

*

Walking back by the hotel, she saw the strollers had gathered into a line: they stood two deep. Before them was the thin man's weapon, which opened like an easel on three legs. On these legs stood a box with a spout in front, and over the back of it hung a black sheet. The thin man was hunched inside it, she saw. So she understood, he was a daguerreotypist, he made pictures of people who came to stay there. There was no mystery after all — John was interested in this new kind of picture.

At the cottage she laid their meal with care. John, like a good boy, came to assist, though she must tell him where each dish went.

'I have the canvas,' Everett said at the door.

They stood the painting on a chair, close to the window. In the clear light each leaf and water-drop gleamed.

'I have not finished the water to the right. But on the left side, all is done.'

'Everett — oh!' John stepped back in survey, then bent close. 'The way that lichen changes from silver to pewter — the subtlest beauty. But the water! The way it builds, fall after fall. The clarity, the plunge of it! The sparkle, the transparency!' He stepped back to gaze more, in frank delight. 'No painter I know has got the curves so true, as to the exact way in which water *falls.*'

The painting was like none she had seen, with that white silhouette bang in the centre. She knew the shape was John, from the lank outline of the hair at the back of the head, and from the tight small way in which the shoulders were pinched.

Over John's bent back Everett looked again to her. In summons? In an appeal she could not answer.

John stood. 'And there' — he pointed — 'the water has the sheen of maiden-hair. But let us dine.'

They sat to the meats she put before them.

'Some tongue, Everett? Now, you may perhaps have read me on the Truth of Water?'

Everett gave a short nod.

'I think I may say I have noticed more, of the changing looks that water may have, than any before me — saving great Turner. I see I must re-write those pages. You have shown me things I had not seen. I thank you, in humble admiration.'

The praise was full, his face had a light — you could say he gazed with love at Everett, who sat face-down, frowning and chewing his lip.

John turned to her. 'Oh but my dear, these pickles have mothered.'

'I am sorry, John.' She spoke with ill grace, he chose not to notice.

'Dearest, I have something to ask of you. Our hosts at Edinburgh have made a request. Are you willing to go to the Philosophical Institution an hour before I come myself? So you may welcome and seat our acquaintances, before the Hall is opened to subscribers.'

'I shall do that.'

'I knew you would. Thank you.' He said aloud to the table, 'I must tell you the subscribers are over one thousand. The lobbies will be packed, to the doors and beyond. I am concerned for my throat.'

He took Everett's hand, where he sat in sombreness. 'With all my heart, dear man, I wish you could be there to hear those lectures. It grieves me that we leave you alone here. And in but a day or two. We shall miss you most keenly — shall we not, my dear?'

She had to look down. But it was Everett whose cup began to dance in its saucer. He put it quickly on the table, and poked at his ham, then hunched down in a choking cough. He stood.

'Excuse me.' He crossed the room quickly, and went into the school-room. Through the closed door they heard a loud odd swallowed gasp.

'Good Heavens! My dear, I am concerned.'

'Shall I go to him, John?' She felt wet tracks on her own face.

'A woman's comfort? And I see you are moved.' He bent close to her face. 'But no, we must let him collect himself. He would be shamed, to think we knew he wept.'

They heard Everett cough, or clear his throat. Presently he came back, and stood by his chair. 'Forgive me. I surprised myself — and you are entitled to know my grief. It's not only you who are going away. My friend Hunt has written, from his voyage to the Holy Land. I don't know when I shall — see him again —' He had to stop for his voice dissolved. He buried his face in his hands, and heaved a giant single sob.

'Is *that* the reason for your grief?' John inspected him then turned to her. 'It's true, he and Hunt are extremely close. They were the first Pre-Raphaelite "Brothers", before even Dante. These are *comradely* tears. The great-hearted young braves!'

He moved his chair, to rest his arm on Everett's shoulder. 'Weep as you must, Everett dear. This is a man's grief — I honour you for it. Why, I am moved myself.'

Quietly, so John did not see, she cried into her handkerchief.

The scullery door opened and Crawley came in, and cleared the plates impassively.

*

She knew, when Everett left, she should begin to arrange and fold her clothes, and think how they would be stowed in the trunk. But she only sat, till she became aware that John was examining her.

When she looked up, he said, 'My dear — how strong is the tenderness you cherish for Everett?'

Heat like the heat in the church possessed her. 'It is true that in our time here I have grown to love him dearly.'

'"Love"? And "dearly"?' He had sat erect.

Her clear voice came. 'What did you think would happen, John? You show me every day you think me a trial to you. *You* encouraged me to talk with Everett. He is a young man, I am a young woman.'

'You say that to me?' His voice had no breath. 'I trusted your honour.'

'And rightly so. I am still a pure wife.'

'That is well.' He nodded some moments, and when he looked up his eyes were frost. 'So it shall be. I charge you now. In these last two days, and after we leave, you shall not speak with Everett when I am not by. Everett knows this, I have told him my will.'

She did not answer.

'Do you heed me?'

She did not speak.

'After Edinburgh we shall return to our own dear home on Herne Hill. I ask, do you look forward to our going home?'

'I told you before, John. To leave here, and go back there to live with you — frankly it will break my heart.'

'What!' His chair fell behind him as he stood tall over her. His eyes jumped, very blue, in a face of fire. He looked as she had never seen him look — as she saw her father look only once — like a grown man beside himself with rage. For the first time ever he frightened her.

Raising his arm, he shouted high-voiced, 'I shall hit you with a common stick.' She lifted her forearm.

But he had stepped back. He closed his mouth tight and took slow breaths. His eyes lost focus, his colour sank, till he had returned inside himself.

He said hoarsely, 'You are my wife. You shall do as I bid. It is plain as that.'

She made no reply. Her forehead jerked, as though a small creature jumped, under her skin. Her left eye creased in a painful wink.

He entered his own room, and shut the door. After a space

there was a scraping noise, as he pulled the box from under his bed. Then she heard the soft slap of leather on leather as he began to pack his books.

13

While sorting their things, when John was busy outside the cottage, she found a packet wrapped in oil-cloth. Its size and shape were odd, and it tinkled with a silvery sound when she turned it. She undid the cloth, and the paper within it, to find square plates of glass: they were the size of the pages of a book. She recognized daguerreotypes, and carefully held one to the light. As she turned it back and forth, the light parts of the picture went dark, and the dark parts came light. But was it fancy dress — a children's party? She recognized the small girl from the hotel, loosely dressed in a fine white gown — her best dress, perhaps. Her face was lofty, her small nose lifted, as she played the princess looking down upon you.

The next plate showed a different girl, who held a cloth like a curtain about herself. She had a shy, uneasy smile.

The next glass almost fell from her hand. She saw wall-paper, furniture, and yet another small girl. But what stopped her dead was the fact that this girl wore nearly nothing. Her white body was breastless. She held a slender arm up high, and turned so she stood like a tiny dancer. But — how could John own such a picture? Who had made it?

But she knew who had made it, it was the man she had seen with the so-thin head. What words did he exchange with John?

On the instant she knew — when John spoke of a 'trophy', he meant this packet. But what, still, did these pictures mean? She sat with the daguerreotypes in her lap. There was a strangeness in John she never would fathom. In his family too there were — strangenesses. She thought of his mother in the old house in Perth — as she heard broken steps descend the stair, till the horror of her life stood at the door.

What to do? She must think fast, for she heard John outside. Quickly she wrapped the pictures back in their oil-cloth, and replaced the package where she found it.

*

She had an absolute need to speak with Everett. But how to arrange it, so John did not know?

There was a red brick wall near their cottage, which she walked past every day. It was just like the wall in Everett's painting 'The Huguenot'. She knew that picture by heart.

Beside the wall she stopped, and stooped, and picked from among the flowers that grew along its base. As she stood, and smelt them, her fingers rubbed the red crumb of the wall. She knew that when the time came, they would say their last words here, sheltered by the wall from windows and eyes, while John arranged some detail of travelling.

Tender as a breath they would steal a kiss, while a fitful sunlight shone on them. Then she would say,

'Everett, do you see? We are just like the lovers in your "Huguenot". It is the painting of yours that I like the best.

He would smile. 'Welcome to my picture, dearest. At least there's no massacre — in 1853.'

'Maybe the massacre is coming to us.' She would speak of John. 'After all we are in a different picture — say Orpheus and Eurydice. You are my Orpheus, my artist, my angel.

Herne Hill is Hades and John is Pluto, who will take me there.'

'He shall not. I shall set you free.' Then he kissed her tenderly, on her left eye, which often blinked.

Such love, such lovers...

In her overflowing eyes the picture's colours swim. They stand, these lovers, by a garden wall: the baked bricks crumble from summers of sun. It is the eve of the Bartholomew's Day massacre of Protestants, and the beautiful redhead, pale with love, pulls tight the white sash round her Protestant lover's arm. The Catholic sign, it will save his life. But though she is Catholic and he loves her, still he is brave and loves his faith too. So even as they clasp each other, still his embracing arm fingers the sash, and tugs to undo the knot she ties. He will die for his faith though it shatters her heart, and she can only implore with her eyes that he heed the danger he will not flee. For now they are together and utterly one. Ivy of constancy winds up the wall, nasturtiums of loyalty bloom by his feet. A light breeze ruffles the white Canterbury bells, so the tiny white trumpets sway like a chime — a symbol of faith.

Such love, such lovers — Everett understands love. I shall go to him whatever John says, among the crowds of the hotel lobby if need be. I shall bid John farewell, to his face, and leave him.

Hungrily she gazed down the village path, but no one came. She went back to the cottage to put the flowers in water. She would place them where she would always see them.

*

Again, in the black dead of night, she woke. If she left with John tomorrow, then Everett would be lost forever, whatever he and she had said. He would meet pretty girls at every party in London. Their big mothers would invite and snare him.

She said to herself, you fool, you coward. So many times she had said, John is strange and a monster, I shall leave him

141

today and go to Everett. It had not happened. She was weak, unworthy, scared of risk and scandal.

No — I *shall* speak, she told herself slowly. An owl quavered its churchyard call.

As she sat to breakfast she rehearsed the words, but there was no place to speak. Crawley was in and out with their things, while John ate standing, directing him.

Her small room was empty. She drew on her cape, and tied on the bonnet she was to wear for the trip. She took a deep breath, the time is now.

She came into the sitting room and saw all their things gone. Outside Crawley stood in the sun, in the shafts of the hand-cart from the hotel. John stood beside him, in the act of taking out his watch. He was smart for travelling, in his new-brushed black coat, and black winter trousers for the city. His hair was sleek.

'Good morning, Euphemia.' He was bright and crisp, as always when they set out on travels.

'Good morning, John,' she weakly said.

She thought, I cannot do it now. I shall tell John in Edinburgh, then write to Everett. He will write back at once, I know. I promise this, Everett, on my soul. Still, like the vanquished, in shame, she walked beside John, behind the labouring hump of Crawley. The wheels of the hand-cart squealed.

Everett stood waiting where the coach would stop, at a distance from a party of hotel guests. The ladies' voices there made a music, as if they had just met. The gentlemen smiled quietly to each other, and scuffed the gravel with their heels.

Her eyes were on Everett all the time they approached. He was thinner than ever, he looked like a knife. She did not hear what he said to John. Then he stood over her.

'Farewell, Countess. Do not forget your drawing — you are the best pupil I ever had. *Bon voyage*. You are in my thoughts.'

Meeting his eyes, she thought, he is like a ravenous wolf. Her eyes must say, I shall write to you, Everett. John leaned in close.

'Dear drawing master — I thank you for your lessons, from the depths of my heart. Take the very greatest care.'

She shook his hand, as men may do. Let John think it odd. The two hands gripped and held as tight, as if each held the other above a cliff.

John touched her elbow. 'My dear.' He handed her into the coach, where the other ladies had already mounted. He climbed in after, while Crawley heaved their trunks into the van, and climbed up to sit outside at the back.

The coachman blew his horn, harness tinkled, the horses stepped. She was deep in the coach and could not see Everett. John beside her sat back in satisfaction.

The coach windows showed a blur of hedgerows, and then the grey waters of Loch Achray. The hills beyond were brown with withered heather. She thought, I shall not go back alone to Herne Hill — I shall invite one of my sisters with me, and never be alone with John again.

'Oh, by the by,' John comfortably said, 'I will add one thing more, to the wishes I mentioned the other night. I am not willing that you and Everett should write to each other. It would upset you, so I forbid it. I fear I have allowed too much to pass.'

She swallowed the yelp she needed to give, she must hold her face so nothing showed.

'You did not say this before —' she began, and stopped. He watched her closely. It was clear why he did not speak

143

before — so she could deceive herself with hope, which he would kill when she could not act.

He was talking still, she began to hear him. Evidently he felt he could comfort her for his voice was stern but kindly too. Would he try to woo her back?

'None of us may have all we wish in life. I have given you much. I have given you the life of wealth. I have given you Venice, and Chamonix, and the Alps. I have given you wardrobes of glacé silk, and the society of lords, and Grand Dukes, and — and — *hussars*.'

He paused, he was not pleased with the sour look she gave, as she moved so she faced away from him.

'Through me you have met our Queen — and the Viceroy of Vienna.'

Her eye gave its ugly wink as she turned and said in bitterness, 'That is dust to me, John.'

Her voice was so sharp that all the coach heard. He muttered under his breath, 'But for me you would die poor doing needlework in *Perth*.' He turned from her.

What was worst, was that there was truth in his words. By not acting, she had chosen — comfort, security and high society. She had murdered love, now she was dead.

One purpose she had. In London she would see her friend Lucy Eastlake. Lucy's father was a women's doctor, and she would ask Lucy to examine her person, and tell her how she was — unusual. Then at least she would learn the worst, and learn too why all hope was lost.

14

She had gone, and his nights were worse. At least, before, he saw her sometimes. Now he had nothing of her. Maybe, as John said, they would not meet again.

And the weather had spoiled. He shivered as he huddled to his canvas, a cold wind threaded the woods.

'Thank God for Crawley.' Before they left, Crawley had made a small shelter for him, of lengths of wood and canvas. He himself had brought a brazier, so hot coals smoked beside him.

My love, where are you? He worked his fingers in the warmth from the coals, to keep them supple. I'm like some old labourer by a hole in the road — all I need is my kettle. His mind filled with dark things, wars, the risen dead.

But to work. His pointed brush, his pointed sight, took aim: he had come to the foreground, he was painting the rock on which John would stand.

He bent close, and dabbed. Gusts flapped the sides of the shelter, and tugged at the boulders which anchored its edge. The voice of William said in his head, Look here, Everett, you've had a lucky escape — you could have been caught in scandal and worse, court cases, quarrels, havoc and distraction. Be thankful you got clear.

145

Away, William — behind me! William had become his private Satan.

There, John — we have you. With two more dabs, he finished the stone beneath John's shoe. The white silhouette was complete, surrounded by rock and water and foliage.

He eyed the shape, which seemed now to hover out in front of the painting. But how, sir, will I 'paint you in' in London? What charade will this be — hypocrisy, betrayal — where I sweetly paint the man I loathe, while both of us know I love his wife? How could she bear to know we do this?

A new gust came, with the force of a gale: it was the freezing breath of the North Wind itself. The hut filled like a sail, pulled for a moment at the rocks on its hem, then lifted and whirled away behind him. Either he, or the wind, knocked the brazier over. He tumbled on the ground, holding tight to his canvas, while coals bounced round him into the stream which, for an instant, hissed and smoked.

He dusted himself, the gust had died. His broken hut had caught among branches. His painting was safe, but two holes were burnt in the skirt of his coat. A few coals still lay on the rock, which, with his foot, he pushed together. They were white with ash, but he knelt and blew on them till they reddened.

He re-erected his easel and picked up his palette, and dabbled a brush in his whites and browns. The rest of the foreground was still to do, and the stone and lichen in front of John.

No, I *shall* paint John in, in London. It will be a sort of link with her, and John must tell me something of her. Yet what a sad link! He had not thought before, how the word 'pain' hides inside the word, 'paint'.

He eyed sharply the corrugations in the stone he must

copy. Had he got the tone right? I don't know if this picture will ever be finished, he muttered as he touched brush-tip to canvas again.

*

In the late afternoon the sky opened and brightened. His paints were put away, he looked at the mountain that stood over the glen.

'I shall do it at last — I shall climb Ben Bulben.'

But first he had to pass farmers' fields, and hedgerows. He climbed through withered brakes, and sharp barriers of gorse. On the shoulder of the mountain he found marshy hollows, where he sank to the ankle in hidden water. But slowly the going changed to thin grass and crags, while the air became keen. The waters of Loch Achray spread out below him, with the valley beyond, like a river of trees, winding away towards Callander.

In the sharp sweet air his thoughts expanded, as the sky became huge. He must look to his future. Back in London the election would soon take place, which could make him the youngest Associate ever of the Royal Academy. If he won that honour, where would his art stop? He thought of his competitors, both the young talents and the seasoned masters. Truth be told, he was better than any of them. Let this mountain be Art, he would climb to the top of it. He had been in a valley, he breathed freedom now.

He loped, and strode, and climbed a steep rise. He kept thinking he had reached the top of Ben Bulben, then found another hump lying in wait. Then, with a last breathless clamber, he arrived.

'My stars, what a view!'

Below him, at last, he saw the whole of Glen Finlas, and

beyond, ringed by hills, Loch Finlas itself. It was so clear that he thought, if I had a telescope, I could see the two of us walking there. It was the place of their love. It was far off, and shining.

It was far, he was high, up on Ben Bulben. Remote but distinct, he saw all of the Trossachs couched like large creatures to the limits of sight. The beauty was — flawless. The sight of it gave him a piercing hurt, that grew so that all unexpectedly he shut his eyes tight as knots, locked his face in a grimace, and called out her name to the void.

Part II
On Herne Hill

'I am your soul, John.'

1

But did they meet? If once you wake, in jealousy's coils, all rest is lost — be it never so dark at the start of dawn.

Nor was she here. Had she left the bed early, so as to hasten to her meeting with *him*?

He was quickly up. He must dress for Town, for the Turner house — and, day of days, for his portrait to begin. So I shall see Everett, who has been all the world to me. Once I am stationed in your studio, dear, so you see no other but me… Squinting into his shaving mirror, he turned his face to the angle the portrait would show.

On the landing, in the dimness, he winced as his finger caught the varnish on the banister — his father's decorator, execrable work.

But there she stood, by the drawing-room window — fully dressed as he was, gazing out to a garden furred with frost. Had her nerve failed? She prepared for the assignation, then did not go.

'Euphemia?'

She was still as ice.

'Of whom are you thinking?'

'Of opera singers, John.' She turned her acid face. 'Of dancers in balls. Of excitement and life.'

Operas, balls — she was of the world worldly, why was she with him? Nor did she speak truth. He strode to the hall and put on his coat.

'Are you leaving, John?'

'I must write my pages for today.' He gazed, he would bind her with his eye. 'And you know where I do that best.'

'Before breakfast? And Sophie, I know, will soon be down.'

Sophie, sweet Sophie — he hung in a hover, his tall hat fumbled in his hand. 'You bid me stay? Since we came home, you have shown little love of my company.'

The tic jerked up the left side of her face. 'I do my duty.' He saw her eyes red, her face grey from sleeplessness.

'Not with a good heart, I think.'

'Don't speak to me of heart, John.'

Heart — oh, he knew what 'heart' meant. Jealous anger flared. But I shall be with him today — I shall fill his eye, and fill his thought.

'I take tea in the City.'

He had shut the house-door sharply. But what a hallelujah of a January morning! He breathed out smoke, his chest hurt from the searing cold. But from here on Herne Hill you saw the bright slopes of London: a thousand threads of smoke idled upwards through clear sky. Behind me, jealousy! Who could think bad thoughts amid such beauty?

He walked quickly, to the gate of his parents' home. What a mercy they lived close by. From sheds at the back came animal noises, geese, a pig, a cluck of hens.

'Master John!' Old Anne, in the doorway, smiled like the sun. 'Mistress is not down from her dressing room yet.'

'I shall be in my room.'

He climbed the broad stairs through warm, stained

sunbeams: the peace of this house.

In his study he sat to his sheaf of papers, while Sanders purred on the easy chair, beside the fire which was already lit. He dipped his pen, and, for all troubles of the night, words came at once. It was always so: in the dark his thoughts grew unwatched, like a tree.

How deep is the science of reflected light — no thing, no person has one colour only, but all are stained by the hues around them.

He did not stop writing, though he knew someone dear now stood behind him. On quietest steps she crept up close, and drew her chair so it just touched his. His left hand reached and found her fingers.

'Pretend I'm not here, dear.'

'You always say that.'

Her whalebone creaked as she raised her hand, and lightly turned his hair. When he paused in his writing, he sat his chair round.

'You slept well, dearest?'

She nodded as she poured a small glass of cordial. 'You told me this book is a present to Father.'

'I hope it may be my least bad book. When is Father due back?'

'This morning — he had business in the wine vaults in Leicester. John — we are both of us glad that you are once more working on a book. I misgave that you did such a mountebank thing, as giving public lectures.'

He stretched his arms wide. 'Dearest, those lectures had a great success. More than a thousand came each night.'

'Even so, dear heart, I always hoped that if you *must* speak in public, it would be from a pulpit.'

A pulpit, Good God! He smiled, his mother brought no

bad thoughts. He took up his pen — but she held him with her gravest look.

'I grieve for you, John.'

What! He was nettled. Would it be his own mother, who sowed doubts in his head. Shortly he asked, 'And why is that, pray?'

She heavily breathed. 'I see every day she has not brought you happiness.'

'We all have our cross to bear.'

She rested both hands on his shoulders. 'My dear son — tell me.'

He wanted to write, not to swing back to grief. Leave me, he prayed, but his voice broke. 'I do not know what devil is in her. Her fits of temper... I forgave her all, of what happened in the Highlands. If it weren't for little Sophie, her sweet sister Sophie, who brings such joy —'

'Forget Sophie.' She munched as she sipped. 'Oh, John, John, John. I fear you speak too lightly of "what happened in the Highlands".'

He made to laugh uneasily. 'I suspected no more than holding hands. The fault is mine, I left them at times in each other's company.'

Her brows knit in a frown as deep as trenches. '*Dear* John, why did you do that?'

'Oh, they were young and I was busy. It was foolish of me, I agree.'

She shook her head. 'My son, you're good — but you are innocent. I dare not say it. Well, I shall tell you. I fear the worst.'

'What worst?' At once he was on the edge of tears. 'You cannot think — that here in London — that she and Everett —' For it would be like the proof of it, if he found she shared his fears.

Her gaze was baleful. 'All I know is, that Father lets her hire a fly, once a week from Crozier's. At our expense. But where she goes in it.... You must stop that, John. Keep her within doors day and night. And your man Crawley, whom you leave to kick his heels all day — have him set his eye upon her.'

'Dear heart, she is not to be shut in a box.' But his voice failed, he was weak as water. Her gaze was full — is any man loved as I am loved? His cheeks puckered and her lips trembled. His head sank against her chest, and a sob he could not stop broke out.

'Dear John.' Her arms enclosed him round. 'I am more proud to be your mother, than if I could be mother to the greatest of the kings of the earth.'

Safe in the nest of utter peace, he shyly raised his tearful eyes.

'John!' she said sharply, 'Please don't make that noise with your nose.'

They both sat straight. How could he write? All thought was broken. Colours, colours — yellow is jealousy, lust is red, and grief and torment are black, black, black. Sophie, white Sophie, purity was there.

'Listen, John. Father is returned.' They heard his strong step on the stair: he was at the door. 'John James, dear heart. What news of Leicester?'

'I thought I'd find the pair of you here. Well, I have had the British Sherry moved far off. I told them to put it on the bottom shelf, with low folk like Harvey's.'

His blue eyes gleamed, his cheeks shone red, from travelling through the icy morning. With his hat off his head his white hair bushed, so he looked like a short Jehovah.

'So, John — the great work, Volume Three!'

'Sanders, go.' She shoed the cat from the chair. 'Sit down, John James, and talk with John. I shall have Anne set coffee and rolls.' She paused by the decanter. 'Some cordial, to warm your blood?'

'At this hour, Megs? Later, later.'

She left in a skirmish of lace and wool. John James stretched his lean legs to the fire.

'Shall we have you all day, John, or do you go into Town?' With his father here, he was a man again.

'I'm expected at the Turner house. And after — I have the first sitting for my portrait. My outline is waiting for me there.'

'You've made your peace with that bounder, have you?'

Bounder? What did his father mean? He was brittle as a struck glass.

'Oh, but my peace was never destroyed. If the young people had a foolish scamper — still I am sure no harm was down.'

He smiled, but his father glowered and growled — then shrugged. 'Anyway, John, you must look to your housekeeping. Your bills always turn out more than you say. Now you have little Sophie to feed — why the dickens should your wife bring her sister to live with her?'

'Oh but father, I am so glad Sophie came. She has saved our house — the little minx. And the devil is in her small pert nose.'

John James sat up, irate and crimson. 'It's to your wife you are wed, sir, dammit and blast it! I've told you times, leave those tiny virgins be!'

He was startled, thrown. 'My wife — yes — why, I get little joy from her company. No more I think than you?'

'Well, John, well.' His father scowled and smiled together.

'I've called her frivolous. It's my money she spends, when she goes to the milliner's. But when she's well turned out — with that *décolletage* — and that way she has of turning her head. She has some spark. If you did your work well, you could be happy enough. Eh? Eh, sir?' His eye of dismay was a bright eye now.

The loathsome old ram! His father in lust — he withered with loathing.

His father abruptly brandished the poker, and smashed a coal so it shattered in splinters.

'Look to you marriage. Make it good, dammit! Do you hear me, boy?'

He trembled like a leaf. His weak voice, of a child at fault, whimpered, 'Yes, papa.'

John James stared a moment, as if in fury — then sat. 'Well, John, enough. As to your expenses, now?' He smiled his curiosity.

'Father, dearest.' They were back on sure ground. 'Well, I did wonder — for this portrait, you know. My best coat is the worse for wear, from all our rambles in the Highlands.'

'John, I have told you, I would have you look well. No man could say you make haste to the tailor's. Lend me your desk.'

His father borrowed his pen, and scribbled a draft. 'You will see I don't mean you to scrimp on the cloth. So, my boy, you are off to the Turner house. I am proud he named you for an executor.'

The relief, in talking of something else. 'I must own I am troubled by what I find there. Some of his drawings — the things they show. The greatest men have weaknesses.'

'Are you making a mystery?'

Quietly he said, 'It is the mystery — in a word — of evil.'

His father sat forward. 'You have found *evil* in Turner's house.'

'Evil — or madness — or both foully mixed —'

But they must stop. He turned to the tap of fingers, where old Anne Strachan stood by the door.

'Mistress said to call you to coffee and rolls.'

'Thank you, Annie. John, let's eat of the staff of life.'

'After you, sir.'

In the morning room his mother sat towards the window. She gazed to his own house, up on Herne Hill. Her lips munched sharply. 'She is a vain, cold *schemer*.'

'Come, Megs,' said John James, 'John is shortly off. Coffee, John? I won't take it myself. I rose at four to catch the stage, and I should lay my head to rest.' He smiled to her.

'And so you must,' his mother cooed. 'And I shall come and sit by you.' Her eyes sparkled, her face was flushed from the cordial.

Their aged endearments — the embarrassment of it. Abruptly he knew, it was time he left. He gulped the coffee though it was scalding hot.

'Father — mother — I run to catch the omnibus.'

'Good day, John.' They blinked, they were used to his sudden goings.

Outside he quickly swallowed air — and gagged to see how the sky looked now. The air had soured, and over where north London hid you saw an odd, sharp-yellow light. Sulphur from the yards where coke was raked. Bile-yellow, it was the sickness of London's soul.

But it was his destination. With his cane he hailed the next omnibus, and joined the men in hats and coats on the open bench along its roof.

*

158

He stepped down from the omnibus in the thick of the city — into deafening cacophony, snorting horses, bawling men, axles squealing for grease. And lit now by a brown-yellow smoke-light, so that hearses and hansoms, drays and handcarts, the teeming crowds and men with head-trays, pressed through a filthy rusty mist which had the smell that roadworks give — the stink of suffocated soil — mixed with drains and horse-excrement. Odd as a dream, a train heaved slowly overhead in falling clouds of smoke and steam, up on arches of moulded brick which were like a travesty of Babylon.

On every side were trade, pride — and misery. Beggars, the blind, a woman with a malformed child that noised like an animal. Pitiable, pitiable. As always he lightened his pockets here, watching the stately carriages that loomed above the toiling crowd. Through the windows you saw the moribund rich — the peerage going nowhere slowly. Their waxen faces, lifted high, were expressionless as the dead. The flunkeys in livery, who hung from straps at the back of coach, had more life in their dozey eyes.

London, our Sodom and Gemorrah in one — all vileness has its capital here. City of sin and perfidy, of pillage and empire. And where she goes — in the fly from Crozier's — at which house she stops, and who she finds there? It must not be — my Everett. Do not have betrayed me, genius youth. You were the King-Queen of my heart, and all my hope for English art. Well, but I come to you today. In your studio I shall strive for mastery.

Queen Anne Street. He had come to the house where Turner died. There old Turner let everything go, except his art. Sooty crumbs of dried-out mortar trickled from black-crusted bricks. Brown paper was stuck behind the broken panes, which themselves were white with dirt.

'Good morning, sir.'

'Clayton.'

The house was as bad inside. In spite of the sweeping, it looked as if the chimneys had emptied on the boards, the banister was vile with gritty black grease.

'Shall I fetch soap and water?'

'If you please, Clayton. May we try again to open the window?'

'I've tried, sir. But the casement's rotten and the glass all cracked. I fear it will fall apart in my hands.'

In the upstairs room he rolled up his sleeves, and rinsed his hands. Even here the ugly, dwarfish Turner slouched in food-stained unpatched gowns, painting in the half-light — Heavens of light!

'A fresh towel?'

'Thank you.'

Glad to be clean, he sat to the table, in a pool of grey light from the dirt-crusted roof-window. To one side lay his catalogue, and the portfolio of drawings he had rescued, to the other the stack of rust-pitted tin boxes, in which the drawings had been packed.

Dear God, let this box show his genius. As he creaked it open, rust came off brown in his hands. Again the drawings were folded in four, and mildewed and mouse-eaten at the edges. Very carefully he laid the first sheet out flat.

He knew at once just what it was, his soul flung wings in leaping to it. The wonder was that those dabs of colour — lemon or rose, and ultramarine — read at once as soaring dawn, with a glow that deepened down the hills but could not reach the sleeping lake. Dashed in a hurry, he saw at once, to catch the instant of changing light.

Great Turner. Master. He closed his eyes, and saw the scene inside his head. Garda or Como, he was not sure, but he knew North Italy — a gentle breeze blew from the sketch, that bore his soul across the Alps. Dear Everett, you have the talent of an angel — yet neither you, nor all your Brethren, have a genius like to this.

With a light heart he spread the next sheet — to reel aghast. The vileness, the shamelessness. He must have had the woman's legs spread wide, and he — the artist — stuck his head between her knees, to revel in these musty folds of the leering, sucking lips. The hole, the pit, stood in the centre, like the sun in other drawings. Worse, he had sought a woman out, who was malformed, as his own wife. The loathsome goat, obscene old man.

He dug his hands into his face as if he could pull out his eyes. When he forced himself to look again, he saw in the corner — obscene cartoons. The hump-back grinning droop-nosed dwarf — who would be Turner — thrust a member like a cannon up against a bulbous dame. Her breasts and buttocks swelled, her nipples stood like Martello Towers, as she uncoiled a giant tongue to slap and lick the swaying trunk.

He had to retch, for burning bile sprang in his throat. Even here it lay in wait for him — the bestiality, the stench, of adult lust. Body into body, was there no escape?

He heard a scratching overhead, and looking up towards the roof-light, saw a claw-foot show, and go. Then another — some bird stepped on the crusted glass.

He shook his head, and soaped his hands again, striving to extract the viscous soil that crept beneath his finger-nails. God give me strength! He had his task.

Again he sat to the old wide table, where Turner drew, and continued to divide the sheets, placing into separate stacks genius — and obscenity.

'These are for posterity — and these, oh surely, they must burn. I shall make sure.'

Above his head came pecks and scuffles from claws that scrabbled on the grimy glass.

*

Leaving the street he stepped sharply back, to escape a trotting troop of horse — in blazing crimson, shining brass, in a shattering clatter on the cobbles. You only saw their jaws and snouts. Off no doubt to a remote possession, to snuff a mutiny in a sea of blood.

But what had these drawings done to his brain? He saw billowing skirts like walking bells — the hot mouth glistened inside those taffetas. And that gross fellow in blaring check — he had to be an auctioneer — had the wolfish eyes of lechery: his trousers hid the lewd fat pipe. Something huge as a bear, inflamed and hungry, reared and dripped inside all life. And I am off to have my portrait painted by the lover of my wife. How the world would cackle if it knew — the shame and the disgrace of it. If it's so, if they do meet... It must not be. My wife is silly, but honest too. Dear Everett, I pray you have been pure.

For protection he returned to an omnibus. But it rocked and jerked, it was crowded and stank. Across the aisle a couple cosied — had he stuck his tongue inside her mouth? Worst, the young woman beside him had a baby at her chest. Its nose and mouth ran, it rolled bright eyes — dear God, get that infant out of my face! Look, it's spit dropped on my coat. And this is what *she* is dying to bear.

'Excuse me, I get off at this stop.'

Gower Street at last, he knew the number. But he could

hardly take a step. He trembled, faint, paused by a lamp-post. Will all go well? What will I find?

It was a run-of-the-mill rich house, spoiled by a portico with columns — as ever, we are enslaved to Greece.

Everett came himself to the door.

'John. Good day. Come in. You are well?'

'I thank you, Everett,' he hoarsely said. But was Everett well? He was thin as bones and white as a ghost. His eyes were stark, he did not look like innocence.

A door opened.

'Mother, dear — John has come. Let me introduce you to a famous man. Father?'

The shy bright lady nodded, the thin bald man held out his hand.

John said, 'Why sir, I have seen you before.'

'He means the Joseph,' Everett murmured, 'In my picture of Jesus in the carpenter's shop.'

'Ah.' The father smiled and bowed. 'My son finds work for all of us.'

'But to pose for the father of our Lord — that I think is *good* employment.' John was pleased with his grace in giving them ease.

'This way, John.'

They climbed the stairs to a large room filled with canvases. Cans of brushes stood on the shelves like flower-pots.

'Why, you've got the best room in the house.'

Everett nodded. 'They have done so much for me.'

His mother's head bobbed round the door. 'Shall I send some refreshment, dear?'

'Oh not now, mamma — we must get some work done first. Go along, old woman, leave us be.'

She smiled with play, and closed the door.

They stood by the canvas, on its easel. There his white shape waited for him, like a shadow he had lost, and found. But Everett, the man is haggard — but young, so young, and weak, I see. All suddenly tenderness flowered in him. The wounded youth — I shall set him free and make him strong. May it be I am his Saviour — of his art, and of his life?

'So we meet again,' he kindly said. His hand strayed, to brush Everett's finger.

Everett shrank at once, and drew in breath. He grew thinner and taller.

'You will need to hold a cane, John. Here.'

He took the stick, which Everett thrust into his face, to make — it seemed — a fence between them.

'Of course, my dear. May I take my station?'

'If you please.'

Seeing Everett so taut — the man twitched and jumped — he found he filled with pleasant ease. Many hours in the studio lay ahead, and through those hours he would quietly work.

The great endeavour began. He stood stock-still, for Everett's gaze became a shaft of ice. He examines me, and so shall I examine him. My wife's lover — or not her lover at all. Are there other maidens I should be jealous of? His pale clear face, small chiselled nose, his fine white skin — he is tired, but fair as a young marchioness. He badly needs his chastisement.

Except, I see, he is not at peace. He jerks and twists, and frowns and blinks — oh I see, his soul is stricken. Is he racked with guilt, at the sight of me? Well, but I can relish this. In a way I have control of him.

But when Everett murmured 'Rest' he avoided talk and trouble. He sauntered in the studio, for he must make himself at home here. He peered and stooped to examine pictures, and at once was blind with awe again.

'Such clarity!' he said aloud. 'No other artist in the world shows such exactness everywhere.'

Such colours too — deep turquoise greens, Venetian reds. There was an oil-sketch of an elderly man, with hot, shy, over-sensitive eyes. It hushed him absolutely.

'Everett, dear — that is *wonderful* work. And that drawing there — but it is — sublime.'

'Which one?' Everett came and stood beside him. 'Oh that. It's a picture to Tennyson's "St Agnes' Eve".' He paused. 'Do you remember? We read the poem in Scotland.'

I have him now. 'I remember that my wife read it aloud — and then you read from it as well.'

'Did I?' And did Everett blush? He swallowed, oh he is not at ease.

'What I love,' John said, 'Is the slender erectness of your Agnes, and the way the line of her sleeve repeats in the snow-topped wall before her.'

Truly it was a perfect drawing, its bold lines fitted perspective's clock. He stayed staring close at it, so Everett would have to speak.

'Would you like it, John?'

Soft as stealth he slyly said, 'Well — I know who truly would like it most.'

'Who's that?'

He only smiled, like the Cheshire cat.

'Do you mean your lady?'

'Well — you both had liked the verses.'

Surely now Everett blushed bright red — and look, his little finger trembles. Oh, I shall catch them in my traps.

Abruptly Everett took it from the wall, and thrust it out,

so it nearly struck him. He must step back.

'Take it, please. It is a present to you both. I shall be glad if it is gone.' he paused — but he was crimson now. 'Or give it into your lady's hands, if you think she likes it more.'

'And so I shall,' he smoothly said, for a cat may play, when it has the mouse between its paws, 'But might you send it, after all? I should be so *extremely* grateful. I shall damage it, taking it by hand.'

'What! By post?' Everett was positively rude. 'How is that necessary? Are you not going back to Herne Hill yourself?'

His own annoyance sprang, for his trick went awry. Shall I be their gift bearer? Even was it possible, that he and Everett might come to blows, a fight?

He spooned his best cajolery. 'I beg of you, do me this favour. It must be framed, and you will know who does that best. I shall pay, you may be sure.'

Everett said shortly, 'All right. I shall arrange it. I expect it will take a day or two.'

John turned and shrugged his indifference now, as if to say — after all, who cares? 'To work, I think.'

He took his stance, and Everett slipped behind his canvas. His bird-crest of hair showed over its top, as he bobbed between his paints and palette.

But he could not be easy in his pose as before. Had he caught them? Had he read the clues? All his thoughts of the day, all suspicions and fears, came together in new blinding knowledge. There was a room, in Bloomsbury, or Clerkenwell, where she took off her shift, he slid his trousers from his bony legs, as they sidled towards the creaking bed. And there they did, as his parents had, as Turner did, as all of bestial mankind did — rutting — coupling — the beast with two backs — the hideousness of copulation, the vileness of the sweaty body. He was not well, the room was an oven, his ears boomed as they never had.

'Hey, John! Steady. Take my hand, you must sit down.'

'I must, a moment. Thank you, Everett.'

He almost fell into the chaise. Everett poured water from a flask.

'Take good breaths. Undo your cravat. You have lost all colour.'

He sipped and weakly murmured, 'Thank you.'

'It's all right, John. This happens when you stand in a pose. The blood drains down. If you looked at your feet, they would be crimson.'

'That must be it.' He brittly laughed. 'I shall be better by and by. So this noble work proceeds.'

*

He arrived home with the early winter dark, to find that she was out.

'Misses sent to Crozier's.' Crawley took his hat. 'The fly came for her.'

'I had not thought she went today. She said no more?'

'Only that she was awaited in Town.'

He drew breath sharply. 'Thank you, Crawley.'

'Miss Sophie is in the drawing room. Ruby already has given her tea.'

'I hear her play.' Quietly he approached the door-frame till he saw where Sophie sat. She played by the light of a single candle.

Heaven! Here is my true joy. On steps as soft as felt on felt, he crept up close behind her. His shadow was gaunt high up the wall.

'And what is the name of this piece, Sophie?'

'John!' She started. 'You made me jump.'

'You play *very* well. But finish, please.'

When the piece was played he drew a chair beside her stool. He had been so tired, now his tiredness fled. 'Do you know what I should like most in the world?'

'What is that?'

'I should like it if we practised handwriting together. May I show you how Cardinal Bembo used to write the letter "a"?'

He lit another candle, and took paper and pencils to the table. 'Did your sister say where it was she went?'

'She said she must see Lady Eastlake.'

'Lofty Lucy? She is not my friend. Look, Sophie, the shoulder of the letter "a" is the most important curve in writing.'

As she copied his letters, their heads touched briefly.

'She has another friend in Town.' Idly he drew the letter E. 'I expect they sometimes meet for tea.'

He searched her eyes, but their gaze was empty.

'Well!' He sat back. 'But isn't she naughty, to stay so late without a word? Was she very smartly dressed, when she got into the fly?'

'Effie is always smartly dressed.' Her brow had begun to knit.

'Sophie, you are wonderful!' He stood both candles on the table, and sat where he could watch her write. So serious yet so beautiful, and all her sight bent to her pen. That piquant profile — so her sister looked, at the age of twelve, when he fell so hard in love. When he wrote his dream-tale for her, called *The King of the Golden River*. A hunched figure knocks at the door of the house, with a steeple hat and a nose like a bugle, while a child in alarm looks to see who it is — did ever a story start so well?

'There, John.' She held her paper.

'That is beautiful! Your "Q" and "u" are truly perfect.'

'Thank you, John.' Her blushing bright-eyed smile destroyed him. His fingers trembled, he had to stand.

'Sophie, I must to my letters. And you — I beg, make haste to Ruby. Say she must cut the biggest slice ever of that cream cake.'

'Thank you, John.'

She slipped, or skipped, or danced away, as he gazed fondly after.

He went upstairs, and sat a while beside his desk. Several times he took his pen, and dipped and put it down again — till he heaved his deepest sigh, and shook his head, and stood. Lord, let me not be wicked, on the day my portrait is begun. He tried to think of the two on the bed, and Everett fair, and all three kissed. Would this raise, or kill, his lust? The excitement grew, but he could not stay. Sophies and Pollies were his joy. Quietly he reach the low drawer of the desk, and without looking pulled the packet out, and slid out the daguerreotypes one by one, like a card-player who will take his time to see the cards dealt to his hand. His breath came hard, the tiny figures shivered in his hand.

When he had slipped the catch on the bathroom door, he hung his waistcoat from the hook. With his trousers and braces at his ankles, he spat on his hands and began his care. He murmured softly, Oh little neat dress with petit point lace, as the tingle began at the root of his spine. Oh little straight nose and tiny waist! A strong heat spread throughout his thighs, he must delay so the coming was greater — till at last in the mirror he made his little-girl face. He pouted and twinkled till his loins came hot with luxury. Faint from delight, he murmured over, 'John, John, John — was there

169

ever potency like to yours? *You* are the King of the Golden River.'

In cleansing water he washed himself, but as he hauled his trousers about his waist, he saw on their flank a jelly dab. With a choke of disgust he rubbed the place clean. Dear Lord, sear and scald my weakness.

He returned to his study. This had been a nightmare day, but as he slowly sat deep peace possessed him. Between the open curtains a moon of gold, an enormous disk, rose like the smile of a god.

*

Still she had not come. He went downstairs, where Crawley had lit the hall and rooms. He found Sophie yawning and sent her to bed, and had Crawley set a cold supper for him.

But had she ever come home so late? Was there an upset with the fly? It had never happened, that he sat alone, and waited while she did not come.

He started when he heard the eerie shriek. From deep in the garden, or the mews beyond — he could not tell if it were person or creature. He caught some odd clink, a metal noise. Then he heard the wordless cry again, but fainter now and further off. For no reason he thought of bones and coffin-lids.

Was he nodding? He set himself upright. No, she was not at Lofty Lucy's. She was with his artist. Who knew in what low inn, or garret? Wherever they were, they licked each other. A sensation came which he had not known, a freezing fury. A thousand times he had wished her away, even into the arms of some lewd beau — and now it happened, he felt nothing but hurt. No excitement now, or hot thoughts of the three of them. Only utter loneliness, deep beyond the deepest pit.

I led them to it, I let them do it. Myself I made my misery. There is no pain compared to this.

Till the thought rose, all uncertainly — is it possible *I* could play the man? She is mine and we are joined. No man but me should enter her. How could that be? But could it be?

The candles went out one by one, but he sat on in the dark alone. He thought, she will be surprised, when she returns from sin thinking no one is here, and finds me quietly waiting for her — as conscience waits at the back of the soul.

2

'Don't you see the pure snow?' Everett said in her ear.

'Snow in mid-summer? I don't think so, my darling.'

But all of the glen was gleaming white, deer moved as if grazing along the ridge. His face bent over her gigantic as God.

'Don't you see?' the bright voice said. 'I think it snowed all night.'

'What?' She blinked. 'Sophie, dear. Close the curtains, please.'

'But I just opened them. John said to.'

'Did he? Give me some moments. I lay awake all night, and only just got to sleep.'

Sophie's face bent over her was like her own face, young.

'You *do* look tired. And your poor eye. Why can't it keep still? Outside it's like the North Pole.'

'Is it, darling? I shall get up, in a moment.'

'It *is* time to rise,' John called from the door.

She sat herself up, with her pillow upright at her back.

'Are you still here, John? I should have thought you would have gone to your writing desk, with your mamma sat down beside you.'

He gave a tiny smile. 'Oh, I shalln't go today. I've got

papers to read.' He turned to Sophie, 'Let's go outside. I think this snow is made for games.'

Sophie skipped up at once. 'May I, please? I shall dress as warm as toast.'

They clattered downstairs. Her head felt like lead as she rose, and slipped on her gown. This is despair. I threw my life away, from cowardice and pettiness.

Drawing the curtains when she came downstairs, she saw John and Sophie at play. John was long-limbed as a grasshopper in his close coat and scarf. He lobbed snowballs at Sophie, and laughed when her own snowball knocked off his hat. Then he clambered up the bank at the garden's edge, whisked up his coat-tails, and slid down again with his arms round his knees. She heard him calling,

'That's what we did in the Alps, Sophie. Only we slid much further, faster.'

She thrust the back of her hand into her open mouth, hard against her teeth. But how much pain was she willing to cause? At least today she would take the step, which she should have taken long ago.

When she looked outside again, the postman stood waving by the gate. John made a pantomime of running to him, so Sophie rocked and laughed.

The postman delved in his bag and gave John a packet. At once he looked up, directly to where she stood in the window.

They were coming, he and Sophie, towards the house, huddled like malefactors over the post. She fastened her gown and pushed back her hair.

'Effie!' He stamped his feet hard so snow covered the mat. 'We have a packet from Everett. Won't you open it?'

'To whom is it addressed?'

'Why, to me, of course.'

'So you open it.'

He laid it casually on the sideboard. 'Oh, I shall, by and by. Sophie and I need a hot drink now. In the Alps, Sophie, they send dogs out with brandy round their neck in barrels.'

'They must be *little* barrels, John.'

John burst out laughing. '*Isn't* she the cleverest little minx ever? But you mustn't be cleverer than your sister. That would never do.'

They went to the kitchen, where she heard clinks and laughs and whispers. In anguish she gazed at the idle packet — she knew Everett's tiny handwriting. Her hand strayed to it, but she must leave it be. And she must dress.

Sophie met her as she came downstairs again. 'John has gone to read his papers. He said, you must start my lessons now. He will give me a drawing class later.'

'Did he, darling? Do play, and let me listen. We shall do dictation and arithmetic afterwards.'

'Yes, Effie.'

She poured coffee and sipped, while Sophie played, sitting very straight.

'That's beautiful, darling. You have practised a lot.'

'Will you play?'

'I'm tired.' She had sand inside her eyelids. But as she sat to the keys, music flowed from nowhere into her arms. She was lifted aching on a sea-surge of melody.

The sound called John to the doorway, where he stood blinking, fingering a small, framed black and white picture.

'You played with — heart,' he said when she paused. 'Look, I have opened the packet that Everett sent to us. It's a drawing for "St Agnes Eve". The Tennyson, do you remember? You read it to us in the Highlands.'

174

He held it up. 'Look, Sophie, it shows a snowy garden like ours. This lady is St Agnes looking out of her window. Do you like it?'

...as she gazed with longing beyond the snows.

Seriously Sophie inspected the drawing. 'It's not a very *cheerful* picture.'

'Well, she is thinking of her lover, and he is a long way away. He is God, of course. He is the best lover all of us can have. But do you like this drawing, my dear? I think the perspective is wonderful.'

She took it from him. At once she was with the lean standing woman who arched her back as she gazed with longing beyond the snows.

'Oh, it's beautiful — so delicate!'

John stood close over her. 'Everett says in his note to me, that he would be pleased if you wished to accept it.'

She came alert. 'Do you mean, as a gift?'

'I think *he* means, as a gift.'

John's eyes came closer, like a cat at a mouse-hole. Her heart banged. She asked, 'Do *you* think I should accept it?'

He was suddenly stern. 'Of course I don't think you should take it.'

'Take it back to him.' She held the picture away from herself.

'I'm not your messenger.'

She placed it face down on a table. 'Take it, John. Post it, send it. Convey it how you will.'

He performed surprise. 'But won't you thank him? And tell him why you return his gift?'

'How may I do so?'

'When you write to him, of course.'

'What do you mean? You know I don't write to him.'

'Oh, I know no such thing.' He cocked an eye at Sophie, in bright conspiracy.

'What game is this, John? You forbad me to write to him, and I have not. Nor has he written to me. Nor do we meet, if that is what you imply.'

Then it was a duel of eyes. She stared till his blue eyes wavered and sank.

He took the picture, then turned, near the door. 'Well,

Sophie — I shall decide what to do with this later. I have to think of Everett's feelings. The poor man is in love and easily hurt. Love does make such a fool of a man.'

She advanced. 'What are you saying, John? And to my sister! What language is that?'

'Oh, I said nothing false, I think.' He stopped again, at the foot of the stairs. 'Are you going into Town today?'

'Yes. The fly is to come from Crozier's.'

'You have visits to pay?'

'Yes.'

He gazed, but she thought, I shalln't say where I go. Let him ask.

He waited, then made an ironic smile. He turned and went upstairs with the picture.

Sophie asked brightly, 'Are you going to see the lady he calls Lofty Lucy?'

'Lucy Eastlake? Yes. I have a great favour to ask of her, which I should have asked a while since.'

Sophie's eyes brightened. 'And will it be a secret?' Sophie was growing used to the conspiracy-game.

'Yes, it will be my secret. And I fear a sad one too.'

At the look in her face Sophie hugged her hand and kissed her wrist. 'Dearest, everyone who knows you loves you.'

'Dear Sophie,' was all she could say, as she bent to kiss her brow, and held her.

*

The new snow, which had been so bright in the garden, was black mashed slush in the London streets. The coachmen wore shawls on top of their capes, and had their hat-brims pulled over their eyes. Against the white, a hurrying sweep's boy showed pitch-black.

Already we are here. The fat columns of the portico swayed and stood still.

'Thank you, Peter.' With care she descended, and gathered her skirts for the dripping steps. The footman bawled her name down the lobby.

In the centre of the wide gilt picture-filled room, the very tall woman stood up from the ottoman. Above her broad skirt, the green satin hugged her sinewy body, and clung to her arms that reached out in welcome.

'My dearest girl — I have been so unhappy for you.' Her jet eyes shone. When they bent to embrace, the older woman clasped her like a mother.

'You're tired, I can see.'

'Lucy — I've lost all my sleep. But you're expecting a party?'

The chandeliers shone, the curtains were tied in drapes and swags. At the sideboard, a servant in a green baize apron buffed the candlesticks.

'One of Eastlake's dinners. But there is time, pray do sit down. I worry for you. Is John difficult still?'

'Lucy, he changes each day. I'm at my wits' end. Now he tells me I am insane. You know he wrote to my father once, to tell *him* that I am mad. And *I* wonder, am I losing my mind? He keeps harking back to what happened with Everett. Which was nothing, and I wish it had been — everything.'

'Does the blessed man *want* to lose you? After what happened — or didn't happen, as you say — he must work very hard if he's to keep you as his wife. That's his only hope.'

'I don't know what John wants any more. He asks so often, am I writing to Everett, that sometimes I feel he *wants* me to see him. John's mother I am sure wants me caught in a scrape. They want him to divorce me, with the bad all on my side.'

'Why should they want that? The scandal would destroy them. The question for me is, what do *you* want?'

'Don't ask what I want. I cannot have it.'

'I only ask, are you saying you want to *leave* John? I know if you stay, you'll be unhappy. But have you thought of what the world will say, if you leave his house for good. He is famous enough, for all the world to talk. Many things would be said, which were not true at all. You must think of the fret of it, whatever you decide to do.'

'Are you saying, I *should* not leave him?' They had come at once to the momentous question, which occupied her every day.

Lucy gazed ahead seriously, as if the question hung in the air before her.

'No, I do not say that. Only that the road is *very* hard.'

'The hardest thing is, that I see Everett never at all. No word, no glimpse, for week on week. Every day I think of him, though he, maybe, has forgotten me. This is what makes me nearly mad.'

Lucy's hand drew near, and held her arm. The hand was kind, the hand was firm. It said, I feel for you, but so it is. 'The cruel thing is — that I am almost bound to see him. At Eastlake's functions, at the National Gallery — the Academy people are often there. And there is nothing I may say.'

Even so, it was like a window: through which, tiny and far, she might glimpse Everett in the present.

'You will tell me how he is.'

The hand was warmer, firmer. 'Of course I will. I shall talk with him, if I may — and I shall tell you all he says.'

'Lucy.' She found that she was smiling, though perhaps she should fear.

Lucy's gaze was steady and kindly too. She rang a small

bell, and the maid brought tea. They sipped a little, then Lucy said,

'Truth be told, I'd almost say, it's a pity you *didn't* make love in the Highlands. At least you'd have had — a woman's pleasure. Enough people in society have done it — and without the excuse of an incapable husband.'

Lucy, don't *you* say this. Is my virtue my fault, after all?

They had come to a pause. The large still damask-hung room was ready: the chandeliers glittered, the epergne reached out silver arms. Tonight there would be loud talking and movement, the collision of crinolines, heads bubbling with monocles. Now it was a clear bright space of waiting. Her life, thought, pain, came all together.

'Lucy.'

'Dear girl.'

The time had come. She sipped, and said,

'Lucy, I have — a favour to ask.' Her heart gave a hollow beat

'Ask, dear girl.'

'You have told me, your father was an obstetric physician.' She gave a nervous smile.

'And so is my brother. But why — what?'

'I wonder, Lucy — would you, yourself, one day — examine me?'

'Dearest girl, I do not understand.'

She was at a standstill. Say more, say less? She quietly said, 'I have a reason.'

Lucy's eye was keen. Does she think, after all, I am with child?

Lucy only said, 'Of course I will. Shall we appoint a day?'

'Please.' They did. She sighed, sat back. The step was taken.

She drank her tea, they talked of London. A maid came in

and closed the shutters. A servant in plush began lighting the candles, with matches that spat and flared blue. A big-moustached man came in briskly, in his waistcoat.

'Effie! How are you? It's good to see you. Lucy, shouldn't we be getting dressed?'

'You see I am dressed, Eastlake. Take your bath. We have a new cistern — you would not believe how little noise the pipes make.'

He came to kiss her hand. 'We could not talk the other evening. Tell me, how were the Highlands? I heard your John made a stir in Edinburgh.'

'Yes, Sir Charles. There were notices in all the Scottish papers. And the Highlands were — often wet, and often lovely.'

'They say he's deep in old Turner's drawings.'

'He comes back all dust from the Turner house. And troubled too.'

'Troubled? What's to trouble him? Many amateurs of art would give their eyes for that work. It's true that Turner was a rum old cove. We artists — But I must take my bath.'

She stood. 'And I have kept my coach waiting. Dear Lucy, I must let you complete your toilette. Sir Charles — I know John would send his regards.'

'I'm not sure of that. Give him mine, in any case.'

As they walked to the door Lucy quietly spoke, 'There is a word I must say, because I know you. You will not thank me.'

'Tell me, Lucy.'

'It is only to say, what we both know. That, in these days, there is a person in London you *must* not meet.'

She could not move or speak.

'You know whom I mean. Because if there were a question

of leaving John — you understand me? If it were said that something improper *had* happened in Scotland, or if it were thought, you had a "friend" now — then people would not ask what John did or did not do as a husband. They would ask only whom you had kissed. They would say, no wonder he does not sleep with her.'

'That is so cruel.'

'The world *is* cruel.' Lucy stood above her on the step. Light came in her face. 'I find I cannot help but love you. Let us hope that others may.' She smiled, her smile said, Don't despair.

'Lucy dearest, I know you want what is best for me.'

They kissed. Lingeringly Lucy let go her arm.

Outside the black slush had a frozen crust, she crumble-splashed to the fly and huddled with wet feet cold inside it. But at least it was possible, Lucy would see Everett, so she would learn how he was now. Also at last a day was set, when Lucy would examine her, and say in what way her body was — strange. It was like the date for her execution. You want to postpone it, and you are impatient to know. But to be told in one breath, that it was a pity she did not love in the Highlands, and that she must not see Everett now — that was too harsh.

Peter leaned in. 'You did not say, mam — where do we go?'

'Home of course — Herne Hill.' She ground it out through bitter teeth.

Peter called to the horse, and the fly slightly rocked. But they scarcely moved.

'Get on out of it!' someone hollered behind them. Looking out, she saw hansoms and omnibuses locked, they were beset all round by drays and wagons. A gigantic percheron stamped hooves like tree-roots. Her agitation grew.

'Peter, no. I've changed my mind. Drive to Gower Street.'

She had not planned to see Everett, but she knew where in Gower Street his family lived. It must be a sign, this blocking of the road. Somehow Lucy's warnings had the opposite effect, she could not be governed by fear for ever. Just the movement of the fly made her more and more sure. This was madness, rashness, but she could not stop.

'Gower Street — we're there, mam.'

'Thank you. No, don't stop. Go up to Euston Road, and wait round the corner.'

The light was failing as she walked back down Gower Street. The wind had sharpened, she butted her bonnet through the bent-down hats that pushed against her like strong waves. But still she walked lightly. I am coming to you, my love.

Only as she neared the house she thought, I am acting desperately. What will I say, if his parents come to the door? Am I out of my wits, as John will tell me?

Across the road stood the sober house: the large, high window must be his studio. No need for the doorbell, with one small pebble at the glass...

She climbed up steps on her side of the road, deep in the embrasure of an unlit door. From here she could look better into the room, already she saw the top of an unframed canvas. A man passed in front of it — and it was Everett. He came to the window and gazed out through the dark. He surely must sense that she was there.

But he turned, and she saw there was someone with him. Everett was nodding, and did not look ravaged. Then John came into the window-frame, saying something that caused both men to laugh. It was like a door banged in her face, so she sat down bump on the step. Men being affable, showing their ease. He does not love me as I love him. John matters to him because he is famous. Everett has forgotten me, or nearly so.

Nor did she know John would be there today. John told her nothing of his intentions.

The bright-lit men passed out of sight. She saw a shirt-cuff reach up high, and the dazzling mantle of the gas-lamp died. She had nothing in her hands.

The light above the street-door brightened, at any moment John would come out. She must scamper the length of Gower Street.

The lights were brighter in Euston Road, but horses neighed. There were bad-tempered shouts, whips cracked in the air. Still she heard the words the hurdy-gurdy man sang, beneath the broad-brimmed corner lamp. He had a bursting bloodshot face but his cracked voice was jaunty —

'Oh, I'd rather go to prison

Than be in love again.'

The anguish of love to a jolly tune, and her own love was a cramping pain.

A woman pressed by, gently patting her baby. She had a pretty, snub-nosed face, and through its tears the baby made bright eyes to her.

Babies, love... The gasp, the sob, tore to empty her lungs; she had leaned on the wall. Would the world see her weep, making a show in Euston Road?

'Herne Hill,' she called, climbing into the fly. The crying fit had stopped. She thought, Everett will go to soirées and assemblies, young ladies and their mammas will be lying in wait. She should have acted in Scotland, her cowardice then had cost her everything.

'Hurry, Peter — it's freezing cold.'

And the day lay in wait, when Lucy would examine her. John was learned, he would not lie: so Lucy would confirm John's word, and tell her she was wrongly formed. It would mean she never could be loved, would mean she could not bear a child, would mean that whether she stayed with John, or left his house to live on her own, or if she saw Everett...

Looking out of the fly, she saw above the roof-tops the evening star. It was at odds with her thoughts. Still it jogged beside her shining brightly, like the light in the window of a happy house as cruelly distant as the sky.

3

He blinked, how could such beauty be? Stepping to him over the dewy grass, through the dawn-lit orchard.

'But you know who I am,' the sweet maid said. Her features were delicate as if spun from glass.

'Know you? Yes...' How could he know her? Seed diamonds woven in her hair were finer than the furthest stars.

'I am your soul, John. I am you.'

'My virgin bride!' As he knelt in tears he clutched her hands, to wet them with kisses. 'We are two, and one.' How was it that he had not known this? Then he heard the hiss beside them.

'Sweet lady!' But she knew no fear. As her small hand caught it, the snake shrank. Its scales were dry, brown-gold, not slicky, its wedge-shaped head seemed not to see them.

'Look, it is but a poor creature of God.'

'Yes,' he mouthed in awe, as he watched the tiny forked tongue flick.

'It is for you, John.' She held it to him, but he winced to touch it, and at once it changed. It grew fat, black and glistening. It stuck to his skin, it coiled round his bare arm like a damp black slug. The garden changed. From the foliage of each tree the long neck and head of a serpent hung down. They gracefully swayed like the curved necks of swans. The black snake was inches from his eyes. It did not strike, instead with a guttural hiss it spat. The venom struck his right hand which smoked as it shrivelled at once to a claw whose black skin flaked from the red-streaked bones, as they dropped separately like stones to the ground. Numbly he watched, aware that beside him the jaws of the snake yawned steadily wider.

'God protect me!' he gasped. Who sent such dreams? He must quit this bed, this house, this town.

'John —' she began, where she lay beside him. With dismay he saw she returned to her sleep: these nights she took the strongest of sleeping draughts.

He needed air. He went downstairs, and, pulling his coat on top of his night-gown, he passed through the scullery into the garden. He made out, in the dark, their apple and pear trees.

There he caught it again, louder — the strange cry he heard before. It was as much like a donkey's bray as like the shout of a person. Were there other voices? He heard shufflings, tappings, clinks of metal or glass — the sounds came from behind the garden wall. The cry came again, full of pain and rage.

He went back into the house for the key to the gate. As he returned he heard muttered whispers.

He opened the gate — to see, very close, the strangest figure. It was so mis-shapen and swathed in rags he could not tell if it was boy or girl, but he saw that its eyes were at different heights in its head — one eye half-way down in its cheek — while the mis-shapen dripping mouth dropped loose. He knew from whose misery the cry had come.

Nor could he stay because a giant figure swept close, whose ragged arm ended in a gigantic hook. Beyond it other mis-shapen figures were trudging or limping close.

He slammed the gate and turned the lock twice. What monsters beset him? Could the wall fail, that closed off the world of demons from his? He remembered his vision, for the start of his story of the Golden River. What if that strange figure with the bugle nose were to come knocking at London doors?

He listened, but heard no further cry. He caught a dragging and squealing...trudging feet? They were taking their leave.

...if that strange figure with the bugle nose...

He was alone in the stillness of his garden. There was no frost tonight and, huddled in his coat, he sat a while in the whicker chair. When he looked up, he found no stars, only the smoke and soil of London dragging softly overhead: the vapours were thick and rough like fur.

The times — this town, this land — were diseased. Would new wars break out, in India, in China? Would unrest increase at home, and flower in public mutiny? He thought of horrors from the past, the dog that bit his face. He thought of the wound his own mother saw, back when she was young in that house in Perth, when the hand that held all was taken away.

In the kitchen he took a cup of milk from the ice-box. He must grow calm. Presently he lit a candle, and, stalking in the house, he saw the large portfolio he had left near the street door. Was this the evil, that infected his dreams? It contained the most vile of Turner's drawings — he would show them in the morning to Arthur Wornum, in the National Gallery. For Turner's drawings had been left to the Gallery, but should its halls — or the catacombs under it — be allowed to house such excrement?

He pushed the case further back on the table. With a shake of his head he went upstairs, stepping quietly not to wake the house.

Coming into their room, he dimly saw her asleep.

'My dear?' he murmured. She did not wake.

He rested the candle on the mantle-piece, to cast more light on her, and sat in the chair near the bed. As he gazed, he thought — but she has a beauty. He could just trace the curve of the vein in her wrist.

But her lips were moving — softly, quickly — she was in her dream as he had been in his. But hers was not terrible. He sat closer, in awe, for he saw in her face — utter tenderness. Gentle as a love so keen that it must also hurt cuttingly.

Her mouth slightly opened to make an oval — and at once he knew her dream. She was with her lover — the adulteress. Then her breathing changed, she began to whimper. He wondered, had *he* caused her fear? — for he had stooped so close, his breath touched her skin. That was what he was to her — an object of loathing.

He sat back in the chair. That was how they stood. He must gaze at the wife who not only loved another, but also hated him. So, if she went, he could say, good riddance! But he found he was perverse, for her aversion drew him to her — as if by coming to hate him, she had won his respect. How strange the heart is! She must be castigated, punished, but the thought of her pain caused his loins to quicken. If he purchased a whip, snaking rawhide from the Argentine... He touched himself. If she sat up, in pain and terror — then could he seize her, beat open her shrine, and sire a breed of heroes?

These were Satan's thoughts, they must be smothered. He took the candle so quickly that it nearly blew out, and hurried from the room.

*

Wornum was a disappointment to him, however. In the plain, cream-painted underground room they stood beneath the high lunettes. With a ceremony of repugnance John opened the portfolio, and sufficient light fell at once on the engorged giant member rammed into the squatting woman whose monkey-face, in profile, squealed in ecstasy.

Wornum bent low and his spectacles darkened. 'My eye! That's a beauty!'

'"Beauty", Mr Wornum?' He pulled down a cartoon

which had scrawled under it, 'Admiral Puggy fires his ten-pounder', in which dwarfish Turner, with a member like a caber, fired into mid-air a plump jubilant girl.

Wornum pressed his fingers together. 'By the Lord Harry!' He scarcely seemed shocked. He had a voice like gravel in treacle: he would live well when not serving art.

'Well, but you know, you should see what else we have in our locked cabinets. Some Japanese prints, showing houses of resort...'

'Thank you, thank you.' He shut off the invitation. Nor was Wornum a Trustee — from the Trustees he could expect a better reply.

At other drawings Wornum tutted, or whistled, or said 'My sainted Aunt!' Finally he gave an ambiguous shrug. 'It may be you are right. These are works by the nation's greatest master. His honour, and the country's too, could be coloured by promiscuous *jeux*. It may be they should not be kept.'

Still John waited.

Wornum sighed. 'I take it you would wish me to consult the Trustees. You will be willing to attend, if they ask it?'

'With alacrity. You need not remind them of the law of the land, concerning traffic in obscenities.'

'Indeed.' Wornum gave a quizzical look. Almost to himself he said, 'But to speak of fire — and for drawings by Turner.' He faced John. 'Well, we both know that artists are a Bohemian set of fellows. You remember what Vasari said, about letting an artist meet your wife?'

'I do,' he muttered quickly coldly. He briefly thought, What tactlessness! though Wornum could not know his case. 'Yet the greatest art is marked by purity, and the greatest artists by pure souls — as I have shown, I believe, in my books to date. I should scarcely call the great Masters "Bohemian".'

Wornum cocked an eye and quietly said 'No?' He conducted John to the door.

All of which was — irritating. He wondered, had Wornum ever opened his books?

In the galleries upstairs he lingered, for he had time on his hands. And Wornum had angered him. Of course there were lewd paintings hanging in galleries, but the greatness of great art went with purity. He went quickly to an Annunciation he loved, by Fra Angelico, and sighed as he drank its light. Here, in their chaste enclosure of gardens, a rose-tinted angel told a virgin that she carried in her womb a holy saviour. The colours were delicate, but ravishing also. Both the Angel and the Madonna had small indoor features — virgin skin, sky-blue eyes — like delicate maidens from an English school.

'Fra Angelico a Bohemian!' He had to scoff.

He passed a small water-colour, which also he loved. The reflected light in the river was radiant, the stone-work of the bridge crumbled like old bread.

'Bohemian?' He could snigger.

Case proved, of course. But he was tired from his broken night, and limped through archways till he found a bench. As soon as he sat he closed his eyes — then brought his head up with a jerk. Had he lost awareness? Did a voice call 'John'? The hairs rose at the back of his neck.

He turned — to see he sat in front of a large painted nude, a 'Venus' so-called, of the Venetian school. She was life-size, as though a real woman sat across the room from him. How very strange, he would never have chosen that place. But why not, for his theory applied here too. The beauty of the nude, in the greater masterpieces, is the beauty of spiritual truth. Even their white pure skin is an allegory. The greatest artists are not sensual men. Only a Wornum would be so crude, as to think that an artist, painting beauty, will be driven by biding lust.

Without fear he looked at the goddess of love: and her eyes met his with a gentle light. Till he noticed that her privates, her genitals, were in the exact dead centre of the painting. Her hand, resting easily, covered that place — but then he saw that her other hand held a sweet bunch of softly pink roses. The curves of her two hands answered to each other, like brackets at either end of a sentence. Then it seemed as though the artist meant to say, that her genitals were at the centre of life, and were lovely and fragrant as the most delicate flowers.

He stared in shock. The devil Wornum was inside his eyes. But as he watched in awe, the picture itself began to change. It stirred, it was ceasing to *be* a picture. A naked woman stretched before him, as once she lay before the artist. Love for the genitals and for the flesh? It was with such love this artist painted. You could not escape it. New eyes were put violently into his head, but he found he was not horrified. Like a gazing child, he watched the picture-woman grow larger, whiter, stronger.

She gazed to him, as if he were her lover. Or was her look a mockery of him, for he was no lover, and she too changed. Live eyes watched him from the picture. But he said, 'It is not me she sees'. She was looking to the artist who had painted her, who doubtless also was her bed-mate. With piercing hurt, he thought of his wife with Everett. 'Heathenism,' he muttered, tightly. 'Sensuality — animality. Aphrodite. Lilith.' The pain of seeing lovers love, when you are shut outside of love.

Was he having a fit? His eyes were ill and hardly his. The orbs of her breasts, the arc of her belly, were domes of golden dawn-cloud light. For a moment he smelt jasmine, orange blossom — some woman's perfume. His eyes smarted — why should he weep? But his heart was falling. He thought abruptly, it is because they are not real breasts — it is because they are in a painting — that I can feel their beauty. If real breasts appeared before him, he would freeze and wince away. He was being seduced, he was under attack. His eyes were on fire, his headache thundered. Effie — Venus — painters — lovers. The foundations of the National Gallery shivered. His fingers strayed forward like the hand of a blind man — like a man who would touch those breasts if he could. His eyes choked with tears. John, John, what is wrong with you? What strange demon have you become, that you can love the image so, and not the thing itself at all. His eyelids spilled, grief dowsed his face, with hot pity for himself.

He must get outside and breathe free air, before he broke apart in splinters. Emerging from the Gallery pillars, he thought, I've never hurt like this. But revelation was breaking on him. The light outside had a blinding glare, as it struck between the churning storm-clouds. The horse in the shafts of the hansom he hailed had sinewy, beautifully lustrous flanks. The young woman before him on the pavement had firm pink breasts and a suave full body. He was so full of paintings, his eye stripped her mantle and the crinoline under it. To the Old Masters she could be a goddess. For it was the same message, which Art and the real world and his own wife shouted. All your life, John, you've fled from the flesh into pictures, and today you see that pictures love the flesh. He said it over: great artists love the full-grown body. They love it with a sensual, animal love. They teach us how it may be loved. You can do what you like with poor Fra Angelico, and all the other painting friars.

Inside the cab he was all a tremble. His wife had betrayed

him and Art had betrayed him. And there was no one to blame but him. He had been wrong from the start, and made a ruin. Where can I go, he asked plaintively as trees, churches, mansions, rattled past. Leaning from the window and looking up, he saw the tall cloud he had seen that morning, standing tall as the Matterhorn high up over London. It was like a hooded Death. It was like a demon or an angel veering as he drew his sword.

*

The journey home seemed to take an age. Alone in the cab with his head sunk down, his thoughts returned to his sorry self. For he was no sensualist. As to women's bare bodies, who was further from warmth than he? Truth be told, as to sensual love — in the heaving, creaking beds of men and women through the world — what was he but a wretched cripple? Or was it because he had been *so* wrong, that he was shown the greater truth?

Raising his head, he mouthed the words, 'To some it is given to be and to do — and to others only to know and to see. Yet those who but see, may still see all. And knowledge and sight make weakness, power.'

Stepping from the cab, as it stopped on Herne Hill, he looked to the west — and was struck dumb. It was an after-storm sky such as he had not seen before. Beyond the horizon, which swelled with housetops, blazed the inferno of the sinking sun, whose red-gold light flung high and wide. It was not the light that amazed him though, but the sheer number of the clouds. He had never seen a sky that could hold so many — in rank on rank for ever and ever. They had round small bodies like ponies or birds: they drove together forward on the strong current of air like ships in an Armada, like buffaloes in the sky. There was ripeness in them. A joyous triumph leapt in him, to see so many stream on together.

'I have seen my vision,' he murmured over, as he stepped from the cab beside his gate. And if, on entering, he should meet his wife — why, he felt large, open, warm. For the words at last stood clear in his head: I was wrong about art, I was wrong about life. I have been as mistaken as a man could be. Love of the body is the clue to art. Your adultery has taught me this. It is wormwood and gall, but I see the way.

He stayed by the gate as his thought roved on. So may I in turn learn to love as a man? Or is it long too late for that? For I am me, I cannot change. But though I cannot change, I still can teach. Young Everett, who was my protégé — maybe in a bed he plays the lover, but his brush, his art, is not sensual at all. He is all exactness: his eye is cold, precise as frost. But I shall show him where he errs. It will be the great turn in his habits of mind — and the saving of this country's art. There was a vast hole in English painting, which he had never guessed before. For where are our great nudes? What artist here paints naked bodies — and with sensual love? We paint trees, and ships, and setting suns — and rolling hills and rolling seas, while people are tiny in our pictures. And if we come close, we paint rogues in a tavern, and portraits, portraits, portraits.

Was it possible a new mission was given to him, all suddenly, born from utter pain? Animal love for the full-grown body, such as Titian and Rubens felt: it was at the centre of their art. I did not see it, I see it now. And, who knows, by seeing so — I may come to join the throng. Even, may I come to love my wife?

Revelation — or daydream? Where had he come? Would he then preach — sensuality? Or would the new light fade, and leave him where he was before, thinking of bodies with disgust, and sneaking off to dream of tiny girls, as he pumped at himself like a milkmaid at the udder?

He entered the house, and knew at once that Effie was again away. Better so, for now.

'Hello, Sophie,' he said, passing down the hall. He found he was annoyed by her piquancy. He would not prattle baby-talk.

He hurried upstairs, and sat to the small desk he kept there, and took his pen, for he must write at once. It only came clearer, from moment to moment — he had come to life's crossroads. For himself, and for all his nation's art. But could he be equal to the task, poor loveless girl-worm that he was? For him, John, to play the sensual man — the world would mock, and he would cry.

He sat, he wrote. Desire, temptation clawed his back, but he did not stop. Small jerks travelled the length of his spine, as he held his gaze to the crimson glow which lay like coals at the horizon's back.

And when next he saw Everett — he had a lesson to teach his protégé.

4

Once more she sat on Lucy's ottoman, while Lucy kindly clasped her wrist. 'But tell me first — what is your fear.'

'It only is —' How could she name it? 'I have wondered if I am — well formed.'

'Well formed. I do not understand.'

Lucy's brow was lightly knit.

'If I am — as women are.'

Very slightly Lucy's frown increased. 'Why should you not be?'

'There are things which John — has said about me. I ought to know — and I do not.'

Lucy slightly raised her head, and drew in breath. She stood. 'Let us not delay. Come upstairs.'

As she followed Lucy's skirts through the turns of the staircase, she saw in a mirror her own stricken face — dead-eyed, and lantern-jawed from fear.

'Let us use this room.' Lucy held the door, into a flower-papered room with a large, old-fashioned, curtained bed.

She murmured, 'I'm petrified.'

Lucy slightly nodded. Her face was simply practical, as she opened the curtains and turned back the coverlet.

While Lucy then gazed out of the window, she took off

the layers of her dress, and her drawers, so she came to the bed in her chemise.

'Please lie.'

Then she saw only the bed-canopy over her, with Lucy a green mound at the base of her sight. Her mouth was open but she did not breathe.

'Please,' Lucy said. She felt her legs parted, and pressed more apart. The bed creaked, and Lucy's fingers softly pressed. She held her breath.

She felt her chemise laid down again. Lucy had stood. She was both grave and smiling.

'My dear girl.'

'Lucy?'

'There is nothing amiss.'

She looked her question — her fear, her doubt.

'You are perfectly formed. You are as all women are — or all women that I know of. There is nothing mis-formed in any way. You are a fit, beautiful, young person — everywhere.'

It was, the unbelievable. But how was it so? Was she truly awake?

'Dear girl, you may believe me. There is little I don't know about the insides of ladies. You should have asked me sooner.'

'I should, I should.'

Still, as she dressed, and Lucy looked away again, the full happiness was slow to come. 'It is strange. I have been so used to thinking that I was — peculiarity.'

'All you need is time — there is no hurry.'

Again the thought was slow to come. 'So my deformity was never in me.'

Lucy nodded. 'No.'

'The deformity was in John.'

Lucy's face was purely grave.

'I do not know if I have words — for what he has done to me.' Yet she had the word. 'He has done me — evil.'

Lucy held her hand strongly. 'I don't know if that helps. He has done you — inconceivable wrong. Worse than simply failing as a man. Still I would say, don't think of it more now, than you have to. A fear has lifted, let yourself be glad. The other questions can wait — they will not go away.'

She nodded — but could she be only glad?

'Let's go downstairs.'

As they went down, she was ready to dance. The corner mirror showed — a young bright-eyed happy woman. But who was she?

They rearranged their skirts yet once more on the ottoman, and Lucy rang the small bell which always brought tea.

'But what must I do? I cannot go back into his house. I do not think I can ever bear to see him again.'

Lucy calmly, precisely, poured the tea. 'After all, you will return to your home, my dear. Your sister is there. You may speak to him as coldly as you like. I would say, say nothing yet, of what we know today.'

'I cannot stay there.'

Lucy gazed some moments into her cup. Then carefully she put it down. 'I see that separation may be the only way.'

'Separation?'

'Separation.'

The word repeated in her head, till she said, 'You mean — I shall live in one house while John lives in another. But still I stay married to him?' Her fear grew, of Lucy's practical sense.

'But of course you must stay married to John. He has not struck you, or taken a mistress. You need see him very little — or almost not at all. But if you leave the marriage, you are — destroyed. Really the world is merciless. You know Carlyle

— marriages *must* not break, for any reason whatever.'

But how could it be — that Lucy, who had just opened the door of her prison, now quietly proposed to close it again? She looked round at the brilliant, damask-hung room. A glass decanter glittered, the epergne gestured still with its silver arms. The scene was elegant, and cold as ice.

'But my feeling for John can be only — hatred.'

Lucy was matter-of-fact. 'Yes, I think that must be so. Better then, in separate houses. Still your name is good — depending of course on how you live.'

'You mean, provided I do not let myself meet — a certain artist.'

Lucy's pity grew graver still. 'Yes, I do mean that. Certainly for now. I grieve for you — with all my heart. To the very bottom of my heart.'

She sat. She nodded. She yearned to weep, or bolt from the room.

They sipped tea. Through Lucy's face she saw thoughts pass, it seemed she would speak, then she did not speak. She caught a glitter in Lucy's eye, so her own eye filled with tears.

'I must go.' She stood. She had reason for joy as well as grief. She needed to hurrah, and she needed to howl.

'Lucy, you have given me very much today. Unbelievably much, and I shall not let it all be taken away. I shall find my way.' She paused. 'I shall ask one thing more. You had said before, you could speak to Lord Glenelg and Lord Salmon — to ask them what the Law says, of Marriages and Separations. Would you do that? May I see them?'

'I shall ask, of course.' Lucy stood too. 'That would be good. Who knows, there may be — another way.'

They kissed. She left.

*

John, she thought, in the fly, going home, you have cost me everything. You have destroyed my womanhood — and then called me insane. Her feeling could only be, absolute hatred. All of her clenched on the thought, John dead. The thought was calm. A judge inside her had passed sentence.

But it was only when she came into the back-kitchen, where Sophie and the maid laughed over their tea, that she saw the means. It lay on the draining-board, they had used it to cut ham — the old bone-handled Scottish knife which she had known from childhood.

'Can we have one, please, Effie? I shall feed it every day.'

'I'm sorry, darling.' She had not caught a word of all Sophie said.

'I said, Ruby's mother's cat has had six kittens, and Ruby says that we can have one.'

'Has she, dear? Let's think tomorrow.'

Sophie pouted, but it was no time for kittens. From the corner of her eye she watched the carving-knife: she saw the knife was watching her. Each time she looked, it had inched a shade closer.

'Kiss me goodnight, darling.'

Sophie gave a grudging kiss, and was led by Ruby upstairs.

She turned down the kitchen lamp, but then, in the half-light, picked up the knife.

'I must put this away.'

But at once the cracked bone-handle snugged into her palm. She turned the metal so it caught the light. Over the years the steel had so worn away that the blade was as narrow as an icicle. And still, if you tried its edge, you would cut off a wisp of skin before you knew it. An old knowledge came to her, from the vengeful clans — thrust deep then cut sideways.

But who was this woman, at charades with a knife? She

was no Clytemnestra, no old Scottish heroine who could kill with a dirk. Still she turned the knife, and thought he has maimed me.

So John found her, in the kitchen dusk, when he arrived home and came from room to room seeking her.

'My dear? Ah, there you are.'

He came where he could see her better.

'But what are you about?' His voice fell a pitch. 'Dearest — oh my dear wife — you must not, it is a sin.'

She would not speak.

'Oh Effie, no. Self-murder is forbidden, whatever the anguish. I should read to you the homily of Dr Snell.'

She needed to laugh harshly, he was so mistaken about her purpose.

His voice dropped further and was deeply tender. 'Dearest — I knew you were not happy. But *such* distress. I am to blame. I have not been forgiving as I ought.'

His dim face was trenched with contrition. This was aggravating — how could she strike?

He cleared his throat, and took an uncertain step. Then he lifted his arms, and held them both out wide towards her.

'My wife — my dear — I — I...'

She had never seen him in this posture — his arms open and high, as if he would embrace her. His face too had filled with uncertainty, such as he had never shown.

She put her soul in her eyes, and he came no nearer. He must have seen, in her eyes, the hatred. He seemed in a tremble, his face forlorn as an abandoned child.

She laid the knife on the table. After all she never could kill anyone with it. And he — he was a feeble, pitiable thing. In a choked voice she muttered, 'Begone, John. From this day on, keep far from me.'

He retreated backwards, his mouth half open. His arm reached behind him to find the sideboard. Shaking his head he left the room, while she thought, I do not need to kill him, now. A great space gaped wide between them. Killing him would bind her to his body, whereas now, within, she was free of him.

Eventually she went upstairs, where she lay in her nightgown, praying he would not come to her. All her thought must be for Everett — who for all she knew had forgotten her, and spoke with other ladies.

The floorboards creaked as John moved in the house. He came upstairs then descended again. She heard him curse as he banged on a chair. She thought of Herne the Hunter, the demon from the ancient trees. Antlers branched from his head. She was on Herne Hill, she was trapped in his lair, where he roved in his trouble as if he turned in a pit.

5

What was worst was not seeing her ever at all. A woman may say no to you, and you suffer to see her day on day. Or you go away, and escape her sight. Or if there is love — in some way you communicate, with letters, signs, a token left. But he had nothing. He was not rejected — and it was as though he was rejected utterly. Love had begun — and in an instant she vanished. The door was shut in his face. Did she pine? Had she forgotten him?

Waiting in his studio — for John was due — he could even be angry that she sent no sign. She could have found a way. But then he had sent no sign to her, except that picture of St Agnes — from which nothing came back at all. Should he try to forget? But always she had piqued him, as if love — fascination — were a barb, that caught in your flesh, and hurt if you turned the other way. Her complete disappearance was a deeper barb, the spike of it jerked constantly.

And if he was indignant — he kicked out his legs where he sprawled on the chaise — why it only showed how spoiled he was. All my life I had everything I wanted, or I was given even more than I asked for — like my talent. It was new to have something snatched away, and shut where he could not come near it. The world should not allow such — disappointment.

Whenever John came — he eyed the portrait — it was strange how completely he made a wall. And she was hidden, behind his back. All the time he painted, a part of him craned to see past John, or over his head, so he found her crouching in hide-and-seek.

Not that John never said her name. He spoke of visits paid, to a lord or to some ball, though the only news he gave was that while he sat and read, she danced a mazurka.

'Then a polka,' he had added, 'She had them all on a leash.' He laughed his tiny v-shaped leer.

Was it to hurt him John told him this? Was it even true? She should not be dancing. But she had told him herself how she loved to dance. She walked like a dancer, easily, lightly. And London just now was filled with balls, to which he was not invited. At night, if he walked the streets at a loss, he passed mansions where vertical men led ladies in gowns up the steps to a portico. Inside were chandeliers in constellations, so floods of light poured from the open doors, while whirling shawls and jumping men passed now this window, now that. He thought he saw her, then it was not her — still, he knew how she would dance. The floor would strain to touch her feet, as the dancers swung from chassée to glissade, sliding smoothly between hopping and gliding. Or when the dance stopped, and she thanked the suave charmer, other greyhounds of the aristocracy, legs long from horse-riding, would saunter near — especially when they saw her husband was odd, and sat beside her with his nose in the *Edinburgh Review*.

Did John tease him to hurt him — when not flattering his art? But then he in turn was false with John. It came so easily — this courteous hypocrisy. Was there, in London, a worse relation between a painter and the patron whom he painted?

Where the artist had grown to hate the patron, but continued because he loved the patron's wife. And where the patron suspected what went on: so he kept his wife locked in a cupboard, but still liked to play cat-and-mouse with the lover. And from what — fascination? Jealousy of the love they had for each other? While all the time he too was obsessed with the painter — his best pupil, his protégé, whose art he still would control if he could. For thus, in a way, it became his own art. So one man may seek to ride the talent of another — as you ride a horse, keen to win the race.

Was that what he had let his talent become? A talent John steered, so John reaped the prizes, because John wrote the praises that appeared in the papers, and it was John's ideas — about Nature, and Truth, and the Truth of Water — which the artist put into paint. Especially when the painting itself was of John! The foul tangle of it all! This portrait would be famous because John was famous, and he in his own young way was famous. It would make a sensation at the Academy show. So it would complete the weird marriage between them, and show how he and John came in one job-lot. While two figures grieved behind the painting. The patron's wife mourned unheard in her dungeon, while inside the craven, truckling artist was the wreckage of another man, who had kissed the patron's wife mouth to mouth, and clasped her hotly sodden in mud while she clasped him in a fury of holding.

He had helped this charade to go on — and he would continue to do so. Because this portrait would add to his fame. It would be praised to the skies, he was sure of that now, and from it would come: commissions. Lord This, Lady That, the poet Tennyson maybe. Who knew? The Queen, herself, in time? For that is the portrait painter's road. It is not the highest road of art, but it is paved with gold, and this portrait would establish him. So he was doing this for fame, and for money in the long run — and, who knew? — a knighthood, even.

But here was John. He heard doors downstairs, his mother's voice then John's, and the creak of John's weight on the stairs.

Was it then diplomacy, or merely weakness, that made him say 'Good day, John. I hope you are well?'

'Yes, I think so, Everett. But you look tired.'

Tired, I should say so, with the little sleep I get. But he helped John to place his hat on the peg, and gave him the cane he should hold in his hand.

'May I resume our progress?' John nodded to the picture.

And, 'Yes, John,' he said, with a courteous nod, when a part of him longed to punch John in the gut, so he folded down winded, while he brought up his knee between John's spindle legs, and crushed his useless genitals — if John had anything there at all — while he took John's red hair, and launched into the feeble fair flat of his face such a punch that his snout would be smashed and destroyed.

'Here,' he said, turning the easel a little. Why was he not man enough to go round to John's house — up on Herne Hill — and kick down the door, and heave John from his path, and find Effie in the room where she was locked, and seize her and love her with all passion in bed, while maybe the household and the neighbourhood watched, and John grovelled whimpering in a corner, and he took Effie's hand, and led her forth, his, and left John's sterile maze behind him?

Instead he said, 'I'm pleased you think so,' when John praised the neat geometry which shaped his cravat. 'So — will you take your stand now, John? So we may go on?'

'Why, Everett, yes.' John took his pose, and at once set his face to look noble and wise. He did not need to do so, for the head was done. What Everett had to paint today was the grey-black bucket of John's woollen coat.

He bent to his brushes, and dabbed at the pigment. No need, now, of crimson lake or aquamarine. What leaden stuff it is, a kerseymere coat! It drinks light and drowns it, leaving just a glimmer, like the scum of light.

'Everett?' John's voice had a lift, as it did when he was close to his baby-talk style.

'May I talk? Do you mind? For my head is finished. And there is something I should tell you today.'

'Not at all, John,' he courteously said, hearing with loathing the cringe in his voice — as though he still sat, a pupil, at the master's foot. 'What is it you want to tell me?'

*

As John spoke, Everett studied the painting's eyes. Had he made John — an atom — squint? He must go back to that.

'I am sorry, John. You said?'

'I said, I see that through the greater part of my life — I have made a *momentous* mistake.'

The brush froze in his hand. Was it possible the news John had to tell him, was that he saw he should never have married?

'Yes, John?'

'For I have taken it as an axiom, that purity of morals makes strength in art. So I have written in my books. And the world has agreed, and praised me for saying it. For that is what the world would like to hear said.'

Everett nodded, frowned, paddling his brown-blacks.

'Whereas I have seen — as in a vision — that the true need

for a great painter is' — he paused — 'a good stout animal sensuality. Moral purity is no substitute.'

Everett blinked, his jaw dropped, while John's eye steadily brightened.

'For think: Giorgione — Titian — Tintoretto — above all Rubens. Is that not the quality they all possess? Human, animal, sensuality.'

He was startled. But John did have this knack of saying things, which made you stop and listen in spite of yourself. He heard himself say thoughtfully, 'Well, John — yes. I think that must be true. I have not heard it said.'

'No, Everett.' John's voice rose. 'It is not said. But that is the fault of our commentators, even such as me. It is the fault of our country, with its puritan soul — even such as mine. It is the fault of our moral fearfulness, and what we have done with the Christian Church.'

Everett frowned. 'What has the Church to do with it?'

'Very much!' John frankly now came out of pose. He shifted his weight, so he stood as he might on a public platform. 'For the great mistake our nation has made, is the degrading of desire. We have come to see it as sordid, base. But Titian, Tintoretto, Rubens — *their* sensuality is great, it is magnificent. It has nobility, it joins with beauty.'

John stopped and rested his hands on his hips, as if to say — Yes, chew on this.

Everett could only stand and gaze, by now in full amazement. What can you say to a man, who shouts about desire as if he stood in a pulpit — and who cannot make love to his wife?

John's gimlet-eye was on him. 'I expect you are surprised to hear me say this.'

'In short — yes, John.'

210

'Yes. I thought you would be.' John munched his lips. He looked down but gave an odd muffled growl, then quickly looked directly up.

'You should not be surprised.' His glare was like an accusing father.

'No?' Precisely Everett laid his palette down, and his brush beside his other brushes.

'Because, Everett, I have you to thank — for this momentous thought of mine, which turns our art world upside down.'

Half he guessed what John would say. 'Me? And how is that?'

'You ask? It is because you forced me to think of desire, all day and all night — when I had little wish to do so. You, and my lady wife between you. With your wretched amour.' John stood taller, broad and square. 'For I should tell you, I know what is going forward.'

He loured like God in wrath — the outraged righteous husband. Would they come to blows? The portrait commission was destroyed. John was panting, Everett heard his breath.

'Going forward? Nothing is going forward. Nothing whatever. And nothing happened in Scotland, if that is what you suggest. Nor have I seen that — *unfortunate* lady — for months, as it has come to be now.'

John's eyes were hard like painted eyes. At last he blinked. 'Is that true, Everett?'

'It is true.'

John worked his lips, his shoulders moved inside his coat.

'Believe it, John. Engage a detective, if you wish, and have me followed. He will tell you nothing, that will cause you distress.'

A time John stared, as he might at an odd, atrocious

painting. Then his eyes lost focus, his hard stance sagged. 'May I sit down?'

'Here.' Everett placed a chair. John sat, but did not sit still. He chewed his lips, continually he rubbed his thighs.

He sighed. 'I know not what to think.' He shook his head in slow heaves, as though it held a lead weight.

Everett poured water from a flask.

John looked up, eyes wide and blue. 'It may be I have wronged you, Everett — and wronged my lady, in my thoughts.' He drew a long breath in and out again. 'Will you take a chair, and sit by me, so I need not look up all the time?'

Everett set his chair a certain space apart. John looked to him with a weary smile. 'Yes, I suppose — I have let my imagination race.' He shook his head and sighed again. 'I do know I have not caused my wife to be — happy.'

Everett kept his face a closed blank door.

John still was making wide grimaces. 'I have been in turmoil, these days — and nights. With thinking of the way my life has gone.' He mused to himself, then gave a wry, confiding glance. 'I understand why I am as I am. And how that has made me — an untoward husband.'

Everett gave a listening eye. John's chair-leg creaked as he got to his feet. He went to his portrait, where his head and chest were there complete, and all his lower body white. He gazed at it in reverie, his chin cupped in his hand.

'You have painted me as a thoughtful saint. But you have not caught my oddity — though I think that you have guessed it.'

He turned back, so he stood beside his portrait. Then there were two Johns.

He took Everett's eye. 'If you paint me, you should understand me. My parents got me late in life, and their love when I came was too great for my good.' Quizzically, he shook his head. 'I was patted and petted and coddled and cooed over, more than any child the world has seen. And in that way they kept me a child.' He glanced to the other, painted John. 'They had the kindest, best will in the world, but they made me girl as much as boy. Or rather, they helped me to stay neither. The soul when it first enters the body is sexless — and so was I, if truth be told. At the same time they kept me to my studies, so I excelled in all fields of knowledge — and thus am I a walking encyclopaedia.' He reflected, then was animated. 'Do you know that when I studied at Oxford, my mother rented the next-door house, and prepared all meals. She sat beside me every day, to help me progress with my studies. She helped much, though she herself is scarcely lettered. And all the whiles she stroked my hair, as still she does, while I sit and write. This is the secret of my "genius" — that I work as a slave who never rests, but have kept within me the quick sight of a child.'

He said it brightly, with a kind of pride, while the other John, pale, mild and mute, seemed to ponder what he said — till abruptly he turned on his painted self. 'Also it made me half a goblin. I do not have all human feelings.' He faced Everett sadly. 'That is why I am not as other men.' He was still, but then his stance grew straight. He stepped forward and hid the other John. His voice was firm, it even twanged. 'But does that mean, that I may not grow to be a man? Tell me, I pray.' His eyes had force. 'Everett, I have suspected you. Possibly I have wronged you. But still you have the greatest talent, of all who came within my care. It may be too that you can help me, man to man. Give me your hand.' He held out his own. His look was strong, and manly too. The painted John, a hovering head, hung at his shoulder like a ghost.

Everett did not give his hand.

John bit his lip and quickly said, 'The animal equipment of a man I have, and it works well, as I do know.' He gave an oddly knowing leer, and a little closed one eye.

'Don't ask my help, John. You do not need it, you will make your way. It would weaken you to hang on another.'

John's hand weakly hovered back. His face had puckered, so Everett wondered, will the baby-voice return?

It did not. John crisply said, with taut eyes like a soldier now. 'You are right, sir. I must stand on my own feet.' As now he did. 'Doubtless I shall find my way.'

Everett placed the chairs where they had been. John stayed standing, watching him.

'But still, my dear — a word upon the thought I had. Do not you think that I am right — though once I should have been the last to say it — that the nobility of Titian and Rubens lies in the greatness of their sensuality?'

Everett had his palette to his thumb again. 'Not all of it.' He preened his brush. 'Do you think, John, it may be that because you were, as you said, very far to one side of the road, that you have gone very far to the other side now?'

John, in his new manliness, stared outright. 'Do you mean I am wrong in what I said?'

'Not wholly wrong, of course.'

'Not *wholly* wrong?' John took the cane, that was one of his props, and grasped it in the middle. 'It is not just a question of right and wrong. It is a question of how important it is — the thing on which I have laid stress.'

'Yes, John. And it is important.'

He spoke too mildly. John gleamed then glowered. 'It is of the first importance. And I shall tell you, Everett, it bears back on your own art too.'

'On my art, John?' Everett stiffened, and laid the palette down again.

'Yes, Everett, I do say that.' John's eye was stern, the grim teacher. 'For look about you in this room.' He extended his arm, to the drawings and paintings — the figures and trees and hands and faces. An elderly woman stiffly dandled a babe. Soft as a breath, a young lover just touched a delicate hand. 'I shall tell what I see. I see the best draughtsman in the world. Every detail you draw is exactly true, so if I went close with a microscope, I still should find every atom in place. And that is a miracle. No one else has such an eye. And the design too is perfect, with every line where it should be. And your colour is rich when you wish it to be — your reds, your blues, your greens, your golds. It is perfect art — as I have told the world. It is true to the stress, which I lay in my books, on *truth* in art, on the *accurate* eye.'

John paused for breath. Everett said to himself, stay calm. 'And then, John?'

'And it is cold. It is a miracle — but the miracle of *accuracy*. There is something wanting, and I shall tell you what that is.' He paused for a moment, guide and master.

'You need not, John. You mean I lack sensual animality.'

'Yes, Everett. You do.'

'Thank you, John.'

He stood quite still, digesting the words. John watched him with saddened kindliness, grave as at a bedside.

Everett's mouth was dry. He slowly said, 'It may be that you are right. I cannot say now. I shall think about it. Believe me, John, really I shall think about it.'

He stood still, pondering. John watched, and waited, as if he said now — take your time.

'I do see, John, that — in the world of art — I may have

been a little like you. That I have stayed "the good boy". I was a prodigy from the age of four. I was so good at doing what one should do — as to how you are told to draw and paint.' He made a mouth. 'I have been the best pupil in the world, and it has not made me the world's great painter. Something else is wanted, I do see that. And it may not be only sensuality. Still — there is time, I think. Perhaps you are right. I shall see if I can — warm.' He suddenly smiled. 'It may be, then, we both should change.'

John smiled too. 'You are right, sir.'

They exchanged a glance, perhaps a little like a father and son, finding they stood on common ground.

John nodded to the painted John beside him. 'Perhaps we go now back to work?'

'It's time.' Everett took his palette again, and chose his brush.

John however stayed where he stood. 'And so, my dear, there are two paths run side by side. Sensuality in life, and sensuality in art. One could think they were one, but they are not. In life, may be, *you* have no want. And in art — well, I am wiser than I was.'

'And yet,' John added, still in his muse. 'I have to say that it grieves me yet — that we may not work together as one.' He paused, then gave an odd, shy, childlike pouting look. 'You *could* help me, Everett — if you wanted to. *If* you are innocent, as you say you are.'

Everett dashed palette and brush on the table-top.

'Don't ask my help, John. Good God! Of all the men in the world, how could you ask me? What do you think has been happening these months? I am innocent, yes. But that doesn't mean I wanted to be. I love your wife. Know that. I do not see her, or plan to see her, or plan — anything at all.'

He stopped, white-faced, panting, glaring, thinking all war breaks out now. And John simply nodded in an elderly way, like a kind uncle.

'Yes, I know that, Everett. Do you think I'm blind? But you may not have her — to yourself, I mean. For I love her too. And it is true — if truth be told — that I had at moments thought — that, maybe, the three of us...'

'John! Know this. It cannot be three. For the love of God, man! What world do you live in?'

'Yes, my dear, I know all that. And even so, I have had — how shall I say? — a dream. Of the love of three-in-one. Dare I say it? Like the Trinity.'

He snatched Everett's hand and held it hard, gazing past him into space with a bright face lit like the sun with wonder. His skin was white, he had sandy hair. His face had a beauty between a god and a girl. His eyes turned to Everett, blue as new-cut sapphires.

'Let go of me, dammit!' Everett snatched with violence, but could not get his hand free. Where did John find the strength? His fingers were crushed.

'No, think of threes, Everett. There is Father, Son and Holy Ghost. Or Father, Son and the Virgin Mary — for virginity is holy and Christ was virgin. But also if you will there is Father, Mother and child, even as my own family was. The first building men made was a pyramid, a triangle. The design of great paintings is often a pyramid. The Gothic arch is a triangle, bending with a three-way love at the end of each leaf on every tree in the world —'

'Good God! Good Heavens! Let go of my hand!' He tore his hand free. 'Slow down your head! Your brain is a runaway locomotive!'

'Forget my brain. We three could make love all in

common, as men did in the early ages. Join us in our bed, my dear, and life and art will all be one.'

'No, John. No. No. No.'

After all John only sighed, and sweetly smiled. 'Ah well — you have an everyday soul, however good your eye may be.'

'Simply, John, don't touch me again. Do not lay a finger on me.'

'Of course.' John looked at his hand fastidiously. 'As if I would want to, after all.'

Oddly, like a visiting connoisseur, he began to saunter in the studio, glancing at drawings and the stray oil sketch.

'Oh, and by the by, before I forget. There is a favour I would beg of you, Everett. My wife asks, will you draw her sister Sophie, who stays with us? Just a small portrait sketch, at a single sitting — she would like it for her mother. On my commission, of course. Could you possibly?'

Everett still was catching breath. 'That would be a pleasure, of course.'

'Then I shall give my next sitting to her. If I may I shall fetch her with me next week — then be a spectator at your work.'

'Bring her, John — and pray tell your wife I am pleased to do this. They are a handsome family.'

'Indeed,' John said drily. His face was closed and opaque.

Everett smiled as he dabbled his paint. It was a tiny request, but it came from her, and ridiculously it seemed as though all doors opened.

'To work, I think.'

John took his stance, and held his cane as in the portrait.

'I am ready,' he said. 'Are you?'

His pose was exact, except that still he looked to Everett.

'But as to my wife —' Abruptly he flashed a dagger glance.

His voice had an edge, like ragged tin. 'She is mine, and all the world shall know it.'

He turned his head to its proper angle, where his mild blue eyes gazed ahead and *saw*. While Everett sharply drew in breath, and scowled like thunder, and grabbed his brush, and stabbed the snakey mound of paint, and dug and furrowed and scrubbed it hard.

*

John had gone, and he sat brooding on the things John had said. Events had made John wild, there was no knowing what he would think or do next. As he sat Everett cudgelled his brow with his knuckles. There is no time to lose, he murmured over — if she still thinks as she did in Scotland. And — there is no way I can send a message to her.

He looked at the portrait — or the portrait studied him. What falsity, hypocrisy. He had made John's nose classical, and given him a chin. Portrait painters do that, and they call it tact, but it's cowardice and hypocrisy. For all his work, it was a daub at last. John's near eye looked asleep. Well, that was because his left eye drooped, when he had to pose for an hour. His lips were pursed, as though he would simper.

Fools would admire it. The servile and the blind. What could you say? It was polite. I hate you, he said to it. He turned it, on its easel, to the wall.

He heard steps on the stairs — had John come back? There was a light tap on the door, a bright glance sparkled. 'Can I come in? Your mother said you were up here.'

He got up. 'Leech! Dear friend. But I'm not good company.'

Leech disposed his lean limbs across the chaise. 'I can see you're in the dumps — I can't think why. What more do you want? The youngest Associate RA ever. Gambart offering the earth to deal with you.'

'You know about Gambart?'

'It's the talk of the town. He's offering you a premium, if you'll cut the Academy and exhibit with him — no?'

'I shalln't, of course.' He made himself move. 'Here — brandy?'

But Leech had stood, as quickly as he sat. 'I'm not drinking here — and you should get out. What? You work here all day and then sit here all night? No wonder you're stale. Shall we eat at the Club?'

'Not the Club — I can't take all that nagging and braying.'

'No? Let's go somewhere low — *damned* low if you like. I need to unwind. I've done four cartoons for Mr Punch this week. Now the engravers will cut them to death — and I need to drown my Muse.'

He had started down the stairs, so Everett must follow.

'Hey, watch your head — ooh! I'm sorry. These are the servants' stairs.'

Leech continued ahead of him, wiry and lithe, and was already talking cheerfully to his mother. He thought, how good Leech is.

His mother fussed as he shook on his coat.

'No, old woman, I shalln't be late. Look, I'm wearing two scarves — I shall be warm enough.'

On the steps they hollered till a cab drew up. 'Where to, Leech? Highgate? You heard that, Cabby — Highgate and look sharp.'

'Yes, milord.'

They swayed in the cab as it skittered over cobbles. Leech's thin face bent close to his.

'Now tell me — what is this grief? Everyone says you're turning hermit.'

Again the questions. His friends would not let him be, they spoke as though he had no right to a secret.

'Oh, it's just Hunt — he's left for Syria. I miss him sorely. Dear Holman!'

'It's not just Hunt.' Leech's eyes were keen, as though he were preparing to draw him for *Punch*.

'And Deverell died. Such a short life — so poor — and his art...'

'Deverell's story *is* tragic. But it isn't that.' Leech sat back. 'It's love, isn't it? You can see it a mile off.'

There he was caught. Before he could say no or yes he found he was swallowing, and blinking non-stop. His mouth had gone shapeless. He made — he heard himself — an unmanly noise. He studied his toe-caps.

Leech gazed at the gas-lamps. The cab came to a stop.

'We're there. You do this one, Millais. The cabby didn't call me "milord". And I don't have Gambart clamouring to pay a double price for my drawings.'

He collected himself. 'Go on, Leech. You get a good screw off *Punch*.'

'A pittance. And unlike you, I've a family to pay for. But I'll cover the ride back. Where shall we sit? What a reek! Say what you'll eat — or shall we drink first? Brandy? Stout? Gin and peppermint? Port and sugar?'

They found a corner, in the smoke-filled roaring barn of a place, in the lea of a huge cask with 'Old Tom' stencilled on it. He took refuge in food, to give himself strength, but still he was weakened, so the chops in front of him rippled and wavered.

'Forgive me — I'm worn out. Just with peering at one inch of canvas all day.'

Leech nodded. 'Don't worry, we'll talk of other things. I'll only say this. I know they say love comes to everyone, but I didn't think it would come to you — not like this. Because you're so ambitious, and wrapped up in High Art. And you're proud, and frankly you're not always kind. If I had thought anyone could get through life without love, it would have been you. And look at you, you're wrecked. I'm *very* glad, it's good for you — however it ends. I expect you don't sleep?'

'I don't.'

'Don't believe you.' He stretched back. 'But I shalln't ask who it is. I don't suppose it's that Edna you used to see.'

'No,' he said balefully. He fell into a study.

'Eat!'

He shook himself, drank, made himself talk Academy, and *Punch,* and Parliament, till, all at once, Leech said, 'Ah, I just realized — I see the problem — the new lady's marri- Forgive me. Have a cigar.'

Surrounded by smoke, he knew still he must say something to Leech. 'I know there's no future in it. Nor are we meeting. Believe me, I'm doing nothing I should not do. But I've got a lead weight inside me, that will pull me into the ground.'

But was he sure there was no future? By saying there was none, he had cancelled the future there might have been. He sank in deeper depression. There was only one necessity, he must find a way to see her. What they would say he could not imagine. Simply if they met and spoke, everything somehow would come to rights.

'But I cannot see her. I can not see her.'

'What?'

He realized he had spoken aloud. What was wrong with him?

'Nothing. I said nothing.'

Leech nodded, and was thoughtful, and did not give

222

further delving looks. 'Look, Everett, your friends are here.'

He peered through the cloudy air of the room, to a table where a man had begun to see them. He had a big square forehead and a short square nose, and held his hand to his brow like a sea-captain trying to make out something through fog.

'Dante — of course. You can meet Dante in any tavern in the town. Don't call him, he's with Fanny. He'll like her for her red thick hair — and her thick neck. But he's coming — hello, Dante.'

'Hail, brother.' Dante pushed back a frowzy cowlick of hair. 'Fanny, do you know these gentlemen? This is John Leech, who draws for *Punch*. Fanny knows many of the gentlemen of London.'

Plump-faced Fanny gave a shining yawn.

Dante inspected him. 'Everett, you're *drunk*.'

'He isn't,' said Leech, 'He's got the blue devils.'

'I don't know what he is,' Dante mused. 'He's not the man he was, at all. But Fanny's tired. Come along, my dear. These low *artist* fellows are tiresome. I'll take you to the poet's den.'

'Bye, *Ever*-ett darling,' Fanny called in husky strong cockney. 'I haven't seen you for *ever* so long.'

'Bye,' he muttered, but he knew he blushed, while Leech exchanged a glance with Dante. As soon as they had gone, he said, 'We should get away, as well. You know what I've a good mind to do? I'll take a cab to Herne Hill, and go and punch the head of — a certain critic.'

'What? Who? Oh, wonderful — your most important patron. You *are* in a foul mood. How has he offended you?'

'Oh, nothing. We disagree about Turner. Let's get a cab, I'm not good for anything.'

'That's true.' Leech touched his shoulder as he stood. 'I'd

better get you home, what you need is sleep.'

'Sleep? I told you, I don't sleep.'

'Well, lie down and look at the ceiling.'

He took Leech by the arm. 'I don't know where I'm going, Leech. But if you wait, you may see me do something, which will make all London stand on its head.'

'Do you mean you'll start a scandal? In a word — don't.'

'And if there's a big mistake, in how the world thinks and how people live...'

'Do big things in your painting, Millais. Not in real life, you'll regret it for ever.'

Big things, he repeated, when he lay down at home at last. It's only words, and I do nothing. There is no way I can even whisper to her.

*

He had to go to a function at the National Gallery. There he met the Director's wife, Lady Eastlake. She said, when they found a quiet moment in a corner,

'A dear friend has told me you travelled with them in Scotland. We all wait to see the portrait you made there.'

He was suddenly woke from his morose sluggish lethargy. 'Half made, truth be told. I am finishing it here. John comes to Gower Street.'

She nodded, it was clear she knew that already. He saw she waited; and the company milled closer.

He said, 'When you see her next, will you say to her — there was a point on which we sometimes spoke — that I have not changed an atom in any of my intentions. I am only more sure.'

They looked round, for company approached. 'Please say something else. She spoke of certain plans she had. Do tell her, delay has dangers. For what she spoke of — there is no time to lose.'

But already she was drawn away, by Eastlake and his moustaches. 'Elizabeth, come please — Lionel is here.'

'I shall tell my friend what you said,' she said, as she glanced briefly back, then was lost in the throng.

But will she know what I mean? he said over. She must not be rash. He was filled with fears. But also something in Elizabeth Eastlake's face made him murmur, I am not forgotten.

He left, there was no way he could stay for the chatter.

On the way back the road was blocked, and he woke from his cave of thoughts to the crowd, and the shouts, and red light in the sky.

'Is there a fire?'

'It's the Vaux Brewery,' the cabby said. 'If it reaches the spirits, you'll see some explosions.'

As he climbed down, a fire-engine passed, ringing its bell, while the firemen whirled rattles for the crowd to part. He ran in its wake, so he quickly came to the front of the crowd. There he stopped, breathless, and gazed ahead in shock with everyone.

Across the plain of cobbles he saw the bleak fortress, spikes of fire at all its tiny windows. Fire engines stood at the brewery's gates, where men cranked pumps while others passed slopping buckets. Constables in domed hats came running with more buckets.

'Wait for it!' 'It's going to go,' the voices beside him said. As he watched, the long roof of the main building sagged and fell in. A turning torn wide blade of flame wheeled upwards in a torrent of sparks. There was a sound as though everyone round him drew breath. The firemen near the gate looked as though they were dancing, firelight sparkled in their lacquered hats.

'Are there men in there?' he asked, 'Firemen?'

'Two,' 'Three', voices said, but already it was late. The walls of the brewery were purely a shell, with nothing behind their rows of small windows but a single, building-high sheet of flame. Then the flame swelled upwards in terrible petals as the entire long wall descended, parting, folding, sliding down in a dull huge crumble, unrolling smoke across the engines and leaving behind the hopping fire crews only an irregular mountain of clinkers — from which crazy claws of brickwork stood up — burning all over like coals in a grate, while giant wooden beams, that stuck out at angles, flared dazzling fires at their broken ends, or blazed along their length with dancing tiny flames like creatures.

'Oooooh.' A great wail, sigh, cry, what could you call it? rose as one from every mouth in the crowd. Those men, he murmured, blinking for his eyes had filled with tears, and every face near him, he saw, was wet.

When the crowd broke he made his way home on foot. He still saw the fire, he saw nothing else. The building was falling, and still he saw the wall stand. Spikes of flame poked like fingers through the windows in the wall. It was a furnace, firemen ran in and out. Those brave men, he repeated. He was ablaze himself. In the dark the world and London burned. He was running more than walking, as if there were somewhere he must arrive before it was too late. Or he was too late, it was late long ago. The fire inside him flared in desperation. Disaster filled the world, and the loss of brave men, but he was not brave. He was worthless in comparison, he was worthless and weak. For if you watch and don't act, and delay and don't act, all burns in a moment, and is lost in fire, and nothing is left but dead burning ashes.

6

As he spoke her eye roved the spines of books. In dark leather, gold-embossed, they made a wall on every side. The paneling about them showed as dark, all waxed and polished by someone's care. She breathed out sadly, for her heart had sunk as his words continued. Then Elizabeth quietly squeezed her hand: her eyes said, 'Wait'.

For Lord Salmon spoke as though he had no bad meaning, though he seldom caught her eye. Either he watched his thumbs rotate, or he spoke at large to the deep-coloured walls.

'Therefore we may not speak of divorce, or of a formal separation.'

Elizabeth's grip hardened. 'Are you saying, Lord Salmon, that the law offers no end — even to a marriage that is no marriage?'

'By no means, Lady Eastlake!' His voice swelled. 'I am saying there cannot be divorce, where — as you say — there has been no marriage.'

Effie and Elizabeth looked to each other. Did he play a game with their understanding?

'For you were right, Lady Eastlake, in the way that you put it. And in the eyes of the law, if the lady is maiden — then indeed there has been no marriage. In such a case, the law declares, there has been but the effigy, or false appearance, of a marriage. The lady is declared never to have been — let us say, Mrs X — but only falsely to have been so named. She is declared always to have been — let us say — Miss Y.' He paused. 'This is what is meant, when a marriage is declared to have been *annulled.*'

Elizabeth frowned. 'In what court is this done? I have never heard of such cancellation?'

'No indeed, for it very seldom has been done. Often, it seems, people have preferred to go without — or to make some other arrangement — rather than that their secret should be known to the world. And one can understand that.' He laid a dry, inquiring look towards her. Elizabeth also glanced to her.

'Please go on,' she said.

'I shall. We speak of ancient Church Law here. An annulment must be enacted in an ecclesiastical court. Marriage is a sacrament, after all. It is a holy event.'

He paused, and she again said, 'Please — Lord Salmon.'

'Indeed. For what is consecrated in marriage is the bodily union of man with woman — not to beat about the bush. Doubtless for the purpose of begetting children, but the begetting of children is not obligatory. The Church is clear, a marriage must *needs* be consummated, or it does not exist. Mere good fellowship is not enough.' He sighed. 'I am not sure the world sufficiently knows the wisdom the Church has shown in this matter.'

She remembered John telling her of the virgin marriage of Mary and Joseph. Was that no marriage, after all, and Jesus illegitimate? But everything was contradictory now. Married, not-married, never-having-been-married — how could she be these different things? The words of Lord Salmon were half like a fairy tale, and half like a problem in algebra. Yet still it seemed the way ahead could be easier than she thought.

He waited. She hesitantly said, 'And so my marriage becomes — as though it had not happened.'

'It is so declared.' She still was wondering: the years I spent within that marriage — where do they go? And the bewilderment and pain of them?

'So I may leave his house, and tell the world I am Miss Gray, and he may have no claim to see me.'

'If you so wish, precisely so.'

She wondered, was it possible she already was free? It could not be, but still she asked, 'And if I did not go home today, the law would shield me from his call?'

'Ah no!' He sat large, like a judge in judgement. 'For as yet you still are a married lady, and subject to your lord's direction.' Seeing her face, he made his tone more gentle. 'Your marriage persists in all its force, until the day that it *is* annulled. For it must be proven first, that there has been no marriage.'

She blinked — there were too many new things. 'How *do* you prove — what is not?'

His eye fell. After a pause, and with a glance to Elizabeth Eastlake, he said quietly, 'It may be proved by an examination of the lady's person, performed by qualified physicians.'

At his first words she was already crimson. How had she not guessed? It must be so, of course. But to think that her virginity must be 'proven', by men in frock coats whom she did not know... She froze, it was unimaginable.

He had turned distinctly to her neighbour. 'And here, Lady Eastlake, you may help, with your connections in obstetric circles. For it must assist the lady's case, if the examiners — there should be two — are known for expert physicians.'

'To be sure.' Elizabeth nodded, and pondered.

But could it be possible, that she would go so far as to press an action — in a court of law? The peering faces, the prying questions, the violation of all her secrets? To be the talk of the town, with the world like an audience spying on her. That too was unimaginable. How could she, ever, go so far?

Still she asked, 'Where are such cases heard?'

'I should expect a case such as this to be heard in the Consistory Court of the Bishop of Southwark. It is hardly a courtroom — they meet in the Choir of old St Saviour's Church.' He smiled. 'Do not expect the Bishop to be there.'

But however hidden the courtroom would be, still the word would spread. The news-sheets would hear of it.

'Should *I* need to be present?'

He looked up again. 'Most probably not. You must be represented by a Proctor. I recommend Mr Glennie, whom you may find in Doctors' Commons. As a diamond he is a little rough — but a diamond still.'

She nodded then, and quiet fell on the three of them. There were no more questions to answer now. The decision was hers — as to whether she acted, or stayed in the shadows. Her head was in a whirl, of possibilities, hopes, alarms, even terror.

She got to her feet.

'Thank you, Lord Salmon. You have been most patient, and most helpful.'

He stood, and slightly bowed. 'Your servant.'

But as they paused by the door, he called distinctly in a serious voice, 'One word more — I pray you, proceed with discretion and care. It may be wise you give no sign, before you have come to be fully resolved. Such issues touch people in delicate places. You cannot predict what they may do — they, or their families.'

He waited, cold and grave, to know she understood.

'Thank you, Lord Salmon,' she said, quietly, clearly.

He gave a quick, small smile, which she carried from the room like a softly spoken encouragement.

*

Rose dresses, lime dresses, lightly rocked like skiffs on a wave, as ladies came and went across the sunlit park. The gentlemen sauntered more sedately, raising their hats, which were like tall chimneys, to each lady they were pleased to know.

'Elizabeth, I have so much to thank you for. I never should have got to him on my own.'

Elizabeth smiled, and drew her mantle close. There was the chill from a recent shower in the breeze, small clouds scudded overhead.

'Dearest — I wish I could have helped you sooner. But just to think — that it may all be done so simply. Are you not pleased?'

'I am, I am — but married, not married, I am turning somersaults.'

'Of course, it is a further step again — to decide that truly you will do this.'

'But Elizabeth, I am so glad that you spoke to Everett. That you told me what he said.'

'I do not mean to be a go-between.'

'Dear friend, we have no go-between. But still his words changed everything. I should not have doubted.'

Though Everett's words were few. But somewhere near — below the ground beneath her feet — was a reservoir of happiness. Springs of pleasure rose from it.

Elizabeth nodded. 'How is John now?'

'He is strange — not that that is new. But he worries me when we retire.'

'You do not mean — he wants —'

'It cannot be. He is strange in the daytime too. His last complaint was about our accounts. He suddenly decided to do them last night, and sent Sophie to say that I owed him fifteen pounds.'

'That's not Sophie's work.'

'He won't let me be. I know his mother is stoking the fire.'

But still she was glad, thinking of Everett — then she saw a rider glance quickly to her. Other men did, briefly, brightly, and went on their way. How odd — it was when she was happy in thoughts of Everett that other men chose to see her.

Elizabeth looked up. 'Our friend.'

Approaching them a splendid centaur, in a sky-blue coat and bright lemon waistcoat, swung his white hat wide as he bowed from his stirrups.

'Your servant, Lady Eastlake, ma'm — and the lady of "the graduate of Oxford", unless I err — the best of a fine spring day to you both.'

In turn he caught the eye of each of them, and nodded to her though he scarcely knew her. Then, erect with self-pleasure, he trotted away.

'That dandy d'Orsay. Though they say he is no bounder at all, he loves his own fine self too much. He's vain as a girl. Society, Society.'

As they walked, other high-stepping horses passed them.

'But the physicians —' she began.

'I shall find good physicians,' Elizabeth said. 'They will be gentle with the speculum.'

'The speculum?'

'It's only — an instrument. No cause for alarm.'

Still she shivered. Must an instrument come into her? They walked in silence.

'So I must decide what I do next. And I must decide this on my own. Oh, Lizzie' — she clutched her arm — 'It is so hard still, that I may not see him. That we may not meet.'

Elizabeth's face grew at once so grave that she had to smile, and jumped into her broadest Scotch, 'Dinna fret, Lizzie, I sha' find the road I have to gang entirely on my own.'

She laughed then, and saw, it was not only men, but women too who glanced to her. So maybe today was all a dream, and in truth she never would be with Everett. But at this moment she was happy in love, and as a result people who did not know her from Adam were pleased to see her go by.

She came back to English. 'But after Lord Salmon, I don't know whether to skip and dance — or what I should do. I am on an edge like a cliff, I could jump, and fall down on the stones.' Still she looked brightly at the budding twigs, which waved to her from every tree.

'We do know you should not delay. Your friend said that.'

'Lizzie, I am glad I should not delay. Though what *is* the first step? I must think well.'

'You will, I know.'

The brittle sun grew sharply bright. On some trees new leaves stood out, in tight lime-green clenches. The tall grasses swayed, there was no stillness anywhere.

'Within, I am already free.'

'Oh, be careful, dearest. Thinking that may have its risks. There are many fences round you still. We cannot guess what John may try.'

As they watched, a jagged gust assailed the cherry tree before them. Clouds of pink-white blossom wheeled, like a sudden shower of snow — or like confetti at a winter wedding.

*

She woke scarcely remembering where she had been. In the crowded courtroom, where everyone watched, she had reached down inside herself, and fetched him out — small though he was — her beautiful Everett, who glistened in his caul like a new-born foal. Seeing he was perfect, the men in wigs crooned 'Oh!' in falling wonder, while he grew to his full height beside her.

There she lost him. She woke knowing she had no moment to lose. With her clothes in her arms she hurried downstairs, then paused, as she dressed, and simply sat. She knew one thing only, she would act today.

Her breathing calmed. The house was still, and the hall lit bright by the early sun. She began to wander from room to room, rearranging the embroideries she had placed, in her efforts to cover the yellow furniture which John's father gave them. This 'nest', as John said — this rabbit-hutch, this cage. It was her home, and not her home. But everything was contradiction. She was married, and no wife at all. Outside she heard a pigeon purr.

She came upstairs. Still no one stirred. The door of John's study stood open, and with stealthy feet she went inside, and sat down at his desk. At once, by instinct or inspiration, she reached and opened the bottom drawer. Without looking she fingered the papers there — and pulled a packet from beneath them all. After all, it needed no long search.

By its feel she knew it, it was the daguerreotypes she had

found before. With care she set them on the desk. The glass plates made a soft clink as she slid them from hand to hand. Still she strutted, turning coyly, the slender breastless uncovered child. She shivered, winced, and shut the packet. With stealth she replaced it, and slipped downstairs on whisper feet.

There another picture waited. Everett's drawing of St Agnes' Eve hung in the alcove where John had placed it. Longingly she gazed at the lean woman there, who herself gazed on beyond the snow. Carefully she lifted the picture from its hook, and clutched it, praying — Everett be there, at my journey's end. There was peace in knowing her utmost wish.

Till she sighed, and, with care, re-hung the picture. She heard the kitchen-maid cough in the attic, soon Sophie would softly call out 'Effie?' She heard John start to snort and honk as he too woke from a troubled night.

*

John had gone with Crawley to town, and the house was quiet. But as she sat to the small table by the window, her eye jerked so the paper shivered. Beyond their garden a plane tree heaved, its branches mottled like a snake's skin.

No more delays, Euphemia. She wrote,

'My dearest Father —'

She stopped and listened through the house. Downstairs Sophie tinkled the piano.

'You are aware that till this last year I have never made any formal complaint to you. There were many reasons for my silence, the principal being of course my great love for you and my dear Mother — fearing to trouble you when you were in great difficulties yourselves —'

She stopped, remembering the desperation, as her parents verged on bankruptcy. Then she heard her father's voice, 'Get to the point, lassie.' Like any solicitor, he looked over his glasses, quietly waiting for her to speak. But he *was* a solicitor, she should have asked him long ago.

Outside the plane tree swayed, sunlit smoke passed through its branches. Gazing out, she tried the words aloud, 'I have therefore to tell you, I do not think I am his wife at all'. She nodded, dipped the pen, and wrote,

' — and I entreat you to assist me to get released from the unnatural position in which I stand to him.' Now she had begun, she would not stop. 'To go back to the day of my marriage — I had never been told the duties of married persons to each other and knew little or nothing about their relations in the closest union on earth. For days John talked about this relation, but avowed no intention of making me his wife.' John's words came back to her, his religious objections, dislike of babies, the desire he had to preserve her beauty — till the day he told her, 'the reason he did not make me his wife was because he was disgusted with my person.' She stopped. 'Disgusted'? There was no better word. 'He then said, as I professed quite a dislike to him, that it would be *sinful* to enter into such a connexion, as if I was not very *wicked* I was at least insane and the responsibility that I might have children was too great, as I was quite unfit to bring them up. These are some of the facts. You may imagine what I have gone through —'

The wet ink glistened, she heard harness and hooves — but they did not stop at her gate. The plane was motionless in every twig. Time waited for her to finish the letter of her life.

'I should not think of entering your house excepting as free as I was before I left it. All this you must consider over and find out what you can do.' She paused again — how should she close? 'Your affectionate daughter,' yes. Then she wrote, 'Effie Gray'.

Setting the letter to dry, she sat for some moments still as the trees, her head lowered.

A pigeon throbbed, the breeze returned. With a sigh she folded the letter small, and sealed it in its envelope. All her marriage was in it, en route to Perth. Then she stood, touched her hair into shape, and went downstairs to Sophie.

7

He hung listless at his studio window, waiting for John. Across the road he saw a peeling locked door up a steep flight of steps. Was that his life — high stairs, a dead door?

The bell rang below, he heard voices — then raised voices. Downstairs he found John talking hotly with his father, while a small girl in dark green attended solemnly. She was Effie in miniature.

'No, sir.' John's voice rode high. 'How can you not see it? That this nation has, in the last thirty years, committed more evil under the sun than any other nation on earth?'

'Evil, sir? And more than other nations? What of the Belgians, sir? What of Austria? Dare I take you for a Socialist?'

'A Socialist? I have more interest in what the Communists say, and in the communes they would try to make.' John gave a singing laugh. 'It's true I also call myself a Tory of the old school. One thing I know — this tumbling rotten society will burst from its iniquity. Blood will gush here, as in Vienna and Berlin. Ah, but here's Everett — Everett, this is my lady wife's sister. Miss Sophie Gray.'

He saw his father, like John, was flushed and breathed hard. 'Miss Gray, I am most pleased to meet you. Please call me Everett. How do you find London?'

'Very busy, if you please. John took me yesterday to see Tower Hill, where traitors had their heads cut off. I was very scared, but I wasn't really.'

They went upstairs.

'This is my studio. And here's the portrait of John. I have finished his head — the most difficult thing — and now I'm half way down his chest. Do you think it is like?'

Carefully she inspected the canvas. 'I think it's *very* like — oh, but you do look funny, John, with just your head and shoulders there, and the rest of you fading away like a ghost.'

John gave a cry. 'Sophie, darling, you're one in a hundred! But you can see from the outline I'm holding my stick.' He picked up the cane, which he held when he posed. 'This isn't my own, but it serves well enough.' Abruptly he brandished it, like a cross farmer. The others leaned back. 'Don't be frightened, Sophie. It's your turn now, to have your likeness taken. I *do* hope my artist friend is willing. It will be *such* a present to send home to your mother.'

Everett brought out his drawing board. 'Of course I'm willing. But can I catch your prettiness, Sophie? Let's move this chair. Will you sit? What do you think, John?' John had come close beside him.

'Oh, but that's a *very* good angle. I shall sit and watch, if I may.'

'Pray do.' They all sat.

'Turn a little away from me, please.' Lightly, in pencil, he touched in her outline. She was like a small animal, poised alert at the edge of its den. He looked again for Effie's face in hers.

John leaned in close to look. 'She has *such* a sweet beauty, don't you think? You must catch that profile.'

Without moving, Sophie sternly said, 'You make me shy.'

John coiled and gave a sharp high laugh. 'The little witch! Oh but she's *so* like her sister was, once.'

'Is she?' He saw her from two angles, for she was reflected also in his large mirror. In the glass they were a curious threesome: the sedate child in green with reddish-brown hair, his shock-headed self crouched over the drawing board, and the pale nervous man in black who stared at Sophie like a mesmerist. Now John did not know he was seen, he stooped and grinned, his look was wolfish. Then, from the mirror, Sophie caught Everett's eye. Brightly, with meaning, a clear look. His heart gave a loud beat. Had Effie spoken to her of him? She looked ahead quickly, as if John must not catch her glance. And when Everett turned back to Sophie herself, again she simply gazed ahead, like any child who was told to sit still.

John had cast his head back, in reflection. 'Of course, you did not know my wife in those days. The tricks she used to play!'

He touched in Sophie's slightly pursed lips. 'I see that Sophie will grow into a beautiful lady, just as her sister did.'

John's stick whisked in the air as he sat. 'Did you hear that? A big beautiful lady, just like your sister? But I don't need for you to be bigger — *I* like you as a *tiny* lady. Tiny girls are perfect beauty. But Everett thinks your sister is beauty. But we all love your sister, do we not?' He stood up and stretched so the stick flung wide. 'Everett, it seems to me, loves her. Yet I still come and pose for him. And he goes on painting me. Isn't that what you call "a pretty kettle of events". And which of us do you think that she loves best?'

'She loves me best because I'm her sister.'

'*There's* a clever answer, eh? These canny Scots. And between Everett and me, whom does she like best?'

Sophie considered, then said slowly, 'I don't think she likes you always — because you can be not nice to her.'

'But is she always nice to me? I think I've been a *very* good husband. And if she needs a friend to talk to, I am sure that Everett —'

Everett stood suddenly, so his chair fell back on the floor.

'That's enough, John. You'll say no more with Sophie here. Hey! Be careful with that stick — you nearly put my eye out.'

John drove the stick hard, with a crack, into the floor. 'But wouldn't that be terrible? If we hurt an artist's eye, so the jelly spilled out. Oh, I'm sorry, my darling, I was exaggerating. And you heard what Everett said to me. That was telling me, eh? But I'm such a lamb — do you know, I shall do just what he says.' He drew his finger across the shut line of his mouth. 'But sit as you were, Sophie. Let Art continue. You know, I have given my whole life to art. To art — but not to artists. Because artists — to be an artist — you don't need to be a very pure man. In fact, it's not good for your art, if you are. To be a good artist, you shouldn't be *pure* at all. Now, isn't that a funny thing!'

'Enough.' Everett stepped forward. 'Give me that stick — it isn't yours, it's my father's.'

John gazed, as if astonished. 'Don't take it from me — I need it for my pose.'

'You're not posing today. Give the stick to me.'

The stick jerked sharply — then John brought it down.

'Oh, *hab'* your stick, Ebewett. Wha' do sain's wan' wi' sticks?' He swerved towards Sophie. 'And maybe I'm a naughty saint. I sometimes do things saints should not. But Sophie —' He stooped close over her. 'Do you know what my father always says?'

'No, John?' She hunched away below him.

'He says, "If you have a stick — you're all right". As if a stick were the answer to everything — to naughty ladies, and naughty men everywhere.' He nodded towards Everett.

'And naughty saints,' she said quickly.

He wheeled up. 'Oh, but that's capital! Isn't she quick, Everett? That was wonderful, Sophie.'

Deliberately Everett said, 'For Heaven's sake, sit, John. I want to get on.' He took his pencil, and nodded shortly, with a smile, to Sophie. Her small quick head came up again.

John looked between them with suspicion. 'Again he is telling me. He sounds at times just like my father. But I must do as he says — for I have to be on watch today.'

Did Sophie's eye catch his again? The movement was so quick he was unsure. John sat, and made to attend. But he could not be still. The toe of his shoe rapped on the floor. His elbow shook, so his cuff rode back as it lay on the chair-arm. His shoulders worked inside his coat, his head quivered with minute vibrations —

Everett jerked his eye back. How had he come to be looking at John, when he should be drawing Sophie?

Nor could John stay. Abruptly he stood. 'No, dammit, I cannot sit. I have work to do in so many places.' He sighed. 'I am heavily burdened — but it is my own fault. I am missed at the Turner House, I am sure. They have not seen me this many a day. You know, Sophie, they keep new towels and heat water for me, so I may be clean as I handle' — his chest swelled — 'unmentionable dirt. Would you excuse me, if I am briefly away?'

Gravely she nodded.

'Everett, may I call in — let us say — two hours?'

'Of course, John.'

He eyed them both, took his hat, and left. He seemed by the clatter to be running downstairs.

Everett looked to Sophie. Could it be, she had a message for him? Her head stayed still.

'Did your sister tie your hair last night?' He examined the silky light in her hair, which hung in close tubes made by curl-papers.

'Yes.' She smiled daintily.

He shaded in her hair, and the light under her chin. 'And how have you enjoyed your stay in London?'

'Oh, very much. Because she is such a good sister to me. And John's mother is always kind when I visit her. But she doesn't say nice things about Effie.'

'No?' He smiled inquiringly.

'I've told her if she says any more bad things, I shall stop up my ears with pieces of bread. We laughed about that. She *is* a funny lady. She told me how she washes her body. "I always do under here, dear, and then I do here and up here. I stand up in the bath with a great big sponge — oh, and I *never* forget to do here." She said this while she gave me tea.'

He had put his drawing board by. 'You *are* good mimic. You draw too, and play?'

'I don't play as well as Effie. She plays better now than she used to. She plays so my eyes go hot and prickly — then I look up, and she's crying too. John says she needs more to do, and he takes her with him to the British Museum.'

'The British Museum? What does she do there?'

'He has given her a *long* list of dates she must copy. Poor Effie, I don't think she sleeps at all. Her poor eye keeps winking in such a strange way.' She paused, then said brightly, 'She's in the British Museum today.'

'What!' His pencil dropped on the floor.

'Yes. She told John she would stay at home. But she told me she would order the fly and go there, after John and I had left. She said she had fallen far behind, in copying the dates John wanted — and she had to catch up without his knowing.'

'John will be pleased,' he quietly said. He was in tumult. When he stooped for his pencil he dropped it twice. He must run round at once to the Museum.

'I must go back to your hair,' he murmured. He tried to catch the curl over her brow. But he could not draw, his concentration was gone. 'Sophie — I've just remembered, I have to go out. I'm terribly sorry, I shalln't be long. But let's go downstairs — I think cook was baking scones today.'

He stood, and Sophie stood. At the door she said directly, 'Will you go to see Effie?'

He did not want to say, and he did not want to lie. 'I should like very much to see her. I am unhappy that she is sad.'

With grave eyes she said, 'She said John is jealous, and will not let her see her friends.'

He said only, 'I am her friend.'

She nodded, as if she had been testing him. They started downstairs.

'I do like scones.'

He smiled — and fortunately, in the kitchen, the scones were there.

'I shall be back soon.'

'Yes, Everett.' She nodded then with a 'canny' look, sly beyond her years. His brows knit — but he could not stay.

He snatched coat and hat, and was on his way. The world was changing and Scotland came back. His feet clipped the London flags like shots, but also he hurried up a path between

244

cottages. The British Museum towered like a Grecian temple, but he half expected, behind the large glazed doors, to find her setting their rooms in Bridge of Turk straight.

Instead of which, in the dim vestibule, he faced stone-floored corridors, and arches leading through other arches. How would he find her? He had hurried pell-mell, he should have asked Sophie more. It would be a nightmare if he lost time searching — running up stairs, and through long galleries — glancing at clocks, and knowing he soon must go back to Sophie.

He began the search. It did not take long, for she was away from her dates and names. As he came into the Egyptian hall he saw a cape and bonnet before a throned blank-eyed Pharaoh, and at once he knew her — was it the way her head sat up from her shoulders? Her face, as she turned, was white as never. One eyebrow shot up oddly high. Her eyes glistened, his own eyes flooded. All he saw was her pale face turning to him, as it turned to him when he lifted her from the mud puddle, with all her hopes of love in him.

There was a bustle nearby, from behind a gigantic scarab came a florid father in strongly checked trousers, a worrying mother in tassled wraps, a fluting aunt with a guide-book held high, and a tumble of children all about them.

'Good day.' He nodded gaily, dismissing them, and they and Egypt disappeared.

'My love,' he said.

*

He hurried back — had he taken too long? And poor Sophie, waiting. He must make it up to her, and give her the drawing she deserved.

It was only as he neared his home that the odd shadow

flickered in the corner of his eye. He turned once and blinked, then walked ahead, for there was nothing untoward behind him.

At the next corner he turned again — and there was no doubt. Behind the lamp-post a figure stood, as though it would hide though that was impossible. The person stayed frozen.

But is it? he wondered. As he began to walk back, he recognized the cloth of the coat.

'John.'

What was strange was that John, even now, did not look at him, but huddled himself as thin as a stake. He was breathing through his mouth.

But he must turn. 'Why, Everett.' His tongue-tip moistened his v-shaped smile. 'Peek-a-bo! I can see you.' He laughed abruptly like a fireman's rattle. 'But my dear, I thought you were in your studio.' He stared hard, as though it were he who just found someone odd.

'My studio? Oh, I had to go out. But I thought you were at the Turner house? Shall we step back together. I have yet to finish drawing Sophie, I am afraid.'

'By no means.' John was almost bluff. 'Go your way, Everett. I have an appointment — in the British Museum. I shall come on to yours when I have been there.'

With a quick glare he turned, and strode off.

He was left in a daze. Had John seen them as they talked? Would she be caught? He, and everything, was shaking and breaking, as if the shops and church-towers of London would fall, so she and he together must run for their life.

'Did you like the scones, Sophie?'

He was glad she looked up pleased to see him. If he could draw her like that, with the large white apron and smile behind her —

'Yes, and cook gave me lots of jam.'

In the studio she sat to her pose at once, as if she would help him make up for lost time. Her small face was closed and doubtful: he worked with the rubber, so as to catch her as she was now. He was surprised his hand kept steady, when all of him was quivering, alive with flame. He felt fragile as a window with a ball flying to it, in the instant when you don't know if the glass sheet will shatter. And John — what would happen when he arrived?

John took another good hour to come.

'May I see? But it's heavenly. A quick sketch but perfect. My wife will be delighted — and your mother too, Sophie. She will be *very* pleased.'

'Yes, John.' They prepared to leave.

John said no more, and gave no clue of what he knew, or did not know.

8

But where were her parents? She waited in the small rooms in Bury Street, which her father had reserved.

'The boat will be late,' the landlady said. 'All the way from Dundee — you can't wonder. At this time of year the storms can be savage.'

She pictured her poor parents, clutching a rail on the heaving deck, while the boat ran aslant the grey wall of water. She remembered how the drenching spray burst over her, years ago. Spring storms — pray God they come safely.

'I allowed a full hour for them to come from the docks. Now I've waited three hours more.'

She picked and unpicked at her tight-pinned hair.

'Don't fret, they'll come,' the landlady said comfortably.

'I can't wait longer, I'm expected at home. My husband will wonder where I've got to.'

The landlady's arms lifted in a smiling shrug. Husbands may be let to wonder. She shook her head as this dutiful wife fastened her mantle then paused in the doorway.

'You will make them welcome?'

'Very welcome. You see the fire is lit and hot.'

In the fly, going home, she worried — what would John say? His ways had become so hard to predict. He might press her with questions, if she were a minute late — or make a loud show of not noticing she had been away. These days the house was filled with nervousness: the maid dropped plates, Sophie cried easily, and she would find Crawley waiting in odd corners, as though he wanted to ask things of her — but then he sidled off.

Her parents in London — it would be a different world. How curious it would be then, to slip away to see them as if she went to meet a lover. Come quickly, ship!

What would be hard, would be keeping her parents' visit from Sophie. But Sophie must not be told yet, in case she gave signs which John could read. Yet — Sophie's keen eyes…

At home, as she came into the room, John rose. He stood, grave and pale at the head of the table, so she must feel like a truant child. The full dishes waited — how long had they waited?

'We have not begun. Sophie was fearful, so I sent Crawley to look for you. Pray, where were you?'

'Oh, I saw Lucy.'

'*Again?*' He gazed round, as if an audience watched. 'My, you must have important business. I should like to know what that might be.' He turned an ear, waiting with theatre to be told.

'I didn't know you had *so* much concern for my business.'

'Oh, *business*.' His face puckered — then he laughed. 'I can show my concern for your *business* interests. Sophie, might you pass your sister that envelope?' He butted his head towards the sideboard.

Sophie neatly obeyed, with eyes as puzzled as her own must be.

'Must you write to me, John?'

'Will you open it, please?' He had become even roguish.

The envelope was unsealed and she opened its flap.

'Why, it has money in it. What is it for, John? I don't understand.'

He waited, savouring her puzzlement. 'It's the money I owe you. I find I was wrong in our accounts. You don't owe me fifteen pounds — I owe you sixty. And there it is, paid in full. I owe you an apology as well as cash — and give it as gladly. Let us sit and dine.'

So his severity was in play. Smiling, he held the chair for her to sit, and passed dishes.

'The parsley potatoes are of the best. Do have some more.'

Through the meal he glanced brightly to her, like a boy wanting thanks for a good deed done. Or, she thought, he is like a dog — who looks to be petted when he brings the stick. She was startled to think of him with such contempt.

When they had finished, he begged her to play on the piano for them. After Sophie went to bed, he stood. 'It's late. Will you come up with me?'

He waited, with a glitter in his eyes like glass.

'I shall sit a little, John. But thank you for caring for my accounts.'

'I am always glad to put matters to rights. Come soon.'

'I shall, John.'

With odd politeness — was it false? — he bowed. She heard him step slowly up the stairs.

She must not go. His play, his smiles, drove her wild with disgust. She was almost frightened by her changes of mood, since the day she saw Everett. John's odd sniff could start a storm of loathing. She hated his nostril and the scar by his lip. She hated the droop one eyelid had. She hated the different sinus noises that rattled and clogged in the holes in his head. And the crumble in his voice which meant he was pretending.

She told herself, it is not good, to hate anyone in the world so much. How could anyone love her when she was so filled with hatred? Most of the hatred she hid from John, and so, with hatred, came hypocrisy.

Tonight, though, she should let herself rest. Her mother and father must have docked by now. She would see them next day, however she explained the outing to John. And if he left early, as he often did, she would not need to explain. Sophie could visit a neighbour's house.

She waited till she heard John's snore, when she went to the foot of the stairs, then crept to their room and slipped beside him to sleep.

*

It was only a question, as the door opened, into whose arms she should fall first. Her mother had a sitting-up-straight way of standing, with her chin tucked into her rigid neck, but her eyes were hot, an oven of care. Her father's face moistly beamed — where he stood with his coat hanging open, as it usually did at home, a lean bald man with tufts of hair standing out to either side of his ears. Already he stepped forward, holding wide arms that clasped her.

'Lassie, lassie.'

She let her face drop on his chest. He pressed her shoulders while her mother, beside them, waited her turn to hold her daughter, who she knew would stay in her arms longer, as they comforted each other and sat down by the fire, where, little by little, she would tell them everything.

*

'The appointment is made,' her father had said. Now she stood at his side in the lobby of the chambers, while the clerk made a show of busy writing. He had a special skill in causing a pen-nib to scratch, in a way that set your teeth on edge. After all, she reflected, it had not been hard to deceive John as to where she went. Was lying so easy? Or was it that he did not care much, how she chose to pass her day?

A voice behind the frosted glass called 'Steynes'. The clerk, at his leisure, wiped his pen and stood.

'Please follow me.'

A black-suited man, with a veined, kindly face, stood behind his desk. 'Mr Gray — I am told you are a Writer to the Signet.'

'A "solicitor", as you would say. Yes, we prefer a different word.' Her father laughed, so both men laughed. 'My daughter, sir.'

'Madam.' He bowed in the older style. 'As you may gather, Mr Gray, I have read your letter carefully — ah, but here is my colleague, Mr Glennie. Mr Glennie is a Proctor. We stand in need of his skills.'

He waved towards the short man, burstingly stout, who just then banged in from the room beyond.

'I mean,' the kindly lawyer nodded to her, 'He is also a "solicitor" in the Consistory Court — that is, in the *Ecclesiastical* Court.'

The proctor's head was a red, hard ball, his coat and knee-breeches were faded green-black. A rank smell of men's sweat enveloped the room.

'Your servant sir, ma'm.' He dully eyed her father, then her. The kind lawyer had them all sit, and sat. At his leisure, with discretion, he resumed their case. The proctor made impatient noises, and turned a dead eye on her father, or on her.

'And so, Glennie,' the solicitor concluded, 'Mr Gray has

proposed to me that he call on the husband's father — at the soonest — in the hope that, as sagacious parents, they may resolve the matter smoothly.'

The proctor grunted. 'A clear mistake.'

His voice was so sharp, she saw her father was flustered. He fingered his lips.

The proctor faced him. 'Sir. Mr Gray. I disagree. You will not go to see the father.'

Her father sat taller, his Scottish twang hardened. 'By your leave, my man, the father and I are reasonable men. I believe we could settle the matter quietly.'

'Oh aye?' The proctor seemed to strut as he sat. 'You haven't the first idea of the risk you run.' He faced her squarely. 'Madam, pray excuse my rough words. But you will not be safe. A father may *bid* his son marry a lady — to spare the shame on the family's name. Whether the son is willing or no.'

Her father frowned. The kindly lawyer shone to her through his glasses.

'Or, Mr Gray, sir, the father may agree with you, but yet the son may not. The son may say, she *is* my wife. Whatever he has said or done before. Do you understand me, sir? By your leave, Madam. The son may choose now to marry his lady. He has the right in law. They are man and wife. He may proceed and do it.'

'Gently, my man, for Heaven's sake. May I remind you that you speak before my daughter?'

But the proctor's clapper-voice only hardened. 'I have eyes, sir, I can see that. Madam — I beg that you excuse my frankness — but you must know the hazard you risk. To end a marriage, whatever the cause — in such a case, people do not act as they are used to. Believe me, ma'm, you must leave the house, before suspicions are aroused. May you not say you will visit your parents? What could be more natural and proper?'

She was still gazing, surprised by his brusqueness. He continued to stare at her — after all it was for her, not her father, to say.

'Yes,' she said, 'That is better.'

'Good.' He bowed his head to her, then turned back to her father, 'Once the young lady is away, sir, letters will be delivered by a man of law, and given by hand both to the father and to the son — stating the case as it goes to the Court.'

'I see your reasons. Yet I had hoped to act more openly.'

'Sir, I commend you for it. And indeed the choice is yours — provided that your daughter concur. I trust your relations with both parents are cordial?'

'Aye, well, in truth —'

The proctor observed him with dull eyes like oysters. He took a brown scattering pinch of snuff, and fiercely inhaled. Her father looked to her, she looked to him. The dank smell of old sweat was strong in the room.

Her father said, 'We shall do as you advise.'

'I congratulate you on your choice, sir, ma'm. We shall have the papers cast. But I may not emphasize enough, that you must act with great dispatch. Such matters never do stay quiet. Someone gets wind of it — before you know it, the plot is blown. Hey, Webster, do you share my view?'

'Oh indeed.' The kind lawyer nodded, and smiled to them as they left. The proctor had picked up a paper from his desk, at which he scowled as though it filled him with rage.

*

254

'With dispatch', the proctor had said, and within two days she stole away from her archives in the British Museum to meet her parents beside the Thames. She walked quickly with her bonnet low — though who would know her in this crush?

She fretted as she waited beside the crossing. Just the fact that matters went forward so fast made her impatient for the end.

But there her parents stood, angularly bunched, before the funnel of a pleasure-steamer down below the embankment. A curtain of steam and smoke throbbed round them, the ship was on the point of starting — it was as if they had only to jump aboard.

They could not leave so quickly, but still it needed only moments before her father told her,

'So lassie, the plan is clear. You shall take Sophie to the station next Wednesday. You'll catch the train in the normal way — you must be there at nine, be sure of that. Your mother and I shall be waiting at Hitchin. There I shall join you for the journey to Perth, and your mother will follow with Sophie by sea. That evening at six the letters will be delivered to the parents' house on Denmark Hill. I doubt not your man will be there at the time. He seems to spend all his waking hours with his folks. Am I right, lassie? Is the plan good?'

'Yes, father dear, it's exactly right.'

'It's a sorry business, after all, but it must be so. We must get you free.'

'I'm not sorry,' her mother said warmly. 'I would take you home tonight if I could. Mister Gray, you were ever too slow. I don't trust what tricks these folks may throw.'

Her father said, lilting, 'Well, dear heart, be that as it may, we still must do as the proctor bids.'

The family nodded, they were at one. As quickly as she came, she slipped back to her tasks.

*

Each day, at home, there was some new turn. It often came in the evening, when they sat at table.

'What are you doing, John?'

She was so used to his reading books, and even writing them, as he ate, that it had taken her a while to ask.

He looked up with mischief-eyes. 'Oh, just making a note of what you said.'

'Why should you do that?'

'Well, I can set down what I see as your un-reason.'

Writing down what she said? Did he talk to lawyers also? To whom would he show such notes? She stood up from the plates and tea-cups.

'Why, John, do you write down what I say?'

He gave an odd, close laugh. 'For my amusement — forget it, please. I may act as I wish at our table.'

He nodded his head sharply for her to sit. She bit her lip, thinking I should not provoke him. Again she saw the scar by his mouth, which the dog-bite caused — how ugly it was, dead-white in his face. The thought grew, he must be talking to lawyers.

'May I see the paper?'

'Oh, but it's mine.' He clutched it to his chest, smiling to Sophie.

She walked round the table and held out her hand.

'John.' She stood over him.

He stood too. 'Be seated, Euphemia. I shall say what you may read.'

'Truly?' She snatched the paper, and went back to her seat,

taking a candle from the sideboard. John took one step, and swung his arm in the air — then he sat too.

'Ah well, Sophie dear, why shouldn't she read them? They're her own words. You'd think she'd remember them, wouldn't you?'

He made eyes to Sophie as she read — though her words looked odd in his neat handwriting. When she had finished she looked up. 'What have you got here, John? What's wrong with what I said?'

'Do you really not see the sullenness there?'

'What's this? A "batch". When did I say that? What's amiss, anyway?'

'What's amiss? At luncheon you spoke of my parents and me as a "batch". After all the kindness you have had of us — not to say the money spent. The *vulgarity* of it!'

'Vulgarity? "Batch", "crew", "brood", "gang" — write them all down. A "covey", a "litter". I'm ready to say all of them.'

'Indeed and worse. But I have written down all you've said. On other papers which I keep locked safe.' His eye slipped briefly to the inlaid cabinet in the corner.

'You aren't well.' She stood again. 'Sophie, come with me. I shall curl your hair and read to you after.'

'Sophie, wait.' He came round the table — his concern now all for Sophie's leaving. 'I've sweets to give you. And I shall tell you the best stories of all.'

'Sophie!' she called.

As Sophie stood, John took her hand. 'Do' go, Soph' Stay wi' Johnny.'

Sophie gazed, troubled, to her.

'Don' be unhappy, either of you. Sophie, you are jus' like Effie was once. Isn't it strange? There is one of me here, and two of Effie with me.'

He seemed to be on all sides descending round Sophie, who stood rigid within his wide limbs, gazing to her with most grave eyes, which even so did not beg for help. John's face, down beside hers, lifted. For a moment he seemed to gloat, holding Sophie enclosed, then he held out an arm.

'Effie, come and join us.' His other arm curled round Sophie. 'You are both my dears really. Let's not be at war. Come, Effie, let us kiss Sophie together. Let us all hold together like babes in one nest.' His face glowed in invitation.

'Effie?' He appealed again. 'Oh dear, Sophie, she *does* look cross. Shall we send her away, so *I* curl your hair tonight?' His face, next to Sophie's, sent a thin smile up to her, sickly, sweet.

Time froze, she did not breathe. But the gleam in John's eyes deepened, his hold on Sophie tightened, as he drew her closer to him while his face slid close to hers. As if twin girls looked up to her, one rosey and bewildered, one sick to death that grinned.

She shut her eyes, shook hard her head.

'Sophie, come at once.' How had she delayed so long? 'John, step back. I mean it — or I shall tear this Turner up.' She held high the tiny water-colour, which she had grabbed from the wall.

'Oh. Oh. Oh.' He stepped back with eyes as wide as his startled mouth.

'Stand by me, Sophie.'

Sophie crossed the room, and stood next to her. John, fish-faced, held his arms towards the painting.

'Sit, John. We will forget this moment.'

It was not the time to give orders to John. A muscle jerked in his neck and abruptly he came at them. His body was broad, his face enraged. Did he think he was powerful and fearful, a man?

'Quickly, Sophie.'

She had shut the door after them, they shivered in the hall. Would he bang the door open? Would he come through the wall at them, like a ghoul?

They just caught a soft whimper.

Upstairs, she soothed Sophie in her bed: they sang a rhyme, she read to her. When Sophie slept she stood on the landing. The house was silent as if John had vanished: she knew he had not come upstairs. Well, she had a purpose now. She stepped to his study, sat in his desk-chair, and opened the bottom drawer.

And if John found her, delving in his private things? It was too late to care for that. Do not provoke him, the lawyer said, but caution could not hold her now.

She pulled out the packet with the daguerreotypes, and began to unwrap the tissue paper.

Her heart tripped as she heard his step on the stair, but she kept her station.

He started, in the door-frame.

'What, pray, are you doing?' His eye glittered, his face came white as snow.

'You tell me, John. What are these plates?'

'You know daguerreotypes when you see them.' But he had no voice, just rasping breath.

'Who made them?'

'Who? But you saw him I'm sure.' He came nearer. 'For I made a friend in Bridge of Turk. As a friend he gave me these — gems of his.'

'You call them *gems?*' She held up the bare small girl to the light.

'Oh, *that*. Put it by, it is not fit.' But did he blush, in that face as white as cotton? 'He could be untoward, my friend.'

Like a striking snake his hand shot out, and snatched the packet as her fingers closed.

'Give it back,' she cried.

'It is mine, I think.'

'But it is my proof.'

'Your proof of what?' As if in carelessness he dropped it down, and casually trod on the broken shards.

'My past was bad, I close it now. You have freed me — and by freeing me you have bound us close. Come here.' He held his arms out wide.

She had backed to the door-frame. 'Stop, John. Come no nearer.'

He gazed then — even in admiration. 'For now, my dear — get to your rest. Another time I shall come for you, then there will be no turning back.'

*

'Oh do come in,' the kind lawyer said. 'Look Irving, here are Miss Gray and her father.'

'Indeed?' The proctor frowned at them while they stifled in his pungent smell.

Her father nodded briefly to them both. 'We are come to confirm that our plans are made. Your letters I trust are ready for delivery. My daughter will depart her house next Wednesday.'

'Oh dear,' said the kind lawyer. His glasses even seemed to mist with distress.

'That's nonsense,' said the proctor. 'There's no chance of that.'

'But you said, my man —'

'I am no one's man, sir. And our Mr Avory is from the office. He does those letters. Your plans must be put back one week.'

She looked to her father, but he already was speaking. 'What do you say, man? We've taken pains, it may not wait. You said to act with great dispatch. We have told some acquaintance. The news will be out before Wednesday week.'

'By no means. News does not travel as fast as you think. And it quickly goes awry. Your plans will all be confused in the telling. Wednesday week is soon enough. Be assured we shall be ready then. Thank you for calling.' Finally he spoke to her, 'Madam — dear lady — I am sorry for this delay.'

Another week — she was filled with fear. But she saw the uselessness of pleading. She nodded.

'Thank you, ma'm,' the proctor said. 'And so — good day to you both. Mr Webster, will you cast your eye on this writ? Hey there — Steynes! Show these good people to the door, will you?'

The kindly lawyer smiled, commiserating, then turned his glasses to the sheet of parchment the proctor had passed to him.

'A week more,' Mr Gray grumbled, putting on his hat in the windy street.

'Father — I don't like this extra week. John gets stranger every day.'

'Lassie, we must hope — and pray too, I think. "The law's delays," as the Bard puts it. Pray God it all comes right at last.'

9

From within his pose, like a hawk, John watched Everett mix colour. His brush played over his palette like a pianist's finger.

But how much, truly, did Everett know? He must make each word he said a test.

'So — tomorrow dear Sophie, whom you drew, goes home.'

'Oh.' Everett barely raised a brow.

'My wife will take her, and pass some days with her parents in Perth.' Did Everett's mouth pull down at the corner? 'They leave by the nine o-clock train.'

'Dash it!' Everett said, 'I've spoiled my white.' His hand had shaken, his face was frozen like a waxwork. He stepped back from the easel. 'Well, John, I expect you will get more work done. You have said you are distracted at home.'

Distracted — had he used that word? But Everett would change the subject, he saw. Everett laid his palette aside.

'I have heard, John, that your father is upset — that our portrait won't make this year's show at the Academy. I am sorry for that. I am going my fastest, but I must get things right. There are still those Highland rocks to finish.'

'Of course, Everett. Next year's show is soon enough.' He

smiled, but thought — rocks in the Highlands? Will he be off any day 'to get the rocks right', and see someone else as he passes through Perth?

For the rest of the session he could learn nothing, though Everett swore 'Dash!' or 'Dammit!' more than once, as his brush made a slip in mixing colours. Did he know already that Effie was leaving? Since the day he caught Everett away from his studio, when he was supposed to be drawing Sophie, everything was uncertain.

In the carriage home he asked himself, would he make her his wife? It was the last night before she went north — and he *had* held his seed, to be strong when they joined. His unfaithful wife. Each night she was unwell, or surly, and he was divided, and unwilling, too. But the time must come. Her ill-will would lapse when she *was* his wife. And he was in turmoil, till the thing was done.

The air burned his throat — the sour breath of London. Then the traffic at the Elephant and Castle was locked.

'Whoa. You there — clear the way,' his driver bawled, they were moving at a snail's pace.

When they reached Denmark Hill, and began to climb, he leaned from the window. Looking ahead he saw a low cloud, black as soot, firm as an animal, with a surface like fur, slide too quickly along the crest of the hill: it was evil in motion.

The road came level and its name changed to Herne Hill. Home at last. But as he alighted a hot gust of wind whooshed in his face, so he clutched his hat.

'Good evening,' he called.

He came in the hall, where a trunk and several cases were stacked. Did they need so much luggage, just to take Sophie home? Effie came from the kitchen.

'John! Tea is ready. We expected you sooner.'

'The carriages were stuck in the Old Kent Road. You're ready for your journey?'

'Yes, Crawley will help us at King's Cross.'

On an impulse he said, '*I* shall take you to King's Cross.'

'Oh, there's no need for that. Crawley can manage perfectly well.'

But his mood was large. 'No, it's fit that I come — to see my dear wife off. And to bid farewell to Sophie. Crawley will help us mind the bags, as you say.'

'Oh.' She smiled tightly. 'Thank you.'

Crawley came in suddenly. 'Madam — oh, good evening, Mr John.'

'Evening, Crawley.'

'Yes. Please excuse me. I'm wanted in the pantry.' He disappeared quickly.

'What's the matter with Crawley? He was hopping as though he had ants in his pants.'

'No, he has helped us.' Her voice was brittle.

'Good evening, John,' said a small sedate voice.

He turned. 'Sophie — my, you look smart in those rosettes. I *am* sorry you are leaving tomorrow.'

'Thank you.' She gave a serious curtsey.

He bowed with ceremony. 'Let us go into the dining room. After you, I beg. I shall say grace.'

They did not talk. Both Effie and Sophie sipped their soup neatly, like figures in a book of good behaviour. He was provoked.

'He's a rum chap — that admirer of yours.'

She turned to stare. 'Are you speaking of your artist?'

'Yes, of course. The poor man was jumping about just like Crawley, I feared he would smudge the canvas.'

She nodded, her brow knit, as though she shared his

bewilderment. Sophie, beside her, took quick spoonfuls of soup like a bird beside a dish of water. He looked between them — they had something hidden. When he caught Effie's eye, she gazed back hard, like a person saying, *I've* no reason to look away.

The soup-plates went, the meat arrived. Abruptly he knew — genius will take these leaps — that Everett would travel to Scotland also. He would say later he went for the rocks, but instead he would take a hotel near Perth. When Effie returned, the deed would be done. For certain she would no longer be virgin. It left him no choice, he must act tonight.

'John, whatever is it?'

He looked up startled. 'Yes?'

'The noise you are making with your knife and fork! Are you trying to cut the plate in two? You said your artist and Crawley were jumping. What about you?'

He looked up with biding eyes. How could she find the courage to snap, in the thick of her intrigue? 'Pray, excuse me.'

He ate dessert with small, precise motions, thinking, Milady, I shall surprise you this night.

Sophie had folded her napkin neatly, and sat up straight.

'Sweet Sophie,' he said. 'I shall miss you dearly.'

Curtly Effie said, 'Get to bed, Sophie. You need good rest for your journey tomorrow.'

'Will you come to do my curl-papers?'

'Of course, dearest. John, you will excuse us?'

He leaned forward. '*Give* me a kiss, Sophie. You must, for it is our last good night. Oh, oh. *Thank* you! *Sweetest* dreams.'

The room was still, he was left to his thoughts. He went to the sideboard, and poured himself a glass, then a tumbler, of his father's sweet sherry. He must be strong tonight. My wife and Everett — who knew what they did? In some squalid hole where, barely undressed — he with his shirt off, she in her petticoat — already they grabbed each other. Her lips ate his thin white shoulders: the thought made him mad, and fired his desire. And Sophie, his dream, was being taken away. He was stricken — but I shall teach you, madam. He had not known rage and lust lived so close. If he thought of her in pain, he could want to hold and heal her.

Is not Effie taking long to come down? He drained his glass, and went upstairs. She was not in their room, she must still be with Sophie. Sweet Sophie — of all his small girls she had the best beauty. As he should know, for he was beauty's harvester. Or did she stay with Sophie in order to keep away from him?

He stayed in their bedroom, and took off his coat. What to do? Should he travel north after these lovers, and track them, then burst in wrath upon them? What strange scene would then unfold, as they cowered astonished? Would he smite them, would he...kiss them both?

'What ails you, John?' He nearly jumped from his skin, she had come behind him. 'I saw your face in the mirror. I have never seen you so.'

He turned — and saw, the time had come. No more running, no more prevarication.

'Euphemia — I know.'

'Know what?'

'Of you and Everett.'

The blood ran from her face, she backed quickly away. 'What! There is nothing to know.'

He moved towards her, his heart beat hugely. 'It's true I have not been to you — as a husband should.' He made to stroke her shoulder. Was it the sherry? He was filled with warm strength.

She stepped back so she knocked against the wall. In a high voice she said, 'Shall we not kneel down, John, and say our prayers?'

She was like a scared child, he was moved. A voice in his head said, Now, John, now.

'I shall do what you have asked of me — many a time. You shall not leave this house unloved. I shall marry you now.'

'Keep back from me.' She was ugly from fear. 'I'm indisposed. Not now. When I return from Scotland.' Her voice was shrill, would she wake the house?

'Shsh,' he urged, in smiling strength, reaching out to clasp her.

'No!' She had jumped on the bed, and down the other side.

'I like playing chase — oh, I shall catch you.' He reached the door first. 'Come to your husband. This is our wedding night.'

As she darted, he caught her, and hugged her so her chest and arms were squeezed. Leaning back, he lifted till her feet left the floor: she gave a breathless croak. The strength of Samson filled him — I *can* play the man. With a lurch he flung them both on the bed, and laid his weight on top of her.

'No more play. Our bridal night is here.'

She heaved up.

'Be still, woman — or I shall beat you first, and marry you after.'

She was arching and writhing, and glaring with venom. With one hand he held her, while with the other he loosened his trousers. He tugged her skirt and petticoat up. After all, he knew how to do these things — where had his manhood hidden, these years?

'Your lord is here. He will come unto thee.'

Her body jerked, she was panting.

'Be still, and wait.'

She pushed, but he held her. The ceiling trembled.

The lord did not come. Would she see he was red-faced, contorted with fret? If his labour should fail...

'I shall conquer you, lady, and lay you waste. Behold, I shall desecrate your holy of holies.'

With one hand he held her, while with the other he worked on himself. She must not hear his whisper, Oh little pert nose and tiny waist, oh little pert nose and tiny waist.

She lay rigid beneath him.

'Help me, wife. I'm seeking to marry you. Oh, I shall wed you! I shall bind you and take you.' He muttered and strove. Almost angrily he urged her, '*Be* as you were, when I first knew you. *Be* like twelve again. *Help* your husband.' He tried to chuck her under her chin, but her head jerked to the other side. 'Rouse up your lord, so he enters your tent. Tell me what you and Everett do.'

'What!' She pushed with her arms and legs.

He closed his eyes: this was abject. '*Say* the words.' All strength left him, he wanted to weep. '*Help* your poor husby.' He lay back, setting her free.

Coldly she said, as she stood from the bed, 'The time is past when I could help.'

He lay half-curled across the bed. He heard himself cringe, 'Don' leave me all on my owny.' Would he grizzle like a baby?

She stood in the doorway and did not speak.

Buttoning his trousers he sat up on the bed. The picture grew clear.

'So, when you leave here, you are going to him.'

'I'm not going to anyone. I'm taking Sophie home. I'm going to see my parents.'

He saw it was true. He nodded slowly.

'Still there was something. The way we all were — in the house tonight.'

She gazed back steadily. He repeated, 'You're going to your parents' house.'

She looked down. He saw the case.

'And you will stay there?'

Her eyelids stayed down.

He breathed out in a long shrug. 'So be it.' He could not say other: it was too late to oppose, or to seek other ways. He gazed across the room at the empty grate.

He sat, she stood. Eventually he looked up.

'We did have good days.'

Her eyes met his but he saw no feeling.

'You remember when we went to Radetzky's ball — with poor Paulizza. In the gondola we all sang the trio from Gounod. We leaned this way, that way, we nearly tipped the gondola over.'

'It was Donizetti. It was "Linda di Chamonix".'

'And so it was.' He got to his feet, while she backed quickly outside the door.

He lifted his coat from the chair-back. 'If you will allow me to pass, I shall leave this room and not molest you. You may turn the key in the lock if you wish.'

She stepped aside so he could pass.

He stopped at the stairhead. 'I bid you good night. I shall sleep below, on the sofa.' He made a laugh. 'It will be like Glen Finlas.'

He began the stairs. Behind him she faintly said, 'Good night.'

'Rest well,' he said, not turning back.

Through the drawing room window he heard cats squawling. He lay on the sofa and did not sleep.

*

When she came down he was already up, while Sophie, in the hall, stood counting the luggage.

'Some coffee?' he offered. He stood by the pot.

'Thank you.'

'Did you sleep?' he asked presently.

'Hardly.'

'Me neither. But I shall sleep tonight.'

She gave a small, crooked smile. They ate their rolls, till Sophie, with her cape on, said from the door, 'Should we not be leaving? The coach has come.'

As they travelled he looked at neither of them, but outside, at flower-sellers still arranging their buckets, at butchers in aprons beside their big blocks.

'Look, chestnuts,' said Sophie. 'May we stop? Effie. Are you deaf?'

She turned her tired face. 'I am sorry, dearest. I was far away.'

He had the coach stop, and bought them chestnuts. As they continued he stole glances at her, but her face was a wall. He found himself blinking, and turned to his window.

At King's Cross he handed them from the coach. Crawley had already jumped down from the back, and called a porter. They processed to the platform, the trolley creaked behind them.

On the platform they stopped, and he took out his watch. 'These infernal machines are never on time.' He bent down, 'Sophie — be sure you post me the best drawings you do. I shall write down what I think, and send them back.'

'Thank you, John.'

'A pleasure to see you, sir.' A voice haled him from behind.

'Oh — good day to you. It's good to see you.' But he did not remember who this was.

She came beside him. 'You know Mr Keir from Stirling, John? This is my young sister, Sophie, Mr Keir.'

He asked, 'Do you go as far as Perth?'

As they talked the shunted carriages stopped with a jolt beside them. Mr Keir took his leave, Sophie got in, the porter and Crawley went off with the cases.

They faced each other some moments. Gently he said, 'I do wish you well in life.'

'Thank you, John.' She swallowed, briefly the tic clenched her eye.

Crawley came back. Down the platform a stout guard blew a whistle. Doors banged shut and Sophie called, 'Come *in*, Effie. The train will go.'

She faced him squarely. 'Good success with your book.'

'Quickly,' he said. She touched his hand, and jumped aboard.

The carriage shook and clanked, and began to roll forward. For a few steps he walked beside them.

'Bon voyage. Sophie, don't eat too much Edinburgh rock.' He waved his tall hat as the train picked up speed.

'So, Crawley.' He replaced his hat. 'We must find our carriage.'

'Mr John.'

Before the station's great glass hood he paused. A still gold light, a strange peace, rested on London. The street was packed with cabs and horses, yet none at this moment seemed troubled by haste.

They arrived at their carriage, Crawley went to the back.

From the door he called, 'No — Frederick. Come inside. I'd be glad of company.'

Shyly, Crawley climbed in, and sat upright. He himself sat back, for the weariness of the night approached. Absently he watched the metal canopies pass, on the first floor fronts of thin brick houses.

'I shall travel soon,' he said. 'You will be glad to see the Alps again, Frederick? I shall need your help in making my daguerreotypes.'

So — his wife had left him, and gone back to Perth. He leaned into the coach's padded corner, and closed his eyes. He felt, as he had not before, absolute exhaustion. But also, as he sank to rest, deep peace. He thought, it's like the peace of death.

*

He tried not to speak at all as he ate. Let his parents think she was briefly away! Explanations he would handle later.

'You saw them to the station, John?'

'Yes, father. They should be in Edinburgh by nine.'

He turned quickly to his mother, who gazed to him lovingly. 'It is so good that you are dining with us. You will sleep here tonight, won't you, dear?'

'I shall of course. I shall not be much in Herne Hill.'

'Dear John.' She reached across the dishes for his hand, and clasped it. 'Are you happy, John James?'

He nodded briskly. 'I am happy with John's plans for our travels together. The peaks, Swiss villages. I don't know that I can climb as I used to.' He drew in a deep breath, as of Alpine air. 'What the devil is that?'

They all heard the strong ring on the front-door bell.

'Who'd call at this hour? No one is bidden.'

'I cannot imagine, father.' He knew at once, some evil had come.

John James had stood, when old Anne opened the door. 'If you please, sir.'

'Well, who is it?'

'I don't rightly know. They insisted they must speak with you.'

'The devil they did!' He left the parlour. From out in the hall they heard him say 'Sir!' Quiet voices talked, while his mother's eye caught his.

'What can it be?'

He found himself cool. 'Be at peace, mother. Be sure that none of us is under arrest.'

'Well.' John James came back in the room. 'They want you too, John.'

'Of course.' He got up nimbly. So quickly come the blows of fate — much sooner than he had expected. Well, he would meet them.

Two men waited in the hall.

'We are sorry to disturb you, sir. But I believe this letter is addressed to you?'

He saw his name, he would not lie.

'Why, so it is.'

But he wanted to laugh, the men in their black looked so like undertakers. One was lantern-jawed and dry, the other had a plump, cherubic face — a boy-face. He had a high, bright voice.

'I am charged to deliver this into your hand.'

'My thanks.'

'And this packet likewise. If you would be so kind, as to give it to your lady mother.'

'I thank you.'

He saw them out, and went back in the parlour.

'This is for you, mother. We each have a missive.'

John James already had ripped his envelope. 'Do you know what this is, John? You don't seem surprised. Is it a writ? Where are my spectacles? Mags, what have you got?'

But his mother only nervously fumbled her envelope.

In the face of their alarm, he found it easy to sit back lightly, and neatly crack off his envelope's seal. With leisure he extracted the folded paper. In an instant like prayer he closed his eyes. He thought he could read it with composure — but the words jumped, he kept losing his place. He was in a tremble.

His father scowled, almost snarled, as he read. 'The devil's in it. What mad prank's this? You said the woman was out of her senses. Well, don't just smile, sir.'

'I didn't know I was smiling, father.' But he avoided his father's eyes.

His mother shook her packet, which made a metallic chink.

'John darling, you're ill. You've both lost colour. Whatever is it, John James?'

His father held him with biting eyes. 'It only is, my dearest Margaret, that the wretched dame is suing our John — to annul their marriage.'

Did she say 'Mercy'? Her shawls and lace shook, she was all in a flurry. With difficulty she fumbled and picked at the seal.

'Mother, dear.' He took the packet, opened it, and gave it back to her.

'Dear Lord!' With a rattling and chinking she drew out a skein of keys, together with some papers folded small.

'What's this? The keys of the house. Are these her accounts?' She blinked and struggled at the papers with her bad eyes, then said, 'The pauper harlot.' She glared at them both. 'I know what I think.'

'Mother?'

'Good riddance!'

He smiled, but John James cleared his throat. 'You're jumping ahead, Mags. Well, sir, will you look at me?'

In fear he faced his father's eyes. His manhood disappeared, he was a small boy in breeches. He must gather his strength, be firm as iron.

'Well what, father?'

'Don't give me your damned dilettante tomfoolery. Is there truth in what is said here?'

His father's passion made him cool. Intemperate old man, he spat when he spoke. 'What is said there is true.'

John James wound his lips. 'The shame of it — the misery and the shame of it!'

From the end of the table his mother wailed, 'What is it, John, John James. You have utterly lost me.'

'What is it, Mags? *What is it?*' He turned — he had his own sarcasm. 'Dear John — my son — why don't *you* say "what it is"?'

'Certainly, father. You will both understand, when you hear everything.' But his voice had gone high, he must speak lower.

'*Tell* me,' his mother begged. 'Will you both torment me to death?'

He lifted his eyes to hers. 'Effie has sued for the annulment of our marriage, in the Consistory Court of the Bishop of Southwark, on the grounds that I chose never to make her my wife.'

'Make her your wife?' She frowned, bewildered, to John James, whose voice climbed, 'Do you not see, Margaret? On the grounds that this "pauper harlot" as you call her — John's wife — is to this day a *virgin*. Isn't that right, sir? And our dear son here tells us it is true.'

Dear mother, her eyes gaped with disbelief. She swallowed, and frowned. 'John, how can this be? Was she cold and hard to you? There are women, I know, that are — ice, down there.'

'No,' his father cut in. 'The fault isn't in her, I see it right enough. She is a vain silly normal *damned* pretty girl who simply wants — what any girl wants who has blood in her veins. It's our John who is ice down there. Eh sir? We have given our lives for you. And *this* is your gift to us? Did you think, Mags, you might one day have a grandchild? Poor Mags.'

John sat, head down, not moving. I must endure this — in the end he will stop.

'How can this be?' she said. 'Our John is such a handsome man.'

His father rasped, 'We spoiled him, Mags. We spoiled him — absolutely.'

It was clear then what must come next. He stood, and with dignity said, 'May I be excused? I shall go upstairs.' As he walked, he had a trip in his step.

His mother reached out her arms to him. 'Don't go, John.'

His father grunted, head down again with his spectacles on, 'Let him go, Mags. I must read these papers through. So should you.' To himself he muttered, 'We shall be the laughing stock of London.'

His mother's voice rose, 'What do I care for that? He's a prince among men. I gave him such love as no mother has given.'

His father's voice echoed in the hall. 'Did you let him grow up? Or did all your love only keep him a child? What price his "genius" now?'

Her chair-legs scraped as she stood. 'You're wicked. I shall go with my John.' Her rustle and flutter of shawls came after him.

'Aye, aye, go,' his father called. 'Cuddle him close. Pet him to death. If I had whipped him half the times I wanted to —'

They lost his voice as, with her arm round him, and his arm supporting her, they climbed the stairs.

In his room she pressed, so he sat on his bed.

'Dearest John.'

'Mother dear.'

She hugged him close, and he was melting and close to tears.

'Whatever has happened, John, I know it's not your fault. You're such a son as a king would rejoice in. I knew from the first she could not make you happy. She was vain and mean always, and spent all your money.'

'No, mother,' he began — she touched her finger to his lips. He shook his head, he must not melt in her arms.

She moved her fingers through his hair. '*Let* the world mock. We shall stand by you.'

Slowly, in her caress, he leaned curling down and lay on the bed. Still her arm reached and fondled his hair. His mouth fell into its old sucking motion, as if he drank on a straw. He thought, it's true, I am no man at all.

There John James found them. In the doorway he stood with malevolent eyes. But his voice, when he spoke, was not harsh.

'Hear me, John. I shall take these papers to Mr Rutter in the morning. You will come with me. We shall give the best account we can.'

His mother appealed, '*You* go, John James. We must spare our John pain.'

His father tutted, then shrugged. 'Well, I'll go. There's one thing. We must make sure we are all in the Alps, when this thing comes to court.'

His mother rubbed his shoulder. 'Do you hear father, John? We shall endure this tribulation. We shall be far off when the scandal-mongers talk. John James, hold me, and hold John too.'

His father rested a hand on her shoulder, but did not reach to touch him. They stayed so a time, in the room that had for years been his own small bedroom.

10

'The world has heard', Lucy Eastlake said, in her next letter, 'And it has heard awry. As I can, I set matters straight, though I say as little as I may.'

She must then guess what the world had said, for Lucy would not tell all. Nor did Lucy know how the world found out, that when Effie left London, she left John for ever. Nor again did Lucy know — nor could she tell — how the name of Everett got joined in the story.

'Go on,' said the horny-lidded eyes, bright in the spongy ducal face. 'You know what they say? The wise husband doesn't let an artist in the house. Have I got it? A word to the wise, eh?'

'Norman,' Lucy said, 'The case is utterly other.'

'Oh aye? What does "other" mean here?'

'It means more than you could ever guess. It means something that exonerates the lady entirely.'

"Huh! She'd need to be a virgin for that. What? Did I touch it? You blushing, my dear? Uh, I don't believe it. A married virgin in London — in this day and age? Pull the other leg. This high moral cant is all a big sham.'

So Lucy must blush. Had she hinted too much? She turned the conversation. But then she was asked, by others again, whether she knew that this John never 'married' his wife, and that was why annulment was sought. The case would be heard in the Consistory Courts. It would not be contested. The 'wife' would be awarded a large compensation.

To which she said only, 'Her family I know claims no compensation. They have chosen to take the high ground there.'

Necessarily, as Sir Charles's lady, arrayed in her favoured greens and blues, she moved widely — and highly — in Society. Now she conversed with Admirals and Generals, now with Viceroys and Governors, now with Bishops and Judges, now with Duchesses and Ladies-in-Waiting. But whether she bent to whispered questions in a tight box at Covent Garden, or leanly towered between yellow columns in the Egyptian Hall, always she found herself the centre of inquiry. What must she say then, but some part of the truth? For the rumours had swelled. Had she heard this 'quiet' husband went home and beat his wife each week? This was why she fled his house in a scene of broken chairs. To go and live with that dauber Holman Hunt, it was said. The lovers were to meet in the Holy Land. But what could you expect, after the husband's long liaison (all Society knew of it) with that pretend-pious Lady Trevelyan? Sir Walter, poor lamb, had no suspicions.

On hearing these extravagances, she stood so tall as to worry the chandeliers. Still there were some people, to whom the truth could not be told because they could not comprehend it. Her very dear friend, old Lady Charlemont, was indignant on Effie's behalf at once.

'I always knew that behind his simper, the "Graduate" was a bounder. The man gives public lectures. Well, dearest Lucy, you know how the ladies flutter when they go to public lectures. You can imagine what happens, when they take their questions to his chambers afterwards. He has filled the Yorkshire Schools with bastards.'

'No, really, my dear, this is a different case.'

'Buh! There's only one kind of case with men. They all are goats and deceivers and bounders, and none more so than my own ghastly Charlemont — before he went at the knees. Men go at the knees, you know, dear friend.'

'No, dearest, but this case is different. He has never once *sought* to touch a grown woman.'

'Stuff.' The big pale eyes glared at her, and no more could be said.

Nor could Lucy make more headway with the most important personage of all, when the Eastlakes next dined at Windsor Castle.

'Lucy Eastlake — they say you know all.'

'Ma'm.' Lucy, in black-turquoise satin, sank in one of her erect lean curtseys, which brought her eyes only to the same height as her Queen's. Victoria did not mind — the short plump lively woman took her wrist.

'You must tell the story to me.'

With fit reserve, she told.

'Poh! I always thought the man a milksop. And what do you expect, if you let your wife loose with a young painter all summer?'

'Ma'm — Euphemia is my friend.'

'And a handsome woman, too — I remember when she was presented. Do you think nothing went on in the Highlands? If you believe that, you'll believe anything.'

'Her innocence will be proven, ma'm. There will be doctors.'

'Oh aye?' Her Majesty's eyes sparkled merrily. 'I rather

doubt it will go so far as doctors.'

'I think it may, ma'm. I have heard the Court seeks Dr Locock himself.'

'What — my own Physician Accoucheur?'

'So I have heard, ma'm. The lady has been so good as to ask me, if I will chaperone her at the time of the inspection.'

'Indeed.' Victoria fanned herself briskly. 'I hope Charles Locock will be wary. Come, dear man. It was good to talk with you, Lucy.'

Somewhat sharply Victoria proceeded, steering the elbow of her bristling German, who stooped to laugh quietly at something she said.

11

But to have to travel back to London again — and all so that doctors could peer inside her.

'Mrs Gray should be with us,' her father said, as they leaned on the steamer's railings. The day was bright, the sea sparkled like gems, the green Northumberland hills slid past.

'Dear mother,' she said. 'But I am glad to have you with me.'

'Thank you, lassie. But still it were best your mother were by, when you see these *physicians*.'

'When I am seen by them. But Lucy will be with me — she's my closest friend. And I must have you, when we see the lawyers.'

Her father sighed, and buried his sight in the waves. She knew he blamed himself, that they had not the money for more tickets to London.

'Well,' she said with a laugh, 'We have to make the best of it — just the two of us on a loose.' She allowed her elbow to nudge his.

He stood up. 'It's good to see you well, lassie. The sea breeze has put colour in your cheeks.'

She said a long 'Aye', going briefly Scottish. 'Father.'

'Lassie.'

'It wasn't good, I think, that I knew nothing at all of what men and women do — before I was married to John.'

'Aye, lass, I think so too. The world has changed strangely. When I was a lad, we knew too much. It was the time of the Regent — we were all young rips. Now we've become like good babbies, and we bring up our daughters to know no more than babbies. And our sons too, to judge by your John. The truth is, we've caused you years of harm.'

She leaned her cheek on his shoulder. 'Dear father, I know you both meant for the best.'

Side by side they watched the green coast pass, and she stayed, when her father went below. She thought, the future is slow to come, if you travel to meet it by boat.

She was alone, in the prow, when London approached. Before her the brown air thickened to fog, as they pushed between hayboats with vast tarpaulins. Lines of steam-cranes puffed hard clouds, and their own paddles became deafening, with ships pressed close on either side.

'Do ye smell the drains?' Her father had come. 'This is the true real grand auld reekie.'

'We won't smell them for long.' She clasped his hand, while warehouses like fortresses gathered round them, and derricks dropped hooks and looping ropes. Slowly the sense grew that Everett, whom she must not see, was everywhere and nowhere here, like God.

It was then but a day, till they waited together in Bury Street, in the rooms where her family had stayed before. The physicians would come. Lucy had joined them, and stationed herself by the window's sash.

'They have come,' Lucy said.

Her father stood. 'I shall go to meet them.' He went downstairs, and presently they heard the landlady's voice, and men's formal voices in the hall. Then came their deliberate tread on the stairs.

'Oh, Lucy.' She settled herself in the bed, sitting up with her gown around her.

'Be easy, dearest.' Lucy held her arm.

Her father came in with two solemn men, both dressed in black and with nearly-white hair.

'Gentlemen — my daughter, Euphemia. Lady Eastlake has kindly agreed to be present.'

'Hello, Charles,' Lucy said easily.

'Lucy! How are you?' Dr Locock was handsome though plump. 'May I present Dr Lee? Robert, you don't know Lady Eastlake? You will when I tell you who her father was.'

Lucy smiled. 'My maiden name was Rigby.'

'You're the daughter of Edward Rigby?'

'And sister likewise — my brother also is an Edward.'

Her father looked so puzzled that she had to smile. 'They are all obstetric physicians, father. I could not have a better chaperone than Lucy.'

In a ripple of courtesies the doctors took off their coats, turned up their sleeves, and washed their hands from the jug of warm water the landlady had brought.

Dr Locock murmured, 'Mr Gray?'

'Excuse me. Lassie. Lady Eastlake. Gentlemen.' Her father left, the doctors loomed over her — and all at once the bright spirit, which she had tried to keep, fled. Nothing was sure. They were men, and not a friend like Lucy. And John had sharp eyes, after all. What if in some way he had been right? Her body had frozen, it would show — *some* oddity. Nothing escapes a grey doctor's eye.

'You have the speculum?' one said to the other.

She shivered, for Lucy had not used the 'speculum'. What

strangeness would the instrument make?

With dismal faces they drooped close over her, she could not make out what one held in his hand. She was far from home. There must be pain. For her life to be decided, as unknown men peered into her, on a strange bed. Why must obstetric physicians be men?

'If you please — might you just lie back. Be so kind as to undo your gown. Thank you.'

Her legs had clenched, they could not be parted. She stared at the bed-knob over her head.

'If you please?' A man's rough skin grazed the root of her thigh.

'Thank you.'

She did not breathe. His hand was gentle, the metal cold. One doctor had disappeared from her sight, the other stood with a mute, cold face. Then he disappeared, and the first doctor stood, while suave fingers pressed her skin.

'Thank you.' The doctors looked seriously to each other, so she knew there *was* something wrong. She must ask them, and she dare not do so.

Dr Locock bowed. 'I am sorry we troubled you. It must be upsetting. I fear you may be cold. Lady Eastlake?'

Lucy was beside her at once. 'There, my dear, let's wrap you round.'

The doctors washed their hands, and fiddled their cuff-links.

'Will you write the certificate, Dr Locock?'

'Why don't you write it, Dr Lee? I'll sign it.'

They dipped to each other like figures in a comedy. She must not wait longer. She sat forward in bed. 'Forgive me — Dr Locock — Dr Lee — may I ask, did you find me — well?'

They peered towards her from the escritoire.

'"Well"?'

'Did you find me — untoward.'

They looked to each other. Lucy said, 'There have been worries — from the course of the marriage —',

'Ah,' the doctors said as one. They turned to each other and then to her. 'No indeed, you are *well*.'

Well, she thought, what a word is 'well'. They smiled, and Lucy smiled. She smiled herself, then sunlight burst into the room, birdsong, music, the bed she sat on rose in the air, and all the world and London smiled. The sun shone into the room with Everett's face.

The doctors, in the meantime, had turned to her father as he came in the door. 'Mr Gray, sir, we should be on our way.' They had their black coats on. 'We have signed the certificate, and shall send it by messenger to the Consistory Court.' Dr Locock paused, and glanced to her. 'I wonder, may I perhaps read to you what we have said?'

She nodded, and he read precisely, 'We found that the usual signs of virginity are perfect and that she is naturally and properly formed and there are no impediments on her part to a proper consummation of the marriage.'

He bowed, and both doctors shook hands with her father. 'Mr Gray, we wish your daughter well for the future.'

Her father took them down.

'Lucy.'

'I told you.'

But they hardly could speak, before she had sobbed in Lucy's embrace — a sob which changed in mid-breath to a laugh — to the bewilderment of Mr Gray, returning, who stood in the doorway and quietly said 'Hem'.

'Father. Have the doctors gone?'

'Is all well, lassie?'

'Aye, father *deer*.' She was drying her eyes.

'Don't mock the Scottish, lassie. They've signed the certificate. Our work here is done.'

'Then let's awa' — to the Highlands.' She sprang out of bed, and leaned up to kiss the high crown of his baldness.

Lucy had put on her cape. 'I shall leave you for now with your father.'

'Thank you for being here, dear friend.' She followed Lucy to the landing. 'So — the sky is clear.'

'It always was. Your understanding was abused.'

They looked to each other, kissed, and parted.

12

The sweltering July closeness is everywhere. Even the wide khaki Thames looks hot, and offers no coolness under Southwark Bridge, where the bargemen lounge in the shade on their flour-sacks. Out in the sun you stream sweat, even if you do no more than nod to the warehouse-hand working the derrick, as a new sling of barrels rocks up through milky air. From the mill beside the bridge breaks a wet wad of steam.

There is shade in the alley between the warehouses, but neither quiet nor coolness where the carts and wagons jam and holler.

Only, across the way, old black-crusted St Saviour's Church looks to house so much shadow and stillness, there must be cold stone deep within. Yet not only in the nave, but beyond the altar-screen with its pious queue of saints, even at the far back, in the ancient back-Choir, still in this spinney of bony columns the humid air breathes like hot wet wool, so the bevy of lawyers clustered there seems bent on performing a dance of the handkerchiefs, as they forever wipe red brows.

For it is here, once each season, that the Consistory Court comes to temporary life — with chairs from the side-chapels, and tables from the vestry draped in purple. The learned Commissary and his two fellow judges wear no wig or gown, but only black coats and bands at the neck, like the proctors before them. Though Effie's Mr Glennie sweats like a roast, it is John's quiet proctor, Mr Pott, whose finely embroidered handkerchief seems the more sodden and sopping.

A judgement is given, certain proctors and clerks flit away between shafts. The Commissary exchanges a quiet sally with his colleagues, then his pouched eyes glance sharply about.

Mr Glennie has stood. Though his glasses mist white on his tight red head, he makes no pause as he presents to the court a deposition, signed by the lady, 'listing the addresses — and their dates — where they resided together. Further deposing that until recently they shared the same bed.

'Two, Mr Commissary, a deposition from her father, one Mr Gray, a man of law, deposing that the said couple had lived together continuously until the last six weeks.

'And three, Mr Commissary, a deposition signed jointly by Dr Lee and Dr Locock.'

All of which is completed quickly enough, and Mr Glennie sits down puffing. Whereupon Mr Pott has folded his handkerchief, and stood to present but a single paper, signed by John in Lausanne the previous week. The paper is a proxy, in which the said husband records:-

One, that, in so far as he knew, his marriage was valid when solemnized;

Two, that indeed this marriage had not been consummated;

Three — in reply to a question on the Lady's conduct — 'that the Lady's conduct had been without reproach'; and,

Four, that he wished the case to proceed with as little hindrance as possible.

It would seem they have seen these papers before, since the Commissary and his colleagues nod their agreement with only the fewest of whispered words.

The Decree is upon us — the Commissary swallowing preliminary pages, and only pausing at the close to pronounce slowly that,

'Having heard learned counsel, we John Haggard Doctor of Laws do pronounce decree and declare that the said marriage between the said John Ruskin and the said Euphemia Chalmers Gray falsely called Ruskin was had and celebrated whilst the said John Ruskin was incapable of consummating the same by reason of incurable impotency. Wherefore we do pronounce decree and declare that such marriage, or rather show or effigy of marriage, was and is null and void from the beginning and the said Euphemia Chalmers Gray falsely called Ruskin was and is free from all bond of marriage with him.'

Mr Glennie, looking down, has raised his brows high. Mr Pott slightly frowns, gazing up to the vaulting.

Rising in one movement, they both have bowed briefly to the Commissary, and tread stealthily across the sunk graves in the Choir. As they leave the Sanctuary, their heads rock in low-spoken affability.

'You know, Glennie, the father did everything for him. I shall tell him, it's best his son doesn't read the decree.'

'Aye, Pott, he seems a sorry fellow. Let the poor soul write his books. It's well no reporters made their way here today. Have you read a word of him?'

'What, books on the arts? They sound like *The Keepsake*.'

'Hah? You're right, sir.' For once Mr Glennie is possessed with mirth — to the point, as they step into the sweltering sun, that he seems liable to hemorrhage from a broadening guffaw. 'You will walk with me back to Doctors' Commons?'

'If we may pause to have an ice on the way. Otherwise, I

strongly fear, the sweat of our brow will be all that remains of us.'

*

His blood effervesced as he gazed in the face of the high full moon. He could climb on the tiles and skip on the roof-ridge, like a tight-rope walker cutting capers in air.

But back to his table and to his letter:

'This time last year there seemed no more chance of what has happened than that the moon should fall, and now you are Miss Gray again. If you could see me I am sure you would pity me for I am scarcely able to write commonsense I am so bewildered.'

So long he had hung, outside the shut door of her marriage. Now, like a miracle, that marriage had vanished. It had gone from the past, as well as the present. Always, truly, she had been Miss Gray.

He looked round the room, at the drawings and paintings pulled out of his portfolio. Against the chairs, against the wainscot, he had stood them in the moonlight — of her in the boat with him, of her sewing, of her seated by the water. The even perfect hollow curve of her profile.

'By the by what am I to do with the little portrait I did of you with the foxgloves? I never sent it to him — This will appear to you an absurd thing to talk about, but I am so crazed with trying to realize your freedom that I am simply unequal to express myself. It is past twelve o-clock — for I could not attempt to write to you till they had all gone to bed — and I have not said one thing I would wish.'

Again he stood, then hurled himself down on the chaise long. His future was clear, there were no big choices still to make. His heart gave a solemn beat.

He sat up — and faced the portrait of John. So, that would stay unfinished. A pity, but it was part of the past.

Back at his table he wrote with decision, 'I feel half frightened at the thought of meeting you again, like the time when you returned to the cottage after visiting your parents.'

There were questions too. For they could not call the banns in some church the next day. The world would say 'Ah! Now we know why she ran from that marriage.' The scandal must be allowed to die.

But that too was the future: this was a moment outside time. He walked in the room, shaking his head and sighing.

Birdsong kindled. Away in the east, the dark blue had turned brown.

'If I remain up much longer, I shall hear Elsie come in to lay breakfast downstairs. So I must finish this. Write me a line by return of post. If I have done wrong in writing to you take no notice of my letter.'

Finally he sealed it. He looked at it, kissed it, sighed, put it down: then picked it up, looked at it, and kissed it again.

13

Now they were back, he did not want to delay. Still it was he who dragged his feet at the threshold — of the large room hung with water-colours, where top-hats nodded and bonnets dipped to picture-frames.

'Come on, John. No hesitations.'

'Quietly, father, please.' Did the old man need to speak so loudly? He must be growing deaf.

'Quietly? We have lain low for weeks. We mustn't seem *furtive*.'

John winced at the noise. 'They won't call *me* furtive. They will know, I have come to review the Show. I just don't want to bang about.'

'Mmff.' His father entered ahead of him, firing hot glances round the room. John followed on soft feet.

'Let's start with dear Cattermole.' John led them to a study of crumbling buttresses, gravestones at angles beneath the yew trees — a country churchyard.

'He knows his Old English so well.' He gazed intently at a weathered finial.

Stepping carefully behind cooing ladies in silks and chuckling ministers in shovel hats they passed down a wall of placid rivers, mellow manors, aged oak-trees.

'Would you call it a good year, John?'

'No, father. The feeling in all of them is too much the same.'

A man with a thrusting beard, importantly reading out the catalogue to his family, paused, and straightened, and stared at them. Well, he thought, it was simply a matter of time.

'What of this church, John. Wouldn't you say the perspective is wrong?'

'Yes, it is, father — oh, but look how the ivy seems to flutter. *That's* brushwork. I couldn't do that.'

The ripple in the ivy passed through the room. Lorgnettes and eyeglasses were turning to them, and bright eyes sparkled through gossamer veils.

'Do let's get on, father' — the old man would dawdle by any bright sunset — 'Oh, for a picture which actually caused me to stop and *think*.'

There were puzzled faces also. A tall ensign across the room frowned, while the young woman beside him talked in his ear. They turned sharply away when he looked back.

'They see us, and don't see us, in the Hell of Eyes.'

'What's that?'

'Nothing, father. But I see we still are the talk of the town.'

'We knew they would talk, John. Courage now. Look, there's David Roberts.'

'Oh my stars, the worst painter in England. Let's go the other way. I can do without *his* condolences.'

'By no means. Behave, now. Good afternoon, David.'

'Good afternoon, sir — hello, John.' The grey-haired, dark-tanned, lean man came. 'I'm glad to see you. You're well?'

'You're showing here, David?'

'One has to, I think. You'll find my Bedouins in the next room.'

They shook hands. From round the room, shy glances came flitting like bats. Well, he thought, let's make it theatre. After all, he was known, and David Roberts was known.

Nor would Roberts beat about the bush. 'John, forgive me — I must tell you all my thoughts are with you. You have endured much. I am glad you are here.'

His eyes pools of sympathy he leaned in close and held John's hands, tightly, warmly. Nearby conversations paused. A crimson Indian major, who evidently gathered that something was up, frowned about him in puzzled jerks.

John quietly said, 'There is pain for all — but it had to be.'

'I'm sorry.' The brown man shook his head sombrely.

His father at once came clattering in. 'John's modest as ever. The truth is, we hurried to make an end of it. John was trapped into marriage. He *was* engaged, you know, to a Countess with a chateau. But that scheming Scotch minx — well, her father had lost all their money in the railways. She had to catch someone.'

'Dear father —' He raised a hand, so his father should pause, but the old man would not stop. 'I did the needful. My Margaret and I had both agreed, that John should be bothered as little as possible. At all costs his work must not be interrupted. But look, John is pale. Do you want to sit down? David, we bid you good afternoon. You understand, this isn't the place —' He spoke too loudly as he looked round fiercely, at nearby motionless backs of necks.

They shook hands with Roberts.

'Come along, now, John, we've been here long enough.' His father was all impatience to get him from the room.

'Not so soon, father. I still must make notes for my review.'

The pictures — he took out his notebook, but in any case

he could not attend for the pictures themselves would not keep still. The branches of old oaks uncoiled claws. A crimson thread slid from twig to twig, and slipped like a snake inside his eye.

'It's time to go,' his father fretted. 'Come along, John. You're white as a sheet, and we've shown our metal.'

'*Please*, father. I am a critic of art. You go if you must. I shall follow my calling.'

He turned now to a delicate wash — of beautiful silver-mauve folds in the clouds — but darkness boiled behind the paper. His skull split with headache. Behind him the dowager murmured a phrase to the bishop. The officer whispered it to the pig-iron merchant, whose mother-in-law said the words aloud. At first he strained to make it out, but soon he knew — there could be no doubt.

'Incurable impotency.'

He turned and all the room looked at him — boldly or blinking, through monocles or spectacles or the sticks of fans, with a scowl, with derision, with a leer, with deep pity, they cried it aloud,

'Incurable impotency.'

He returned to the clouds, but now they boiled, erupting from the picture frame. They made smoke in his head, and when he turned yet again he saw that the crowd had drawn up in a line. In black or brown coats, in light shawls or bell-skirts, they tipped and rocked. They bent at the knees with their hands on their hips, or stuck their thumbs in their ears and made children's grimaces. In the centre of the line a chimney sweep grinned as he brandished his brush. A black cat arched on his shoulder and hissed.

'Incurable impotency,' they cried as one.

'John, you're not well at all. Quickly, we must get you

home. Your mother was right, we should never have let you go out.'

Meekly he let himself be led to the door. On the steps he stopped. Though the sky was clouded, its whiteness was blinding.

'Come *along*, John.' His father tugged at his arm. He would fall in the street — but had he gone blind?

Turning briefly he glimpsed the lethargic crowd, jawing on as ever, beneath the high rows of all the water-colours which he had not had time to see.

14

'You don't mean the man is coming here,' William said.

'He insists on it.' He tightened the clamps which held the portrait to its easel. 'He need only come once, and the picture's done.'

'But after his wife has got "engaged" to you. As you put it.'

He took up his china palette, and began to place colours. 'I doubt he knows that. We have told very few.'

'He will know. Well, it's his funeral. But coming here, to be told by you how he should stand — after the tricks you played in the Highlands. Was he blind?'

The palette trembled in his hand, cold fury seethed. William *must* be frivolous. 'Nothing wrong was done in the Highlands. And she left him because her marriage was misery. Anyway, he's coming today for the hands.'

'The hands?' They turned to the portrait, where all was complete, except for two small spaces to either side of the coat.

'I offered to use someone else's hands. But no, he wrote, it must be his own paws. *I* don't want him here. He'll come and be bland like a sheep made of sugar, and then, at some stage, he'll play his games. I loathe the man so I could throttle him.'

'Don't you think he wants to throttle you? My stars, the show you both make of this precious daub, while you hate each other to death. And this marriage to his wife. Thank God you've put it off, at least. Next summer, right? That's a breathing space.'

'Don't take that tone. And she was never his wife. Still, we had to wait. It would all look wrong, if we bolted off to Gretna Green. Nor should we meet in the shadow of John. It *is* a long time, but she must be sure. We must both be sure.'

'Be sure?' William frankly scoffed. 'For God's sake come to your senses, man. It will look all wrong next year as well. It will look all wrong to the end of time.'

The hand that held the palette shook. 'Don't try me, William.'

'Don't try you? Do you think I'm scared, as the others are? Because of your "fame". The point is, do not make this match. You should turn your back on the whole sad story. You were his "protégé", and you're still not free. Fine, you turn your back on him. But let his lady go as well. You're like the story of the apprentice, gone wrong. The apprentice should marry his master's daughter. Instead you've run off with your master's wife. And that will make scandal, from Land's End to John o'Groats. Do you think the family will stand for that? Ask father. Ask mother. Ask Colonel Millais, ask the cousins and aunts. That's why not one of us is going to be there. Turn your back on that mess for the love of God, and find a woman all your own. Or she and the past will dog you for ever. Do you think you can ever set up house in London? Wake up, man. Lead your own life. Let her go.'

It was too much. Of itself the china palette left his hand, dashing for William's head with its load of cobalt and madder. William ducked, and the china shattered, pitting the wall-paper, while a clotted slime of red, blue, yellow and green oozed in long tracks towards the wainscot.

'Blast! *Blast!* BLAST!' He strode up and down. 'Get out of here! You silly fatuous *ordinary* man. Never come back.'

'Oh, I've gone.' William was half-way out of the door. 'You'd better calm down before your customer comes. You look like a bad actor.' He clumped downstairs.

Surveying the mess, he stood clenching, unclenching his hands. It was pure mistake to speak to William.

A palette, a palette. He rummaged behind his drawing-boards, and pulled out an old wooden oval with its thumb-hole. The cracked crusts of dried colour were furry with dust. He rubbed it with turpentine. But to use my first palette, to finish John — let it be a good omen for the portrait.

There were noises downstairs — while a many-coloured puddle grew on the floor. He set his mouth: he half-saw already John's accusing stare. And still he had time to open the portfolio with his drawings of her. He snatched a glance at her pensive sweet face, mouthed 'I love you', and closed it again.

They were at his door. 'Yes, old lady?'

'Your subject is here, dear. Oh — oh! William said you had an accident.'

'Yes — when you go down, do please send Elsie with the mop. John, come in.'

John entered slowly. He was grave as at a funeral, erect, even stately. He ignored the spilled paint.

'Good day, Everett.'

He did not hold out his hand, but stayed near the door, his cape still fastened, pale with reserve. Everett met his fever-eyes.

'Do get along,' he said to his mother. 'So John — your hands.'

As if he came to from reverie, John started. 'Oh — yes — hands are important. The hands' — he held his own before him — '*are* the man.'

They stood some moments, in which John waited balefully.

'John, please take your cape off.'

'Yes.' John moved slowly. There was a tremor in his elbows, as he folded the cape neatly and set it across a chair. He looked up, blue-eyed. 'Oh, I'm sorry.'

'Why is that?'

'I didn't bring my old hat — don't I need to be holding it?' He was suddenly at a loss.

'Don't concern yourself — look, I've painted the hat. For now you can hold another one.' He wondered, will John play the child?

'But can I? Will it look the same?'

'Let's start, I've got my palette ready. I had an accident with the other one.' He winced as he nodded towards the wall.

'Oh, Everett,' John laughed, 'Your "accidents".'

Shortly he said, 'John, please stand still' — John was full of small movements, as though insects, inside his clothes, ran up his limbs — 'I'll do the right hand first. Take the cane, if you would.'

'Ah! Your father's cane — once more in my hand.' John gripped it, swung it once in the air, and planted it hard on the floor. He lifted his head. 'Am I standing right?'

'That'll do — no, bring your hand this way.' He darted forward to adjust John's cuff, and, without thinking, touched John's fingers. Stepping back, he saw that John had frozen. He breathed through his mouth.

There was a tap on the door. Everett opened it to a flustered small figure.

'Oh, Elsie. Yes, it's over there. Here, take some turpentine, use that first.'

Little Elsie limped in, with a big pail of soap and hot water. The tiny cap, pinned to her curls, bobbed as she crouched low by the wall.

Brush in hand, he stared at John's fingers, lightly curled about the head of the cane. Presently John said in a sing-song voice,

'Have you ever seen mountains, Elsie? I was in Switzerland this summer.'

Elsie gazed up with timid eyes.

'The Matterhorn there is an enormous peak — and do you know what I did? I lifted my coat-tails and slid down the slope — just as I used to when I was young.'

Elsie giggled, she had excited eyes. Everett gave a sharp cough. 'I'll lay in your left hand now. Hold *this* hat, if you would.'

'My, Elsie, your master *is* working fast. Look, he's "laid in" my right hand in the time it took to scrub the wall.'

'Thank you, Elsie,' he muttered. Blushing, and with a clanking curtsey, Elsie dipped so the pail banged the floor, and left.

'*Look* how well she cleaned it!' John said. 'Now there's clever hands! She *does* have a small build, doesn't she? But can you paint both my hands in one day? I shouldn't want you to hurry.'

Tersely he said, 'John, it's all right. Can you let your fingers curl — just as they will.'

Gradually John eased his fingers. The small hand looked delicate, it could be a woman's. Everett studied it closely, and for a time the only sound was the soft scratch of bristle on canvas.

'Everett —'

'A moment, John.'

'Did I speak amiss? You sounded quite gruff.'

His eyes rose to John's, which were liquid, soulful. 'John, it's best I concentrate. We can talk afterwards — if we must.'

'Yes, but I wanted to help your work.' John let his pose go and waved the cane. 'Because, Everett, you mustn't think that I mind *very* much now — what you and a certain lady did many moons since.' His voice was airy, his eyes were arch.

He looked hard at his palette. 'We had better not speak of the lady.'

'Oh, but why ever not? My own wife, as I thought. I have suffered, it is true — great pain, be it told. But I have travailed in my spirit, and prayed long and hard, and, in short, I'm happier now. I was young and foolish when I wed.' He shrugged blythely.

'I can't take it so lightly. The lady suffered greatly at your hands.'

'Oh, come now.' John laid the cane down. 'She went to all the balls they gave in Venice, and had a merry time shopping as well — on the allowance my father gave her.' His eyes grew roguish. 'She chatted for hours with each gentleman caller.'

He gripped the paint-brush so his nails hurt his palm. 'I beg you, John —'

'Oh dear!' John pretended to duck. 'Will you throw this palette at me?'

Deliberately he set down brush and palette. 'For both our sakes, John, I think it's best we don't speak of the lady — or of the past — or of her and you —'

'And what of the future?' John inquired. 'Will you tell us of that.'

He looked at John, looked down, then quietly asked, 'Do you want this portrait finished, John? We can do that today. Or we can leave it — for good. Here, you can take it with you now. Any good painter can add the hands.' He began to undo the clamps.

'Add the hands?' John's voice rose. 'That would not do at all. For shame, Everett, that you should think such a thing. So. Well then, let us keep mum, and silent as mice — of important things.

Look, I've taken my pose again. Oh, but where's the cane? Do I need it still, now you are about my left hand?'

'It's best that everything is as it was. Yes, let the cane be there. Besides, I shall come back to your right hand.'

He re-set the clamps, and took his brush. Almost at once they were as they had been, with John standing motionless before him. From his distance he examined John's small, soft knuckles.

John seemed presently to be at rest in his pose. Everett quietly continued painting, while the light from the large windows wheeled in the room. From time to time, from outside, came the clash of horse-shoes on stone, and the creak of carriage-springs. When he said 'Rest' John yawned, stretching his arms.

'You are close to finishing?'

'Nearly there — will you look?'

John pursed his lips. 'Mmm. I shall wait till we arrive.' First one then the other, he stretched his legs before him, like a dancer toeing the floor. 'A touch of cramp. But since we've paused, you can tell me — what else are you painting?'

'Oh.' He was unprepared, the question seemed innocent. 'Well, there are other portraits. It's true I also have a "subject".'

'May I see it?'

'It isn't finished.' He nodded to an easel across the room, on which a loose cloth hung.

'I still am curious. If I may, Everett?' He spoke as though they were in no way at odds.

'Oh — but of course, John.'

He removed the cloth, and John, who had come close, stepped back again.

'This is no Deluge! Good Heavens! Is the world on fire?'

'I saw a fire.' He was lost a moment, remembering. 'I saw firemen die — from bravery.'

'Everett!' John was motionless. The left side of the picture was incandescent, not yet complete: white canvas showed through stripes of flame. Out of the inferno a fireman, wearing a gleaming helmet, carefully trod down burning stairs, while a boy in a night-shirt hung round his neck. Under his arm he held a small girl, whose legs kicked behind her as she stretched for her mother, who stood on the bottom step reaching out, while all love and thankfulness showed in her face. The fireman was handsome and serious. Through a window half blocked by smoke, you saw a night sky over roof-tops.

'It is — superlative,' John said. 'Who has caught firelight so exactly? On skin, old and young, and on different materials. And then the contrast of the fire's rage with the coolness of night out there.'

'I meant it as a tribute to those brave men — and to all who do such work.' He gazed at his own painting. 'I have become an auxiliary.'

John blinked.

'I go to the fire-station some nights a week. Sometimes I ride with them to a blaze. They don't let me do much. I hold the hose — or the horse. Still, I've seen everything from close to. Look, I brought my hat home — for the reflections.'

From a shelf he brought down the shining-black, crested helmet.

'It's made of hard leather like a sailor's hat. Then, in the black lacquer, everything shines.'

He turned the leather helmet, so the reflections of the windows in it smoothly stretched and curved.

John's finger momentarily touched the hat. 'I did not know you got so close to your work.'

'I don't know that I did. I have changed a little, I think.'

John gleamed to him. 'We all change, whether we will or

no.' He turned back to the painting. 'Of course, you know, one might ask where her husband is? Could he not have brought the children down, before the fire had got so far?'

'Well, well.' Everett moved his hand with annoyance. 'The husband is — away. The children were upstairs — the fire caught quickly —' He fumbled, and saw John watch him fumble.

'What will you call it?'

'I thought, "The Rescue".'

...all love and thankfulness showed in her face.

'Good, Everett. You like the thought, I think, that you rescue women in distress.' John's look was abruptly merciless.

'John!' Did John *want* for them to come to blows? Fisticuffs in the studio, the lover versus the abandoned husband. But John went on at once,

'By the way, did you know my man Crawley has had to wed?'

He stared, then said, 'You mean — young Crawley's to be a father?'

'It's our chamber-maid, of course. What do you expect? But it isn't only our servants who have — hot underclothes.' His blue stare was frank, a prosecutor in court.

Everett bit his lip a moment, then coldly said, 'I thought you had come to like "sensual animality".'

'Oh!' John gave a yelp. His eyes glinted brightly.

Everett went on, 'But I'm glad — for Crawley's sake. Give him my congratulations.' He smiled, his mood warmed.

'*Your* congratulations! But I'm not glad of it. There will be noise in the house. That Ruby of his sets the chairs all awry. She drops the cutlery.' John sighed, and returned to 'The Rescue'. 'But as to your latest work — the brushwork is *wonderful*. The flame-tips. The woman's face. The reflected lights everywhere. As a technician of optics you are *transcendent*. Thank you for showing it to me.' He waved for the cloth to be replaced.

Looking back at his picture, as he brought the cloth down, Everett thought, John is right, I also have helped rescue — someone.

'A-hem!' John waited. 'The final lap, I expect?'

'It may be, yes.'

He bent closer to his canvas, for the daylight had begun to dim. John coughed once of twice, and cleared his throat.

'You won't guess where I'm bidden tomorrow.'

'Mm?' he inquired. He had one brush between his teeth, while he painted with another.

'I see the Chair of the Trustees of the National Gallery.'

'I thought you were always round there, John.'

'Oh no, this is a special meeting. They are drawing to a conclusion on a matter of' — he spat the word — 'obscenity'.

'Obscenity?' He lifted a brow. What new cut would come from John? But John was still again, his brow knit in thought. Then he sighed, and seemed again at ease in his pose.

'There.' Everett stepped back, and laid his palette on the table of paints.

John looked up shyly. He asked, 'It's finished?'

He took a great breath. 'I can't do any more to it.'

John rested the cane. At his leisure he came, and stood by Everett.

Finally he said, 'Oh, Everett — *that* is a portrait.'

Side by side they gazed at it. It was far from all fires, and keen with cold light. The white torrent frothed and churned gold brown, while the humping rocks shone silver with lichen. In the centre, the mild man towered on his crag: he wore smart black over teeming water. His face was keen and not unkind, his blue eyes gentle as the Saviour's. His hands were small and ladylike. He looked pale, you might say ill with thinking, but he stood erect. You might say, here's a *noble* man.

John's voice was hoarse when he said at last, 'I must say — in all the circumstances — I'm proud you discovered this man in me.' He coughed a small laugh. 'I almost don't mind how he hides those fine rocks.'

Everett found he too was hoarse. 'That's the John that I admired.'

'Thank you, Everett.'

'So.' John stepped back. 'You will dispatch the canvas to Herne Hill? I shall arrange for my father to send a draft, then we shall discuss how we may exhibit it.'

'Yes,' he said, in an exhausted voice. The tirednesses of many months' painting were collapsing together on him.

At leisure John fastened the clasp of his cape.

'Everett, though painful considerations have come between us — I hope they may not end *all* our intercourse.'

He woke. 'Intercourse — what do you mean?'

John's hand wandered in air. 'I should like to feel we can still at times meet — and talk together — on questions of art —'

'What questions?'

'More —' The hand fluttered here, there, like a moth at a loss. 'I have dared to wonder, whether you might design me a piece — for my classes in the Working Men's College. Something to carve in wood or stone.'

'I'm not a sculptor.'

'Oh, you're wrong.' All at once the stray hand seized Everett's shoulder, and gripped tight, digging in. 'Remember how we worked together in the cottage, when you drew the kissing angels — when a certain party was away. You have both architect and sculptor in you. I *know* it. Be my pupil yet. In spite of all. It still can be. Given my guidance, you may be *great*.'

With energy Everett pulled the hand away, and, as best he could, threw it from him.

'After all that has happened, how could we possibly meet to speak?' His strength had gathered, he stood solid as a new-built house. 'Understand me, John, because I understand you. You mean to show me that what happened with Effie doesn't matter — because to you she did not matter. To me she is everything — that she wasn't to you. It is best we part now. I shall say no more.'

John still was rubbing his wrist. 'You hurt me, Everett. That wasn't kind. I shall leave, as you ask. But take note of this.' His lips worked a moment, then he too set his shoulders. He stood taller, you could think lightnings played round his head. Everett thought, he will denounce me again, call my story-pictures mawkish, say my talent is for turning art into cash. But John drew breath — and then spoke seriously, quietly.

'I was not wrong in the dream I had. With your genius for painting and mine for ideas we could have made works greater than yours or mine alone will ever be. Never mind Raphael, pre- or post-. We could have led in England a new Renaissance. It will not happen now as it might have done. Neither you nor I should rejoice at that.'

He stopped there, and only looked at Everett steadily, till Everett dropped his eyes again. He thought, and presently said,

'That may be true, John. As you say, it cannot happen now. I do not rejoice at it.'

'Well — well.' John gave an enormous shrug — then smiled. 'In any event, you will know my thoughts. I shall review you, never fear. I shall mark your progress — let us pray it be good.'

Were the words double? But he said, 'Thank you, John. And I shall read what you write of art.'

'Then I may thank you.' John started down the stairs, but continued to speak. 'In truth, I do not know if I shall write more of art.' He gave a long sigh. 'In these past months I have had much to think of — during my *exclusion* from society. I have been derided by all, and, worse, I have been *pitied*.' They turned to the street door. 'I was not made to be a martyr. But it has been given to me to feel, how those estranged from Society feel. The excluded, the helpless, the miserable.'

He opened the door himself — though Everett had reached for it — and stood a moment with the bright street beyond him.

'Of what will you write, John, if not of art?'

John spun back with eyes like lamps. 'Of social justice, Everett. I was half a Communist before all this, and by God I have a mind to go all the way now.'

He was so surprised he could only exclaim, like some shocked dowager, 'A *Communist*, John?'

'Aye, and a red-hot one!' He smiled, seeing Everett's jaw had dropped. 'Well, but a part of me is Tory still.' He held out his hand. 'Shall we make the gesture?'

'Of course.'

He was surprised still by the muscle in John's grasp. John's face, close to his, was pale and worn, yet also urgent, then teasing and coy like a child in delirium. As their hands held, John's different souls came and went quickly.

'God be with you,' John said, starting nimbly down Gower Street.

'And with you,' he called.

John waved, but did not look back.

Dearest, he murmured, re-climbing the stairs, How came you ever to be with him? That marriage seemed more than ever impossible. But already he was forgetting it, as though it belonged many years in the past. She was a free young woman: and she was his now.

15

He looked at his portrait, where it hung on his wall, then thought, but what vanity — to set the picture of myself above my own mantle-piece. He had hung it there, where the light was good, so as to examine well Everett's work. In the first days he had allowed himself sometimes to think, Well — that is not a bad-looking man. But his thought was now, How sad it is, that all I have left from my marriage, and the great friendship — as I thought — of my life, is a single picture — of myself alone.

Was any man alone as he was alone? Before, he had almost never been by himself. At school, at Oxford, in London, in Venice, his days were busy with more friends than he wanted. Now he had fallen from Society. He did not want to go out, nor was he much invited. Were they sparing him, his 'friends' — sparing his shame? He had committed no sin, yet he was disgraced. He had become a curiosity. Nor could he tell whether people looked oddly at him because of his story, or simply because his worn face said — Distress. And what was so untoward? So he kept his wife six years a virgin — our Lord Jesus was a maiden man. His Mother was virgin, yet She bore Him.

The house was quiet, Crawley and Ruby had gone to bed. He was glad of their company, but they were like nephew and niece to him, and could not be closer. Little Sophie was long gone, the young light of the house.

He stood. He was not tired, and he had time, if he wished, to write more pages — or read more pages — or to study the new missal, which he had bought with his father's help. He had time for all those things he had wished to do more of, when he was burdened with a wife. And now that time hung useless on him, like a suit of clothes many sizes too big.

'I am — lonely,' he said over. His eyes smarted, he could weep with self-pity — but he had done that, too, many times these months. His society was his parents, and he was weary to death of spending every night there.

Walking without aim between the rooms, he heard again the strange cry he heard sometimes at night. He thought of banshees, ghosts — what spirits haunt the dark? Then came a knocking, something wooden cracked and broke.

Quietly he turned the back-door key, and stepped outside. There was a radiant full moon, so he saw clearly the fruit-trees, the lawn, the rustic table and chairs they had put out for their summers. The light was silver and without colour, it laid an even beauty everywhere. Then again came the cry, or roar — it was muffled but filled with pain. It came from behind their garden wall.

He had brought the large key to the back-garden gate: the rust-crusted wards scraped as he turned it. Cautiously he pushed the gate back, and stepped into the mews behind the houses. He saw no one at first. There was a place, at the end of the lane, where the rubbish from all the houses got piled. Between clearances it could grow to a mountain, but what was wrong, as he looked, was that the mountain moved. Were there five people there? Seven — a dozen? In old torn clothes with sacking lagged round their heads. If they turned and saw him in the moonlight...

They moved stealthily, but he heard rasping wood, tearing

fabric, a clang of cast iron. Methodically the scavengers were sifting the rubbish, he made out the heaps of what they took. They had small carts, old perambulators. One of them moved wildly, shaking and hitting — he could not tell if they were boy or girl, but something was wrong, there came a hoarse snarling with no clear words. All the time a man's voice answered steadily — a father perhaps? He saw the large vague shape, stooping and burrowing as he talked.

Till the cry, or roar, came again. The wild figure hurled its head: it loped towards him, braying. He saw it was a girl — as she saw him, and stopped. She was mis-shapen, with one eye lower in her cheek than the other: the ooze from her mouth shone in the moonlight. Seeing him she grunted, surprised and frightened. Behind her, the scavengers had stopped their work. They had turned towards him. Their faces were blotched with cold, bruises, dirt, so he could not make out their features. He feared — would they rush at him?

One of them came, the others turned back to their sorting and searching. He was huge as a bear and shapeless in rags, his right arm ended in a frightening hook. Ignoring John, he muttered soothingly to the girl so her noise sank to a whimpering bleat. Then you saw that he looked shapeless because he wore three coats, ripped in huge tears that gaped over each other: inside them was a tall, lean man. The hook in his hand was a warehouseman's grapple, which he must use as a tool in his sifting.

So there were no banshees, there was no danger. They were strangers to him, he was nothing to them. When the man straightened, he touched his forehead to John, and took the girl's elbow to help her back.

'Stay.' Had he spoken? He surprised himself. 'Would you care for — refreshment?' The girl was still, the man stared. 'Thirsty work?' He nodded towards the heap.

Ahead of them he walked back through his garden gate, and left it wide open. He did not look back. He went into the scullery, and found a loaf and milk and wine, and brought them out to the garden table. The man and girl stood in the gate, with someone else beyond. He gestured towards the moonlit table, and cautiously they came. He went back in the house for a corkscrew, plates and beakers, and found a large cheese and a ham, and brought these too.

He held a rustic chair for the girl, then sat himself, and motioned for those who found chairs to sit. By now they were joined by two or three more. A young man wore a soldier's tunic, with the frogging torn and hanging loose. Another, in a wide country smock, proved to be an elderly woman, emaciated, with eyes like ferrets, hungry and wary. She took the cheese and by hand broke off a large piece.

He nodded to the grapple that lay on the table. 'You've worked in the docks?'

'Aye, a spell. The docks, the shipyards. The cokeyards too.... I was down at the Arsenal — for a spell. It's difficult, leaving her alone.' He nodded to his daughter, who leaned clinging to him.

'Yes,' he said. He had still his gentleman's reserve about prying, and his guests were wary. He saw they were ready to run out through the gate, if someone in the house should give the alarm. Did they think he was deranged, an eccentric relative who slipped his bonds at night? He caught them nodding to each other, exchanging looks and hidden grins.

He filled the man's glass, and his own. 'Good health,' he said, 'To you, your daughter.' He turned to the soldier, who he now saw had lost an eye.

'The Crimea?'

They were not at ease, but he found he was. He had no

fear, though the long knife he brought lay on the table. Here was society's other side. I shall dine with the abandoned tonight. He knew they would not stay long with him.

The full moon shone on the curious party. By its silver light they came and went, giving up their chairs to others who came. A man on two short wooden legs came in — they gave him better balance, perhaps, for he stood waist-high. He wore at an angle a battered top hat, which evidently he had found among the rubbish.

'It's a fine night to be sure,' his Irish voice said, 'Good evening to you, sir.' With a sudden deft twist he swung himself onto a chair.

'You are welcome to my table,' said John. 'A glass of hock?'

*

He was descending from an omnibus at the National Gallery, when he glimpsed her. At the foot of its steps the milling crowd parted, and he saw her for a moment, attended by family. But who could she be? She was nearly a woman, but slender as string. Her dead-white, perfect face was pinched, with enormous solemn little-girl's eyes. Something was wrong — he thought of that illness when girls never eat. She had a nobility, she was touched by death. His heart stopped as he knew — such a woman I could love with a grown man's love.

But the parting crowd closed, she was already gone. He looked up at the sky, where a dark cloud lifted. He should not think of love, this fateful day: important work waited. He climbed the steps of the Gallery.

In the lobby he found no delegation of Trustees. That's poor, he thought. They hide their heads from the harder duties. Wornum was there, however, flushed but sombre.

'Good day, sir — I hope I see you well.'

'Well enough for our work, I think. You in good health, I hope?'
Wornum led them down stairs. 'Your writing goes well, sir?'

'It has taken — a turn. I am writing a book not for
connoisseurs, but addressed to the working people of England.'

'You don't say.' Wornum fingered his lips. 'Smith, Elder
like the plan?'

John gave a sharp glance. 'I shall find a publisher. And if
not — still the book will appear. I have the means, I think.'

'No doubt. Well. And here are the drawings.' They paused
in a corridor by a small table.

'I believe they are all there.' Wornum opened the portfolio,
and together they leafed through it. As the yellowing papers
slid past his eyes plump buttocks rose like rising dough,
breasts globed and glowed like juice-packed fruit. Scents
started in his nostrils — civet, roses, the body's sweat.
Members stood like castle towers, then leaned as further
drawings came, spread legs, lewd hands, the lower lips... And
everywhere the folds and bulbs were drawn as well as sin
could wish, the Devil and genius hand in hand.

'Yes, that's my list,' John said.

Wornum opened the door into a small, enclosed yard,
where a brazier had been placed. A man in a buff tunic stood
by with a poker.

'Morning, Bigsby,' Wornum called, 'Not a nice day.' Low
torn clouds drove fast overhead, gusts snatched at the
drawings when he opened the portfolio.

'Better give them a twist,' Bigsby said. 'So they get truly burnt.'

When the drawings were twisted they were like Christmas
bon-bons, but still you saw, at their ends, bent bits of
women's bodies. A stout member looped like a snake from
his dreams. A woman's sex grinned like a mouth. He felt a
spasm of hatred for all coupling, rutting brutes.

'Press them down, Wornum. We must get them all in.'

When the brazier was full, Bigsby took out a box of lucifer matches. Wornum shook his head. 'And these from our finest painter ever.'

'I knew great Turner,' John said. 'I called him a friend. And yet there was a mad, bad part of him. He will be the greater when these scars are gone.'

Wornum nodded. 'And the law is the law. These are unclean works.'

Still they paused. Looking up, John saw at black windows grey faces pressed close — elderly faces, with mustachios or beards, who retreated when he found their eyes.

Bigsby held the matches to Wornum. 'Will you, sir?'

Wornum looked to John. 'Sir?'

John made a demurring movement. 'Mr Bigsby — please.'

Bigsby struck a match, so small flames of phosphorus danced on the box. When the match blew out, he bent close to the brazier.

'Would you step up, gentlemen, so we stop the wind?'

The three men stooped close round the brazier, while Bigsby pushed flaring matches through its holes. The flames took and blazed, so presently they all must stand back from the scorch.

He stared into the heart of fire, where breasts withered and shrivelled. Fat buttocks crumbled. A penis, in the curling paper, turned to black lines on a white sleeve of ash, which hovered for a moment, then shivered to dust.

Wornum shook his head. 'Poor old Turner. He called himself Admiral Puggy, you know.'

'You are right — poor Turner. We have helped him, I think.'

'I wonder, will it be judged so?'

John smiled with his nose. He picked up the poker and thrust in, crumbling the burnt black crisps.

'Let's get in from this wind. I feel that with this fire a chapter is ended. The world is bleak, but the future is clean.'

Still, as he passed through the galleries before leaving the building, he was troubled again by twists in the pictures. At the last moment, as they passed from his sight, he caught coiling and shudders. All was still when he stopped, and faced each painting squarely, but again when he walked the canvas moved. Branches stretched fingers, the painted vines writhed, and the thin line of red which he knew already crept like a serpent from several Gardens of Eden, so he wondered, was he followed by invisible snakes?

...catching London unawares!

Leaving the Gallery, he paused on its steps. London, and his new mission, lay before him. Across the great square with its smirking new lions, sparrows lifted like elation. The sky was wild, lit by a white glare, so the shower-shot city seemed real and unreal — the streaked mansions, the high-stepping ponies. From the far side of the square came shouts from some accident, mixed with the blare of an army band. They played a dead march, a hero had died: he made out the draped coffin, born on a gun carriage. Beyond the far-off bleached facades, soot-laden smoke poured from the river's clamouring steamers.

Everywhere he looked, wealth mocked destitution. The driver of a hansom cracked his whip at a poor man, who could not stand erect but had to walk crouching, who was taking too long to cross the road. At the foot of the steps, a man in a silk hat waved his cane at a woman who reached a clawed hand to him. She was bent over what looked like a bundle of sticks, though he saw it must be her child: as he watched she covered its wizened face, and laid it very tenderly down on the flags. Her head sank slowly to her knees, and then, for all the movement she showed, you might have thought she too had just died.

Axles creaked, hawkers shouted, below him the crowd dragged past without end: he saw surly faces, sleek faces, faces sick with corruption. Great city, city of pain, heart of empire, you cry for Judgement. Let Everett's Deluge fall in thunder, catching London unawares! Like flaws in glass he saw threads in the air, so he whispered in awe, the serpents are flying. Be free my snakes: claim each sinner, they are your food.

But slowly, he thought, he must keep his mind clean. Indignation, like despair, can make you mad. There was a wild edge to his thoughts: he must not, in solitude, let disorder grow. For a moment he remembered the string-slender girl, whom he glimpsed as he came to the Gallery's steps: would he ever meet such beauty again?

He came down the steps, stepping into his mission. Before him human suffering cried for its poet, the wrong men did, their heartlessness. The soullessness of our new world. Above him, glass serpents wound through the air. With gloating eyes, a torn mask in the clouds grimaced. Behind him, from an alley, a black cat slid: on pads quiet as air it followed him. When its tiny muzzle curled, it showed needle fangs: its fur was fine as a prince's velvet. It passed through railings and bollards as though they were water, with a frightening slowness drawing closer to him.

16

She was lost outside their house — but how had she come there, wearing only her chemise?

'Everett? Dearest?' There was no one to see, only thick leaves and the sheared stubs of branches.

'My dearest.' His warm voice breathed in her ear. She quickly turned round.

'Why can't I see you? Are you here, or not here?'

'No one can see me now,' he said. 'I have become invisible.'

His voice was close, inside her head: she saw only bushes on every side.

'Touch me, please. Hold me. I need your arms.'

'I cannot touch you,' his sad voice said.

She woke in alarm. Everett! She was cold with premonition, he had become a ghost. Her mother was right, she had waited too long. Now the year had passed, and she had lost him.

She drew on her gown — her mother would be up, she knew. She padded to the nursery, where her mother sat crouched by her new tiny brother.

'I don't know if there will be a wedding, mamma.'

Her mother sat upright from the crib.

'But we expect him here in two days. Lord save us! Has he written?'

'What if he has died — suddenly, in some accident?'

'Died?' Her mother looked here, there, bewildered.

She told her dream. 'He is a spirit now. I cannot see him.'

'This is all from a dream?' Her mother frowned with impatience. The baby burbled loudly, and she bent to walk her fingers on small steps to its neck.

She thought herself, yes, it was just a dream — why should it be true? 'Since I knew John, I remember my dreams. He writes his dreams down, and tries to read them.'

'That John of yours had many dreams. This little piggy — Come, play with your brother.'

She looked at the baby, then held out her finger so the tiny hand clutched. The baby blinked to her with elderly eyes, while her mother moaned, 'At my age to have been with child again. Ooooch!'

'You're only forty six, mamma. It will be lovely, I think, to have the christening right after our wedding.'

'There!' her mother said. 'So you do expect the wedding to happen. I think you dreamed you could not see him, because for a year you could not see him. You should not have left it so long. You should have taken the man as soon as you could.'

She sat back in trouble. 'It caught me in the heart, mamma — to have a dream that he had died. And Lady Eastlake was very sure, that we should wait at least a year — so all the scandal is forgotten.'

'Lady Eastlake! What is she to us? I have been filled with fear these many months.'

In a low voice, with fierce urging, she said, 'He *must* come. I know he is true.'

Her mother gave a sighing shrug, and bent to chuck the baby among its chins.

Come, my love, on swiftest wings! I was wrong to make us bide so long. I have let us pass in the shadow of death.

Her mother looked up. 'At least you still wish for your brother to bear the name "Everett"?'

She laughed then. 'Of course I do.' She bent beside her mother, so they crooned together into the crib, where the new Everett bounced and flapped both arms.

'There, little lambkins.'

'Effie!' Sophie came running in. '*Can* we ride the pony?'

'In the afternoon, dearest. I have the flowers to order.' She got to her feet.

'At least your eye is better,' her mother called after her. 'I hated to look at you, winking and blinking. It spoiled your beauty absolutely.'

'Thank you, mamma *deer*,' she said. Still she thought, as she left, But something has died. His love can have died, in the year gone by. Dear God, let this marriage not be a mockery like the last one.

*

With the work of the day, preparing for flowers and food and guests, the dream grew faint. She was tired but filled with expectation, when she walked, with Sophie on the pony, in the afternoon. Steadily they climbed the hills over Perth, while the town and the North Sea widened below them.

'But the wind is strong — my hair's all dry.'

'It's the west wind, darling — a lovely warm wind.' Between the clouds the sun was gold, the hills rose clear and golden round them. 'Darling, there's MacPherson's farm. Shall we see how his lambs have grown?'

'I think they will be big sheep now.'

Still they went to the farm. She left Sophie there, happy by the sheep-pen with a bowl of sheep's curds, and climbed on up the hill till she walked on the ridge.

'God help us!'

The wind was so hard that her bonnet blew off, she had to untie it before she was strangled. Still it was a blessing wind: she turned her hair to its gusts as if under a hand. She used to come here as a girl, this was her true home in the world. She remembered her dream. Perhaps it meant after all that she had his love, though he himself had not come yet: this wedding would be a step into the dark.

The descending sun peered below the cloud, like a parent lifting a blanket to look at you. If I could I'd cast myself adrift on this wind, and let life blow me wherever it will. But there's Sophie, I have let it get late. We must hurry down before dark comes.

Sophie talked of the wedding as they came down the hill. 'But isn't it strange — that it was in our house that you were married to John, and it will be in our house that you get married to Everett?'

'Yes, my dear. That is our way.'

'I think the English do it better. They get married in a church. Then if there's a second time — well, you can go to a different church.'

Effie kissed her. 'Sophie, don't be a trial to me. At least it isn't the same room. We shall be using the *big* Drawing Room.'

'But won't it be empty? I don't think many of his family are coming.'

'There's his brother William. You'll like him, I think. He sings, and catches fish, and teaches arithmetic and also paints.'

'That's too many things.'

Effie kissed her again and nudged the pony. 'Let us get on, dear. It's dark already.'

Dusk had fallen by the time they came back, but their way was lit clear by the line of new gas-lamps. Then, as they turned a corner, she saw the big shadow that awaited her. In this street there was no light at all, evidently the gas supply had failed. Both street-lamps and houses showed not a glimmer — no cabs came, no one walked.

'Don't lets go this way,' said Sophie.

It was as if a black curtain crossed the road, it was like the darkness in which Everett hid. She was troubled, and drawn to it.

'Our eyes will get used to the dark,' she said. 'It will be an adventure.'

She nudged the pony. It was like crossing a threshhold, stepping into the shadow. She felt blind for a moment as though she had no eyes, then she made out the hulking shapes of houses, between black trees like tumbled towers. But she could not be afraid in this dim place, for the wind had dropped and in the warm June night the gardens breathed out a thick sweetness of scent — jasmine, rose-scent, stock.

'Come on.' Sophie tugged again.

But she could not hurry: it was like the rich darkness inside passion, as she imagined passion to be. Oh Everett, she prayed, let us make love with passion at last — we have waited so long. She remembered the dream she had long ago, of a man made of mud who clutched her drippingly: that man was Everett. He lived in the thick of the dark, even death, this Everett of her dreams. She remembered the words she heard then, The King of the Night is coming to you: those words spoke of Death and Love at once. Into what darkness was she stepping? She was filled with hope, and yearning, and dread.

*

A weak voice in him whispered, 'You *could* cut away.'

He lingered on the rim of the great hall of King's Cross. His bags had gone on ahead of him, William would follow by a later train — for William had said he would come, after all. And from early that morning he felt simply — empty. Scotland was long ago. Seeing her was long ago. Only last month he saw a girl that he liked. Was he travelling simply to keep his word?

His ear was caught by someone singing, to accordion music, across the station. 'Twas early one mor-ning just as the sun was daw-ning...' The melancholy song was sung so sweetly that he himself hummed it under his breath. Peering between bent porters, he saw the musician, on a faraway bench. She had a bright red skirt, and a shawl round her head, and as she sang, and worked her accordion, her whole body swung from side to side. Her face was lifted high, as though she read the words on the roof-beams. She was perhaps nineteen. It was only when he was near enough to trip over her, that he realized her open blue eyes were blind.

She could not see him — and he could not take his eyes from her. But whistles blew, he ran for his train. Poor girl, he repeated, as they gathered speed through suburbs. Poor — she must be very poor. If he could stop the train, he'd run back and pour out a till-full of cash.

They were passing factories. Below the viaduct a foundry erupted — molten iron splashed, he too was blind. 'Oh never leave me, how could you use a poor maiden so?' The blind girl's hair had shone like copper. Only now he took in the words of her song. 'Oh, don't deceive me.' Was he such a lover, not true at heart? Women love and men are faithless.

He watched the hedges and cows slide past, and cornfields and fields of sheep. Effie dearest, he murmured absently. Ahead was a blankness, like a wall of white mist.

Cities and villages ended, and even trees and pastures stopped. There was only bleached rock and flaring gorse — a dejected donkey, crows among stones. They raced on, between bleak hills, shaking and rattling, rocking and clanking, as if at any moment they would leave the rails and career away crazily over the heather. They must be among the Scottish borders, and now, in glimpses, the past came back — a look she had sent across the room, which slipped behind the head of John. It was urgent as if she meant to eat him, it had alarmed him but it thrilled him more. Its shock was fresh like yesterday.

Hours passed. For a time he slept. He woke, changed trains. At Perth station, finally, he took a cab.

'This house is Bower's Well, sir. Shall I drive you to the door?'

'There is no need. I have only a light bag with me now.'

His heart was loud as he began the walk. The large house had a tower, and gables and wings — and all in new brick and new stone. He reflected: but of course, the house was re-built. It was in the old house here that John's family lived, before the Grays came — then one of them married Euphemia Gray. He had fallen among ancient, inbred clans.

'Everett?' Sophie sprang from the shrubbery, then the whole family trooped round from the back of the house. They were carrying bowls.

'Everett,' Mr Gray called loudly. 'We rejoice that you are come.'

'Mr Gray, Mrs Gray.' The younger Grays were all named to him.

'Countess.' He and she touched hands. Her face was white, and urgent with that look of need which made his soul dissolve, so all he could do was yearn to hold her.

'You must be tired,' her father said. 'A dram I think will set you straight.'

He was shepherded in by the herd — the horde — of brothers and sisters, who inspected him with curiosity. Her face was luminous, and very pale and tired too.

*

William, when he came, spread ease, and asked about everything except the wedding. On the eve of the wedding old stories came out, till William asked her, 'What *is* it that happened to John's mother here? Your sisters give hints, but don't quite say.'

'Ah, aye,' Mr Gray nodded. 'It *is* a story to tell, on a late summer's evening, seated round a fireplace, as we all are. Daughter, say.'

She had been nervous all evening, but sat back now. 'It's not a pretty story — but I shall tell it, as she told it to me. You must know it happened in old Bower's Well, the house that stood on this site before.'

The small fire they had, without needing its heat, crackled and lit their faces. Outside the summer sky was bright. Everett sat with glazed eyes, basking in the music of her quiet Scottish lilt.

We are back in the time of the Regent and Buonaparte — in 1817. Young Margaret Cox, the niece of the old inn-keeper John Thomas Ruskin, sits in the drawing room, sewing by the window. Is there something heavy in the steps outside, that makes her glance up? But the door has already banged sharply open — so she sees John Thomas, in the cutaway coat they used to wear then, standing in the door with a wide dead stare. His hand clasps a red rag to his throat, as if he needed to hold his head onto his body. Is he trying to speak? As she hurries he staggers down into that leather chair William is sitting in. When she bends over him he draws back his hand, so she sees the yawning ragged wound, white and blue sinews laced with blood — she finds she is gazing *inside* his neck. His eyes start eagerly, as if he's proud to show her what he has done.

She gasps, and shouts frantically, trying with both hands to hold the wound shut, though the blood jets onto him and her. It is not clear if the horrible rasp of his breathing comes from his mouth or from the wound.

'Get a doctor — get me water — get a towel.'

She's a practical soul and too busy to faint. While others run or collapse, she clasps the wound tight. Did he use his razor? The doctor is coming, but John Thomas has lost so much blood.

'There is little we can do.' The doctor pulls her away. The old man, tightly bandaged, hardly moves. The doctor has turned to care for young Margaret Cox, who sits quite still, white-faced, seeing — she will see it for life — the old man in the doorway clutching his throat, with no chance of stopping the pouring blood.

'It was the following year,' she concluded, 'That she married her cousin John James — that is, John's father. She told me herself. That is why she never could come back to Perth. It's like a curse, in a story by Scott. And that is the history of old Bower's Well.'

William nodded. 'So, *that's* her story. There *is* something black in that family's blood. I wonder how John will end his days?'

'That's more than we know,' Mr Gray said. 'We need some cheer. Young Everett, will you pass that flask?'

He poked the fire, and told other stories, as the bright night lengthened and the horror in the life of John's mother grew faint.

Behind him Mrs Gray got to her feet, and he at once stood also. 'We must get some good sleep. We are busy tomorrow.'

They all retired. And if she and Everett, awake in their rooms, listened for each other's breathing as they once had done in the cottage, they would hear only the long soft rumble, like a steady surf, of other people's sleep.

*

Mrs Gray came downstairs. 'Lord save us, Mr Gray. It's already late — I've never known her like this.'

'It's no surprise.' Across the table from each other, they sighed and shook their heads together.

He rose. 'I think I'll go and see her.'

'Oh aye? Then get ye to her, Mr Gray.'

He paused at the stairhead, outside her door.

'Lassie?' He pushed the latch.

Faintly he heard her say 'Father', and crept in.

'My dearest girl.'

She sat in brown dimness, before the closed curtains. When she looked up, her white face and black eyes made him think she had fever. He sat near the bed.

'What do you fear, lassie?'

Her hand reached out and clasped his tightly. 'Father, I don't know if I can be married. I don't know if I am — if I am ' — she cast — 'cold'.

'*You're* not cold, Effie,' he said. 'You have been hurt — but I do not think you're hurt to death.'

It was the timbre in his voice that caught her — some humour in the kindliness. She thought, I have been making theatre. And the time had come.

'Father *deer*.' She stood.

He stood too, and took her arm, as he would in leading her to the minister.

*

He found himself alone in the large long drawing room, which was filled with light, and crowded with roses — crimson, pink, yellow, white — and carnations in vases mounted on stands. He felt brittle as a glass with cracks, held by fumbling fingers. Was he ready, unready for his fate? Outside the room, the event had gathered like a building wave: he heard women's voices, the first guests had come. Through the window he saw William, on the lawn, fooling with the brothers and sisters. He drew in a deep breath of the gathered scents — almost you could lift your feet from the floor, and lounge on the soft dense cloud of them.

The door opened, and strangers came in. They stared at him, and each other, till one of them asked, 'Are you the new gruim?'

'I beg your pardon.'

The man frowned and said loudly, 'The *gruim!*'

He slightly bowed. 'I am he.' Without reason he thought, new groom, new broom.

'Ooooh!' their Scottish voices rose. They looked to each other with rising brows — as though he were an exhibit, he thought, which they expected to see in a frame or a cage.

Like a rescuer, William came in briskly. 'Are you set then, brother?'

'I think. You see, I got that coat with the new high collar.' He turned in his black frock coat, then mused, 'Isn't it funny, how love will play hide and seek? It can carry you somewhere, and then — just abandon you. Another day it comes back, and you don't know where it hid.'

William frowned. 'And where are you now?'

Abruptly he stood tall and smiled. 'I'm dithering on the threshold, William. What else do you expect a *gruim* to do?'

'Tidy that buttonhole,' William said. 'And move your shoulders, your new coat looks as if it's still on the rack.'

'Look at *you*. You're smeared with grass.'

'Who cares about that? Smile man, you look as though you've got a raging toothache.'

By now the room was nearly full, an elderly man was pushed against them. 'So you will be the gruim, puir soul. Here — will you no take a pinch? It will put *heart* into ye.' He thrust out a snuff-box the size of a mustard-pot, and proffered a tiny ivory spoon.

'I thank you, no.'

'Noo?' The man sighed. He cavernously sucked in a spoonful himself, and rubbed his blinking eyes.

'Everett,' William nudged him sharply. In the doorway the minister had appeared, and made his way, through nods and greetings, to their end of the room.

'Good day to ye.' He shook Everett's hand, and exchanged a word. Then Sophie appeared, in a tiny white dress that John would have loved, and loudly said to everyone, 'Sssh.'

A sigh — a rising 'Oh' — travelled through the gathering, as Effie came in on Mr Gray's arm. Within her white veil she was pale and grave, her taffeta rustled and shivered its lustre. Behind her came Sophie, with a face just as solemn, and a trip in her step as though everyone watched her.

The time had come. Everett murmured then, 'Be with us, Lord', and took his place beside her.

When the words that marry them are completed, the guests mill close — there are handshakes, kisses, touches on elbows and pats on the back — and he himself is smiling shyly. Presently, before all of them, he lifts her veil — *strange* white face, and brilliant eyes — and light as a breath he gives a kiss.

But a new pause comes. The elder Grays have both retired but presently reappear at the door. The gathered crowd parts as they advance, with Mrs Gray holding in her arms Effie's new brother, crumpled, red, impatient-looking, wrapped round again in white. Thus the wedding party becomes a christening at once, and a soft tender common gasp passes from uncle to minister to grandmother to aunt, and out through the servants who are in the room also, in their Sunday best, for the shared celebration.

*

When they had changed their clothes, and made sure of their bags, they travelled with a retinue down to the station. The wedding party jostled and called round the carriage, till they both squeezed into the window, waving to everyone and slipping to each other bright, shy smiles. The engine fumed, the wheels spun then gripped, and the small train pulled away from Perth.

'Lord's sakes!' She sat back on the first-class upholstery. 'Thank God we are by ourselves at last.'

'What a performance!' He came from the window and sat facing her.

'Everett dearest — after our long pain, after all we have endured, you are truly happy that we are wed at last?'

He sat forward and clasped her hands in his. 'My dearest love — you don't know how happy — how happy —' He had to stop.

'What is it, my darling?'

His face was writhing, he had started to pant. 'How happy —' he began, but the words broke in his mouth. 'How —' he said. His eyes screwed tight shut, and sprang with tears as the sobs overwhelmed him.

He sat back and turned so he cried at the window. She moved to his seat, and put her hand on his shoulder — then he heaved in yet bigger convulsions. Were they tears of relief, from the year's frustration, or tears of grief for where his life had come? He did not know why, or where he was. He turned and gazed to her in speechless appeal, then dug his head into her lap, sobbing freely as her arms came round him.

She held him close and soothed his shoulders, gazing bleakly out to the shining Tay.

*

He was coughing and blowing his nose as they arrived at Glasgow station. They took the boat for Rothesay, and as they thudded down the Clyde they changed their clothes.

She was firm. 'They must not think us young marrieds.'

Still the hotel porter smirked, as he let them into their room.

'Charming spot.' Everett scowled at Rothesay harbour, choked with funnels and masts. 'Does it always rain, this side of Scotland?'

'It will be lovely on Arran. Oh, but this bed — can you feel? The mattress seems filled with rocks!'

When she stood, he touched her, and bent and kissed her gloomily. 'My dearest wife.'

'Everett, please. You cried all the journey. But what's that noise? They must be unloading coals. Oh, this bed — I know I shan't sleep.'

'And look at this chair.' He caught her mood. 'The wicker's coming all undone. Be careful of the chair-arms — you could get cut.'

Still, when they lay down, he reached out and touched her uncertainly. His hand was cold, like a spider inside a glove.

'My sweet.' He touched her breast, then took his hand away.

She turned her large-eyed face to his.

'My dear — we only sleep, tonight.'

'Yes,' he said, they could do no other. They lay side by side with open eyes. Outside there came a new racket of coals, clattering down their metal chute.

*

She entered first.

'But what a lovely room — I told you Arran was beautiful.'

The room was flooded with late-afternoon light. Beyond, the shoulders of Beinn Nuis glowed purple, patched with yellow gorse.

They unpacked quickly. Almost too busily, she hung her clothes. Everett smoothed his jackets on hangers.

'That's everything,' she said. 'Let's go out and walk on the front.'

'Let's,' he said, but he only stood. The warm room was so radiant, you would think the sun had stepped indoors with them. He waited.

'I love sea air,' she said quickly. 'It was so fresh when we came.'

They walked to the end of the quay and back. She sniffed

as they re-entered the hotel. 'Ah, dinner. I'm hungry as a hunter.'

When finally they were back in their room, he stood tall over her. 'My bride — my wife.' He kissed her tenderly.

'Oh.' She went completely still. Carefully he undid the brooch that fastened her jabot, and kissed her again. Her fear grew as he unbuttoned her blouse, kissing her lightly and speaking gently. Kneeling, he undid her skirt at the waist, and helped her to step out of it.

'My dear dear love,' he said, 'All our lives we have been coming here.'

Wearing only her shift, she stood by the bed as one stands by a chasm. He stood in his shirt, his legs fit spindles. It has to be, she thought, though she froze with fear. Catching her eye, he blew the candle out.

She gave thanks for the darkness, in which still she made out his loving face. Quickly she kissed him, and rested back. Be with me, dear God. More than ever she knew, this is not the right time — but there was no right time. He was nervous too, his hand moved roughly. As his hold strengthened, her soul slid through the keyhole and out of the room.

It was done, it had hurt, she lay still in the dark.

When he lit the candle, she made out dots of blood on the tangled sheets. Sitting up, she huddled the blanket round her and slowly shook her head. He stretched back long-legged in the chair by the bed, tousled, troubled. In silence their glances flitted briefly to each other, across the sunken wreck of love.

*

He had put the candle out again, and she lay back waiting for the years to pass. His touch was gentle, but he was soothing her to sleep, not love.

338

She was pushed, flying, by a steady wind from the East. Farewell, my heart, I cannot stay. Gulls swerved round her, and screamed with hooked beaks as the wind grew ferocious.

'What's happening, lassie?' Her father was by her.

She knew but she dared not say. The horizon turned black and rose in the air as it grew towards them, in a towering hill made of water and foam that streamed constantly *upwards*. Deep-green, transparent, through which you saw wrecked ships rolling pell-mell.

'Why, it's Everett's Deluge. He has sent it at last.'

'It will kill us for sure.'

'Well, why not? But take a deep breath.'

The wave lifted them into its soaring swell. From inside its waters she saw the roof-tops of Perth sliding fast underneath them. Their heads broke surface, high on the crest where the air was keen.

'Take breath, father.' She heard him say, 'Lassie.'

They slid on a rolling hillside of water, which settled slowly to level sea. She knew they were high up because the clouds were so low that she could reach out and touch them. Perth and all Scotland lay drowned far below, where fish swam through fireplaces, eels nested in cupboards.

'Look, there's Sophie — and mother too.'

'You must be soaked, George.' Her mother paddled to them in the small cockle-boat. 'And your best frock-coat — for shame.'

As they clambered into the tipping boat, she saw other boats — row-boats and dinghies — dotted away across the bright surface, which rose and fell like a sleeper's breathing.

'Is no one drowned?' her mother asked impatiently. 'Where's Mrs MacDowd?'

'But where is Everett?' she cried.

'Look Effie,' Sophie called, 'The water's run off.'

'Everett,' she wailed.

But the world was washed clean. Old Perth looked new like Paradise, as they grounded in the branches of an apple tree. Slate roofs and grey stone were scrubbed so they shone. The hills beyond Perth were radiant emerald, except where the heather was purple and gold. Boats leaned against chimneys at crazy angles, while people shouted for ladders from parapets.

But where was Everett? She could no longer stand, for the many leaves of her skirt opened wide, while her pelvis parted. Everett in the dark lay beside her. Still he caressed her. Still the dream held her, lasting whole nights, or seconds. A dancing warmth grew — were there fireflies inside her?

'Dear love,' he breathed. No change would come, then the change was coming, the mountainous wave of her dream rose growing and warming and widening through her.

'Come to me,' she said, clear awake.

*

Little by little, over the following days, they told each other all of their lives. They discussed where they would live, and his plans for his art. He described the blind girl in King's Cross station.

'You liked her?'

'She was poor, she was beautiful, she showed no grief. She moved me — I wondered —'

'You must, of course.'

'You're sure?'

'Oh yes. If you paint her, it will be like a gift to her.'

'Which she could not see. I would call it "The Blind Girl".'

'You could have someone with her, who saw what she

340

could not. I could find the clothes for them. I've a lovely red petticoat, that's all old and tattered, just like the one you said she wore.' She loved colours, both bold and subtle: they agreed how the colours in the picture would be. She paused, then drew a long breath. 'I was a Blind Girl.'

He squeezed her hand.

'Where is the portrait of John?' she asked.

'Oh, he gave it to Dante Rossetti for safe-keeping. His father was determined to stick a knife through it. I don't know who will see it now.'

She was silent.

On their last day they passed children who played round a bonfire. On the crackling branches they threw cut summer grass, which their father — she supposed — had scythed.

Children: she held his arm. 'I used to cry every time I saw a child.'

His hand came firmly to her arm. Still her eyes smarted, when only a little smoke blew in her face. Looking round, she saw his eyes were wet.

Dusk was falling, a parent called, the children grew quiet and serious. Summer grass, the dreams of youth. Her heart pricked, their glances met. They both saw here too was a picture to be.

As they walked on she brightened. If they were blessed with a family, she would have Everett paint every child. Not only pictures with subtle meanings, for the likes of John to read, but pictures to touch the heart at once. Of every mother in England, and every father too. She gazed over the twilight sea. Everett was diffident, but she would be there.

After fifteen days they climbed back on the steamer, and thudded for the mainland. The sharp breeze blew spit of spray in their faces. She swallowed and blinked, and clasped closer hold, while he in some way seemed all about her. Below them the water divided and foamed. Gulls screamed, the sea whipped, and the sky whitened steadily, while heather and hills, and white peaks beyond them, seemed gathered and sweeping from all sides to meet them, as if the mainland found voice and its people were calling, Yes, life begins here.

PICTURE
ACKNOWLEDGEMENTS

The author wishes to give thanks to the following sources of illustrative material and/or permission to reproduce it. *'Everett understand love'*, John Everett Millais, 'Love' © Victoria and Albert Museum, London; *'Closely, please'*, John Everett Millais, 'The Countess as Barber', The Pierpoint Morgan Library, New York; *'I feared I had given...'*, John Everett Millais, 'Design for a Gothic Window' (detail), Private Collection; *'Such love, such lovers...'*, John Everett Millais, 'A Huguenot on St. Bartholomew's Day Refusing to Shield Himself from Danger by Wearing the Roman Catholic Badge' (detail), Private Collection; *'...as she gazed with longing...'*, John Everett Millais, 'St Agnes' Eve', Private Collection; *'...all love and thankfulness...'*, John Everett Millais, 'The Rescue', National Gallery of Victoria, Melbourne. *'It must not be told'*, *'I am your soul, John'*, *'...if that strange figure...'*, *'...catching London unawares!'*, collage illustrations by the author from nineteenth-century editions.